a GROOM of ONE'S OWN

a GROOM of ONE's OWN

USA TODAY BESTSELLING AUTHOR

EMMA ST. CLAIR

To the Appies fans who made this possible...

Thanks for loving this team of imperfectly lovable hockey players and for supporting the author whose imperfect brain was stuck listening to them yammer on in her head for months.

CONTENT WARNINGS

This is a light and funny romcom, but I want to help readers feel safe! Here are some topics that are touched on in the book:

- Parents passing away due to car wreck (past)
- Parental abandonment (past)
- Older relative with dementia (current)
- Parent with chronic illness (current)
- The gooiest golden-retieveriest MC
- Misuse of glue gun

Spoiler alert: No one dies. There is no sex in this book. You will get a happy ending with no cheating and minimal angst.

ABOUT THE APPIES

The Appies is a fictional AHL team located in the also fictional town of Harvest Hollow. We wanted to create a hockey team with the vibes of the Savannah Bananas. (If you don't know the Bananas, do yourself a favor and look them up. You're welcome.)

You'll first meet the team in *Just Don't Fall* by Emma St. Clair and *Absolutely Not in Love* by Jenny Proctor, both part of the Sweater Weather series.

All of the Appies books can be read as standalones, but if you'd like to read in order, this is the reading order: Just Don't Fall, Absolutely Not in Love, A Groom of One's Own, and Romancing the Grump (with more to come).

There are special edition paperbacks for Just Don't Fall and Absolutely Not in Love you can find at https://emmast clair.com/appiesversion or by searching "Appies Version Just Don't Fall" on Amazon.

CHAPTER 1

Eli

I LEAN FORWARD, elbows on my thighs, one step away from the classic head-between-the-knees position to prevent fainting. Clearing my throat, I ask, "To sum up, my options are…?"

The immigration lawyer, with his wispy comb-over and a stain on the center of his baby-blue tie, gives me a tight smile. A pitying one. Which is all I need to know.

I drop my head into my hands with a soft groan.

"I'm afraid you're out of options," he says. "You'll need to return to Canada at the end of the month or risk deportation and a much bigger issue. That is, unless you were planning to get married in the next thirty days." He laughs.

I don't.

Malik, the Appies' manager sitting to my right, doesn't.

And Grant, the no-nonsense team lawyer in his crisp black suit and stain-free tie, absolutely doesn't.

Deported.

Married.

DEPORTED.

MARRIED.

Breathe, Hop, I tell myself.

Easier said than done. I wonder how likely it is that this guy keeps a stock of paper bags in his desk for situations just such as this.

Grant glares at the immigration lawyer, whose very unfortunate and very unlawyerly name is Mr. Pebbles. "You, of all people, know getting married solely for immigration purposes is considered fraud."

Mr. Pebbles holds up both hands like he didn't just suggest—or joke about?—this exact thing. "Don't shoot the messenger," he says, which doesn't even make sense in this context.

Is this really the best immigration lawyer Grant could find to consult? Maybe in the small town of Harvest Hollow, yes. But neither Asheville nor Knoxville is too far. I don't know why Grant didn't consider someone from either of those places. Unless ...

Unless there really are no other options.

My insides have coiled into a knot so complicated, it would take a surgeon to untangle everything.

And to think I got out of bed thinking it would be a perfectly lovely day. No practice. No meetings. I slept late, relishing the warm cocoon of my sheets. Rolling out of bed at nine o'clock felt positively indulgent.

Mom sat crisscross applesauce in her favorite chair in the living room, perky and pain-free. I joined her. While she drank coffee and read a book, I sipped a smoothie and checked stocks. Markets opened strong. Things looked good. All in all, a lovely, lazy morning.

During the hockey season, very few days stretch out with zero plans. If not practice and training, it's filming social media content—both for the team and my account—giving interviews, attending charity events, and so on.

My only plans for the day were to take Mom to the acupuncturist. Then, I hoped to stop by the animal shelter before it closes. Dogs make me happy. Visiting the sad dogs who need homes makes me *really* happy. Technically, I don't think I'm supposed to keep coming in if I *know* I can't adopt one. But the shy woman who works there, Bailey, doesn't seem to mind. She also doesn't seem to know who I am, which is refreshing. She's become something of a personal project. More like a challenge.

Can I get her to say more than four words in a row? If so, how many?

At my last visit, she said two sentences in a row, *and* I almost got her to laugh. There was the tiniest huffing sound before she swallowed it down, which is a win in my book. I've started counting her blushes. Keeping a mental tally, my achievements glowing like a scoreboard.

But my hopes for this lovely, aimless day were ruined by my phone, which wouldn't stop ringing after I set it down.

"Your fans are calling," Mom said.

But it wasn't my fans. It was Malik, requesting my presence at the Summit, my first sign that today would turn into a five-alarm dumpster fire. The second sign of the impending apocalypse was seeing Grant in Malik's office. I should have turned and run.

Instead, Malik drove us in tense silence to this immigration lawyer's office, which smells like old sub sandwiches. Then I listened to them argue about terms I only vaguely know and understand. P1-A and O1-A and petitions for renewal and so on.

What I do understand: I have to go back to Canada to file a new visa. But this could take time, and there's no guarantee I'll keep my spot on the team. The Appies may be an AHL team, but we're arguably as recognizable as any NHL team now, thanks to social media.

Guys are *begging* to get traded here. And I have—or had, until now—no intention of going anywhere.

How did this even happen? Between the team's administrative staff and me being a functioning adult, there's no good reason. I could have gone to Canada in the off-season this summer and taken care of this. Had I remembered or been reminded by the people who manage this stuff that I needed to do so.

When I first got signed to Denver and moved stateside, I was eighteen. Mom handled talking to the team about the visa stuff. I have a *vague* memory of hearing about the cap on my visa. How I could renew here after five years but would need to go back to Canada after ten. I also remember thinking this seemed like a problem for Later Eli.

Hello, Later Eli. I wish I could say it's good to see you. But it's really, really not.

I lean back in my chair, playing with a pen I found on Mr. Pebbles's desk. "You're sure there's no loophole? A clause? An extra payment option?"

Grant's eyes cut to me. "No. You'll go back to Canada, apply for a new visa, then wait for processing. Any other suggestions"—he glares at Mr. Pebbles again—"would be fraud and"—now he glares at me like any of this was *my* idea —"is not condoned by the Appies organization."

"No one suggested fraud," Mr. Pebbles says, though I'm pretty positive that's exactly what he suggested. He runs a hand down his tie, finally noticing the dark stain I've spent half this meeting trying to identify. Ketchup? Soy sauce? Chocolate? His frown makes me wonder if *he* even knows its origin. *Gross.*

Now, though, I have much more pressing concerns than the mystery stain. Like, for example: *deportation.* What this will mean for my spot on the Appies. The rest of this season, my career.

And what this will mean for my mom.

I lean back in my chair, staring up at the ceiling and picturing Mom's smile this morning. The way the sunlight made her hair look more gold like mine, like hers used to be before the white crept in. I imagine the happiness draining from her face, replaced by worry and disappointment.

Mr. Pebbles puts both elbows on his desk, which is cluttered with papers. "I only meant if Eli is dating someone, you could push the timeline up a little. Or, you know, a *lot.*"

He waves a dismissive hand like neither fraud nor asking a woman to push up a wedding timeline are serious things.

I've watched enough episodes of *Say Yes to the Dress* with Mom to know he's wrong, at least about the second one. I'm sure there's a meme somewhere, featuring Boromir from *Lord of the Rings* and the words *One does not simply ask a bride to move up her wedding date.* I'd love to see Mr. Pebbles try telling a bride not to take a change in date seriously.

You know what's hard to take seriously? A lawyer with a last name like Pebbles. That's what.

Malik leans forward in his chair, catching my gaze. His brown eyes are hopeful. *Way* too hopeful. "It would just be like fast-tracking a relationship. Aren't you dating someone? That girl with the ... um ..."

I can't blame the man for not knowing details about my current girlfriend. Considering the fact that she doesn't exist.

I drag a hand down my face and look away. "I'm not seeing anyone I was planning to propose to in the next month."

It's not, technically speaking, a lie.

I'm *not* dating anyone I would propose to in the next month. In fact, my dating life is blanketed in a thick layer of dust and cobwebs. Not for lack of trying, either. Oh, how I've tried. Maybe if I wanted what most guys in my position—young, professional athletes—want, it wouldn't be hard to find company. Something casual.

But I'm a not-so-closet romantic, and I haven't dated someone seriously in a good, long while. Which is no one's business in this room but mine.

"But you could at least discuss the idea," Malik suggests.

"Somehow, I don't think she'd be on board with this." Because she doesn't exist.

"I'm not hearing this conversation," Grant says, actually putting his hands over his ears.

"Once again, it's not fraud if the marriage is legitimate between two people involved romantically who were planning to get married anyway," Mr. Pebbles insists.

Grant glowers, the hands over his ears clearly not blocking out any sound. He looks ridiculous this way, and if I were in a better mood, I'd snap a picture and send it to the team group chat. "Please stop saying the word *fraud*."

As we ride back to the Summit, me in the backseat like a child and Grant and Malik arguing up front like two parents on the cusp of an ugly divorce, I stare out at the mountains. I've grown used to this view. I *love* this view. Even though I've spent more collective time on other teams and in other cities, the Appies feel like family. Harvest Hollow feels like home.

I could lose all this if I leave in a month. My teammates,

some of whom have become the closest thing I've known to brothers. My career, which has grown exponentially since I transferred to the Appies.

And this won't just affect me. It will have just as much impact on my mom.

"We'll get this sorted out, Hop," Malik says as we pull through the gates for the Summit's player and staff parking.

I meet Malik's eyes briefly in the rearview mirror. "Exactly *how* will this get sorted out?"

My leg bounces and I shift, pressing a hand on top of my knee, like that will be enough to quiet the anxiety coursing through me. Malik parks, then shoots Grant a quick look before twisting to face me.

"Would it be so hard to move things along with whomever you're seeing?"

Ah, yes. The girlfriend I made up spur-of-the-moment twenty minutes ago. *Her.* I should have known the not-technically-a-lie would come back to bite me.

"If you're going to commit fraud, I can't know about it." Grant swivels around, directing his trademark pinched expression toward me. "Think: deportation with little hope of playing hockey again anywhere. No team would *touch* you."

Malik turns to Grant. "It's not fraud if Eli and his girlfriend decide to rush things along for practical reasons. I've heard of plenty of people getting married on the DL for a variety of reasons. They could do it now legally, at the courthouse, then have a big wedding and celebration later. I don't see what the big deal is. It's not like Eli's trying to pay someone to marry him."

"Which would *absolutely* be fraud." Grant gives us both one last look of warning, his personal version of a fraud deterrent, then slams the car door. I can see him muttering to himself as he walks away.

Malik studies me. "So, are you thinking about it?"

I frown. "About going back to Canada?"

"About asking your girl to marry you sooner than later."

"Not going to happen," I say instead of telling Malik the truth—that there's no *her* to ask.

"Are you against marriage?"

I blink at him. "No. I *want* to get married."

To someone I love. Not so I can stay in the states. Like Grant said: it's fraud.

Even my nonexistent girlfriend agrees: Real men don't commit fraud.

Malik nods. "And she doesn't? Or …?"

Or … she doesn't exist.

"Worst case scenario, I'll just go back to Canada until we get it straightened out. If it takes six months, that puts us at the end of the season. I could be back for training and—"

"The immigration lawyer said it could be months before things get processed. A year, man."

Am I sinking? It feels like Malik's leather seats are suddenly sucking me down into them. I definitely didn't hear Mr. Pebbles say anything about a full *year*. It must have been one of the many times when I zoned out.

"I can't promise Larry would hold your spot."

I sink just a little bit farther. If I had to describe the Appies' team owner in one word, it'd be *hungry*. While hunger is what drives me to be the best at my position, Larry's hunger is the ugly kind. The *greedy* kind. The kind wanting to feast on more money, fame, recognition—as much as he can get and in any way he can get it.

Larry is the single person I don't like inside the Appies organization. It sucks that he happens to be the owner.

I swallow past a growing lump in my throat. Feels like a boulder.

"I'm sorry, man," Malik says. "I'm sure it will be fine. Just … talk to your girl. We all do things and make sacrifices for the people we love. Maybe she'll surprise you."

Somehow, I don't think she will.

———

Mom tries to convince me we should cancel her acupuncture appointment by doing jumping jacks to demonstrate how good she feels. Her version of jumping jacks looks more like some kind of dance you might see in a boy band video, only done very, *very* poorly. Her arms flail up as her legs come together, completely incorrect form.

Normally, this would make me laugh. Today, I shake my head, holding back a sound that I'm afraid might be a sob. "We're going."

When she clasps her hands together under her chin, pleading, I wag a finger at her. "Nope."

"But I feel good. *So* good. Need me to do jumping jacks again?" She lifts her arms above her head, already starting in the incorrect position.

I finally get her in the car by plying her with promises of sweets. "Cheesecake, cookies, or ice cream. Your choice," I tell her.

And she holds me to this after her appointment, telling me she wants all three. "You said my choice. And I choose all three."

"I meant your choice of *one*," I say, pushing open the door for her while waving goodbye to Dr. Wei, her acupuncturist.

Needles make me sweat in places I'd rather not mention. I fully blacked out the last time I had immunizations. But acupuncture helps Mom, so I can manage sitting in the same building, trying not to imagine her with tiny needles in her skin. I always wait in the living room of the old-house-turned-acupuncture-clinic, doing something inane like responding to comments on my latest TikTok videos.

Today though, I'd rather think about a face full of needles than my visa issue.

Mom loops her arm through mine as we cross the wide porch. A group of jack-o'-lanterns left over from Halloween slouches on the steps, their smiles softening as they slowly cave in on themselves.

"Then you should have specified," she says, giving my arm a squeeze.

She's got me there. And even if she didn't, I still wouldn't say no. I almost never do, unless it's something that would be harmful to her health, like skipping out on appointments.

Because today is a good day, we walk the few blocks to The Toasted Pecan Bakery. The air is crisp, but the sun is high and bright, making this late fall day feel more like summer than a precursor to winter. It's so nice I can almost forget about my morning.

The lawyers. My visa issue. Having to tell Mom.

So far, she hasn't picked up on my mood. But then I make the mistake of only ordering coffee. Which sounds puny compared to Mom's cinnamon roll, chocolate caramel muffin, and slice of French silk pie. None of which are cheesecake, cookies, or ice cream but all of which satisfy her sweet tooth. For now.

Mom presses a hand to my forehead. "You don't *feel* feverish."

"I'm not sick."

"Well, you're *something*," Mom says. "Not hungry for *you*

has always translated to something being wrong. Like the time you stole those batteries from the store."

I groan. "Will I ever live that down? It was a two-pack of double-A batteries, Ma. I was seven."

"And your guilt kept you from eating dinner. Otherwise, I'd never have known. Not when you buried the batteries in the backyard to hide them from me." She laughs. "Remember getting worried about growing a battery tree?"

We're still standing at the counter, and I'm thankful there's no post-lunch rush. "Yes. I do remember."

"Good thing you chose hockey instead of a life of crime." Mom pats my arm. "You'd make a terrible criminal."

"Thanks," I mutter, but the mention of hockey only makes my stomach clench more. Same with the mention of being a criminal.

Because I'll be honest—over the last few hours, I've been considering Malik's suggestion. Or some version of it, since there is obviously no girlfriend in the picture like he thinks.

Which means, I guess I *am* thinking about a life of crime.

A *temporary* life of crime. More like a *season* of it. A brief *moment* of crime.

And when you compare getting married to stay in the country to something like selling drugs or robbing a bank, it's hardly even a crime. Not if you grade crime on a curve.

It would be less a life of crime and more a moment of ignoring some minor laws.

"For here or to go?" the man behind the counter asks.

"To go." I turn to Mom. "I still want to go to the shelter before it closes."

Her smile is wide. "You and your dogs. When are you going to bring one home?"

"One day," I tell her. We both know I'm too busy, and her

health is too up-and-down to add in the responsibility of a dog.

As we retrieve our order, the guy behind the counter clears his throat. "And could I get an autograph? I follow you on TikTok."

"Of course." I end up signing one of the white pastry bags for him. It's still folded neatly, my scrawled signature contrasting with the neatly printed Toasted Pecan logo.

"I could sign too," Mom teases, and the guy gets flustered.

"Oh, um, sure?"

"Kidding. You wouldn't be able to sell it on eBay then," she says with a laugh.

"People do still use eBay, right?" she asks me on the way out.

"Probably? I don't know."

"I heard of another site recently—OnlyFans? Is that similar?"

I almost spit coffee all over the sidewalk. "That's not—*no*. It's not like eBay, Ma. Never mention that site again. And please don't go there."

She cackles, and I realize she knows exactly what Only-Fans is and was totally messing with me.

"What's the next stop on your sweets quest?" I ask, desperate for a subject change.

"We can head home since you have plans."

"I thought you wanted to eat your way through Asheville's desserts?"

Mom shakes the bag in her hand. "I'm fully stocked on sugar. At least for the afternoon." She pauses. "Why don't you ever take me with you to the shelter?"

"I didn't think about it," I say.

Which isn't exactly true. I know she'd probably love it. I

have thought about bringing her before. But going to the shelter helps me unwind. It boosts my mood if it happens to dip. And as much as I love her, it wouldn't serve the same purpose if Mom came with me.

I also have a sneaking suspicion she'd probably try to set me up with Bailey. "You need a nice young woman," Mom's said more than once. "Not those hockey hussies always hanging around." Bailey falls into the nice young woman category. And I've had enough of people trying to push me into relationships today.

"I'll bring you sometime," I tell her. "But not today."

She hums, like now her mind has turned from solving the mystery of why I'm not eating to why I want to go to the shelter alone. So long as she's not trying to figure out why I had to go into work this morning, she can Sherlock her way around anything else.

"Don't forget—I'm hosting book club this week," she says.

"How could I possibly forget?"

Mom laughs. "It's not that bad."

I grumble, but in truth, I'm grateful Mom has her book club. Even if I never, ever want to be home when all the ladies are over. I'm pretty sure the last time I accidentally walked in, Janice took a picture of my butt. Janice is pushing eighty. I felt like a prize steer at some kind of livestock show. I half-expected to receive some kind of ribbon or get auctioned off at the end of the night.

Even so, book club is one more reminder of what's at stake.

Mom's roots in North Carolina are even deeper than mine. Mostly thanks to her book club friends, but also the abundance of practitioners and homeopathic experts here in Asheville. None of whom ever tried telling her that fibromyalgia is a fabricated illness the way her doctors in Canada did.

Not to knock Canada—I'm sure many doctors here would suggest the same thing. Overall, the medical community seems unsure what to do with chronic illnesses. More than any other place we've lived, we've found the best care here and the best routine. An acupuncturist, a massage therapist, and a chiropractor as well as a great rheumatologist. Mom's health and her spirits have never been better.

Mom won't *want* to go back to Canada. She *shouldn't* go back. Unlike me, she has dual citizenship. If my dad hadn't been such a controlling, manipulative jerk, my sister, Annie, and I might have gotten dual citizenship too, avoiding this whole situation. But he was a garbage human, one who drove a deep wedge between my mom and her family before he took off.

Now, she has me and Annie, who's still in Montreal and visits occasionally. Always unannounced because Annie loves chaos. And surprises.

Mom won't stay here without me. I know it. Ripping me out of *my* life means ripping her out of *hers* as well. And I simply won't do that to her. Which means ... I guess I need to find myself a wife.

CHAPTER 2

Bailey

"I TOLD YOU—I don't want whatever you're selling."

A deep scowl on a pale, deeply lined face accompanies this proclamation. The look paired with her words almost have the power to make me feel ashamed, like I *am* a solicitor who knocked on her door with a clipboard selling magazine subscriptions.

Instead of what I actually am, which is her only granddaughter. The one who brought the pho she really loves—rare beef, no onions of any kind—and her favorite flowers, peonies—which are not in season right now so a lot more expensive. Next time, I tell myself, maybe I'll bring her carnations.

I won't. I know I won't. Because she may not remember me, and she may not have been all that kind before she lost her ability to remember, but Gran is all I have.

She glowers at me like a queen enthroned among the pillows, the perfectly curled blond wig atop her head acting as her crown. Today, it's the Classy Dolly Updo wig, one of seven Gran purchased from an Etsy store specializing in custom wigs modeled after Gran's number one hero, Dolly Parton. Out of the bunch, my personal favorite is the Dolly Layered Bouffant wig. I tried it on once and almost felt like I could conquer the patriarchy or solve the literacy crisis. So, I get the appeal.

"It's Bailey, your granddaughter." I manage to dredge up a smile from somewhere. Feels like it was scraped off the concrete. "Your son Peter's daughter."

I am very careful not to use past tense when talking about my dad. It's better when I don't have to tell her again as though for the first time that he died a few years back. Better for us both.

And for the assisted living facility, which suffered five-hundred-forty-seven dollars' worth of damage one of the times Gran found out (again) her son was dead. I've never seen someone rip down a curtain rod and wield it like a sledgehammer, but it was a sight to behold. Before three of the staff could stop her, she took out two windows, a television, and a set of Hummel figurines belonging to the woman rooming with her at the time. Who knew those things could be so expensive?

Now, Gran has her own room. Likely because of that incident. Or perhaps the one where she knocked Mr. Winters off his motorized scooter and stole it, making a break for the emergency exit.

When they called to tell me about it—complain, really, threatening to kick her out yet again—I had to put the phone on mute to smother my laugh. Not about possibly losing her spot. It was the mental image of Gran tooling down the road

with the Dolly Teased Mullet Bangs wig—the only appropriate one for an assisted living jailbreak, IMHO—blowing in
the wind as she fled.

Before Gran can decide she should drive me out by
throwing whatever's within reach, I hold out the soup and
flowers. "I brought you pho and flowers. Are you hungry
now?"

"I could eat a baby," Gran says.

I wince. Where did *that* comparison come from? I decide I
don't want to know. Maybe she's been watching *Game of
Thrones* again. I haven't seen the show or read the books, but
eating babies sure sounds like it could fit into that world.

As I locate a tray and start arranging her soup, Gran sits
up, straightening her pink pajama top. It's silk and has pearl
buttons down the front to match her earrings, probably. She
tucks the paper napkin in the neck, as delicately as though
it's linen.

"Thank you," she says primly.

I almost fall over because Gran is not big on thanks. She
never was—even before her mind became more like a sieve
with very large holes. She wasn't the soft and cuddly
grandma so many people seem to have but more the
demanding and cuttingly critical kind. So, I'll tuck away this
thank you like a tiny gift.

But then she reaches for her bedside table and tries to
hand me a five-dollar bill from her Vera Bradley coin purse.
"Here's your tip. That will be all."

I sigh and take the bill. I'll give it to Hannah when I leave.
Later, she'll slip it back into Gran's wallet.

I was planning on a longer visit, but Gran, now convinced
I'm a DoorDash delivery person, frowns and shoos me out
with her chopsticks. I'm not in the mood to fight, so I wave
goodbye, thank her for the tip, and make my way to the front

desk where I find Hannah filling out paperwork and listening to a true crime podcast. I'm grateful she hits pause because the host was saying something about decomp. I'm not squeamish, but I can't handle dead body talk right now.

"Can you slip this back in my gran's wallet?" I hold out the bill Gran gave me.

"She thought you were the DoorDash driver again?" Hannah's smile is soft. She clasps her hands on the desk, flashing the rings on almost every finger. Hannah is the definition of bling. She's even got some gold accents wound into the thick knot of braids on top of her head.

"Yep." She still hasn't taken the money, so I wave it at her. "Here."

She shakes her head, her smile faltering. "Keep it."

"I can't take her money." Even if I'm the one currently footing the majority of the bills for this place, everything not covered by her social security.

Hannah sighs, then pulls open a drawer and retrieves a sealed envelope with the facility's return address stamped in place, my name scrawled across the front in messy script.

The pitying look in Hannah's eyes makes dread pool in my belly, sour and heavy. "I'm sorry, honey," she says.

I take the envelope with two fingers. "Is this going to ruin my day?"

Hannah's sigh is bone-weary. The sound of someone overqualified and underpaid at a very difficult job. "Just … keep the five."

She presses play again on her podcast, and I walk out the front doors with the envelope still held between two fingers as a deep voice discusses rigor mortis.

———

If freeclimbing were a thing I ever thought about doing, my grip on this letter would be tight enough to keep me hanging on the sheer face of a cliff. You'd never catch me climbing a cliff, but it sounds downright pleasant compared to dealing with this letter. Its cheerful font is a slap in the face, a direct contrast to the not-at-all cheerful threats it contains.

Threats, I tell you! Because the assisted living facility where my grandmother lives is clearly run by a terrorist cell.

Too bad I have no choice but to meet their demands—a twenty percent price increase to their already exorbitant monthly costs. Which insurance and all the governmental things only cover nominally to begin with.

Where am I going to get an extra twenty percent? What even *is* twenty percent of her current monthly payment? I need a calculator. What I would love is not to be the sole adult left to handle these details.

I often miss my parents with a deep, throbbing ache. Their voices, the sight of them bent over books or the laptop glow reflecting in Dad's glasses. But in moments like this, when I have to be more *adult* than I feel qualified for, I miss them with a sharp tang of bitterness. Usually accompanied by a few moments of *why me* and *poor little orphan Bailey* before I tell myself to shut up and deal with the hand I've been dealt.

Which is: losing my parents to a car accident just months before college graduation and now being the sole caretaker for Gran on a nonexistent budget.

"Oh, Bailey ..."

The moment I hear Beth, my most favorite and also most nosy coworker, sing-song my name, I shove the letter into my bra.

Just like the completely normal, fully functioning adult I am. One of the paper's sharp corners immediately pokes delicate skin where no woman ever wants a paper cut, and I wince.

It's the same knee-jerk reaction I would have had as a kid when caught with my hand in the cookie jar. A cookie jar would be a lot more fun—and tastier—than this missive. Why, exactly, do I feel the need to hide the letter?

And why did I shove it into my bra? That's easier to answer—because scrubs don't have pockets. Or, at least, *mine* don't. They're the bargain scrubs. No pockets. And made of a fabric only a stone's throw from burlap. I really wish I could afford the softer, pocketed kind. Because as I turn to face Beth, I am rewarded with what is most definitely a paper cut on my nipple.

"Yes, Beth?" I echo in an equally melodic voice.

I know from the smug grin on her softly lined face exactly what she's going to say. My heart, already racing a little, picks up the pace again, clearly going for a PR on its late afternoon sprint.

"Your boyfriend's here," Beth says, clasping her hands over her chest in a gesture that somehow makes her look about fifty years younger, like an elementary school girl with a crush.

I can't blame her. But I also won't reward her teasing with an acknowledgment.

"Hot Puppy Guy," Beth clarifies after a moment. Clearly, my response of staring blankly is not what she's after.

Like there's more than one man she teases me about.

"Oh, him." I roll my eyes. But I also move to the door to see for myself. There's a tiny window in the door separating the reception area of the shelter from this multipurpose room. I have to stand on tiptoes, but peeking through the glass, I confirm there is a veritable Viking bouncing on his toes with his flannel-clad back turned toward us.

Hot Puppy Guy. Also known by his real name, which Beth pointedly and forever pretends not to know: Eli.

I allow myself a moment to indulge in the view. Impossibly broad shoulders. Perfectly messy golden-blond hair. And if he were looking this way, I'd see blue eyes that somehow manage to be warm despite their deep blue color. He just needs a little bit longer hair—perhaps with some tiny braids—and an ax to complete the look. A leather skirt wouldn't hurt.

Vikings do wear leather skirts, right? Or ... kilts? Historical accuracy aside, I'm sticking with this mental image.

Eli's face is the kind which could both launch a thousand ships or sell out whole product lines from a print ad. Sharp, chiseled features softened by full lips and a perpetual smile. The varying levels of facial hair he sports—from clean shaven to a trimmed beard—all look good and flatter his angular jawline.

He could probably shave his eyebrows and still rival the last twenty years' worth of *People Magazine*'s Sexiest Man Alive.

Whatever he does for work, it must involve some kind of manual labor. Like pulling trees from the ground by their roots. Or carrying old ladies across the street. Building homes without the use of any electrical tools. And yet, despite what could be an imposing physique, Eli is a total softie. He's sweet. Goofy. Thoughtful. He clocks almost as many hours visiting dogs as some of our volunteers do. Though they're doing it to look good on resumes and Eli comes in just because he likes dogs, honestly.

Speaking of volunteers, several of the college girls are gathering at the front desk like flies to honey. Or is it bees to honey? Between the two insects, these women are definitely *flies*.

I remind myself that I have no right to feel protective. Eli is *not* my boyfriend, no matter what Beth says. Still. I'd like to take the push broom and sweep the volunteers right out the front door and right into traffic.

Okay, that feels a little too mean.

I'd just sweep them outside. If they *happened* to step in front of traffic, that would be on them.

Irrational jealousy rises in my chest as Katrina—the lord of the flies, if I'm sticking with my bad bug analogy (and I am)—does her best contortionist impression, bending herself practically in half over the top of the high reception counter. No doubt to get closer to Eli. While also giving him a clear view of her cleavage. And demonstrating her flexibility.

Like I said: *flies*.

Katrina says something I can't hear. Eli jolts a little at the sight of her, then pointedly fixes his gaze in the opposite direction from the low-hanging boob fruit she's dangling right in front of him. Right at a poster about the importance of spaying and neutering your pets.

No one ever said the ambience in an animal shelter was romantic.

"Hot Puppy Guy is a *snack*," Beth says, and I do my best not to visibly cringe as I step away from the door.

"He has a name," I remind her. "It's Eli. And you can't *say* things like that."

"You can't tell me not to." Beth crosses her arms. "You're being ageist by implying I'm too old to use the term *snack*. Or to appreciate a *snackable*"—I flinch again—"piece of man."

"Beth, *please*. It's as much about objectification as it is your terminology. He's not a *piece* of anything. He's a *person*."

"I'm not *objectifying* your boyfriend. I'm *appreciating* his personhood. Like he's a fine wine. Or a Van Gogh."

"You are literally illustrating objectification right now. And, once again, Eli is *not* my boyfriend."

But I sure wish he were.

Not that I'm even in the market for a relationship. I absolutely and categorically am not. Clearly, I need to have a talk with whatever part of my subconscious keeps forgetting that very relevant fact whenever Eli shows up. It's probably the biological impulse to naturally select the biggest and strongest male for procreative purposes.

Procreation is something I need to think about even LESS than I think about having a boyfriend.

The cost of vet school means my focus needs to be work. No distractions. Definitely no boyfriends. Not even super-hot Viking men who love dogs.

I'm in my spinster era. Every twentysomething has one of those, right?

Aside from a lucky lotto win, saving up enough to minimize student loans will take years. Especially if I consider the letter still jammed in my bra. The one I keep forgetting about until a corner pokes me in a very sensitive area. Again.

I *really* need to pull this envelope out when Beth isn't looking.

She claps her hands. "Stop drooling and go."

I take another step away from the door. "I'm not drooling."

Still. When Beth looks through the window, I wipe my chin. Just in case.

"Hm," she says in a faux-thoughtful voice. "Looks like Katrina is trying to demonstrate yoga poses and—"

"On second thought, I'll head out there."

Beth's smile widens into a smug grin, and she tucks a white curl behind her ear. It immediately springs right back out. "That's what I thought," she says. "Maybe this time you could actually, I don't know, talk to him about more than dogs."

Doubtful. Not because I am incapable of carrying on conversations that don't revolve around animals. But more because every time I'm around new or unfamiliar people—and I don't consider people *familiar* unless we've been close friends for at least a year—my shy tendencies kick in hardcore. Forget tongue-tied; I become tongue-tangled.

My normally neat and organized thoughts get jumbled, like someone dumped an alphabetized file cabinet out on the floor then took a leaf blower to it.

"I make no promises."

I hesitate by the door, and Beth gives me a hearty shove. "Get out there before Katrina takes her top off in a desperate attempt to steal your boyfriend."

I don't even bother arguing again that he's not my boyfriend. Or that Katrina won't take her top off. Honestly, I wouldn't put it past her.

Taking a breath, which does nothing to slow my racing heart, I step through the door.

And there he is—his back still turned toward the reception desk. The three volunteers scatter at the sight of me. Totally busted in their ogling. I'm not their boss, exactly, but as a full-time employee, volunteers fall somewhat under my purview. Katrina answers the phone, which has probably been ringing since Eli walked in.

I approach him cautiously, stopping a few feet away to give his flannel-clad back an appreciative glance. Not an objectifying stare. If I were objectifying, I'd be looking at his butt. Backs are totally neutral zones.

"Here for more puppy therapy?" I ask, proud I'm not only able to get words out, but funny ones at that.

When Eli turns and I catch the expression on his face, I

immediately regret my attempt at humor. Not funny. Not even a little.

Clearly, my words hit a little too close to home. Eli looks ... terrible. I mean, relatively speaking. About as terrible as this man *can* look. Still very, very attractive, but his infectious smile has been replaced by a frown, and his blue eyes look haunted.

It actually *hurts* to see such a normally bright and sunny man look so sad.

Immediately, I want to fix it. Especially after sticking my foot so far into my mouth.

"Sorry—bad joke," I say quietly, waving a hand and hoping he doesn't see the flush creeping up my neck. "It's just an expression. Studies have shown that being around dogs can cause a release of oxytocin, serotonin, dopamine, and endorphins. So, it's like a kind of therapy. Not that you *need* therapy. Or that there's anything wrong with therapy. I saw a therapist for a while. Just for, you know, *reasons.*"

I clamp my mouth shut before any other words can possibly escape. My tongue tangle is in full effect, only instead of *keeping* me from talking, it's indiscriminately spraying out words with the force and imprecision of a firehose.

The only thing that saves me from disappearing into a pit in the floor is Eli's smile. A real one. Slow and warm like melted cheese—ew, no! Not cheese. Like melted caramel —better.

If my ridiculous babbling can lighten his mood and make this man smile, I'll gladly contribute to the cause.

"Good to know," he says, still smiling.

Good to know *what?* That I went to therapy? That being around dogs can help release a cocktail of happy brain chemicals? That I have a real problem with oversharing?

I swallow thickly, afraid to open my mouth again lest I confess something else. Like the fact that I still have an overdue book I checked out of Asheville's public library seven years ago, or how I once threw a piece of ice across the cafeteria at a boy I liked and it left a welt on the back of his head.

In lieu of speaking, I extend my arm to the swinging door that leads to a hall of what we call our meet-and-greet rooms.

Eli nods, still looking amused I'm *sure* at my expense, and runs a hand through his floppy blond hair. If not a face model, Eli could totally be a hair model. Or whatever that official job title is. A shampoo spokesperson? Follicle featurer? A harbinger of hair?

Eli beats me to the door and holds it open for me. I refuse to swoon over his gentlemanly vibes, but as I brush past his broad chest, I do take a deep inhale of his scent.

I don't know what exactly the different notes are, but the sum total ends up being masculine and heady without being overwhelming. Like a spicy-hot, manly cinnamon stick. Possibly the best smell in the world. Followed very distantly by the fresh bread smell when you walk into Subway. I have to shake off thoughts of what it would be like to stand next to Eli *inside* a Subway.

Eli plus freshly baked bread? Perfection.

I lead him to the first meet-and-greet room where people can see how they vibe with different potential pets. Our shelter has three of these rooms, all identical with an uncomfortable bench nailed to the wall, a few scattered toys, and a drain in the floor. Excited dogs often equal excited bladders. And it's a whole lot easier to clean up this excitement when you can rinse it right down a drain.

Typically, we would walk potential adopters through the second door that leads to the kennels and let them pick a few dogs to meet one at a time. But Eli isn't typical. For one, he's made it clear he can't adopt a dog. His job—whatever it is— requires he keep hours that aren't conducive to pet ownership. So he's said. Which is a shame, really. I've seen the longing in his eyes when he's playing tug-of-war with a lab mix, the widening of his smile when a tiny mutt climbs in his lap, the way he brightens when I walk into the room with any dog at all. The man should have a dog if for no other reason than it lights him up inside.

I've never asked what he does that won't allow him to care for a pet. I don't ask him any questions. That would mean crossing over some invisible line I've set for myself. And fighting against the shyness holding my words hostage.

Technically, I shouldn't let Eli keep coming in to hang out with the dogs.

Technically, I don't care.

The second reason Eli isn't like other people who come in is that he lets me pick the dogs for him. After his first time here, he refused to go in the kennels. He said it made him too sad to see all of them lined up and waiting for homes. I remember the way his eyes widened, how his gaze traveled down the long row of enclosures, at the noses pressed between bars. His swallow had been visible, throat bobbing in a way that made me sad at the same time as it made me want to remove a layer of clothing for fear of spontaneous combustion.

Eli forgoes the bench to sit on the floor cross-legged, like he's a Kindergarten student waiting for reading time. Not a grown man whose frame is so large he makes this room look Lilliputian.

He makes me feel miniature as well, which is normally something that would bother me. After being teased mercilessly about my height—or lack thereof—when I was younger, I normally don't like any reminder that I'm what my best friend, Shannon, calls a pocket person. Eli's largeness, instead of making me feel smaller, somehow makes me feel safe.

Not that Eli has ever acted in some kind of overtly protective way toward me. Outside of my dreams, anyway.

Creepy as it might make me sound, Eli *has* starred in my dreams a few times.

Most notably a recent one in which he was some kind of centaur-unicorn with his handsome face and broad chest attached to the body of a purple horse. Complete with a pink mane, tail, and glittery horn.

That one was trippy and definitely in the PG-13 category. Me, riding on his back, gripping his mane between my fingers. The searing kiss he gave me after I slid down his flank.

Freud would have a field day with all of this.

But it's my *subconscious!* I can't control what my brain does when I'm sleeping! If mine wants to have sexy centaur-unicorn dreams featuring Eli, I can't stop it and I'm certainly not going to judge.

My subconscious has good taste.

"Are you okay?"

I jump at Eli's question, realizing I've been simply standing here, staring into space while thinking about kissing his centaur-unicorn counterpart.

I give my head a little shake. "Sorry. I'm just, um, thinking."

About you shirtless and with a purple horse body.

"Must be some good thoughts." Eli grins and, for the second time in the last few minutes, I blush. "*Very* good thoughts."

I've never been more grateful that mindreading powers

only exist in fiction. I'm sure if Eli knew about my dream version of him, he'd run screaming from the room. I'm worse than Beth and her snack comments and overt objectification!

Needing a breather—and to get on with what I'm supposed to be doing—I open the door leading to the back room, which connects to the kennels. "Any special requests today?"

Eli hesitates for a moment, and then the same lost look returns. The one he had in the lobby a few minutes ago. "Maybe ... a dog who looks like they need a hug?"

If I didn't already harbor a crush the size of the Appalachians, this comment would be enough to send me over the edge. I give him a quick nod and duck back into the kennels before I can do something like ... well. I don't know what I'd do.

Kiss him like the centaur-unicorn of my dreams, perhaps? Definitely a bad idea.

Ugh. Someone as good looking as Eli should really possess the personality of a cave troll just to balance out the scales. It's a travesty of justice for someone so attractive to also be so kind. Completely unfair. Especially when I have no good defenses against him.

My crush didn't even start because of Eli's looks, though they certainly add to the whole package. It's his energy that draws me. Aside from today, there's a brightness to him, a sort of vibrant energy that emanates from him like each cell in his body is a tiny sun.

In this analogy, I'm a planet stuck in his orbit.

Whenever he comes in, just being near him lightens my mood. Not that I'm a super melancholy person. I've actually been accused of being too optimistic and believing the best about people—neither of which are bad things, in my opinion. But ... there aren't a lot of joys in my life right now. Eli coming in is pretty much the highlight of any week or month.

I realize this makes me sound super sad. Like my life is *so* empty that a random guy cheers me up when he comes in to see the dogs.

Let me emphasize this: when he comes to see the *dogs*. Not to see *me*.

I take a few moments in the kennels to collect myself. To give my twitterpated heart and overactive imagination a stern talking to.

Once I feel a little more grounded in reality, I walk past the kennels, looking for the dog who most needs a hug. The ones who have been here for a while and know the drill practically throw themselves at the door. *Pick me! Pick me!* their barks and effusive tail wags say.

In truth, all of them could use a hug. Our facility is a no-kill shelter, and it's pretty great as far as shelters go. But it is old. And, like any nonprofit, funds are stretched thin. The facility would be much better if we had outdoor runs attached to the kennels so the dogs wouldn't be cooped up inside except for twice daily walks.

"Which of you needs a hug from a hottie today?" I ask and am rewarded with a lot of enthusiastic butt wiggles and shrill, desperate barks.

But as I pace, my mind keeps circling back to one dog in particular. The one dog I probably *shouldn't* bring out to meet someone. Still.

I leave the kennel for the main back room, where a small black dog trembles in the single row of small kennels. The latest stray Animal Control picked up isn't adjusting well to the shelter. To put it mildly.

The vet had to sedate her so we could shave off the clumps of matted fur covering her body. She's trembling, and every time a door slams or a dog barks from the kennel room, she jolts. I've grown so used to the steady barking, I almost don't hear it anymore. But Doris practically had a panic attack when we walked her in there, so for the time being, we're keeping her out here in the row of small kennels usually reserved for dogs recovering from surgery.

I've been talking to Doris all morning, attempting to win her over with kind words, which have been ignored, and dog treats, which have been left untouched in a small pile near the front of her kennel.

The look she gives me is pitiful. "Hey, girl," I say. She gives the tiniest thump of her tail. Progress? "You definitely look like you need a hug. Do you *want* a hug? That's the question."

Her pointy ears flick back, almost like she's saying, *A hug, you say? Hard pass.*

But I can't shake this feeling. The same instinct that often helps me pair the right person with the right dog. Beth says I have a gift. I think it's more that, after so many years of being the quiet person who's hardly seen *or* heard, I have keenly developed powers of observation. I can quickly get a good sense about both humans *and* dogs. When people or families come in to adopt, often, I just *know*.

I bite my lip, debating as I look at Doris. Finally, I get one of our slip-on leashes and open her kennel, coaxing her out with a treat. Not one of the crunchy dog biscuits Doris has ignored, but one of the soft and chewy treats that stink like high heaven but must taste like doggy delicacy.

It works. Doris gingerly accepts this one from my fingers and allows me to slip the leash over her head—a good sign.

Slowly, giving her time to smell anything she wants to smell, I walk Doris toward the door, talking her through what we're doing. I have a habit of talking to the dogs as though they have a very good grasp of English and at least a high school vocabulary.

"You're a lucky girl today," I tell her. "You're going to meet Eli. Don't tell anyone, but he's my favorite. He said he wants a dog who looks like she needs a hug, but you know what? I think *he* needs a hug, Doris. I have this weird feeling like you two need to meet today. Just be yourself, okay? He can't adopt a dog, so there's no pressure to perform. It's not a rejection when he doesn't take you home. But also ... don't get too attached for the same reason."

She gives me a look that either says she understands and agrees or she thinks I'm bananas for talking to a dog. "How about this—if you can cheer him up, I'll give you an extra bonus treat, okay? The good kind."

Her tail wags at the word treat. Perfect. We have an understanding.

With a last deep breath, I walk back into the meet-and-greet room with Doris, hoping my instincts are still on today.

Eli looks up, his shoulders more slumped and his expression darker than when I left the room. But he perks up immediately when he sees Doris, his face brightening and softening at the same time.

And dang it—I've never been jealous of a dog, but I sure am now. I'd like to be the one putting that look on his face. The one who walks into a room and has that kind of impact.

I gently slip the lead back over her head, setting her loose in the small room. "Eli, this is Doris. Doris, Eli. I'm not quite sure how this will go. She's new and still getting the hang of things, so she might not ..."

There's no need to finish my sentence. With the kind of grin that could disarm nuclear warheads, Eli holds his arms out wide.

Doris, smart girl that she is, climbs right into his lap.

I can't blame her. If Eli were opening those arms to me, I'd walk right into them too.

No, I'd *run* and take a flying leap.

Eli doesn't move while Doris settles in his lap, as though sensing her need to take things at her own pace. Slowly, he lowers his arms, bracketing her in while still giving her plenty of space.

She sniffs one of his big hands, then the other. Eli waits, motionless but still smiling, letting Doris run the show. She tilts her head to look up at him. Then, slowly and tentatively, she stretches up and gives the blond scruff on his chin a solid lick.

Even his chuckle is soft, as though he knows a full laugh might scare Doris. "That's a good girl," he says.

My heart gives a solid thump. I ignore it. It thumps again, harder this time, and I tell it to kindly go back to its regularly scheduled programming.

With Eli's focus on Doris, I am completely at liberty to stare at the impossibly attractive man before me. I remind myself of what I told Beth earlier—*don't objectify him*—and then add my warning for Doris—*don't get too attached.*

Doris, however, is listening about as well as my heart. After Eli passes her smell test (I could have told her that he would), she settles in on his lap and rolls over, presenting her belly for scratches.

Eli gently strokes her belly. "We're going to get along just fine, aren't we, Doris?" His smiling eyes meet mine. "And to think you doubted me."

"It's not that I doubted you—"

He smirks. "Uh-huh."

"I just wasn't sure how it would go. Doris has had a rough time adjusting so far."

Eli's happy expression recedes, and he gazes down at

Doris, who is now shamelessly butting her nose into Eli's palm. "She has a sad story?"

His somber tone makes my chest tighten.

"As with most of the dogs who end up here, we don't really know. From the looks of things, she'd been on her own for a long time. You can see how thin she is, and her fur was one big matted clump. It's why we shaved her so short."

"Well, I happen to think you look beautiful with a buzz cut, D. You're a stunner. Don't let anyone tell you different."

Gah! My heart! It feels like each of Eli's kind words is piercing me like an arrow, tipped not with poison but some kind of love potion. There is a cupid laughing maniacally somewhere. I just know it.

Doris curls into a ball and closes her eyes as Eli scratches behind her ears. He gives me a smug look, and I feel it all the way down to my toes.

I hold up both hands. "I stand corrected."

"Never doubt me again," he says.

I clear my throat, feeling a weight in his words I know he doesn't intend. "Never."

Normally, when people visit with dogs, I'll pop in and out of the room, checking to make sure things are going okay but giving them plenty of space. Trading out one dog for another as people try to get a sense for what one might be the best fit.

With Eli, I've started spending more time in the room. Mostly because he invites conversation, pushing me into feeling almost comfortable around him. Also because I just like being around him.

I stay today because it's almost closing time, and there's not much else to do. And because Eli's dampened mood when he came in has me concerned. Even now, with his smiles and his teasing, he's not at full strength. Like someone has been messing with his dimmer switch, powering him down to a fraction of his normal glow.

I slide down the wall, sitting directly across from him with my knees pulled to my chest. As he snuggles Doris closer, Eli's gaze falls to my forearm, which is freshly marked up thanks to a feline encounter earlier in the day.

He frowns. "You're scratched up again. Cats *really* don't like you, do they?"

I glance down at the angry red marks. "I really do *try*. But no—the cats have clearly sent out an all-feline bulletin about me. It's a conspiracy. They're plotting my demise."

Eli laughs, and pleasure thrums through me, a warm slide of happiness. "How's that going to work if you plan to be a vet? Can you have a canine specialty or a no-cats policy?"

Sighing, I say, "I'll have to find a way to peacefully coexist with cats."

"Ah. The suck-it-up-buttercup plan."

"Pretty much."

"I have faith in you." Eli's blue eyes twinkle—almost but not quite at full strength—as he shoots a smile my way. It sends a chain reaction through my body, this one on the cellular level, a molecular game of telephone delivering what I'm sure is the very wrong message.

This is not the first time Eli has flirted with me. He also flirts with Beth, who's twice his age. And with Cyn, the part-time vet tech, who's almost Beth's age and seemingly incapable of smiling.

But Eli *never* flirts with Katrina and the other young and pretty volunteers and staff who fawn all over him.

In other words, Eli only flirts with the women who aren't really viable options.

I'm so, *so* glad I fall into the flirt-because-I'm-safe category.

"How are the vet school applications going?" Eli methodically strokes Doris's back, and she sighs like she's having the best sleep of her life. Maybe she is.

I make a face. "Fine."

Better if I could work up the nerve to ask the vet who works here part of the week for a recommendation. But Dr. Evie is highly intimidating. There's a reason she's better known as Dr. Evil around the shelter.

"I'll bet you aced your test," he says. "Which one was it again? The MCAT or the LSAT?"

"It was the GRE. And I did well." When he raises his eyebrows, I grin and drop my gaze to my hands. "Fine. I *did* ace it."

Which is good because those tests are not cheap, and I didn't want to pay to take it again.

"I knew you would." He sounds almost proud, which makes me feel ridiculously happy.

"You couldn't know that. You barely know *me*."

"Or maybe I know you better than you think, smart girl."

Now, there's a thought that just about breaks my brain.

I'm always shocked Eli remembers or seems interested in any of my life's details. He has a way of coaxing information out of me during his visits the way I coaxed Doris out of her kennel with soft words and a treat.

I feel a sudden stab of guilt, realizing I don't do the same for him. Not because I'm not interested. But it's just *hard* for me. Even when he makes it look so easy.

My shyness is a product of both nature and nurture. My parents were academics and researchers, Dad in literature and Mom in biochemistry. Both the very stereotype of the absent-minded professor, better with books and beakers than people.

Though they absolutely adored me, their only and

perhaps accidental daughter, my childhood was a little too quiet and solitary. They encouraged independent study, independent thinking, and just, well, being independent.

The sad part is that I've always been drawn to people. I remember aching to have the kind of childhood I read about or saw in movies where kids gathered in groups to play outside. Sleepovers. Parties. Riding bicycles and coming home at dusk, happily exhausted and smelling like damp leaves and fresh air. Our house was way outside of Asheville with beautiful scenery and some land, but no neighbors nearby. No possibility of easy friends.

I think my parents assumed I was like them: self-sufficient and nerdy enough to let books be stand-ins for other people. While I am bookish and admittedly nerdy, I've also realized I fit into the little discussed category of people known as shy extroverts. As in, I get energy from being around people. But I am in no way outgoing or talkative or socially brave the way people typically imagine extroverts.

Especially because, after a childhood spent cloistered up in our house or in the university campus library or my parents' offices, I don't always know what to say or how to interact normally when I'm around people. The whole tongue-tangle thing.

It's a challenge.

But I'm tired of shyness being my excuse. Eli asks me questions even though we barely know each other. I can do the same for him.

What to ask?

Now that I'm trying to drum up my courage, all rational thought has left my brain. My fingertips tingle, and my pulse is racing. I'm suddenly reminded of the letter in my bra when I shift and it crinkles.

Thankfully, Eli doesn't hear it. His shoulders are slumped

again, and there's a tiny crease between his brows as one of his big hands slowly strokes Doris's back. I can still read the sadness in the uncharacteristic stillness of a man who usually possesses border-collie-energy mixed with golden-retriever-happiness.

I think of Beth's challenge to talk to him about something besides dogs, and I have a little argument with myself.

Talk to him!

No, thanks.

Just ask if he's okay.

He's fine.

He's not fine! Look at him!

Yes, he is fine. Fiiiine.

Not THAT kind of fine.

Eli sighs, as if to prove the mouthy part of my subconscious correct. He might be fine-looking. But he is not fine inside.

Before I can talk myself out of it, I ask, "Is everything okay? You seem a little down today."

My voice is hardly more than a whisper, but Eli's head snaps up like I shouted. I grit my teeth and force myself to hold his gaze. No sense being a coward now.

He offers up a lopsided smile, but his eyes are still sad. "That obvious, huh?"

I offer him a shaky smile. Shaky because adrenaline is surging through me. Sad what a tiny bit of bravery can take out of me.

"You're flying at half-mast," I tell him, then hope it wasn't a terrible thing to say.

But Eli chuckles, looking somehow pleased. Maybe that I'm talking to him like this? Hopefully he hasn't noticed the lopsided way our conversations have always gone. But how could he not have? He's always the one talking, and I'm always the one answering.

I feel anxiety trying to take me down in a death spiral, and I focus for a moment on slowing my thoughts, slowing my heartbeat, slowing my self-judgment. It works. Slightly.

"I've been better." Eli drops his gaze and his smile, smoothing his hands over Doris again and again.

It takes a few long moments for me to land on an appropriate follow-up question. At least, I *hope* it's appropriate.

"Is there anything I can do to help?"

Eli's reaction to my question this time is slower but somehow almost as dramatic. No—*more* dramatic. It's as though my offer struck him like a stone between the eyes, stunning him.

His hands stop moving, resting lightly on Doris's dark shaved fur. His shoulders stiffen. Almost comically slow, he lifts his head to look at me again. His expression seems dazed, almost bordering on surprise.

He opens and closes his mouth several times, then he tilts his head to the side, as though assessing me.

Is he...? *Wait.* Is he actually considering taking me up on my offer to help? Is there something I could really do for him?

My body's response to this wildly exciting yet completely terrifying prospect is to start sweating profusely under my scrubs. Behind my ribs, a rave is going on, with my pounding heart providing the bass.

I force myself to swallow and remind myself to breathe as Eli's blue eyes track over my face. He seems to arrive at some conclusion, because he relaxes with a soft sigh and an even softer smile.

"Unfortunately, Bailey, I don't think you can help."

"Oh."

Disappointment, sharp and bitter, lands with surprising force. At the same time, the blow is softened by a bright ribbon of pleasure curling through me. *He knows my name!* A tiny thing, really, especially when he's been coming in for months. But we hardly ever address each other.

When did I even tell him my name? The very first time he came in?

And he *remembers?*

It makes me double down on my bravery, which is starting to feel a whole lot more like recklessness.

I shake my head and cross my arms. This presses the edge of the letter against my skin. I ignore it.

"Try me," I say, before the courage fueled by stubbornness dissipates. "Maybe you're wrong. Maybe I could—or would —help."

He tilts his head, and even under the harsh lights, his hair glows gold. "Why?"

I'm not expecting the question. Or his piercing gaze. "Why ... do I want to help you?"

He nods, and I look away, my gaze landing on a poster about feline leukemia. A very sad cat stares back. I search for an answer that doesn't include confessing my schoolgirl crush.

"You don't even know what I need help with. And to quote you from earlier," he adds, and I can hear the smile in his voice even though I'm not looking, "you barely know me."

Again, the gentleness in his voice softens his words. But hearing the echo of what I said moments ago stings a little. Mostly because it's true. Especially compared to how much information he's managed to get out of me over these past six months or so of visits.

But while I may not know much about him, from the time

I *have* spent with him, I do feel I know who he *is*. Maybe I'm fuzzy on the details like job, hobbies, and personal history, but I know Eli's *character*. You can observe a lot from watching a person interact with animals.

An unfamiliar desperation to prove Eli wrong claws its way through me. Paired with a palpable, aching need to fix whatever it is that's bringing him down. A desire to be the exact and only person who can help.

I lick my lips, which are suddenly almost as dry as my mouth. "I know enough," I tell him. "I know you're kind. I know you care about animals, which says a lot about a person."

"Who doesn't love dogs?" he asks, scoffing a little.

"You'd be surprised. But you don't just love the easy ones or the pretty ones." I tilt my chin toward Doris. "She's hardly let anyone near her, yet she's curled up in your lap. Most people want puppies or dogs who look like they might be purebred. The good-looking ones and the young ones. The *easy* ones. But not you. You love them all. Even—maybe *especially*—the ones no one else does. You have a big heart, Eli. A good heart."

And ... now I've done it.

I gathered my courage, attempted to partake in normal conversation, and then gave the equivalent of a villain's monologue.

Except instead of revealing the motivations for my evil plot, I've likely just revealed way too much about how I feel about *him*.

"So, yeah," I add quickly. "I want to help because you're a good guy."

So many more reasons. But this is the only safe one.

Eli is quiet for a long moment. The kind of pause that feels like the pulling back of the ocean before a tsunami. I briefly consider bolting from the room, claiming some emergency. A fire! An escaped dog! My period! I force myself to sit still and stay silent.

"I appreciate the vote of confidence," Eli says, *finally*. "And the kind words. But I still don't think this is something you can help with."

He stops, then meets and holds my gaze with an intensity that freezes me in place.

"That is," he continues, those blue eyes blazing, "unless you want to marry me."

CHAPTER 3

Bailey

I CHOKE ON A LAUGH. No—literally *choke*.

And I guess, technically, I'm choking on my own saliva, not laughter. Caught in the embarrassing and unlikely situation wherein a handsome man makes a statement—or a joke?—about marriage, then you inhale your own spit and almost die.

Maybe, I think as I hack uncontrollably, *dying would be preferable to this current humiliation.*

Eli is beside me in an instant, crouching inches away, Doris cradled to his chest with one arm. He reaches out to me with the other, grasping my shoulder and giving me the smallest shake. His eyes—the pure, crisp blue of Norwegian fjords, which I know because I googled Norwegian fjords once after he came in—are wide and panicked.

"Are you okay? I'm sorry. Bailey, I—"

I cut him off with a wave of my hand, trying to wheeze out something dismissive like, *I'm fine, really,* or *Just leave me here to die.*

But my words are unintelligible, and his concern increases as he tugs me forward, then attempts to slap me on the back. All while keeping a small dog tucked protectively against his body.

Doris must have seen some *things* in her little life because she seems totally nonplussed by my near-death experience. Then again, maybe she doesn't care because Eli's solid presence has lulled her into feeling secure.

This situation is utterly ridiculous. *Eli* is ridiculous. Yet still so very, very attractive. This image would make a good inspiration for a monthly calendar. The theme being: Hot Men Saving Women from Certain Death While Holding Dogs.

I'd laugh if I weren't still attempting to clear my own airway. But I do manage to suck in a gasping breath. Finally.

How absolutely mortifying.

Then again, the payoff for my stupid choking incident is grand. Eli's warm hand is now sliding up and down my back in gentle strokes. I'm sure it's meant to be comforting and it is, but his touch also ignites something fierce and hot, a sizzling burn just below my skin.

The scent of him, which if bottled up and named would be something like Viking Warrior #3, has a dizzying effect, scrambling my thoughts.

Because did Eli really say something about *marriage?*

That can't be right.

"I'm sorry," he says again. "I didn't mean to ... ah ..."

"Make me choke on my own spit?" I wipe my eyes, which are brimming with cough-induced tears.

"Almost kill you with a marriage proposal." Eli's mouth kicks up on one side.

I blink at him. "You really *did* say marriage."

"Ah, yeah. I did."

Eli blows out a breath, and he's so close, I feel it brush my cheek like the softest caress. One of his hands is still warm and solid on my back, the other holding Doris, who has gone back to sleep, her nose tucked into the front pocket of Eli's forest green flannel shirt. The tips of his ears are pink.

"But you were joking, right?" I ask.

There's no way this man needs help finding a fiancée. No way he'd be asking *me*, a person he's had minimal interactions with. Someone he's not even dating. My brain is whirring along, sounding like the old laptop I recently threw out, which sounded like an airplane taking off every time I turned it on.

"Yeah. But kind of no?" He gives his head the smallest shake, his smile sheepish. As I stare—because I'm *totally* staring right now—his cheeks turn the same pink as his ears. "It's not—ugh. Not like a *real* marriage."

"A *fake* marriage, then?" If my voice sounds flat, it's because that's how I feel. Like his words are steamrolling me into a pancake.

Are fake marriages even a thing outside of Hallmark movies and romance novels?

"I mean, it would be real on paper. But not like a *marriage* marriage. With all the, you know, marriage parts."

"Marriage parts," I repeat dumbly.

I have been reduced to Eli's echo. But it is impossible for me to locate any fresh words of my own. My brain tripped over this whole marriage concept, and now I'm trying to scrape myself up off the figurative sidewalk.

"So, there's this visa issue," he says. His hand has come to rest on my upper back, his fingertips brushing the bare skin of my neck.

Does he know he's touching my skin? Does it have anywhere *near* the impact on him that it has on me? Clearly not.

"The immigration kind, not the credit card kind. Complicated, long story. The point is, if I don't get married in a month"—he winces at this, and I do too because WHAT—"I'll be deported to Canada."

He gives these words a moment to sink in. They do. Deeply, like the roots of an old oak. Deported? I think first, irrationally, of all the dogs who won't get their pets. And of not seeing him, of having the bright spots in the otherwise dishwater gray of my life.

Selfish thoughts, I realize, when I should be thinking of the man who will be deported. Canada, I realize, feels as fictional to me as Narnia. Up North, snowy, a vast expanse on a map that's never seemed real until this moment.

Eli clears his throat. "But I didn't really think ... I mean, you wouldn't ..."

He didn't think *what?*

I wouldn't *what?*

My thoughts have been tossed haphazardly into an industrial dryer where they're tumbling around on high heat. Around and around. Mixed up. *Heated.* If Eli's cheeks are rose-petal pink, mine must be Valentine's red.

"Wow. I'm bad at this," Eli says with a chuckle that sounds less humorous than a funeral dirge. "It's not like you or anyone else would want to marry me anyway. For money or whatever reasons."

His eyes flick up to mine, and I swear there's an unspoken question: *Would they?*

Maybe even … would *you?*

I wish I could say this didn't have some part of me standing up, jumping and waving while shouting, *Me, me, me! You had me at* For money! *Yes! I do! Put a ring on it!*

It's the same part of me suddenly aware that I *still* have a letter poking me in the boob that very much has to do with money and my desperate need for it.

And would it even be a hardship to marry this man? The one snuggling a dog, whose face is inches from mine. The one with kind blue eyes and the kind of scent I'd like to wrap myself up in like a warm sweater.

"Can we, uh, just forget I asked you to commit fraud?" Eli asks, and his fingertips do a tiny dance at the top of my spine. I fight to keep still and not tremble. "I'm clearly beyond help."

"I …"

My thoughts are still tumbling, but now it's more like one of those lotto ball machines, and as I open my mouth to speak, I'm not at all sure what word will separate itself from the rest and pop out of my mouth.

And I'll *never* know because that's when the door opens, and Dr. Evie—aka Dr. Evil—walks into the room.

She freezes, one hand curled around the doorknob. Her blue eyes—which are not fjord-like but rather the gray blue of harsh slate—narrow at me first. Her delicate features manage to be pretty even when she's glaring in disapproval. Professionally shaped dark eyebrows, lashes I suspect are extensions, and the kind of perfect lips that gave cupid's bow its name. All of her deceptively pretty features might lead one to believe she is nice. One would be mistaken.

While her doctorate is in veterinary medicine, Dr. Evie has a secondary degree in finding flaws and pointing them out with clinical—and maybe joyful—precision.

All while looking just like a Disney princess.

"What's happening here?" she asks, closing the door behind her with a decisively judgmental half-slam.

I scramble to my feet, eyes still slightly wet with cough-induced tears, cheeks still flaming from all the talk of *marriage*. This looks *bad*. I am not supposed to be hanging out with a prospective pet owner. Definitely not sitting practically nose-to-nose.

Absolutely positively not talking about marriage.

"Sorry, I was …"

The explanation—or excuse?—I was striving and failing to come up with completely leaves my mind when Eli stands, towering over us both. His presence doesn't just suck all the air out of the room. It sucks *everything* out. Air, thoughts, words, feelings—all gone.

For half a second, I'm grateful for the reprieve. For the distraction of this giant man saving me from making up some kind of lie. I am a terrible liar. And it's not like I want to tell Dr. Evil about the confusing conversation she just interrupted.

But then, I quickly realize my relief was naïve.

Because Dr. Evie's eyes track up, up, up until they land on Eli's face with surprise and then interest. The protectiveness I felt when Katrina was angling her body toward him earlier is nothing compared to how I feel now. It's all I can do not to put myself as a barrier between Dr. Evil and the man, though I have zero claim to him. The urge only increases when her lips curl into a poison-apple smile.

"Well, hello," she says. "I didn't expect to see *you* here."

My stomach drops. She and Eli know each other?

But where her face shows familiarity, his expression is blank, borderline wary, though he doesn't seem necessarily surprised that she recognized him.

Weird.

Dr. Evie's eyes take on a predatory look I don't like even a little bit, and her posture shifts from grumpy boss into siren mode. It's subtle, but I don't miss the slight arch in her back and the coy tilt of her head. As she steps around me and closer to Eli, her hips sway. She practically *glides.*

Like a gorgeous poltergeist.

When Beth and I aren't discussing Dr. Evie's penchant for biting criticism, we're rolling our eyes at her uncanny ability to channel sex appeal while wearing a white lab coat. I swear, the woman has her scrubs and coat specially tailored to accentuate her figure.

I don't *like* the woman, not even a little bit. But it's imperative that I *pretend* to like her. Not only to keep this job, but also because I need her recommendation for vet school. Which means I can't punch her for the way she's looking at Eli.

"Hello, Eli," she says in a sultry voice that does not belong in an animal shelter. "I'm Dr. Evie. Eli, Evie."

She laughs, like it's the funniest thing ever how both their names start with E.

I frown. Okay, so she *definitely* knows him. But if they know each other, why is she introducing herself? And why does he look so uncomfortable?

Eli circles his arms a little tighter around Doris—either in an attempt to protect her or use her as a canine shield—and takes the smallest step back.

"Hello," he says stiffly. No smile.

Why does this make me so unreasonably pleased?

Doris gives a low growl as Dr. Evie steps closer. She pauses, eyes narrowing before they flick back to me, instantly shifting from sultry to sharp.

"Doris hasn't been cleared for adoption yet," she says.

"And I wouldn't think hockey players have the time to care for a dog."

Busted! I wonder exactly how much trouble I'm going to be in for bringing Doris out. And for Eli's visits when he's made it clear he can't adopt a dog right now. And for—*wait.*

Hockey player?

I make note of Eli's broad shoulders and the way his thighs are testing the tensile strength of his pants seams. Professional athlete makes sense. Which I guess means his job is not bare-handed tree removal.

But wouldn't I have heard about this? If Dr. Evie recognized Eli right away, Katrina and the other volunteers always drooling over him probably know who he is.

Come to think of it, they probably *do* know. I assumed they always congregated when he arrived because he's attractive. Which could still be true. But I bet they just never mentioned who he is. And why would they? We don't interact much. If they're the cool girls, I hang with the *other* crowd—the shelter's social equivalent of the band geeks or nerds.

Though they're both decades older than I am, Beth and Cyn are the only ones at the shelter I really talk to. I've always felt a little bit more on the outskirts when it comes to the college-aged volunteers and staff. Losing both parents early will do that to a person. I feel infinitely older than twenty-three.

Hockey, huh? I study Eli again, trying to picture him in skates, a stick in hand, and ... whatever hockey players wear. A jersey? Pads? A helmet? Try as I might, my imagination has very little to draw from when it comes to this—or any— sport. I've never seen a hockey game despite Harvest Hollow being home to the Appies, a wildly popular minor league team.

One which Eli apparently plays for. It totally tracks. Still, finding out this fact leaves me strangely shaken for reasons I can't really explain.

"Are you hoping to adopt a dog?" Dr. Evie asks Eli.

Eli seems to shrink away from Dr. Evil's attention. The expression on his face returns to the lost look he wore when asking for a dog in need of a hug.

He drops his gaze to Doris. "I, um ..."

I clear my throat, which feels slightly raw from all the cough-trauma. "Eli was actually interested in our volunteer program," I say, hoping he'll play along.

"You want to volunteer?" Dr. Evie asks him with an arch of her brow.

"Yes," Eli says quickly. "The Appies do a lot of volunteer work, and I was interested in ..."

His gaze meets mine, and it's strange how we suddenly seem able to speak soundlessly from across the room.

"Walking dogs a few times a month," I say. "I was just about to get the volunteer application. To, um, keep things official. As we do."

"Well, then—why don't you scurry along and get it?" Dr. Evie says, dismissing me with a wave of her hand.

I may have covered for Eli—and myself—with the volunteer lie. But now I'm going to have to leave Eli alone with her. I shoot him an apologetic look, but his expression is still carefully void of emotion.

Thankfully, I know exactly where the volunteer applications are, and I'm back in record time.

Not a moment too soon, either. Doris is practically burrowing her face into Eli's armpit, and Dr. Evil looks about ready to toss the dog out of the way to pounce on her prey.

She has one hand, with its French-tipped nails—far too

pretty for someone in a hands-on job like hers—on Eli's arm. He looks about ready to bolt, Doris in hand.

"Got it!" I say. A little too loudly. A little too brightly. "Paperwork." I wave the single printed sheet for good measure.

Dr. Evie frowns and takes a step back, sliding her hands into her lab coat pockets. I swear, I can see her fists clench. "Oh, good."

I set the paper on the bench seat and pick up Doris's leash, holding it out to Eli. "Want to put this on her? First step in training. You just tuck the strap through this metal ring and slip it over her head."

I demonstrate how to work the simple leash, hoping Dr. Evie will leave. She doesn't. Which is a shame because Eli and I really didn't finish our conversation.

At least, it felt very unfinished to me. My brain is now populated by a bright constellation of question marks.

Eli, on the other hand, just seems eager to get away from Dr. Evil. Smart man.

Doris allows Eli to loop the leash around her neck, staring adoringly at him the whole time. He leans close, murmuring something in her ear, and I do my best not to melt into a puddle.

When he carefully sets Doris down, Dr. Evil doesn't even try to hide her blatant perusal of his body. I only hope I'm hiding how much I'd like to claw her eyes out.

Totally unearned jealousy, but there it is. Or maybe it's *somewhat* earned. Don't I get some kind of claim based on the pretend marriage proposal? And the fact that I liked him divorced of the knowledge that he's a hockey player?

"I'm glad we'll be seeing you again," Dr. Very Evil says, stepping closer to Eli. "Hopefully soon."

He barely gives her a nod, then catches my eye and holds out Doris's leash. "Here you go, Bailey."

Am I imagining it, or do his fingers linger on mine?

Probably all in my head. At least, based on the way he bolts from the room a moment later, volunteer application in hand.

Dr. Evil glances at me with narrowed eyes the moment the door slams behind him. "Why didn't you tell me Eli Hopkins was here?"

I swallow, not wanting to admit exactly how often he's been coming in. If she asks around, she'll find out pretty quickly. I guess it's a good thing most of the staff is afraid of her—or more likely sees her as competition—and wouldn't say a word.

"I had no idea he was a hockey player until you said something."

She laughs, then stops when she realizes I'm serious. "You didn't recognize him?"

I shake my head slowly.

"You don't follow him on TikTok?"

"I'm not on TikTok."

"Oh, sweet Bailey," Dr. Evil says with a cluck of her tongue. "You're so *young*. If you're not on TikTok, how do you spend all your free time?"

Her patronizing tone grates, but I remind myself I need to stay on her good side if I want a recommendation.

"Working mostly." I clear my throat. This is a perfect segue. And I've got just the tiniest bit of bravery left over from my conversation with Eli. Just enough, it turns out. "I'm actually applying to vet school."

"Oh." She blinks as though surprised. "I had no idea."

Of course, she didn't. Despite it having been on my application to work here. And the way I drop hints every so often, hoping she might offer to write me a recommendation and I can avoid the ask altogether.

I take a breath, hold it, then let it out slowly. *Nice and easy, Bay. Just ask her.*

But she speaks before I can. "I'd be glad to write a recommendation letter if you need one," she says.

"Really?" That was way too easy. It smells like a trap.

"Of course." She gives me a sly smile as she puts her hand on the door. "It will be an even better recommendation if you can keep Eli Hopkins coming in."

And ... there it is.

She must see me blanch—because *really?!?*—and she forces a laugh. "Kidding," she says. "Of course I'm kidding."

I don't get the impression she's kidding. At all. Which now makes me feel all kinds of ick. Even though I should be focused on the important part: she said she'd write me a recommendation!

One step closer to vet school. Now I just need to get over the money hurdle. My stomach squeezes at the thought, and the letter in my bra reminds me of its presence.

Of course, then my mind zips straight to Eli and the mention of marriage and money.

"Thank you," I say, the words sounding stiffer than they should.

"Of course," she says breezily.

But I have to wonder if she would have agreed so easily without Eli.

As I'm putting Doris back in her kennel, my mind circles back to the *professional hockey player* I've been hanging out with a few times a month without having any idea. Why is this hitting me the way it is? Or ... is it the hockey player info combined with the whole marriage idea?

I think about how he normally puts me at ease and the way he coaxes me to talk.

So, he's famous. A big deal. With me, he's just Eli.

Ha! The man isn't *just* anything. Even without the fame, his presence is practically too large for a room to contain.

I wonder if he'll come back in after this. Dr. Evil probably scared him off. Or maybe our conversation did. The idea of never seeing him again sends a wave of disappointment through me.

Way to ruin the highlight of my week, Dr. Evil.

But she's not done yet.

She pops her head back in just as I'm about to start administering the various meds that go along with the evening feeding.

"Oh, Bailey—I almost forgot," she says. "The reason I was looking for you was to ask for your help bathing one of the cats. He made quite a mess and rolled around in it."

Her smile is as sweet as a honey-covered dagger. I don't miss the way her eyes drop to the scratch on my arm. It's no secret that I'm universally hated by cats. It also could just as easily be a volunteer's job to bathe a cat.

Dr. Evil's already gone when I mutter, "There's nothing in the world I want to do more than give a cat a bath right now."

CHAPTER 4

Eli

"DUDE, WHERE'S YOUR HEAD?" Van smacks the side of my helmet with his stick as he skates past me.

"Right here," I grumble.

But it's not. My head is nowhere near the Summit. It's caught up in a worry vortex, cycloning around my uncertain future.

For days now, I've been trying to think of some kind of plan. Some way to skirt around immigration laws. To make it so I don't have to leave these idiots and rip my mom away from the life she's built here. Any alternative to moving back to Canada. Some kind of plan B or C or D or XYZ.

I am also pretending my half-hearted proposal attempt to Bailey, a woman I barely know, and the subsequent nonsensical explanation before I bolted, didn't happen. What was I even thinking? I don't have an answer for the temporary

56

lapse in judgment that lead me to blurt out a half-cocked joke-proposal to the sweet, shy woman working at the animal shelter.

Based on her reaction—which was almost choking to death right in front of me—I think I can rule out the whole find-a-wife option.

And now, I'm too embarrassed to face her, which means not going to the shelter, which is not helping my mood. She may have joked about it, but the dogs really *are* my version of therapy. Maybe Bailey has a part in it too, something I only realize in hindsight now that I've wrecked things with her.

When I was little, Mom sometimes would pick a chapter book to read at night. Often I fell asleep only to wake up to find her still reading, silently then, and many chapters ahead. One book that stuck with me was about a boy who lived in a house with a doomsday clock in its walls. Kind of creepy reading, but I loved the thrill of fear, and Mom did a great job with the voices. Too good, maybe.

The story comes to mind now. That's me—a man with a doomsday clock in my walls. And every day that I don't do *something*, the deadline moves closer and my mood gets darker. I swear, I can almost hear the minutes ticking away.

Alec knocks into me, his bulk hefting me into the wall. For a moment, we're locked in the hockey player's version of a romantic embrace. If we didn't have our helmets on, his face would be far too close for comfort.

I grunt and shove him off.

"We're going to have to start calling you Speed Bump," Alec says, skating away.

"Ha ha," I say. I'd like to release a little of my current tension by wiping the smile off his face. Briefly, I imagine his grin with a few teeth missing, and I'm almost happy.

Tucker laughs, and I have a sinking feeling that I've just gotten a nickname to replace Hop. *Great.*

"I approve," Tucker says, turning backward to shoot me the kind of grin that makes me want to chase him down and knock him into the wall. "Speed Bump suits you."

I manage to ignore the guys' ribbing, but when Coach calls me over, I can't ignore *him*. He may not call me Speed Bump, but I'm sure he's thinking it. I am useless on the ice today. If I keep this up, he'll replace me with the overeager second stringer in Saturday's game.

The idea further darkens my mood.

I expect a lecture, but Coach's stern expression softens when I skate over. He puts a hand on my shoulder, his dark brown eyes meeting mine.

"I know you've got a lot on your mind, son," he says. "But until you're not here, *be* here."

I try not to react to him calling me *son*. But every time Coach does it, something inside me expands, like a desperately needy part of me is preening under the idea of anyone at all claiming me as their *son*.

Stupid.

After I shake off that feeling, Coach's other words sink in: *until you're not here.*

Not *if.*

Until.

In other words, he already sees this as a done deal. Me leaving the team. Going back to Canada. Losing what I've built here.

Whatever expanded in my chest moments ago shrivels up and crumbles to a fine powder. The hidden clock inside me ticks away, picking up speed.

I swallow and nod, forcing a smile that feels like it doesn't fit. Like it was designed for a completely different person, a totally different face.

"Hop?" Coach gives my shoulder another squeeze.

"Sure thing, Coach."

"Malik said you might propose to your girlfriend?"

Malik has a big mouth. I briefly squeeze my eyes shut, like that will make the words disappear. How long will the lifespan of my little lie be?

"Uh, maybe," I hedge.

Coach grins. "My daughter's getting married soon, you know."

I do know. Coach passed out save the date cards a few months ago in the locker room. A black and white photo of a couple with mountains in the background. I vaguely remember sticking mine in a drawer somewhere in the kitchen. Probably need to find that and actually, you know, save the date.

That is, if I'm still here.

Coach's expression now mirrors the one he wore when he passed out the cards—pure pride.

"We're doing the whole big wedding thing," Coach continues. "Some of you will be there, I hope. Anyway, what I wanted to say is that Millie—that's my daughter, Amelia—said she'd happily marry Drew with or without the giant wedding. To be honest, I wish she would. It would save my money *and* my sanity."

He chuckles lightly, lifting his baseball cap to rub the top of his balding head. Even though he's making it sound like the wedding is a giant pain, he also looks like he could talk about his baby girl getting married forever. Meanwhile, I am officially done with this conversation and eager to get back to practice where I can hopefully find someone to knock into.

"I'll bet."

"Think about it." Coach grins and gives me a hearty slap on the back. "When it's love, you don't need all the bells and whistles. Just each other."

I get that. When it's real, the relationship is what matters. Not the cake or the flowers or whatever else.

But you *do* need an actual woman to marry.

———

Despite having been useless at practice and not feeling remotely social, I join some of the guys at Felix's loft for dinner. When someone offers to make you homemade lasagna, the answer is always yes. Especially when the someone is Felix and the recipe is his grandmother's. He makes a few alterations so it's less of a cheat meal for us. More protein, gluten-free noodles, and I happen to know he adds finely chopped spinach to the sauce for guys who hate vegetables—the same way moms sneak vegetables to picky toddlers.

Maybe ricotta will improve my mood. Ricotta therapy should totally be a thing. If I can't face Bailey again after having embarrassed myself so badly the other day, ricotta will be my poor substitution for puppy therapy.

"You've lost your spark, Speed Bump," Alec says as I set a plate down in front of him. The rest of the guys seem content to laze around while Felix finishes the food and I set the table.

Do none of the guys have mothers who worship Emily Post and her many, many manners?

I roll my eyes at the nickname, which unfortunately seems to be sticking. "I'm not a *Twilight* vampire," I mutter.

"I said *spark*, not sparkle," Alec says.

Van snorts. "I don't think men *spark* either."

He tugs at his V-neck, the only style of shirt he wears. Says the way his chest tattoos peek out makes women go crazy with curiosity and the need to see *all* of his tattoos.

It's a solid strategy, I guess, and it works for him. Van isn't often alone. Not unless he *wants* to be. And I've never known him to want to be.

He might be the only guy on the team as extroverted as me. I'm not even sure if, for him, it's about having the company of women so much as ... *company*. Period. But I'm not about to suggest that to him. Or say that even though he may not often be alone, I suspect he's *lonely*.

With plates and silverware for everyone, I take my seat between Van and Logan, who passes me the breadbasket. A big bite of garlic bread is the best way to avoid contributing to the conversation so I jam a whole piece in my mouth before handing the basket to Van.

Logan kicks me in the calf under the table. Not hard. But hard enough to draw my attention. "For real—are you okay, man?"

I shrug and work to locate an acceptable response as I swallow down the last of my garlic bread. "*Okay* is a relative term."

"That's a no," Felix says, bringing over the steaming pan of lasagna.

His oven mitts look like a gift from his girlfriend, Gracie, who's a professional cellist. The relationship is fairly new, which means Felix has been smiling more. A *lot* more. He's also held almost every team scoreless for the last few weeks with his save percentage up to .920, so none of us are going to mention the oven mitts.

They're pink and have music notes all over them. His apron sticks to the theme, the stiff black fabric printed with the words *Nothin' but Treble*.

"Does *baby* wanna talk about it?" Van asks in a tone like I'm a kid with a skinned knee, crying over a boo-boo. Or throwing a tantrum over not getting the biggest chocolate chip cookie.

The man who happens to be my best friend on the team treats almost everything like a joke. Even when he's serious. It's hard to know which he is right now. I'm not in the mood either way.

Someone tosses a piece of garlic bread at him. Van catches it and takes a bite, smiling around a wide grin. "Thanks."

"No throwing food," Felix says, slicing the lasagna. As the guys hand him their plates, he dishes up heaping squares. "But seriously, Hop—you okay?"

Van swings his gaze back to me, and he's not the only one. They all look curious. Even Camden and Wyatt, two of the newer guys who joined us for the first time tonight, are listening intently. I definitely don't want one of my first interactions with these guys off the ice to center around my stupid predicament.

From what I *know*, they're decent guys. Camden is as quiet as he is fast. Wyatt rivals Nathan in surliness and Alec in the pretty-boy looks department, though Wyatt is the lighter version with dirty blond hair and pale gray eyes. Neither Camden nor Wyatt has said much tonight. Maybe because conversation keeps circling back to me and my mood.

If I were Nathan, no one would question me being grumpy. But everyone knows I'm the sunshine on the team, not the dark cloud.

Maybe I should have just gone home. But even aside from book club being at the house tonight, being around Mom when I'm keeping a secret leaves guilt hanging over me like a dense smog. I am the air above L.A. during rush hour. The longer I wait to tell her, the worse I feel.

But telling her makes it *real*. Until then, I can just handle breathing in my own smog.

And handle the guys pressing me for answers.

"Well?" Alec arches a brow. "What's the tea?"

"Who said anything about tea?" Van's lip curls. As though tea in any variety is akin to poison. In most cases, I'd agree with him.

"It's an expression," Logan says. "To spill the tea is to share gossip."

"Well, aren't you fancy with all the terms," Van says, using quote fingers around *terms*.

Logan lifts a shoulder, the same side of his mouth titling up in a half grin. "Parker."

Logan's girlfriend, Parker, aka the Boss, is the team's social media manager. As well as the slang and pop culture professor, it seems. For now, even though she's not here, she also makes for a good distraction.

Not *quite* good enough.

"Forget I mentioned tea," Alec says. "Why are you suddenly acting like an Oscar-the-Grouch-Eeyore hybrid who skates like he's wearing cinder blocks on his feet?"

I pass my plate to Felix, and by the time it returns, my appetite has disappeared. Still, I slide my fork through the lasagna, cutting it into messy little squares oozing with cheese and sauce. If I can't even enjoy this, I'm sunk.

"Doesn't matter," I mutter, spearing a piece of lasagna. Normally, I'd have shoveled most of the plate into my mouth, not be basically playing with my food.

"It's about a girl," Van says, speaking around a huge bite of lasagna. A string of cheese is caught in the dark stubble on his chin, making him look ridiculous.

"Or lack thereof," Alec says.

"Woman," Felix corrects without even looking up from his plate. "Not girl."

"Okay, a lack of *women*," Alec says.

"It's not that," I say, but the turn in conversation has me thinking about Bailey.

How round her eyes got when I mentioned marriage. The way her cheeks flamed red. The surprising warmth of her skin under my fingertips.

Bailey is cute. Pretty, even. It's not like I didn't notice before, but it was more a detached observation.

Fact: Bailey is pretty.

But the other day, I noticed her with a whole different set of senses. In the swoop of my stomach as I crouched in front of her, rubbing her back. In the sharp need to lean closer, the tug right in the center of my chest, the buzz of my fingertips.

Feeling: Bailey is pretty.

It was ... disconcerting. Especially considering the way I was already falling all over myself with words. Add in the sudden visceral awareness of her, and it's a wonder I could form any coherent syllables at all.

Not that it matters. I don't need to be noticing Bailey. Or anyone. How poorly that conversation went only makes me less enthused to discuss any of it now.

"Your face says it's a woman problem," Logan points out unhelpfully.

I take a bite of lasagna, just to keep from having to answer. The taste of garlic and fresh basil and whatever other kinds of magic Felix baked into it almost makes this whole line of questioning tolerable. Almost.

"If you don't tell us, we can't help fix it," Felix says.

"This isn't fixable."

The words come out harsh, and I'm never harsh. It

surprises even me, and I set down my fork and wipe my mouth, ready to get up. But Logan sets a hand on my arm with just enough pressure to give me pause.

I could fight him off, but I stay where I am. It feels like defeat, waving my own threadbare white flag. More like a pair of dirty white socks run up a flagpole in a rainstorm.

"You don't know that," Logan says.

"I do."

"Let us help. Eight heads are better than one." Nathan is the one who says this, and I'm pretty sure that's more than he's said all day. He runs a hand over his hair, tied in a bun as usual, then goes right back to eating like him speaking up isn't unusual.

Someone drops a fork, and Felix coughs violently, needing Camden to pound on his back.

"The oracle has spoken," Logan whispers next to me, quiet so only I can hear. Halfway between reverent and sarcastic.

I choke back a laugh.

"Dude," Van says, somehow less shocked than the rest of us at Nathan's sudden desire to take part in conversation. "The saying is *two* heads are better than one."

Nathan shrugs but doesn't offer any explanation. I think he's built with a shutoff valve inside him that activates when he talks too much. Clearly, it's been tripped.

"But seriously," Van says, pointing his knife my way. "Are you going to tell us or not?"

Maybe Nathan is right. Though I don't think the guys around this table could possibly know more than the lawyers or even Malik or Coach, it would be nice not to feel so alone in this.

I glance around the table, meeting everyone's eyes in

turn. "You have to promise not to talk about this with anyone else. Swear it."

I'm not sure why I'm insisting. When I get sent back to Canada, they're all going to know. Or whenever Coach or Malik or someone on the Appies staff lets it spill. But it still feels shameful, like the kind of secret you hope stays in a dark closet somewhere. Plus, if I decide to talk about the marriage part of it, I'll need this promise. Not that I'm going to do it. I'm not. But still.

Logan holds up his pinky and arches a brow. "You want us to pinky promise?"

I snort. "No. A vow of silence, maybe?"

"A vow of *violence*."

That's Wyatt, and for a moment, no one responds. I think we're all a little stunned that the new guy spoke at all. Much less suggested something.

Alec breaks the silence with a laugh. "I like alliteration. And violence." Then leans over and kicks Van under the table.

Van groans and doubles over, dramatically rubbing his shin. "The *hell*, dude?"

Alec crosses his arms over his chest. "I knew I liked you, Wyatt. Vow of violence. Who's in?"

"So, we're kicking each other under the table and—what? Promising not to talk about whatever's making Eli a grumpy Gus?" Van asks.

When I realize they're all looking at me, I nod. "I guess."

The next minute or so is a whole lot of violence and kicking under the table. It honestly makes me feel better. Strangely normal. That is, until the guys stop kicking each other and turn toward me, waiting to hear why they just agreed to a vow of violence.

"I'm being deported."

Not exactly true. I mean, if I don't leave on my own, sure. But using that term seems like the best and quickest way to catch everyone up to speed real quick.

It works. The room goes silent. The kind of silence that's somehow painfully loud. An intense *lack* of noise.

I already regret saying anything, but now that I've started, why stop?

"The only way to potentially stop it from happening is if I get married in the next three weeks."

This is met with laughter, not silence. Uproarious. The kind punctuated with guys banging on the table or slapping each other on the back. I think Van is crying. The only two not laughing are Logan and Felix, who are clearly the only sharp tools in this shed.

I cross my arms, leaning back in my chair. "And you wondered why I didn't want to tell you."

"Wait. Wait, wait—you're serious?" Alec wipes his eyes, then peers around Logan at me.

"About being deported or getting *married?*" Van asks, laughter still in his voice.

"Why doesn't everyone shut up and let Eli talk?" Logan suggests, though the tone of his voice sounds more threat than request.

So, I do. I explain about how P-1 visas work, something I know more about now after late-night googling. About limits, renewal, needing to go back to Canada, blah blah blah. The unknown timeframe and the possibility I could get traded considering how long these things sometimes take.

"What about your mom?" Felix asks.

This makes the table fall silent again. All the guys—even Cam and Wyatt—know how close I am with my mom. Kind of hard to miss when the woman bakes game day cookies for everyone. She's even convinced Parker to sneak her into the Summit to decorate lockers. Mom always picks a random person, and I'm trying not to take it personally that she hasn't picked me yet.

I twirl my knife on the table, seeing my own distorted reflection spin and spin. "I haven't told her. But I don't think she'd stay here alone."

Twice now, I've almost picked up the phone to ask one of Mom's book club friends if they could take her in or help drive her to appointments while I'm gone. Be her support. But what stops me is the fact that I can't tell someone else before telling Mom. It's also a lot to ask of someone, and I know I'd be a wreck worrying if she's okay.

I also think she'd say no. She would talk about missing Canada—she doesn't—and missing Annie—okay, that she does—and how we stick together. Look. I'm very aware for some, maybe even most guys, living with their mom from age eighteen to twenty-eight would be laughable. Unhealthy. Bring on the mama's boy jokes.

But Mom and I have always been close. And even before her diagnosis, when she first started having health issues, I made myself a promise I'd take care of her. For her part, I know she feels the same sense of loyalty to me.

Van shifts in his chair, counting on his fingers as he speaks. "You're hot. You've got money. You play hockey. It's like a trifecta of marriage material. How hard could it be to find a wife in a few weeks?"

I picture Bailey, red-faced and choking. "About as hard as you think. Multiplied by a lot. Plus, I don't want to get married like *this*."

"We can't let this happen," Van says, like he has any say in the matter. I appreciate his naive declaration of support, which sounds like it belongs in a war room, not at Felix's dining table. "Unacceptable."

"We're in it together," Felix says, his voice subdued but firm as he repeats what Alec always has us say before a game. "Family."

"Family," the guys repeat. I say nothing because there's a tickle in my throat and a stinging in my nose I need to push down.

Before I do something dumb like cry at the dinner table.

Alec pulls out his phone, shoving his empty plate out of the way. "Doc or spreadsheet?"

"Come again?" I say.

"For the list of potential wives," he says.

"We're not making a—"

"Spreadsheet," Logan says. He shrugs when I glare. "More efficient for adding data."

"Spreadsheet it is," Alec says. "Do we have any women to put on the list? Anyone you've dated recently or thought about dating?"

I don't say Bailey's name, but I do think it. "No."

"We could start with characteristics you're looking for and work backward," Felix suggests.

Van's grin is sly. "I'm happy to help with the list of characteristics."

"Your 'characteristics' would only be physical attributes," Logan says wryly.

Van shrugs, still grinning. "And?"

"It takes more than looks to make a marriage work," Wyatt says from the end of the table. He speaks like he knows, which makes a dozen questions sprout up in my mind.

"Is there really no woman who comes to mind?" Alec asks.

Only one. A quiet, unassuming woman who's pretty in

the kind of way that sneaks up on a person. One whose smiles and blushes I count, who makes me happy.

I *like* Bailey. Legitimately. She's a sweet woman. Shy. Kind. Thoughtful. She treats me like a normal guy. Didn't even know who I was or that I play hockey, which means points for her.

"A woman willing to be my fake wife? No," I say firmly.

"She'd need to be your *real* wife," Logan points out. "Legally speaking."

"Then, definitely no." I'm not about to drag sweet, shy Bailey into my problems. Especially not like this. Not when it includes fraud.

"That's okay." Alec's brows draw together as he taps on his phone. "Spreadsheet to the rescue."

"A spreadsheet won't save me," I say, wishing it could. I stand, grabbing my plate. "I need to head out. Can we help with dishes?"

Felix catches my eye, hesitating for a moment like he's trying to read me. And I think he must sense my need to escape because he gives a quick nod and picks up his dishes. "As much as I'd like to help with this endeavor," he says. "I've got to kick y'all out. Don't worry about the dishes. Just carry them to the sink. Gracie's coming over."

Camden arches an eyebrow. "You're going to have your girlfriend do our dishes?"

Felix blanches, as though just now realizing how his words sounded. "*No*. I'll do them. I just want the place clean and you guys gone before she gets here. Now get out."

He does everything but sweep us out of his loft with a broom, then slams the loft's metal rolling door shut.

Van grabs me by the shoulder before I can escape down the stairs. "Night's young. We're going out."

"Nope."

"Let me rephrase," Van says, squeezing my shoulder harder. "You *need* to come out."

"You're not going to find a wife by staying home, Speed Bump," Alec says.

"He's not going to find a wife in a bar," Logan points out.

"Shut up. Come on." Alec grabs me by the back of my shirt, steering me toward the stairs, and I decide not to fight.

The alternative is heading home, where I have to pretend everything is fine in front of Mom. At some point I'm going to crack and spill everything, and I'm not ready. Yet.

"Fine," I say. "But don't push this whole finding a wife thing. I'm just going out to go out."

"Of course," Alec says easily. *Too* easily.

Van doesn't even pretend. Pumping a fist in the air, he shouts, "Let the great wife hunt commence!"

CHAPTER 5

Eli

MISTAKE. Coming to Mulligans with the guys was a mistake. Telling the guys about the whole marriage idea too. *Especially* that.

For the last hour, Van has been parading women in front of me like I'm ABC's newest Bachelor while Alec taps furiously into his phone, presumably updating his spreadsheet. What kinds of notes he's making, I shudder to think.

Nathan, who might have scared off women with his glare, went home when we left Felix's. I was counting on Logan to put a stop to the foolishness—maybe because of Parker's invisible good influence on him. But he's been watching the whole display with unbridled amusement, smirking around a bottle of beer. I wasn't sure what to expect from Camden and Wyatt, but they walked in and went right for the pool table like it was some kind of billiard siren.

Which leaves me at the mercy of Van and Alec.

The two usually don't get along all that well, but apparently finding me wife candidates is the perfect bonding experience. Glad I could be of service.

While I know the guys took the visa stuff seriously, especially after Felix asked about my mom, everyone seems to think this wife hunt is all good fun.

"Dude," Alec says. "No way you're going to snag even a *girlfriend* like this. Much less a wife."

"I told you I'm not interested in looking for a woman to marry. At least, not in a bar."

"This is about your future. At least look alive, man. It's like you body-swapped with Nathan."

I wish. Then I wouldn't be *here*.

But Alec is not wrong. I can feel the heaviness bearing down on me, a weighted blanket of discontent. I stare down at my shoes, a new pair of Vans. I have a thing for skater shoes. Maybe because growing up, we never could afford them. My kid self would lose it if he knew how many pairs I own now. A small consolation at the moment.

Being moody doesn't suit me. It's like wearing a jersey ten sizes too small. But I'm not able to shake the doom and gloom tonight. It's even worse than before lasagna, which means ricotta therapy was a fail. Or maybe it was simply offset by this whole fiasco.

"I can't be sunshine all the time," I say, taking a sip of my beer, wondering if I should just head home.

Except … book club. We left Felix's early since Gracie was coming over. It's only eight o'clock, and Mom's book ladies have been known to linger.

Van walks up with a woman on each arm and the kind of look I want to smack right off his face. Both blonds—one with straight hair, one curly. But their faces are indistinct to me, probably because I'm not interested. It's not them. It's me.

I shift in my chair, looking across the room longingly at Wyatt as he lines up a shot at the pool table, laughing at something Cam says. I suck at pool. But I'd much rather have a cue stick in my hand and be losing to the new guys than have an overeager Van thrusting two blonds my way.

As though invited—to be clear, they were not—the women drop onto my lap, one on each knee.

I glare at Van between their shoulders. Despite my sport of choice, I've never been in a fight. Not even on the ice. Van says this makes me a unicorn of hockey. I think it just means I'm measured and even-tempered, easy to forgive.

But now?

Now, I'd like to throw my first punch. At my teammate. In a bar. Where he's trying to "help."

"Our boy Eli seems to have lost his smile," Van says to the women, who giggle as though he waved a magic giggle wand. "See what you can do about that, hmm?"

Both women nod enthusiastically. I'd put money on the fact that they would say yes to any guy who wears an Appies jersey. Or *any* kind of jersey. I start to get up, but Van comes around behind my chair, resting his hands a little too firmly on my shoulders as he leans close to my ear.

"Remember: you're doing this for your country. *This* country, not Canada." He hums the opening bars of "The Star-Spangled Banner" before slapping me on the back and loosening his grip.

The women settle in and lean in close, their arms snaking around my shoulders as the mix of their perfume makes me sneeze. I glare at Van, but he only grins and heads back out. Probably to find more potential victims.

I sigh, giving the women pressing in on either side a

cursory glance. I want to be polite but don't want to encourage conversation.

Or anything else.

"I'm Eli." Nice and neutral. No hint of flirtation. Nothing to give off any hope. "And could you actually … use chairs?"

When they stare blankly, like my request for them to vacate my personal space is outlandish, I reach to the side, grabbing chairs. Then I gently but firmly urge the women off my lap.

"Hockey's hard on the knees," I say, which is actually true. Even if that's not why I don't want them sitting on mine.

Unfortunately, this doesn't stop them from draping themselves over me. Fabulous.

"I'm Brenda," purrs the one with the straight hair, dragging a fingertip up my forearm.

"Kellie," the other woman says in the same kind of voice. They sound like throaty babies. Like two-year olds with head colds. "Kellie with an -ie not a -y. In case you want to put it in your phone."

I definitely do not.

Alec grins as he taps on his, probably entering Kellie with an -ie into the spreadsheet I hope I never have to see.

"Brenda and Kellie," Alec says. "Like the original *90210*."

The women stare blankly, and I shake my head.

Alec sets his phone on the table for the first time since we got to Mulligans. "*Beverly Hills, 90210*? Am I the only one who streams nineties TV shows? Never mind. I'm getting a beer."

Which leaves me shifting uncomfortably as I try to decide how to politely extricate myself as the women press closer, making me the middle of an unwanted Eli sandwich.

"Eli?"

Oh, no. No, no, no, no. Don't let that be—

I glance up and wish I had done more to extricate myself from the women on either side of me. Where's a TARDIS when you need one?

Because a few feet away, Bailey stares. A baby deer, wide-eyed and blinking in undisguised shock. Her eyes dart from my face to the women petting me like a zoo animal. I don't miss the way her expression falls. Her surprise morphs into disappointment.

Not that I can blame her. This looks … *bad.*

I'm a caricature of a professional athlete. The kind of man who treats relationships—and women—like paper plates.

Though it's a stereotype for a reason, there are also plenty of athletes who don't fall into that category. Me being one. I've dated, but always with a more serious intent in mind. Never casually. Always hoping I've found someone who could be more.

Except, that's not how this looks. It's not how *I* look.

Two women rather than just one? No biggie—just a typical night at the bar!

And it matters to me. Deeply.

"Hey, Bailey. I, uh … " There's nothing more I can say while I still have Brenda and Kellie on either side of me like twin Barbie gargoyles.

If my mom were here, the disapproving look she'd give would be enough to burn a hole through my shirt.

Bailey's cheeks flush, reminding me with a slice of regret how easily I can make her blush with a teasing word.

Happy blushing. This is most definitely *un*happy blushing.

She's already starting to back away. In a long overdue move, I hop to my feet, dislodging the two women as politely yet firmly as I can. Brushing past them, I ignore their twin huffs of annoyance and step into Bailey's space.

"Hi," I say.

"Hi." Her lips tilt up, then quickly drop, her smile landing somewhere near her shoes.

"So, what's up?" I wave, then drop my hand because, *really, that's the conversation starter I'm going with?* "You're here ... in a bar."

From somewhere behind me, I hear Alec, who returned with a beer just in time to witness this, snort. I ignore him. But I agree with the sentiment. It's like my brain has been transported back to middle school when I tried and failed to make conversation with my cute lab partner in science.

So, dissections, huh? How about that dead squid?

"You're also in a bar," Bailey points out, her smile widening.

"Yeah, but you're ..." I don't know where that sentence is going, but probably nowhere that's going to do me any favors. I clamp my mouth shut.

I'm fidgeting, suddenly full of energy that feels like it's erupting out of me. Probably leftover embarrassment from Bailey catching me at the exact moment she did. Or from the fact that in our last conversation, I halfway proposed.

I shove my hands in my pockets, then feel awkward and pull them back out, crossing them over my chest. But I saw something on TikTok recently on body language, and the guy said crossing your arms over your chest looks hostile. Or like you're trying to show off your muscles.

Unfolding my arms, I drop my hands to my sides where they hang like anchors.

Why am I suddenly so aware of my hands? How is it that they feel huge and clumsy, like I'm standing here in street clothes but wearing my hockey gloves? What do I do with my hands normally, and why can't I just do that now?

Bailey laughs softly. "Tell me the truth, Eli—did you think I *lived* at the shelter?"

I laugh too, pleased that she's teasing me. Or ... flirting? Is this the Bailey version of flirting? The way the pink in her cheeks deepens to red tells me maybe it is.

Somehow, this dispels my nervous energy. I grin. "*Do* you live at the shelter?"

"If I don't return at midnight, I'll turn into a pumpkin."

"Noted." There's a tiny pause, and I clear my throat. "I'm sorry about ... that." I don't realize I'm shaking my head until a lock of hair falls into my eyes. I brush it away. "It really wasn't what it looked like."

"It wasn't you with two women practically sitting in your lap?" Her smile is wry. One brow arches, and I chuckle.

But I'm also seriously glad Bailey didn't walk by a minute sooner to see the women *actually* on my lap.

"You're messing with me. Yes—it was that. But it just happened and—"

"It was me." A heavy hand lands on my shoulder, one attached to Van. "I'm a very bad influence. Are you looking for a bad influence in your life?"

"*No,*" I say. The word comes out somewhere between a growl and a groan. "She's definitely not."

Bailey laughs. "No, thank you."

"This is Bailey," I tell Van, debating on whether I should give him some context or if doing so would make the whole thing worse. Or give him the wrong idea.

Too late. Van looks pointedly between us. I can almost hear the gears in his head grinding to a stop. He turns fully to Bailey with a smile.

"I'm Van. I play hockey with this fool."

I don't like the way he's looking at her. Or smiling at her. Or standing so close to her.

"Nice to meet you."

Bailey's voice is muted, soft enough to make me want to lean closer so I don't miss a word. Or so Van's not closer to her than I am. She reaches forward, her small hand disappearing in his palm. When Van lifts it to his lips, his eyes are on mine, daring me to react. I don't take the bait.

Even though I'd like to rip her away from him, yank Van by the back of his shirt collar, and drag him right out of Mulligans.

The flush in Bailey's cheeks spreads, reaching the tips of her ears and even her neck. A swell of protectiveness rises in my throat.

I crowd closer, nudging him away with my shoulder. "Dude, she doesn't want your germs. Sorry," I tell Bailey. "He's incorrigible."

"I've been called worse," Van says, looking pleased with himself. "What's *incorrigible* mean?"

"Google it," I tell him.

This earns me a laugh from Bailey, even though she still looks hesitant, like she's not quite sure how to respond to any of this. Shy Bailey is back, it seems. She takes the tiniest step closer to me, like I make her feel safer.

Good. I like that.

With no warning, Van curls an arm around my neck and starts to ruffle my hair. "Dude. Get off!"

We scuffle, and I shoot Bailey an apologetic look from under Van's armpit, which is not a location I ever want to be. She watches, her toffee eyes wide.

"So," Van grunts, his mouth way too close to my ear. I'm used to having the guys invade my space, but usually it's on the ice. The feeling of Van's beard on my neck in this bar is *too* close. "Is she the next hopeful Mrs. Eli Hopkins?"

Now I'm the one with him in a chokehold, breathing hard

and speaking right into his ear where he's not possibly able to misunderstand me. "Shut up about that. Okay? She's a … friend."

The last thing I'm *ever* going to bring up again around Bailey is the whole marriage thing. It was a disaster, even if I didn't intend to even tell her. I picture her on the shelter floor, eyes glistening and cheeks red from coughing. No—definitely not doing that again.

It took me months to get her to feel comfortable enough to talk to me. I'm lucky she's still talking to me now after even joking about my situation.

"Right. Because guy and girl friendships work *soooo* well," Van says on a laugh.

"Yeah, like you'd know. Have you ever tried to be friends with a girl?"

He doesn't answer. He doesn't need to because Van lives firmly in the men-and-women-can't-be-friends camp and cannot be convinced otherwise.

I let him go, shoving him a few feet away, but he comes right back. Like a virus you can't shake. Or gum stuck to your shoe.

"Sorry about that," I say, brushing my hair out of my eyes and straightening my shirt. I realize one of the pockets of my jeans is inside out, and I tuck the lining back in with my fingertips.

"It's fine," Bailey says. "I'm actually—"

"Bailey!" At a table near the back, a woman with short dark hair waves wildly. Two other women sit slack-jawed and staring like this scene is straight out of a telenovela. It's close enough.

Even more so when arms snake around my waist from behind as Brenda and Kellie—whom I'd forgotten all about—

make what can only be called a last-ditch coordinated, amorous attack.

"Uh-oh," Van mutters.

Though I think it should be pretty obvious to anyone watching that I am *not* interested, the presence of Brenda and Kellie has an immediate effect on Bailey. Her smile fades, and her eyes dim. She steps back, her shoulders curling as she folds herself into a smaller and smaller space, like she thinks she can disappear.

"I'm with friends," Bailey says, taking another step. "And it's obvious you're … busy."

"I'm not busy."

I clench my jaw, removing Brenda and Kellie's hands from my body with less gentleness than when I pushed them from my lap. It takes some effort. When I push away one hand, another appears like a hand-Hydras.

Finally, I take a huge step away from them. Toward Bailey.

I've completely invaded her space. We're nose to nose. Or, I would be if she were taller. More like her nose to my collarbone.

I lean close. "Can I meet your friends? Or buy you a drink?"

Bailey saws her teeth over her bottom lip, glancing again at her friends then behind me where I imagine Brenda and Kellie are regrouping. "Um."

"Please?"

I don't even care how desperate I sound. Because Bailey's presence is a strong wind, blowing away the thick, dark fog I've been feeling.

I wish she would also blow away Brenda and Kellie, who step forward again like some kind of synchronized stalking team, trying to hook their arms through mine. I wiggle away from them and curl one arm around Bailey's shoulders until I'm practically draped over her like a shawl.

Her hair smells like cinnamon and cotton candy. Suddenly I'm starving.

"*Please*," I repeat, this time in a whisper. I bend, my lips brushing her ear. This is more touching than we've ever done, and I half expect Bailey to evaporate in a puff of smoke. "Help me, Bailey-Wan Kenobi! You're my only hope."

"Are you afraid of the big bad wolves?" she murmurs.

"*Very*."

"Fine. You can join us." She glances back once more, where I imagine Brenda and Kellie are pouting. I don't look. "They do have very big ... teeth."

That has me laughing as I start to guide her toward her friends, my arm still curled around her shoulders. A burst of happiness blooms bright in my chest when she relaxes into me. I give her shoulder a squeeze. "You're funny."

"Don't sound so surprised."

"Hey, in my defense, up until this week, I could barely drag more than two sentences at a time out of you."

Bailey's elbow finds my ribs, a teasing poke. "I tend to be a little ... reserved when I first meet people. Or when I'm not comfortable with them yet."

I grin. "So, you're comfortable with me now?"

"I guess so."

"Good. And sorry again about back there. My teammates were trying—and failing—to set me up. Mostly against my will. I should have extricated myself before then."

"*Extricated*, huh?"

"Don't sound so surprised," I say, echoing her words from a moment ago. "I'll have you know I aced the vocab portion of the SAT."

"Good to know. But as for the need for extrication ..."

Bailey sticks her lip out, and I find myself suddenly distracted. "Poor little hockey player with all the ladies after him."

Grinning, I pull her closer with the arm around her shoulders and use my other to tickle her lightly. She giggles, a sound that lights me up from the inside out. "Don't mock me."

She bats my hand away. "I said what I said, hockey player."

"I see how it is. Now that you know who I am, that's all I am to you—a hockey player?"

"Pretty much."

As we cross the bar to her table, I take Bailey in for the first time, and my brain goes on a brief hiatus from working. Until now, I haven't even noticed that she's not in scrubs. She's *always* in scrubs.

But not tonight.

She's dressed in a dark skirt that falls just above her knees. Legs bare, despite the chilly fall temperature outside, and she has on ankle boots. Her blue top is soft and loose with a wide neck, revealing delicate collarbones. It's the first time I've seen Bailey's hair out of a ponytail, and it hangs loose around her shoulders.

She glances up, as though feeling the weight of my attention on her, and the smile I get is one I haven't seen before. Still hesitant, but more open than usual, like she no longer feels the need to make herself small around me.

Pretty, I think with a hard swallow. *She really is pretty.*

The whole thing throws me. Seeing Bailey here at a bar in normal clothes is disconcerting in the same way it is to see your doctor at the grocery store.

I blink and try to readjust the box Bailey fits into. From shelter worker to ... *this.*

The soft smile and the flush in her cheeks are the same. The shy demeanor too, though she's definitely more comfortable. Maybe she's had a beer? Two? I need to focus here—on the things I recognize. To hold them as anchors.

But my eyes are drawn to her bare legs. I tell myself not to ogle. Even though they're absolutely ogle-worthy. Ogleable. Ogle-icious.

Anyway. No ogling. *Nogling.*

I force my attention back to Bailey's face, feeling my skin prickle with awareness. Brenda and Kellie are long gone. I probably don't need to keep my arm around Bailey.

I keep it there anyway.

Van steps in front of us just before we reach the table. "Sorry we got interrupted," he says. "Where are we going?"

"I was buying Bailey and her friends drinks," I say.

"Sounds good."

I look at Bailey. "Is this cool?"

Bailey hesitates, like she's weighing various options and outcomes. Finally, she sighs and then looks between me and Van, then peeks past him at the table. "Fine. My friends would be more than happy to meet you. I may not know hockey, but some of them do. I apologize in advance for the fangirling you're about to be subjected to."

"I love fangirling." Van tugs at the collar of his shirt, adjusting for maximum tattoo teasing.

"You would," I mutter.

We reach the table with Bailey's three friends, one of whom looks significantly older than Bailey, and all of whom are actively staring.

Bailey drops onto the nearest chair, patting the one next to her and looking up at me expectantly. I waste no time sitting down and scooting a little closer to her. Van pulls a chair over from another table and turns it so he's straddling it backwards. He turns his baseball cap at the same time, as though he needs his hat to match his chair.

"Everyone, this is Eli and Van," Bailey says, her voice more bold and commanding than I've ever heard it. "Yes, they play for the Appies. That's the hockey team in town, if you don't know. Be cool. Don't ask intrusive questions. And no"—here she gives a long look to the younger, dark-haired woman directly across from Van—"they will *not* sign any of your body parts."

"Eli won't," Van corrects. "But I'm happy to sign anything at all if you ask nicely."

I roll my eyes. "Ignore him. He was raised in a cave by trolls."

"Not wolves?" Bailey asks.

"Nope. Definitely trolls."

Bailey does introductions, and I try to remember, though my brain is buzzing. Shannon is the loud one with pale skin and dark hair, and I think Jenny is the name of the one with glasses, rows of tiny braids, and light brown skin. Her disposition reminds me a little of Bailey. She speaks so softly, it's hard to hear her over the music.

I realize I've met the older woman at the shelter—Beth, with her white curls and wide smile. I'm too distracted by the feel of Bailey's leg pressed against mine under the table to take in much else. I'm wearing jeans so I can't feel her skin, but just knowing hers is bare is enough.

I have a brief argument with myself about being shallow for noticing Bailey now that she's wearing something other than scrubs. But my awareness started the other day. When she was in normal work clothes and had her hair in a messy ponytail.

And I've always liked Bailey. Even if it's only lately that I started to realize my visits to the shelter are maybe as much about her as they are the dogs. Her quiet steadiness calms me. I've enjoyed the challenge of seeing what questions will actually make her talk.

So, see?

Not shallow.

We're friends. I feel affection because we're *friends*, just like I told Van when I had him in a headlock.

She smiles up at me, and my gaze falls to her lips.

Not *terribly* shallow. Maybe more than just *friendly* feelings. A *mild* sense of attraction.

"Good to see you," Beth says, her white curls bouncing around her face as she smiles. "Almost didn't recognize you without a dog in your lap."

"How's Doris?" I ask.

Bailey's smile widens. "Better. Still doesn't like the other dogs or most people, but she's eating."

"Who's Doris?" Van asks, looking confused.

I ignore him. "Can I buy everyone a round of drinks?" It's only as I look around the table that I notice the birthday balloons and a few gift bags, brightly colored tissue paper peeking out of the tops. "Wait—whose birthday is it?"

All conversation stops. And from the way everyone's eyes fall to Bailey, I don't need anyone to answer. I spin, angling myself toward her and resting my arm on the back of her chair.

"Bailey—is it your birthday?"

She stares down at her hands, twisting a napkin in her lap. But she's smiling. "It's not a big deal."

My arm is still on the back of her chair, and I let it fall forward until it brushes her shoulders. "Oh, I happen to disagree. Where I come from, birthdays are a very big deal."

Shannon furrows her brow. "Like, birthdays are a big deal in Canada?"

"Yeah, Eli," Van says, leaning back in his chair and crossing his arms. "You have Canadian birthday traditions I don't know about, *eh?*"

"Yeah. We do."

We don't.

But no one else at this table knows that. Honestly, I've found that the American understanding of Canada begins and ends with maple leaves, Mounties, and the apparent universal appeal of Justin Trudeau.

Oh, and *eh*. Just add *eh* to unlock your Canadian achievement badge.

I grin at Bailey, staring pointedly until she lifts her gaze to meet mine. For half a second, looking at her warm brown eyes, I forget where I was going with this.

"In Canada we have a whole set of birthday traditions."

Bailey tugs at the end of her hair, twirling a strand of it around her finger. I find this little show of nerves endearing.

"Like what?"

Like … I don't know. But I'm good at spontaneous. Much better at living in the moment than thinking ahead. And I'd highly prefer to just have a fun evening making Bailey's birthday special than worrying about my time ticking down.

I grin and give the end of her hair a playful tug. "You're about to find out."

CHAPTER 6

Bailey

I'M PRESSING COOL, wet hands to my cheeks when Shannon saunters into the bathroom at the bowling alley, whistling. Her smug smile tells me the cold water has done nothing to tame what feels like a permanent flush in my cheeks.

Of course my closest friend knows I'm flustered. And exactly why. Even if I hadn't mentioned my crush on Eli before, I'm sure it would have been obvious tonight.

Can I help it if the man makes me shine brighter? Feel lighter? And blush like a schoolgirl with a crush?

Shannon leans a hip against the counter and brushes a strand of dark hair off her cheek. Oh, so casual. *Too* casual. Somehow, she also manages to make her floral nightgown paired with bowling shoes look trendy and cute. Whereas I'm drowning in ugly pink fabric and certain I'll wake up tomorrow to find some kind of bowling-shoe fungus on my feet.

I tug at the neckline of my own nightgown. It's the kind I see women with tufts of white hair sporting in my grandmother's nursing home: a thick pink material with decorative buttons down the front and tiny flowers. It should fall to my knees, but the ruffled hem hits me mid-thigh. Which makes me wonder if it's a child's nightgown—usually I'm swallowed up in fabric, not worried about things being too short. Paired with orange knee socks and bowling shoes, I look like I lost a bet. Or several.

Instead, it was Beth—whom I'll find a way to get even with later—who picked out my clothes for me as part of Eli's supposedly Canadian birthday shenanigans. Our whole little group is now dressed in a random assortment of sleepwear. Well, Shannon, Eli, Van, and I are. After the Walmart shopping excursion, we lost the other two. They gave excuses about early work mornings, but I think it was more the idea of bowling in nightgowns that didn't appeal to Jenny and Beth.

"Those Canadians sure love celebrating birthdays," Shannon says, crossing her arms.

"Yup." I rip off a paper towel from the dispenser and pretend like the rough brown paper is actually helping to dry my hands. Anything to avoid looking at Shannon.

"It's weird, though." Her voice takes on a thoughtful tone as she taps her chin. "I've never heard about Canadians doing a special birthday extravaganza."

Me, neither. In fact I highly suspect that Eli, for whatever reason, made the birthday thing up.

Which would mean this entire night—from the round of drinks at the bar to bowling in the silly clothes to the as-yet-unfulfilled promise of waffles at my favorite diner—is only because Eli wanted to make my birthday more fun. Not because it's the "Canadian way."

The idea makes me ridiculously happy. But I need to find a way to tone it down to a manageable happy. A *reasonable* happy. I'm getting way too many ideas.

When the reality is that Eli is a nice guy. A fun guy. A guy who seems to enjoy making other people happy, even people he's barely friends with. Like me.

This has nothing to do with him crushing on me the way I've crushed on him for so long. And I'd really love for it to have nothing to do with his visa issues. Like this night is some weird way to ease me into his marriage-fraud idea.

"I don't know much about Canada," I say. "Other than like … hockey and snow and poutine. Is that a Canada thing or a Wisconsin thing? Sounds gross, either way."

I'm babbling and I know it. Which won't in any way help curtail my too-smart friend's suspicions. I'm at least grateful I didn't tell her about the whole mention of marriage. If Eli's pretending that never happened, so am I.

Even if, deep in the recesses of my brain, I can't stop thinking about it.

From what Eli said, he's going to have to go back to Canada. I was already sad when I thought about not seeing him again. After tonight, it will be worse. I'd rather not face that fact on my birthday. But the thought has been there, like a steady hum of a refrigerator or the Muzak in a department store.

"Oh! And the Ryans! They're Canadian," I add. "Reynolds *and* Gosling."

Shannon snorts. "Nice try, with your sad little Canada facts. But you know I'm like a bloodhound." She makes a show of sniffing the air. "And I smell … *romance* in the air."

I squeeze my paper towel into a tiny, tight ball before

tossing it in the trash. But when I try to brush past Shannon, she blocks my exit. Her hands on my shoulders are surprisingly gentle. Yet also totally inescapable, like she's a mama hawk and I'm the baby she's grasping in her talons while flying above the tree line. The way my stomach is pitching and rolling, I can practically feel the ground dropping out beneath me.

"You like him," Shannon says, her eyes roving over my face like she's trying to find something she misplaced.

Rather than denying it, the way my panicking heart is telling me to, I roll my eyes. "Who wouldn't? But it's nothing. Just a tiny crush on a man who seems manufactured for the sole purpose of making women crush on him."

"It's not nothing, Bay." The softness in her tone grates on me, even as it soothes me to know someone cares. "You deserve a crush on someone like Eli. Especially after losing so much."

Her jaw clamps shut as I glare with the fiercest look I can muster. "Can we just not? It's my birthday."

Shannon sighs. "I know. I just love you. And you've shouldered a lot."

She trails off. But she doesn't need to finish. And she's not wrong. I just would rather not think about my parents not being here to celebrate my birthday. I already feel guilty that I haven't thought about that in hours. Not since Eli showed up and made the night special.

"Anyway. It's not like it matters," I tell her. "Eli doesn't like me. He's just a really nice guy."

And he's moving back to Canada.

Unless I—or someone else, like maybe one of the women from the bar—marry him.

"Nice?" Shannon asks.

I double down. "Very nice."

He is. Nice. Thoughtful. Fun. Funny. Hot. Sweet.

I've had a front row seat to so many of these qualities at the shelter. You can learn a lot about a person by the way they talk to a dog. But tonight, I've seen all these same qualities in another setting.

Eli paid for everything tonight. He made sure my friends felt included. He got protective when a drunk man stumbled into Jenny, knocking her glasses down her nose. Eli stepped in between them, pinning the man with a hard stare until he apologized.

It was Eli's suggestion that we stop by Harvest Hollow's one and only Walmart before bowling—*Part of the Canadian birthday tradition*, he said. And of course, he paid for the clothes *and* the bowling and I bet he already picked up the tab for the sodas and copious amounts of French fries, which are somehow better at the bowling alley than any restaurant in town.

The entire night, Eli has buoyed the mood, keeping things fun and light. Though I usually hate being the center of attention almost as much as I hate birthdays, somehow Eli has made me feel special without making me feel as though I've been followed along by a giant spotlight. Almost like this man who barely knows me somehow knows me well enough to know what I need. Which is to enjoy my birthday without having all the unnecessary birthday attention.

So, yeah, my crush hatched, sprouted wings, and flew away hours ago. It's an entirely new animal.

Which is why I desperately need to get my feet back on the ground. Preferably not in these bowling shoes.

I also need to stop using so many flying analogies.

With a smile and a little bit of muscle, I manage to extricate myself from Shannon's mama-bird grip. "Really. It's no big deal. He's barely a friend. It's just my birthday. Nothing more."

As I push out of the bathroom door, the noise and flashing lights and smell of bowling alley and beer hitting me, Shannon stays put.

"You keep telling yourself that," Shannon calls after me. The door swings shut on her voice, punctuating her words.

But I've already forgotten because Eli is leaning against the wall in the narrow hallway, grinning at me. My feet skid to a stop.

He couldn't hear us … could he?

No—definitely not. There's '90s rock pumping through speakers overhead, plus the satisfying *thwack* of pins being struck and a tangle of voices and laughter. Still, my pulse ratchets up as my heart does a little terrified shimmy in my chest.

Even dressed in a bright green muumuu covered in lemons, which is what Shannon and I picked out for Eli and Van to wear, the man is enough to make my breath catch. Or perhaps it's because the loose house dress has slipped off one shoulder, revealing a swath of tawny golden skin. Toned. Rippling with muscles even as he just stands here, doing zero athletic activities.

As I watch, Eli tracks my gaze, which has caught on his bare shoulder. With a small smile that looks far too pleased, he slides the fabric of the lime green muumuu back up, covering the skin I was admiring.

I almost boo.

"You look like you're about to protest." Eli's mouth curves in a wide smile—a pleased one.

Am I *that* easy to read? Apparently so.

"I was just looking for scars," I say, scrambling for any kind of excuse for my rude staring.

"I've got plenty. Though the hallway of a bowling alley probably isn't the best place to show them off."

"Probably not," I agree, as though this is perfectly normal bowling alley conversation.

"Maybe later?" He arches a brow, and a thrill moves through me at what sounds like an invitation.

But an invitation to—*what?* Check out his scars?

I think I lost the thread of this conversation. If I ever had it. My skin burns with a feverish flush, and I can't find a safe place to look. Not at Eli's face, with his mouth tipped up in a half smile and his blue eyes, intent on mine. His shoulders are too broad, his collarbones too inviting.

You know it's bad when you find yourself obsessing over clavicles.

I'm saved from myself by a huge yawn. Even though it's only ten-thirty, I'm suddenly exhausted. I have an embarrassingly early bedtime. Beth told me once after I didn't answer a string of texts around ten o'clock that her eleven-year-old niece stays up later than I do.

I believe it.

"We should probably head out." Before I get any *ideas.* "I'm getting tired."

"What about waffles?"

Immediately, I can see a Belgian waffle, butter glistening in every square, syrup pooling around it in a sticky lake. "I just—" A yawn cuts me off, and I cover my mouth with my hand. Who knows what my breath smells like after beer, a Dr Pepper, part of Shannon's chili fries, and a few handfuls of Skittles. "Should probably get some sleep. I've got the early shift tomorrow."

Eli lifts his hand. I think he's going to tuck a strand of hair behind my ear, the one that never stays put, but instead, he gives it a gentle tug like he did earlier, then lets it fall back against my cheek. His fingertips graze the side of my neck. I shiver.

"You're sure?"

"Yes?"

"You don't sound very sure." Eli leans closer and drops his voice to a sultry whisper. "Waffles, Bailey. *Waffles.*"

Has a breakfast food ever sounded sexy?

"Fine." I give Eli a playful shove, mostly because my sense of self-preservation kicks in. Having him this close is dangerous. "Let's see who else wants to go."

Because I need the buffer Shannon and Van provide. The two of them have been flirt-bickering all night, and it's the perfect thing to diffuse the probably one-sided electric tension I'm feeling.

"I need to head home." Shannon is suddenly beside me, the bathroom door swinging closed behind her. She gives me a loud, smacking kiss on my cheek. "Happy birthday, B. Do you think you can give the birthday girl a ride home?" she asks Eli. "I drove her because her car totally sucks."

"Hey! It drives!"

"Barely," Shannon says.

So, maybe it needs new tires. And has a dashboard lit up like Christmas with all the flashing lights: Check Engine, the little oil can symbol, and something called ABS something or other. One day I'll have the extra cash to get all those things fixed. Or at least checked out.

Not anytime soon with the money I just sent off to Gran's nursing home.

"I've got her," Eli says, and I like the way that sounds— maybe a little too much.

We say goodbye to Van and Shannon in the parking lot,

and then Eli leads me to a black SUV and opens the door for me. When he takes my hand to help me up, I exhale a happy sigh. I manage not to protest when his palm slides away from mine. After making sure my legs are properly tucked inside the vehicle, he closes the door and jogs around to his side.

As he climbs in, he pulls out his buzzing phone, frowning as he glances down at the screen. "Sorry—it's my mom." He lifts the phone to his ear. "Hey—what's wrong?"

His frown deepens, and worry pinches my chest. I'd like to reach out, to place a reassuring hand on his arm. The same way he did the other day when I was coughing.

Eli didn't hesitate or overthink the gesture. He just came right over and made sure I was okay.

I want to do the same, but I can't quite bring myself to be that brave.

The call ends before my bravery arrives, and as Eli shoves the phone back in his pocket, I tell myself that in ten more seconds, maybe I would have worked up the courage to touch his arm.

"I have to go," he says, dragging a hand through his hair, his jaw tight. "Something's wrong, but she wouldn't tell me what on the phone."

My bravery chooses that moment to kick in. "I'll go with you."

"Yeah?"

Eli's brows shoot up, and it's then I realize he might not *want* me to go with him. We've gone from randomly running into each other in a bar to me meeting his mother. Which is a lot of ground to cover in one night.

I twist my hands into the fabric of my nightgown. "Or I could just grab a rideshare or you could—"

"Not a chance." Eli shakes his head. "But buckle up," he

says, and I get the sense he means both literally and figuratively.

I fasten the buckle with a satisfying click, wishing it were a little easier to secure the rest of me.

CHAPTER 7

Bailey

I DON'T KNOW what I expected—not that I expected in any way to be going to the house Eli apparently shares with his mother—but it was not this charming bungalow. Hanging baskets overflow with ferns and the door is painted flamingo pink. I'm sure it would all be more cheerful during the day or if the porch lights were on.

Don't like his house! I tell myself, with as fierce of an internal voice as I can. *You cannot like Eli and his house too!*

But it's too late. I like him and his adorable, perfect house.

"Mom chose the color," Eli mutters, fumbling with his keys.

I almost tease him about it, asking him if he holds to the stereotype that pink is a feminine color. But I don't know if Eli is the kind of person whose tension eases with jokes or if it would make him wind tighter, adding more of an edge.

He's been intensely focused since his mom called. I'm sure he knows where the brake is, but he opted to use it sparingly on the twenty-minute drive. I couldn't quite bring myself to place my hand on his arm or shoulder, even though I sense touch is important to him.

But I did allow myself to indulge in stolen glances, watching the way Eli's jaw clenched in the glow of street-lights and headlights. My hands, balled into sweaty fists in my coat pockets, ached to smooth away the lines bracketing his mouth.

His nerves transferred to me on the drive, and there's a nervous fluttering inside me. I don't know what kind of emergency this is, or even if emergencies with his mom are a normal thing. Health stuff? Mental health stuff? A burglary? Hopefully, she'd call the police in that case. While there are a lot of cars parked along the street, not one has red and blue lights.

Eli pushes open the door, and when he glances back to make sure I'm following, I scurry after him.

"Mom? What's the emergency?" He flicks the switch on the wall just inside the door once, twice, then three times in quick succession, frowning when the hallway stays swathed in darkness. The only light comes from the end of the hall, a soft, flickering glow.

"In here," a melodic voice calls from somewhere in the back of the house. One that does not sound in any way like it's in crisis.

Eli must sense this too because his shoulders drop as he sighs, muttering something under his breath about crying wolf. His eyes meet mine in the dim hallway light. "I'm sorry in advance," he says.

I don't get a chance to ask what for. His shoes are loud, the hardwoods creaking out a chorus of complaints as he stomps toward the back of the house. I'm a few steps behind, drinking in details as my eyes adjust to the light. I was hoping for framed photos, but instead I get strange artwork in glass frames: a swatch of ripped denim, dozens of ticket stubs lined up in neat rows, and a framed receipt I can't quite read.

I want to linger, squinting in the dark at the tiny print on the faded paper, but I hear an excited voice say, "You brought someone with you?" The voice pitches higher. "A woman? Well, where is she?"

Eli's voice is too quiet for me to make out the words, only the low rumble that tugs at me like a kite string. I hesitate outside the open door, the toes of my ankle boots just shy of the square of light cast from the doorway. It's clear even though my view is of one corner of the room—all book-shelves—that there are other people in the room. The low murmur of voices, the sound of a glass being set down on a table.

One more brave thing, I tell myself, drawing on the birthday wish I didn't make to help my feet move again.

But before I've taken a step, a woman rushes through the door, almost knocking me over. There's a gasp, and then I'm receiving perhaps the best hug of my entire life.

Tears prick my eyes for no logical reason, and I try to somehow suck them back into my tear ducts before she releases me. There's something about a genuine hug from someone you've just met—or in this case, not yet met. No pretense, no prerequisites. Completely unearned. I hug her back, my hands gripping her sweater.

I somehow manage to not look like someone about to burst into inappropriate tears when she pulls back, openly appraising me with a soft smile before she tugs me into the room.

Which is completely full of women. Every chair—many of which look as though they've been dragged from other rooms—and cushion, even some of the floor space is taken up. Eli stands in the center of the room, rubbing the back of his neck and looking as though he has many, many regrets.

"Well, aren't you just *perfect*," Eli's mom whispers. There is a soft chorus of *aws* around the room, and my cheeks invent a new shade of red.

"Mom," Eli hisses, pressing his fists in his eyes.

But she only grips my hand with unrelenting force as she openly stares at me. Her hair probably used to be the same pure blond as Eli's, though now it's liberally streaked with snowy white and knotted on top of her head. They share the same blue eyes too, but their facial features don't have a strong resemblance.

Her smile is wide, clearly with so many wrong ideas in her mind.

It's at this point I consider how we're dressed.

I'll blame not thinking about this beforehand on the tension strung tight as Eli rushed home for the supposed emergency. At least my coat hides some of the nightgown. I pull it tighter with the one hand I still have the freedom to move.

"Um," I start.

Leaning close, she says, "Don't explain. It's more fun that way."

"Mom," Eli groans. "Let Bailey breathe."

"Let me have a moment, Elias. This is the first woman you've brought home in … well, *ever*. I should get a chance to appreciate it."

My eyes dart to Eli's. The tips of his ears flush red, and he glances away from me quickly. *Elias?* The first woman he's brought home?

Really?

"It's so lovely to meet you, Bailey." She gives my hand a last squeeze before finally letting go. I think my fingers have gone to sleep. "I'm Margaret. Everyone calls me Maggie."

"Or Magpie," Eli says. "Magnanimous. Margo."

Maggie rolls her eyes. "Quiet, *Elipses*."

Okay, I get it—their thing is messing with each other's names. It's … kind of adorable.

"And this"—Maggie sweeps an arm wide, gesturing to the room full of women, all grinning, most waving—"is book club."

I manage a small wave with the hand that still works, and then Eli steps between Maggie and me. "Tell me about this electrical emergency."

Maggie shrugs. "Started a little while ago. Half the lights in the house just don't work."

There are candles on the coffee table, none matching. From the scent lingering in the air, at least one is pumpkin spice, another vanilla.

Eli pulls the cords on the ceiling fan. The blades spin and stop, but the lights don't click on. He points above the mantel, where one recessed light shines brightly. "That one still works. And the power is still on. I hear the heater."

Maggie shrugs again. The move feels a little too practiced, but it's not my place to say. "It's the strangest thing. Some work, some don't. I don't know if it's a power surge or something with the breaker box." She laughs. "To tell the truth, I don't know where the breaker box is."

"It's in the kitchen. I'll check." Eli meets my eyes. Hesitantly, he asks, "Will you be okay?"

"Of course she'll be okay!" Maggie links her arm through mine. "She's with me."

From the set of his jaw, I get the sense that's *exactly* why Eli asked. With a heaving sigh, he walks out, presumably toward the kitchen. It's funny to see him like this. Different from his normal brightness or even the low mood when he came to the shelter the other day. This is more of a gruff concern, his worry working itself out in grumpiness.

The room holds its breath while he goes. Then, it erupts into sound and motion as soon as he's gone. Voices clatter together like dishes in the sink after a meal, and I'm ushered to the couch where two women shift apart to make room for Maggie and me—barely.

If I were claustrophobic at all, I'd be breathing into a paper bag right now. As it is, my shyness rears its head, and my tongue cements itself to the roof of my mouth.

"Would you like something to drink?" Maggie asks. "Water, tea, wine?"

"Vodka?" a woman asks from her seat on the floor. Her face is heavily lined, her hair bright purple. A red bra peeks out from a hole in her ripped Metallica t-shirt.

"There's also decaf coffee," another woman says, holding up a mug that reads *Deck the Falls* with a fall leaf pattern.

"We're big drinkers at book club," Maggie says. "Something for everyone. What'll it be?"

"I'm fine," I say, my voice scratchy, sounding almost unused. My heartbeat is louder in my ears than my words.

"Let me know if you change your mind," Maggie says, then proceeds to introduce everyone in the room, assuring me it's fine if I forget.

Turns out there are only nine women. It feels like dozens, perhaps because the room is so small and over-crowded with furniture. I only remember one name,

Rachel, and only because it was my mother's name. She's seated beside me and, thankfully, does not remind me of my mother in the slightest. This Rachel is tall and full of angles: sharp nose, firm jaw, a pointy shoulder pressing into mine. But her smile is kind, her eyes gentle.

My mother was short like me and soft everywhere, from her gentle curls to her creamy skin and wide hips. Every so often, growing greedy for affection, I'd sink into her lap while she was reading, trying to stay still enough to be forgotten. Hoping she wouldn't shoo me away so she could work. The only thing not soft about her was her voice, which I remember being as tight as a guitar string.

Maggie leans into me. "Why don't you tell us how you met my son? I didn't even know he was on a date tonight."

Her expression is so earnest and so hopeful, I don't want to explain that it wasn't a date but more of a chance meeting turned birthday celebration. So … I don't.

"Eli volunteers at the animal shelter where I work," I explain.

Not wholly the truth, at least not *officially*, but probably easier to explain than the reality. He at least has the volunteer paperwork, even if he never plans to bring it back.

Maggie's eyes widen. So does her smile. The tiniest dimple appears in one cheek. "You work at the shelter?"

I nod, and she goes on to talk about how much Eli has always loved dogs, but they never had one because she was a single mom and too many apartments don't allow it. I'm on the cusp of getting Eli's whole life story, but he walks into the room.

"I can't find anything." He found a hat somewhere, and it's jammed down low, shading his eyes. His hands are in fists on his hips. "It's not the breakers. It's not even whole rooms or particular sockets. It seems totally random. Almost ... intentional."

Next to me, Maggie shifts, settling deeper into the sofa and taking a drink before answering. "How strange," Maggie says. "Then again, it is an old house."

Eli's not buying it. Neither am I. Maggie seems far too delighted with the whole situation and not in the least concerned about why half the lights in the house aren't working. Heaving a sigh, Eli walks over to a tall floor lamp in the corner and starts fiddling with the cord.

"What kind of books do you read?" I ask, desperately needing the focus in the room to be anywhere other than me.

"Our books vary as much as our drink choices," the purple-haired woman on the floor says. "And unlike some book clubs, we *do* actually read and discuss books."

"Among other things," Maggie says, then turns to me. "We all suffer from chronic illness of one kind or another. Or several."

"Except me." Beside me, Rachel touches her chest. "Nurse practitioner."

"She's here in case someone dies," says a woman in a floppy hat.

Maggie shakes a finger. "Not true! We just all love Rachel. And remember--dying isn't allowed during book club. It's in the rules."

What are the other rules? I find myself wondering.

"Fibromyalgia and rheumatoid arthritis for me," Maggie says cheerfully, like she's announcing a prize she's won. "Though we try to keep that kind of talk out of these evenings. Can you believe they wouldn't let me name our group the Chronic-Ills of Narnia? Get it—chronic ills? Chronicles? Such a missed opportunity."

A woman with closely cropped white hair and a tiny nose

ring presses a mug of tea into my hands. I don't protest, though I didn't ask for anything and I didn't notice anyone leaving the room to make it. When I lift the mug to my nose, it smells like Christmas morning.

"Cinnamon herbal tea," Maggie says. "Decaf so it won't keep you up." Her gaze slides to Eli, then back to me. Her smile is sly. "But if you have late night plans, I could find you something with caffeine, I'm sure."

I take a sip of tea, which is thankfully just the right temperature to save me from having to respond. Maggie reminds me of Eli—overwhelming in the best kind of way. Still, there is a lot to process. All the new faces, the names I've forgotten, the various unnamed chronic illnesses I'll now be wondering about. I have some googling to do.

Suddenly, the lamp Eli's been messing with turns on, brightening the whole room. A few women gasp. And then they all clap, like Eli just performed a perfectly executed magic trick.

Maggie grins. "Well, would you look at that! It's a miracle."

Eli stares at the lamp for a few seconds, then slowly turns to his mom with narrowed eyes. Keeping his gaze fixed on her, he walks to the center of the room and reaches up toward the ceiling fan. But instead of pulling the cord again, he reaches inside one of the glass globes and gives the light bulb a few turns. It immediately turns on.

"You solved the electrical issue!" Maggie says. "Thank goodness!"

"Mom," Eli says slowly, crossing his arms over his chest. His eyes are narrowed, but I can see the amusement in the tilt of his lips. "There is no electrical issue. The light bulbs have all been loosened just enough not to work. Do you happen to know anything about that?"

Maggie presses a hand to her chest. "Me? Heavens no. Why would I go around unscrewing light bulbs? Who has time for that? Maybe we have a poltergeist."

I stifle a giggle, dropping my gaze to my mug of tea before glancing back up at Eli. He shoots me a look that's half apology and half exasperation before stomping out of the room, presumably tightening all the light bulbs in the house.

"There's no poltergeist," Maggie whispers, leaning close. "I just wanted to meet you. When Eli texted he was taking someone—a woman—out for her birthday, I had to orchestrate something. It's what a good mother does."

"I think my therapist would have something to say about that," the purple-haired woman points out.

"You unscrewed all the light bulbs in the house so you could meet me?" I ask.

"Just the easy to reach ones. Made it a little more of a mystery to figure out since it wasn't *all* the lights." Maggie grins deviously, and I find myself smiling right back. "I am of the opinion that if you really want something, you sometimes have to make your own luck, even if it's risky."

I'd like to have her write that down on an index card so I could stick it on my fridge.

"Mom," Eli mutters from the doorway. "Please. You can't do things like this."

"Like what, Elisha?"

He only shakes his head. "Bailey, I'd better get you home."

Just the mention of home has me yawning. Still, I hate to think about this night ending. Hands down, it was the best birthday of my life.

"She hasn't finished her tea," Maggie protests.

"I'll give her one of my travel mugs," Eli says. Before he disappears into the kitchen, he waves goodbye, shooting the women a look just as disapproving as the one he gave Maggie.

"You can join us any time," Maggie says. "Chronic illness or not. Do you read?"

"Yes, but—"

"Good. What's your number? I'll put it in my phone."

We've barely exchanged numbers when Eli appears. I stand, and Maggie does too. Eli pours my tea into the travel mug while Maggie wraps me in another hug.

"I'm sure I'll be seeing you again soon," she says. "*Very* soon. With or without my son. You don't need him as an excuse. And the offer to join book club is always open."

She releases me and steps right into Eli's open arms. "I love you," he tells her. "Even if you're conniving and nosy."

"You say *conniving* and *nosy* but all I hear is *caring* and *concerned*," Maggie says, turning her head so she can give me a wink.

I've hardly buckled my seat belt and plugged my apartment complex's address into Eli's GPS when my phone buzzes. Once, then again and again and again. When I glance down at the screen, I'm surprised to see six new texts, all from Maggie.

"My mom loves GIFs," Eli says, his lips curling up in a smile. "And memes. You might be sorry you gave her your number."

I doubt that. Losing my mom and dad when I hardly felt like an adult myself left a gaping, parent-sized wound inside me. Maggie just stitched it up part-way with a hug, a few kind words, and an invitation to join her book club.

As much as I know for certain my parents loved me, open affection was not a thing in our household, physical or verbal. Love was just a thing we all understood to be true. A given, like the way you trust the load-bearing walls will keep the house from crumbling down around you even if you don't ever really think about or acknowledge them.

But I've always been a child who craved these givens, and I'm not sure my parents ever understood that, even when I tried to tell them as an adult.

I decide to save Maggie's texts for later, sliding my phone into my purse. Exhaustion falls over me, a heavy snowdrift of a feeling, and my eyes flutter closed as I snuggle into Eli's leather seats.

"Cold?" he asks, and I nod without opening my eyes. "I'll turn on the seat warmers."

Within moments, I groan softly as warmth radiates through the bottom and back of the seat. "Thank you," I say through another yawn. They're coming rapid-fire now, like the tail end of a fireworks show, one right after another.

"I just pushed a button for the seat warmer." Eli sounds amused.

"No, I mean for everything. The drinks, the Canadian birthday extravaganza, all of it."

He snorts. "Don't forget the nightgown."

"I think I prefer your muumuu." I tug at the hem, running my fingertip along the ruffle at the bottom.

Eli fiddles with the radio and settles on an indie rock station. The acoustic guitar lulls me toward dreamland, though my brain wants to keep circling back to one niggling worry.

"Does your mom know about—"

"No."

"What will she do?" I ask without opening my eyes. I'm not sure I could if I tried. They're sandbag heavy, and I'm sleep-weak. "If you have to go back to Canada."

Eli doesn't speak for a moment. When he does, I jolt, realizing I started to doze.

"She won't stay here without me. Even if she's built a good life here. She'll go where I go."

I think of Maggie's bright smile, the room tonight crowded with love. And support, probably, considering what she said about chronic illness. I don't know much about fibromyalgia or rheumatoid arthritis, but I can't help but wonder if I happened to see one of Maggie's good days.

"Is she okay? With her health, I mean."

"She has good and bad days. We go to Asheville a few times a month for different treatments. A lot of doctors don't really diagnose or deal with chronic illnesses. Especially in women. This has been the best place we've found for support. Not just because of her book club. But it does help."

I press my hand to my throat, wishing that would ease the ache there. It doesn't.

Eli continues, a hint of defensiveness in his voice, "I know it might seem weird that I'm so close to my mom, but she's amazing and did so much for me when I was growing up."

"I don't think it's weird. I think it's pretty great."

"I'll do everything I can to make her happy," Eli says quietly.

Even commit fraud, I think.

It's in this moment I realize that Eli doesn't just want to stay in Harvest Hollow for himself. In fact, it may not even be the primary reason. If he and his mom are this close, he wants to stay so *she* doesn't have to leave. A deep ache settles into my bones.

"How would it work?" The question slides out easier when I'm drifting in this state of semi-sleep. "The marriage thing."

I've heard it said that anyone would do anything given the right set of circumstances.

Like, you might not *think* you'd rob a Wendy's for a Frosty and some cheesy bacon fries ... but spend a few weeks stranded on a desert island with only coconuts for sustenance, and you might change your mind about thievery. That's just one hypothetical.

Another *not-so* hypothetical: I never thought I'd be tempted to marry someone for money.

I probably wouldn't have even dreamed up my current scenario. The desert-island-Wendy's situation is far more likely. Which is saying something, considering I live about six hours from the nearest beach.

But here I am, sitting in an awkwardly silent car with Eli, turning over his offer in my mind. Asking questions about it out loud. Keeping my eyes closed because I'm a coward.

Even without looking, I am aware of a shift, the tension vibrating between us. I sense it the way I've always insisted I can smell snow in the air.

"It would need to be a real marriage," Eli says finally. "I'd need the certificate, for starters. Everything else is ... negotiable."

I'm sure he means practical things: the wedding itself, the housing particulars, how long this would last. But my hazy mind goes to other negotiable things: whether it would include kissing, sharing a room, making public appearances pretending to be a real couple.

"It's a huge ask," Eli continues. "And I don't have much to offer other than ... money." His voice sours with this last part, like he plucked one of the lemons from his muumuu and took a big bite.

That's not true, I think. He has lots of things I want, none of which have to do with money. The trouble is, they're not things I think he wants from *me*.

And also ... I do need money. Every time I walk past the

desk in my bedroom where the letter from my grandmother's facility is stuffed in a drawer, I feel like I'm going to dry heave. Several times lately, I've considered giving up on vet school altogether, since I'll be paying off loans until I've got gray hair. Or no hair.

The idea of having to worry less, of sharing this burden with someone else … well. I hate the wolfish desperation clawing at the pit of my stomach when I think about it.

"Don't take this the wrong way, but I didn't think minor league players made all that much money."

Eli laughs, and the car slows. We're probably at a red light, nearing my house. I wish now I'd given him the wrong address for his GPS, sent us on a wild goose chase so I could enjoy his company and his heated seats.

"I'm really good with the stock market," he says, and I'm not sure he could have said anything that would have shocked me more.

I've never understood anything about the stock market other than to know Martha Stewart went to prison because she somehow cheated the system. It's not something I'd have immediately placed in the box of things I know about Eli.

But okay. Eli—Hot Puppy Guy—is a stock market person. Which means in addition to everything else he's got going on, he's smart too.

Unfair.

"I handle a lot of investments for the guys," he says, and the word investments should *not* sound sexy. "Plus, the Appies get a lot of endorsements because of social media. We're not the typical minor league team."

I have more questions, but they're tumbling over one another then getting lost in the soft edges of my current sleepy state.

"Do you," Eli starts, then pauses. "Are, uh, finances an issue?"

I want to laugh. Because "issue" is a bit of an understatement. But Shannon already brought up my car. Exactly how many broken-down areas of my life do I want to reveal tonight?

"Vet school is expensive," I say. "I've been saving so I'm not buried in student loans."

I peek over, a little afraid but needing to see Eli's reaction to this. He's frowning, and I fully expect to hear him ask exactly how expensive vet school is or to admit he was thinking about something less.

Instead, he says, "Are you planning to move? For vet school, I mean."

I close my eyes again, letting myself relax again in the warm hug of the heated seat. "I'm applying to UNC-Asheville and Tennessee, so I'll stay here." I pause, considering my words. But sleepiness has loosened my inhibitions. Or maybe just my tongue. "My grandmother lives here in an assisted living facility. I don't really want to leave her alone."

Even if she couldn't care less. The last time I went to see her, she called me Jezebel and tossed a large-print edition of a Harlequin romance at my head.

"Are you her only family?"

I know the question Eli's really asking, and I appreciate the careful way he asked. It makes me wonder about his own family situation. People with happy and healthy relationships with both living parents are more likely to ask things like *What about your parents?*

"My mom and dad died in a car crash two years ago," I tell him, feeling like a terrible person when I yawn immediately after.

My eyes crack open as Eli sets his hand over mine, curling

his fingers over my knuckles. His thumb does a quick sweep over the skin at my wrist, making me shiver. He only glances away from the road for a second to meet my gaze, but his eyes are kind. After a moment, he releases my hand, and I hold back the sound of protest that wants to escape at the loss of contact.

"I'm sorry, Bailey. That's … wow. I'm really sorry."

"Thanks."

I blow out a shaky breath and let my eyes fall closed again. Confessions are easier when I can't see his handsome jaw in the dim light from the dashboard. His car, I couldn't help but notice when he first turned it on, has exactly zero maintenance lights flashing.

"So, you're the one who takes care of your grandmother?" he asks.

"Financially," I clarify.

"Did your parents have a trust or something set up?" His voice is so hopeful.

Kind of like I was when I first walked into the lawyer's office to discuss my parents' estate. I mean, I was also broken and sad and kind of a walking zombie, but I was hopeful at least for some kind of financial boon to help keep me afloat while I drifted in grief.

"My parents were apparently not great at financial things. They had a reverse mortgage on their house." I don't need to explain because the noise Eli makes assures me that in addition to stocks, he has some understanding of what that means. "There was very little left over after everything was settled."

So, now Eli can guess exactly how sad my financial state of affairs is. Which is to say: very sad.

The kind of sad that might make a person think about getting married in exchange for some kind of financial benefit. Honestly? The idea of just not doing everything *alone* appeals to me as much as the ease of the monetary strain.

My thoughts have the kind of soft haze of near-sleep, but I can clearly picture the pink door on Eli's house. The way his mom hugged me, the offer to join her book club.

All that might all go away if Eli has to go back to Canada, his mom with him. No more book club. No more hockey. No more pink door. Or centaurs.

Wait—centaurs?

"Who's taking care of you, Bailey?"

Eli's words settle over me, soft as snowfall, only warm not cold.

"No one," I murmur.

"I could," Eli says, and now I'm really not sure if I'm dreaming. Because this is the exact kind of thing I wish someone would tell me. "I would."

A single, solid thought breaks the surface as I'm slipping down, down, down.

"I'll do it," I say, a smile on my lips. Because I'm proud of myself for being brave. For wanting something and then saying so. Out loud.

Unless I'm dreaming?

"I'll marry you, hockey player."

I think Eli responds, but his words slip into merely a steady rumbling ribbon of bass, pairing with the hum of the tires on the road and the cocooning warmth of the seat as my mind drifts and then winks out.

———

A whispered voice, low and close. Hands scooping me up. A warm, safe chest. One I want to nuzzle into, so I do. I could stay right here forever. A masculine scent—one that calls to mind cozy fires and cinnamon rolls.

A lovely, lovely dream. I sigh, allowing myself to fall deeper into the warm comfort, and the sway of calming motion, a soothing drug.

"Which one is your apartment, Leelee?"

Apartment? My dreams don't usually include my dingy apartment. Something tugs at me, pulling me up from sleep. A niggling thought that grows louder and more insistent until it yanks me completely out of sleep and into the present moment.

Where I'm currently being held against a firm, solid chest encased in a scratchy muumuu.

Eli. Eli is carrying me in his arms across the parking lot of my apartment complex.

I am utterly embarrassed at the way my hands are linked around Eli's neck, as though even in my sleep, I wanted to get closer to him. My cheek is pressed against a swath of skin just above the collar of the muumuu, which must have slipped while he carried me. He smells better than any birthday cake could. I am shamelessly plastered against the man.

I can't bring myself to look at him. I also can't bring myself to move, though I should. I should take my hands away from his neck where my fingertips brush against the longer strands of his hair. I should lift my cheek from his chest, insist he put me down on my feet. I'm an adult. I can walk.

But I don't want to.

I'd like to cling to this moment as long as possible. To what felt so much like a dream, because it is like a dream: the famous hockey player who just spent the evening making my birthday so special. Making *me* feel special.

"Did you call me Leelee?" I ask, for some reason zeroing in on the least important part of this whole situation.

"Do you like it?" he asks. "I was trying to think of a nickname for you."

He's trying to think of a nickname for me. This tiny fact has no business making me so happy.

"Bay sounds like either a body of water or the sound a beagle makes."

I snort. "Yeah, let's avoid that. So, Leelee." I test the name out. It's cute. Sweet.

"I think it suits you."

Well, in that case…

"I mean, if you don't mind," he adds.

"I like it."

"Good. Now, I really need to know where I'm going. I think I've walked by the same building three times. But I'm not sure because they all look the same."

They do. I guess that's true of all apartment complexes, but it's especially true here. In a town so filled with charm like Harvest Hollow, I think they had to actually pump in ugly to make this complex, with its stark brick buildings and windows that seem way too small.

I lift my head from Eli's warm chest to see where we are. "That one." I point, then decide to lay my head back on his chest. Why not?

I'm sure that's the post-midnight Bailey talking. The one with fewer inhibitions. The one who wants to take both hands and wring every bit I can out of this moment. The one who—

Wait, wait, wait. I freeze as I remember, every muscle, even the ones I didn't know I had, constricting until I'm a block of stone. *The one who said she'd marry Eli.*

CHAPTER 8

Eli

THE MORE I walk around Bailey's complex, trying not to think about how she feels curled up against my chest or about her bare leg touching my arm, the angrier I get. It's the secondary emotion, stemming from concern. But anger quickly bubbles up, overshadowing my worry.

This complex is a dump.

More than a dump. It would make dumps look like a Hilton.

First of all, there's no security gate. Anyone could just drive in here, especially given its proximity to the highway. It's not well-lit, partially because there aren't a lot of lights, and partially because, out of the few it does have, they either don't work at all or they're flickering like they've been yanked straight out of a horror movie.

There's clearly no security guard of any kind. No cameras.

Essentially, we're walking around a total death trap. A serial killer playground.

I don't like it. At all.

As I walk toward the door Bailey indicated in her sleep-soft voice, I have an internal debate. Have I earned the right to say anything?

Bailey and I are tentative friends. Maybe *definitely* friends after the time spent together tonight. And if what she said before falling asleep in my car was for real, she agreed to be my fiancée.

For the moment, I'm trying to shelve my thoughts and questions about that, ignoring the weird flurry of hope in my chest battling the worry twisting in my gut. My focus is on getting Bailey home safely tonight.

But whatever part of my brain still connects to my very basal caveman ancestors wants to march back to my SUV, toss Bailey inside (gently), and drive her back to my house. After putting her seatbelt on, of course.

Safety first! Even when being a Neanderthal.

The part most likely steered by my frontal lobe tells me to think long and hard before trying to tell Bailey she can't— sorry, *shouldn't*—live somewhere without proper safety features. Mom's always told me I'm too protective. I say there's no such thing.

A thought pings around in my brain like a loose cog. If she's serious about marrying me, it won't be an issue for long. But I don't know that I can count on the words that spilled out of Bailey when she was curled up in the front seat of my car with her eyes closed.

Will she even *remember* saying it? And if she does ... did she *mean* it?

I don't really want to ask that either, unsure whether I want the answer to be yes or no.

Actually *marrying* Bailey? The idea sits on the surface of my mind rather than sinking in. Because I never—not one single time—thought marrying someone so Mom and I could stay in the country was something I would do.

Sure, I tossed it around as an idea, joked about it with Bailey, confessed it to the guys and let them believe they were helping me on a wife hunt.

But at no time did it ever seem like it would become a tangible thing, a real possibility, a verifiable option involving a woman, a ring, and a marriage license.

Bailey shifts, her hands moving a little as she clings to my neck, her sigh soft and content. I clutch her a little tighter to my chest. The same cinnamon-cotton candy scent fills my nose, and I wonder if it's her shampoo or body wash or some kind of perfume. It makes me want a cupcake.

I enjoyed tonight—more than I expected. I saw a different side of the woman who, up until now, occupied a solitary square in my mind. Bailey existed in the animal shelter, in scrubs, the shy woman who I liked to coax into smiling and blushing and talking. Now, the edges of that square have dissolved, and I'm not sure where she fits.

Other than in my arms. She definitely fits here. Which *also* is something I didn't expect.

As though my thoughts are traveling by osmosis to Bailey and she agrees wholeheartedly about fitting here, she snuggles deeper into me. Burrowing, really, her nose landing somewhere near my collarbone.

"Are we there yet?" she asks through a huge yawn.

It drags a yawn out of me too, even though I'm wide awake. On high alert, because in this sketchy apartment complex, someone has to be. Nearby, I hear raised voices, an argument, mostly muffled behind closed doors. A semi blasts its horn on the highway, the sound startling me.

"Is this the right one? 4B?" I ask, glaring toward the darkest and most remote of all the apartments. I should shut up. I tell myself to shut up. I can't shut up. "The one on the first floor, all the way at the end of the building near the woods. The one with all the lights burned out."

My pointed questions, statements really, spoken in a voice that's guitar-string tight, finally rouse Bailey enough to open her toffee brown eyes. Not that I can see the color right now. It's too dark.

Standing in front of her door, we're literally shrouded in a pool of shadow. The next working light has to be a good fifteen feet away. And it's pulsing on and off, so dim the moths aren't even interested.

"I put in an order for maintenance to fix it," Bailey says.

That makes me feel worse, not better. "How long ago?"

A long pause. "Um, three months. Maybe four."

I don't realize I've tightened my arms around her, crushing her to my chest, until she taps my arm twice.

"You can put me down now, hockey player," she murmurs.

Right.

Bending carefully, I angle Bailey until she's standing. She smooths down her nightgown and takes a quick step away from me. I watch as she roots through her purse, presumably looking for keys. It would help if the light above her door wasn't burned out.

She glances back at me, the barest of smiles on her lips. "Do you ever wear a coat?"

I glance down at my muumuu, which is surprisingly comfortable if not very seasonal. Especially right now, when all I've got on underneath is a pair of athletic shorts. I didn't realize how warm Bailey was keeping me until she wasn't cradled to my chest.

"No? I mean, sometimes when it's really cold, I do. I tend to run hot."

Bailey opens her mouth, then closes it and turns back to the hunt for her keys, forearm-deep in her purse. I really hope, considering my safety concerns, she usually walks to her apartment with her keys in hand. And maybe some mace.

"Do you have a taser?" I ask.

Bailey's keys clatter to the ground. "What?"

And that's when, as though conjured by all my imagined worst-case scenarios, a tall figure steps around the corner, gliding out of the shadows like some kind of wraith. Bailey shrieks and lobs her purse full force at the person's face.

I'll give her this—she may live in the most murdery apartment complex I've ever seen, but she's got good instincts.

Right now, she also has *me*. Almost the moment the purse is thrown, I step between her and the wiry man who's now clutching his face with a groan. My hands are curled into fists, my whole body coiled like a spring. It's the moment before the puck drops, and I can almost feel the stick in my gloves.

I wish I had a stick right now. In a pinch, it would make a great weapon.

"Now, why'd you go and do that?" the man says.

"Jesse?" Bailey curls her hand around my arm and peers past me. I can feel the heat of her body against my back and hope she stays right there.

"Yeah," the man groans, kicking at her purse. "Who'd you think it was?"

Bailey's purse capsizes, spilling its contents everywhere. Receipts, a tiny notebook, pens, coins, and a fat wallet bursting at the seams. Either Bailey carries a lot of cash, or she has a problem with credit cards.

A tube of lipstick rolls to a stop at my feet. Bailey bends

to pick it up, and I put a hand on her hip, gently urging her behind me again before I let go. It's clear she knows this guy. But it's still creepy as hell how he was waiting in the darkness for her.

I'm not letting Bailey anywhere near him. My instincts earlier may have been a bit on the caveman side, but they were also correct. This apartment complex is *not* safe.

"Who are you?" I demand.

Do I use my most intimidating voice? Absolutely I do.

Bailey gives my arm a squeeze, and I'm not sure if this means she likes the protective vibe or is telling me to back off. I'm going with option A.

Whether she likes it or she doesn't, the protective vibe isn't going anywhere. The dial is now set to maximum strength.

Until Bailey whispers, "He's just my neighbor."

Just her neighbor. Who steps out of the darkness late at night right when she happens to be coming home. Still weird. And suspect. I don't dial back my protectiveness at all.

"Who are *you?*" the guy—Jesse, I guess—snaps. Then there's a pause, and he leans forward. I can barely make him out, squinting through the darkness. His height and the slightness of his figure reminds me a bit of Gabe from *The Office*. "Wait—you're that hockey player. *Dude.* Why are you wearing a muumuu?"

Bailey tries to step around me. This time, when I clasp her hip and maneuver her behind me, I don't let go. Not even when she lets out a little huff of frustration. Or amusement? I'm not sure which. Instead, I squeeze her hip lightly, holding her steady.

I ignore both his statement and his question. "Why were you lurking outside Bailey's apartment?"

"I wasn't *lurking*. I was taking a walk."

"At this hour? In the woods? Walking by Bailey's apartment door?"

Her hands glide up my back until they rest just below my shoulders, warm and firm. My muscles start to loosen, little by little. But not fully. Because there will be no relaxing until we're not having a conversation in almost pitch-black with a guy who takes midnight strolls past Bailey's apartment door.

"That's his place," she whispers, pointing.

I glance over, keeping Jesse in view, to see the next apartment down. Okay, so maybe he has reason to pass her apartment. I still don't like it.

Especially not when he asks, with venom in his voice, "Wait—are you two dating?"

We might be getting married, I think. But I don't say that. And the press of Bailey's hands on my back sends a signal that she's got this. At least, I hope I'm reading this correctly.

"It's late," Bailey says softly. Much more kindly than I would. "Goodnight, Jesse."

"Fine," he grumbles. "I'll see you around, I guess."

I watch until he's back in his apartment. Bailey's hands remain on my back until the lock engages, her palms slowly tracking back and forth. I like them there. She steadies me, and right now, I need a bit of steadying.

This has been a long night. I feel a little like Bailey's purse: tipped over with everything inside me knocked loose and scattered.

"I don't want you staying here." This probably shouldn't be the first thing I say when I release her hip and turn to face her. Already I miss the warm comfort of her hands on my back.

Her eyes narrow. "What?"

I tip my chin toward the broken light above her door, then the one that should light the walkway. "It's not safe."

"I *live* here," she says, defensiveness edging through her voice.

"Maybe you shouldn't."

She sets her jaw and crosses her arms. But her eyes don't match the rigid posture. She looks like she's about to cry.

"This is what I can afford," she says, lifting her chin, and it breaks me a little because I recognize the look.

For years, Mom raised me and my sister, Annie, in apartments like this. Ones with little to no security, near busy roads, with arguments you could hear outside. Without any support from my biological dad and none from family, Mom did the best she could. Annie and I knew we didn't have a lot, but Mom made life as big and as fun as she could for us, keeping the worries and stresses I know she felt locked-up tight.

The thing about kids, though, is they know. Maybe not the specifics. But Annie and I picked up on her body language, her moods. We recognized the exhaustion behind her bright smiles and didn't miss the way bills sometimes piled up or the pantry and fridge emptied out. It didn't help that I picked an expensive sport.

I promised myself that if I ever went pro, I'd take care of Mom. Annie too, though she doesn't want my help and prefers making her own way. It took some time because not all my contracts were super lucrative, but finally, because of my investments and because of the Appies, Mom and I are in a good place.

I find myself wanting to wrap Bailey up in that same protection. Not just because of the whole marriage thing. I can recognize this as a separate longing, a need to keep her safe. Tonight, Bailey has gone from acquaintance to actual friend. A very pretty friend. And once people move into my circle of friendship, I can't help but want to move them into my circle of protection too.

I can also recognize how hard it can be to accept help, the sense of pride that comes from wanting to do it all alone. Of not wanting to seem weak and helpless while also being desperate for a hand.

I take a few beats to consider my words, crossing my arms over my chest. The temperature is finally starting to get to me. Probably because a light breeze just picked up, reminding me of how inappropriately I'm dressed for late fall in the mountains. The longer I wait, the longer I'm keeping Bailey out here too. She has a coat, but her nightgown isn't meant for discussing potential marriage proposals outside in these temperatures.

"Do you remember what you said in the car?" I ask.

Slowly, Bailey nods. "Yes."

"Did you mean it?"

Rather than answer, Bailey crouches down and starts shoveling things back into her purse. Something I wish I'd thought to do for her. I retrieve the lipstick that's still near my foot. I squint to read the color name, curious what Bailey's color is. Immediately, I feel stupid for checking. Also, it's too dark to see.

When Bailey stands, turning to face me, I can't read her expression any better than I could the lipstick label. Wordlessly, I hold it out to her. She hesitates, and when she finally reaches for it, her fingers brushing mine, I close my other hand around both of ours. Holding her there.

I want to repeat the question. Or ask another. I've got a whole line of questions. But I just stand here like a dummy, keeping her in place. Bailey's hand feels so small in mine, her skin soft. I stroke my thumb over her knuckles, seeing her shiver in response. Or … maybe it's just the fact that it's cold and she's in a nightgown.

She's much too slow to answer. Which is probably an answer in and of itself. I'm shocked by the bitter taste of disappointment. I barely had time to even hope. And what, exactly, was I really hopeful *about?*

I release her hand and the lipstick, then step back. "I'll just—"

"Yes," Bailey says. "I meant it."

She pauses, as though giving her words a moment to land. They do.

My pulse kicks up and I swallow fast. Bailey really offered —she actually said—she'd be willing to … marry me?

The quick thrill is steamrolled almost immediately by a whole host of questions and worries. Things that I hadn't thought to consider because *marrying a woman I barely know* wasn't really a consideration.

I say nothing, my brain firing too fast to corral words into any kind of order.

"I have a lot of questions, and there are a lot of things we should probably discuss," Bailey continues. "But … yes. If you need someone to do this so you can stay, so your mom can stay, I'll be that person for you, Eli."

The light breeze chooses this moment to really pick up, blowing my muumuu well higher than feels appropriate. Even if I do have on shorts underneath. They're the only shorts I had in my car, and they're *short*. Even in the dim light, my legs are ghostly white.

Fantastic. I tug down the hem, and Bailey coughs, trying and failing to hide a giggle.

"Okay," I say, agreeing with a stupid, two-syllable word to something life-alteringly large.

"Okay." Bailey's smile is stolen by another yawn. "Can we talk tomorrow?"

"My phone's in the car, but I can give you my number?"

This feels so backwards, giving Bailey my phone number *after* she's just agreed to marry me. *Marry me.* The words are electric, jolting me every time the idea moves through my mind. It's not a wholly unpleasant feeling, which surprises me.

Should I hug her goodnight? Kiss her on the cheek? I don't know how to end an accidental, sort-of first date involving a platonic marriage agreement.

I hold out my hand. Stupidly.

Bailey glances down at it for a moment before shaking it. Once. Firmly. Like we've just made some kind of bet. I'm grateful for the darkness covering the flush I'm sure has risen in my cheeks. Her smile is highly amused, but then softens to something a little more tender.

"Thank you," she says. "For worrying about me. Jesse's harmless, but—"

"Is he?"

She nods. "Yes. A little odd, and sometimes a bit snappy. But he's all bark. No bite. Not unlike Roscoe."

I grin at this. Roscoe is one of the first dogs I remember meeting. He's still there, so I get to say hi every so often. Apparently, it's hard to find someone to adopt a dog with no teeth. Especially when he hates everyone on sight—except me, whom he only just tolerates. He still growls and gums the heck out of me. I know if he had teeth, he would use them.

"I like Roscoe better," I say, and Bailey laughs.

"You and me both." I glance back toward Jesse's apartment again, imagining him on the other side, ear pressed to the door.

"He won't bother me," Bailey says. "I'm safe. I'll be fine."

I don't argue. But nothing about this situation feels *safe* or *fine*. "Okay."

"Thank you for making my night so special," she says. "Best birthday ever."

"Really?"

"Really." Bailey smiles, then turns away, unlocking her door.

I want to go inside first, just to check and make sure it's safe. To open closet doors and crouch to look under the bed. Test the windows. Lock every door.

I force my feet to stay planted. I can't say the same for my mouth. "Is there a patio? A back door?"

Bailey pauses, one hand on the door as she gives me a glance over her shoulder. "A small patio. There's a sliding glass door. Why?"

"Just wondering."

Because it's a first-floor apartment with no security and there's a sliding glass door and woods nearby and a guy who maybe is or isn't as harmless as Roscoe. *That's* why.

"Okay. I'll text you tomorrow so we can talk about … everything," she says.

"Goodnight, Leelee."

She smiles. "'Night, hockey player."

I wait to hear the sound of her deadbolt engage before I jog back to my SUV and grab my phone, dialing Van and hoping he's alone.

He answers on the first ring. "Yeah?"

"I need a favor," I say.

"What kind of favor?"

"The kind involving being a bodyguard for the night."

"Cool."

What people may not know about Van is that he's this

guy. The one you call when you need a favor like this at this hour. The one who will say yes before he even knows what he's being asked to do. Especially if it involves protecting someone. He almost rivals me in that department.

"I'm going to text you an address. Meet me there and wear warm clothes. If you have a sleeping bag, bring it. Two, if possible. Or blankets."

Van laughs. "Are we camping?"

"More of a stakeout."

I explain about bringing Bailey back home, the lack of security at her complex, and a strange neighbor who likes taking walks in the darkness that just so *happen* to mean arriving home around when she does.

When Van speaks again, all traces of amusement are gone from his voice. "On my way."

CHAPTER 9

Eli

THE FIRST THING I'm aware of is something nudging my thigh. A persistent push, growing slightly harder. A kick?

I groan, feeling the stiffness in my neck, then blink open gritty eyes to squint into painful sunlight.

I'm … outside? And based on the ache and cold in my lower half, sitting on concrete. That's dumb. Why would I sleep outside when I have a top-of-the-line mattress at home?

Then the reason floods me. Bailey. Her safety hazard of an apartment complex. The memory of her neighbor stepping out of the shadows like the creepy love child of Gumby and Gabe. Gumby Gabe—a much better name than *Jesse*.

My hand closes around the sneaker-clad foot nudging my thigh. I blink up at Bailey, who is glaring down at me.

"Why are you sleeping outside my apartment?"

Van chooses that moment to saunter around the side of the building, covering a yawn with his hand. His dark hair, which he's been growing out, is sleep mussed, but otherwise, he looks a lot more awake than I feel. There's a sleeping bag slung over his shoulder and, surprisingly, a book under one arm.

Van reads books?

"Since we're all awake and happy now"—Van's steps slow, and he stops completely when he takes in Bailey's expression, now spearing through him—"or at least *awake,* am I done with guard duty? I need to take a leak, and it felt disrespectful to let loose on the patio plants."

Bailey makes a choking sound, and I clamber to my feet, the blanket Van brought me puddling around my feet. As grateful as I am for his help, it's way too early for talk of peeing in potted plants.

"You slept on my patio?" Bailey manages.

"His orders." Van points to me.

"You're good to go. Thanks." I gather up the blanket and toss it at him. Maybe with a little more force than necessary. It lands on his head, and for a moment, he's cocooned in fabric. "I'll get your coat back to you at practice."

No way am I taking it off now. The morning air is well beyond crisp. Not muumuu weather at all. My breath gusts out of me in tiny wisps of cloud. We've got a later morning practice today—no ice time, just the weight room and then a strategy session with the coaches. I'm going to need to add in some serious stretching time beforehand to work on the cricks I'm feeling. The effects of sleeping sitting up on concrete.

"See ya," Van calls, already jogging toward the parking lot.

When he's gone, I turn to Bailey, fully expecting her

annoyance to have blossomed into anger. I had no right to stay here, after all. It's a few steps beyond intrusive. Instead, her brown eyes are almost gold in the morning light as she offers me a soft smile.

"You stayed," Bailey says, wrapping her arms around herself. She's drowning in a puffy coat that looks warm but too big, blue scrubs underneath.

"I needed to know you were safe." I stuff my hands into the pockets of Van's coat, my fingertips immediately brushing against something sticky. Feels like an unwrapped peppermint. Gross. "Are you mad?"

"Not mad," she says. "Just not used to … *this*."

I hear a lot of unspoken things in that one word. A lot of ways Bailey hasn't been cared for in the past. A lot of ways people have let her down, or maybe not shown up at all. Plus, without her parents or other close family besides her gran, she's so *alone*.

Wanting to show her the care she deserves feels like a challenge. And I've already got ideas.

Holding her gaze, I offer up what I hope is my most endearing smile. "Better get used to it, future Mrs. Hopkins."

———

"I'm getting too old for this, Elvis."

I startle at the sight of my mother sitting on a chair just inside the front door. She has one eyebrow arched dramatically and a mug of coffee in hand. It's the kind of look you'd give a teenage boy sneaking in after a wild night out.

Not an adult man coming home with a crick in his neck after protectively sleeping outside someone's door.

On the drive home, I thought exclusively about two things: drinking coffee and telling Mom about Bailey and me getting married. Which probably needs to involve a little priming the pump first, like telling Mom Bailey and I are dating or *have* been dating. That it's pretty new but serious. Imminent engagement serious.

But any rehearsed thoughts have vanished from my head. A mom lying in wait will do that to a person.

"I don't have a curfew, Mom. I'm an adult. Remember?"

"Remains to be seen." She grins, and the one arched eyebrow turns into a pair of waggling ones. "Did you and Bailey have fun?"

Fun has at least three syllables. "Definitely less fun than whatever you're imagining."

Mom takes a sip of coffee as I toe off my shoes by the door. "You don't need to be embarrassed, Elijah. If you can't talk to your mother about sex, who can you talk to?"

I slap my hands over my eyes. "Anyone! Anyone else! But we don't need to talk about sex because, again, this is not *that*."

I drag my hands down my face with a groan, feeling the grit of stubble on my jaw. My mother doesn't believe in boundaries. Or, if she does, she treats any topic I don't want to talk about like a starter's pistol. I need to get ahead of this—and fast—or I'm going to mess up and tell her the actual truth.

"But ... if there's more coffee, I would love to talk to you about some things."

"I love *things*," Mom says. "Would these things involve Bailey?"

"They would."

She squeals and tries to clap her hands, forgetting about the coffee she's holding. I pluck the mug from her hands before she gives herself a second-degree burn. She pops out of the chair with more energy than should be possible this early.

Another good day. I can tell by her fluid movements and the easy way she stretches up to kiss my cheek. I hand back the coffee and lift the chair, urging her toward the kitchen with it like I'm some kind of lion tamer.

It feels a little bit like that.

"I'll make more coffee," Mom says. "And chocolate chip pancakes! Plus eggs so you can have your protein."

Most mornings, I make breakfast for us both, leaving hers in the fridge if she's still in bed. But on days where she has energy and the pain is more of a low hum than a loud roar, as she describes it, Mom likes to do as many normal things as possible.

"And bacon?" I ask.

If I'm about to tell the biggest lie of my entire life to the person in it who means the most, I'd at least like to do so with bacon. Also, the more cooking she's doing, the more likely her full focus and attention won't be on my face, where she might be able to read the lies flashing like numbers on a scoreboard.

"And bacon," she promises.

"Sold."

Half an hour later, I'm finishing the last of the chocolate chip pancakes, bacon long gone, feeling overstuffed and also overly pleased at the way I was able to convincingly pull this off. Somehow, I don't even have the shroud of guilt for lying I felt sure would be hanging over me. It hardly felt like a lie.

Mom bought every word of the story I spun about going to the animal shelter so often because of Bailey. About keeping it on the downlow because I wanted to be sure before I brought her home. I even said things were moving quickly, though I didn't quite have the bravery to define exactly *how* quickly. I probably need to talk with Bailey about details before I announce my plans to propose.

And I already have plans.

"I knew there was a reason besides dogs you were always going to the shelter," she says. "And why you didn't want me to go with you. Though it took entirely too long for you to bring Bailey home. I love her."

I grin. "Good. I'm not surprised the two of you hit it off."

Despite being mildly horrified by the lengths Mom went to last night to meet a woman she suspected I was on a date with, I loved seeing the way Mom embraced Bailey. And the way Bailey didn't run screaming from the house or hide in a corner when she had to deal with meeting not only my mom but also the whole book club.

"Of course we did. How could I not love anyone who loves you?"

I open my mouth to argue about her use of the word love, then realize I'm going to need her to believe I love Bailey. I'm going to have to get used to saying it, to thinking it. Even if it's not the exact truth.

I enjoy Bailey. Nuh-uh. I *love* Bailey.

I care about Bailey. Nope. I *love* her.

I like Bailey. No. I *love* Bailey.

I'm sure I'll get used to it after a while. As I take our plates to the sink and start to wash up—thanks to Mom, I'm a firm believer in the adage that whoever doesn't cook, cleans—I consider how long *a while* is.

Is there a certain length of time we'll need to stay married for legality's sake?

What if I get traded to another team?

What about when she starts vet school? It's not guaranteed she'll go somewhere nearby.

Will I still need to at some point go back to Canada and handle the P-1 visa stuff, or would the marriage cover it?

I'm not sure who to even ask these questions to. Certainly not Grant. Gracie, Felix's girlfriend, had a lawyer friend who visited recently. Maybe I could ask her. She's probably someone I could trust but is far enough removed from my life and the Appies that it would feel a little safer.

"Is Bailey coming to your game this week?" Mom asks. "So I won't have to sit alone?"

My game this week—*right*. More of my focus and attention definitely needs to shift to hockey or I'll never shake the Speed Bump nickname.

"I'll ask her," I say, an idea taking shape in my mind.

No matter how many times I tell her to stay home, Mom comes to every game. Usually alone, stuck jammed between two drunk strangers. At our last home game, I remember waving up at her, my smile slipping into a frown as I took in the way she was hunched over to avoid the man next to her in his Appies foam hat—shaped like the tiny mountain range on our logo—who was waving, of all things, a set of maracas with wild abandon.

Mom's smile was big, but the next day, she stayed in bed late, complained of a headache, which turned into a two-day-long migraine. Her book club friends, despite being very avid fans of hockey *players*—particularly the calendars from years past featuring my teammates shirtless—rarely want to go to a *game*. Too much noise. Too many jostling bodies. Just … too much.

I might have to pull some strings with someone in the office to get a group of seats, but I bet Parker would be willing to work her magic. Especially once I tell her *why* I need tickets.

The game would be the perfect—and very public—place

to propose to Bailey. Perfect *because* it's so public. I don't want there to be any question about the marriage, no chance for the word *fraud* to even be whispered on the wind. And maybe the best way to preempt any accusations is to make things as big as possible.

Go big or go home—to Canada, in this case.

I drop a quick kiss on Mom's head. "I need to get ready for practice, but I'll let you know about the game."

But I need to talk to Bailey first. And then Parker so I can coordinate the biggest, loudest, impossible-to-question-its-legality surprise proposal possible.

CHAPTER 10

Bailey

THOUGH I SPENT an entire evening with him the night before and woke up with him outside my apartment door, the sight of Eli walking into the shelter has my nerves buzzing like a neon sign. Maybe because the last time he showed up here, it was as Hot Puppy Guy.

Now he's Hot Agreed to Marry Him Guy. I'm suddenly grateful to Katrina for taking a break at this moment so I'm the one at the desk.

Eli gives me a lopsided grin, shakes his hair off his face in a way that *could* scream Justin Bieber circa 2011 but instead just looks boyishly adorable, and slides some papers toward me.

"I did my homework," he says. I don't miss the way his fingertips drag over mine as I take the stapled pages. "Do I get a gold star?"

"We don't have gold stars. Only dog treats. Want one for being such a good boy?"

Dog treats, Bailey? REALLY?!?

Those words sounded outrageously more flirtatious—and possibly stupid—than anything I have ever said.

I immediately wish someone would pull me out of the room with one of those giant hooks that seem to always be lying at the ready in cartoons to drag terrible singers off the stage. I would also accept a giant version of the cranes in those rigged machines in arcades. If one dropped into the room right now, I'd grab it and hold on for dear life to be pulled out of this situation.

Eli laughs, looking absolutely delighted with my answer. "I've been a *very* good boy."

I dip my head to hide my blush, pretending to scrutinize Eli's application. His handwriting is surprisingly neat. I would have expected a messy scrawl, not neatly masculine block lettering.

Can handwriting be sexy? Skimming the page, I decide that yes, yes, it can.

Already, I see several interesting pieces of information on the form (his middle name is *Hagrid?*), but I'm not going to read the whole thing in front of him right now. Definitely later. Maybe with a highlighter and a stack of multicolored notecards.

"Our application is only one page." I frown, running a thumbnail over the three staples in the top left corner before I start turning pages. "Why are there—"

Eli's big hand curls around mine. He links our fingers together, settling our hands on top of the papers so I can't look. It's a weird angle to hold hands, but I'm not complaining. I like the way my small hand looks wrapped in his, seeing his neatly trimmed nails next to mine with their chipped pink polish and chewed off ends. I like the warmth and steadiness of him. Maybe a little *too* much.

"Those pages are for later," he says. His smile hits me like a sunrise, starting off slightly warm and building until I'm slammed with the full force of it. He gives my fingers a playful squeeze. "And I'll take a rain check on the dog treat."

It takes me several seconds to make sense of his statement, which goes back to my earlier question. "Oh. Cool. Um."

If I thought conversation with Eli would be easy after spending an evening with this man, having him literally carry me in his arms to my front door while I hoped the way I was inhaling his scent wasn't totally obvious, I was dead wrong.

In truth, I *hadn't* thought about it. Maybe if I'd known he was coming in today, I would have done some kind of mental prep work, but I didn't. Now I'm frustrated with myself for making things weird. First, by my solid C+ attempt at flirting, and then by being unable to string together words with multiple syllables.

This whole marriage thing will have zero chance at believability if I can't speak to Eli with some degree of normalcy. Maybe it's like exercise, and I just need some time to warm up my figurative muscles.

Maybe not.

Eli releases my hand and taps the papers. "Is there some kind of approval process? A waiting period before I can start officially volunteering?"

"You can jump the line a bit since I can vouch for your character."

I mentally give myself a pat on the back for formulating a full sentence that landed somewhere between friendly and flirty. And didn't mention dog treats.

Eli leans his elbows on the counter, angling forward and batting his eyelashes at me. "You like my character, Leelee?"

That nickname again! I went to sleep remembering how it sounded in his deep voice, amazed by the fact that he thought about giving me a nickname at all.

And the flirting! I used to think Eli flirted because I was in his *safe* category. But it feels very different now. This doesn't feel like general friendly flirting. Starting sometime last night, his flirting switched gears. It feels real. Arrow-sharp, aimed right at me with a precise eye and steady hand.

His previous flirting was like child's play. Junior level. Now, I'm getting his A-game, and he's playing to win. I can't even begin to keep up. The number of things that have changed in the last twelve hours is dizzying.

Guess I better get used to all of this. Eli showing up out of the blue. Holding my hand. Nicknames. Flirting with me. Even if it's for show.

Which it is, right? A show?

The realization immediately pops the bubbles of happiness fizzing up inside me. Then he smiles at me again, sending a whole new wave of effervescence through me.

Oh, who cares why. Eli is here and smiling at me, and I'm going to just bask in it.

No, I decide. *Basking is not enough.*

I'm going to be like Roscoe, the toothless dog with the nasty attitude who, just today, saw a sunny patch of grass and went for it. He dove and rolled and shimmied on his back, tongue hanging out with the pure enjoyment of the moment.

Only when Roscoe finally got back on his feet and shook off did I realize he'd been rolling on a dead bird. (What is it about dogs wanting to roll on dead things?)

This comparison is officially crowned the very worst of all

the analogies I have *ever* thought up. It might even be the worst in the world, the most horrifically terrible analogy ever imagined.

Still—despite the dead bird and the fact that in this comparison, I'm the toothless dog rolling on it—I want to relish every moment with Eli with that level of enjoyment.

Dog on a dead bird enjoyment.

"Bailey?"

Eli's voice startles me, and I realize my derailed thought train has left me standing here for an uncomfortable stretch of time. My cheeks burn, but he only looks amused.

I clear my throat. "Officially, you have to go through training. It's minimal. But I might not have enough time today."

"So," Eli starts, a smile lifting one side of his mouth before moving to the other, "I'll have to come back and see you again, then."

"You will."

If possible, Eli's smile grows wider as he leans even further over the reception counter. If possible, my brain just exploded, leaving only a cloud of pink dust and tiny pieces of heart-shaped glitter.

"Do I get to be trained by you?"

"I usually handle that part, yes."

"Then I *definitely* need training," he says. "Lots of it. And Leelee?"

"Yes?"

If Eli leaned any farther over the reception counter, he'd fall in a heap at my feet. "I am a *very* slow learner."

Volunteer training is the last topic I thought could make me twitterpated, but my heart is absolutely doing some twittering and pating. It feels about ready to leap out of my chest and straight into Eli's arms.

"Somehow, I doubt that," I tell him.

"I'll happily prove myself to you."

The way he says it, voice gravelly and firm, it sounds like a promise for something greater, something I really, really want.

Even though at face value, he's promising to show me how slow he is at learning.

I shake my head, biting back a smile. "You're kind of ridiculous. You know that?"

His smile doesn't dim in the slightest. I think it actually jumps up in kilowatt usage. "Thank you."

Beth appears from the back, whistling a vaguely familiar song. She's tone deaf but loves music, so she is always whistling or singing something no one can recognize. Whenever Cyn and I work together, we try to guess the songs. We're never right.

Beth's eyes widen when she sees Eli. "Hockey player!" she says, beaming with delight and hustling around the counter to squeeze him so tightly, a little *oomph* wheezes out of him.

I'm jealous I didn't think to hug him. And of how tightly she's holding him and, for the love of *Christmas*, how long this hug is going on. Is she going for some kind of record?

I also don't know that I like Beth calling him *hockey player*. It's *my* nickname for him. Which I guess I must have used a lot last night. Now that I'm thinking about it … yeah. I did.

Hey, hockey player—watch your elbows.

Nice gutter ball, hockey player.

Can I steal a French fry, hockey player?

I blush again thinking back over my boldness last night. Who even was the woman who said those things?

Is that what one beer, a birthday, and a late hour does to my confidence—sends it skyward like some kind of rocket? Maybe there's another version of me. Nighttime Bailey, who wears ugly nightgowns while bowling and flirts shamelessly with a famous hockey player.

Anyway, back to the point at hand—I suppose if I wanted to have a nickname that's just for my personal use, I should have chosen more creatively. Not the man's actual profession.

But … I've already claimed it. I kind of love calling him hockey player. It's so obvious and literal that it feels edgy. And in a weird way, like I'm jokingly taking him down a peg somehow. He's not Eli Hopkins with the bazillions of followers on social media, all of whom seem to assume this weird familiarity with him, like cozying up in his comments gives them some corner of the Eli market.

To me, he's just *hockey player*. And though it's the weirdest arrangement ever, one I'm still very unclear of in terms of details, I can safely say I've claimed more than a corner of him.

When we get *married*—I try to swallow and find my mouth totally dry at this thought—I guess I'll really claim all of him.

Technically and legally speaking, of course. Not in the other … *marriage parts*—to quote Eli's phrasing—ways.

Right? I mean, I'm assuming. But then I look at Eli, still trapped in a Beth hug, and realize we need to sit down and clarify some things.

Although I might opt to send a surrogate. I'm already filled with pre-shame at the *idea* of talking to Eli about the specifics of what our married life—*another attempt to swallow*—will entail.

Eli catches my eye over Beth's white curls, clearly signaling he needs help. I walk around the counter, ready to yank Beth back by the neckline of her scrubs. But she finally lets go and pats his cheek, going from extended bear hug to grandmotherly affection in the span of a few seconds.

"Good to see you again. Hope you had fun last night with Bailey. She seemed a little grumpy this morning."

I did? Honestly, waking up to find Eli sleeping outside my apartment might have been the best event that's ever happened to me before eight in the morning. I'm surprised I wasn't glowing when I came into work.

"Hey," I protest weakly.

"Kidding," Beth says, then mouths to Eli, *So grumpy*.

"I can see your lips moving," I tell her. "And I wasn't grumpy. Just tired. I was up late."

This is the wrong thing to say. That is, if I don't want Beth to get the wrong idea. Too late! She's already got the wrong idea. I can tell.

"Mm-hm," she says. "I'll just bet you were."

"Oh!" Eli says suddenly, and I could give him a medal. Best Timing or maybe Best Distraction or Best Non Sequitur. "I have something for you in the car. Be right back!"

He takes off like a shot, the bell above the door almost ripping right off with the force of it. Beth looks me up and down like I'm the tea leaves at the bottom of a cup. Only she's not trying to read my future, but my very recent past.

"Up late, huh? Do we need to have *the* talk?"

Beth has to know I know about sex, so I'm not sure what talk she means. I only know I probably want to preempt it at all costs. And now I'm blushing at just the idea of talking about sex with Eli right outside.

"Eli filled out an official volunteer application!"

I practically scream the words and then snatch the stapled pages off the desk, waving them in her face.

"Why is it so long?" Before I can stop her, Beth takes it from me, flipping through to the pages Eli told me to save for later. "Oh," she says with a chuckle, then presses a hand to her heart. "*Oh*."

I don't know what that means, and I don't get a chance to ask because Eli bursts back in. This time, the little bell does fly off, coming to land by the fake potted fiddle-leaf fig.

"Oops," he says.

But I'm distracted by what I can only call a candy monstrosity in his hands. "Is that for me?" I ask.

"What, this?" He holds it out, then pulls it back before I can touch it. "It *might* be for you," he says.

I'm still staring, head tilted. Looks like a drinking glass with a whole bunch of candy exploding out of it. "A candy bouquet?"

"Yep." He's so unabashedly proud and it makes a ribbon of pure joy roll out like a red carpet inside my chest. "Here."

I take it from his hands, not missing the way our fingers brush but distracted now by his present. I hold it as carefully as a newborn kitten.

He made it, I realize, seeing the wispy strings of glue hanging off the candy bars like shiny cobwebs. One of them catches on my wrist. *Eli* made *this*.

For me.

I will not be a grown woman crying in the lobby of an animal shelter over candy. I will *not*.

"Don't look too closely. It was my first time wielding a glue gun."

"You used a glue gun? For me?"

"First and *last* time." He chuckles, then leans forward to tug away a strand of glue, twisting it around his finger. "I stopped by a florist and a gift shop on the way here, but neither had what I wanted. So, I went to Walmart for a vase. They all looked like they were vases from Walmart, so I bought a box of pint glasses instead—the rest are in a box in my car if you want them—and a dozen different kinds of candy bars. I don't know what you like yet."

The *yet* is my favorite part of the whole string of sentences that just flew out of his mouth. But it's a toss-up because I like them all.

Eli is babbling, the way I sometimes do. Does he realize? It's really adorable. Beth must think so too because she still has her hand pressed to her sternum, the other clutching his application.

He rocks back on his heels and starts listing things off on his fingers. "Then I got dowel rods and a glue gun from the craft section. An adapter for my car when I realized I was going to have to put this together in the parking lot. My SUV looks like a crime scene. I'm not sure who the victim was—other than my interior—but the weapon was definitely a glue gun."

I brush my fingers over the candy bars. The basics: 3 Musketeers, Twix, KitKat, Butterfinger, Hershey (regular and special dark), Snickers, and Crunch. And then some out-of-the-box choices: Symphony, Whatchamacallit, and a Bueno.

"My favorite," I say, tracing my fingers over the last one with a smile. "I love hazelnut."

"Got it."

The way he says it makes me think that from now on, Eli is going to buy me every single hazelnut thing he sees. I'll probably have a hazelnut tree sitting in a pot tomorrow outside my door where I found Eli this morning. Do hazelnuts even grow on trees?

I hug the glass to my chest, still hoping I don't embarrass myself and ruin the moment by becoming a weepy mess. "Thank you," I whisper.

"Hey." Eli frowns, his eyes bouncing across my face. "It's just some candy. It's nothing."

"It's not nothing," I say fiercely. "I *love* it."

Eli reaches out and gently loosens my fingers from around the pint glass. "Don't break the glass, Leelee. I don't want to have to take you in for stitches."

I don't love the idea of breaking the most favorite thing I've ever been given. But the idea of Eli taking me to the hospital does something to me. Since my parents died, I've had trouble with forms. Specifically, the emergency contact part. Shannon is my best friend, and so she's the one I pick, but she also has a big family, and she's probably the name on twenty other forms. And has twenty people to put on hers.

I don't have a *person*, as Meredith Gray and Christina Yang called it.

And why do forms have so many blanks for emergency contacts? Do other people really have that many people for their list? I just want *one*.

"I have something else for you," he says, and I have a ridiculous desire to tell him he needs to stop. It's too much. But maybe I'm feeling greedy today because I say nothing. "It's digital."

Suddenly, Eli looks nervous, shifting his weight and giving me a sheepish smile. "Are you free the night after tomorrow?"

I don't want to confess I'm almost always free. "I think so."

"Good. I have tickets for my next game. Enough for your friends to come," he adds quickly, like he expects me to say no.

Beth makes a little squeak, and both of our heads whip her way. Clearly, I'm not the only one who forgot she was there.

"Ignore me," she says, and I swear, she's crying, fat tears

falling on his application. "Go on! Pretend I'm not here again."

"*Good* tickets," he says. "And I have a jersey for you. Can't have you showing up in scrubs."

"Hey! What's wrong with my scrubs?"

Eli gives me an assessing look that I swear is like a laser heating through me. Never mind that over my baggy blue scrubs I have on a too-big zippered hoodie.

"Not a thing. You look adorable in scrubs. But if you're coming to an Appies game, you need Appies gear."

"But whose name will be on the back of my jersey?" His face darkens, and it only makes me push more. "Maybe Van? He's a fun guy."

Eli's heated look turns molten, and he shakes his head slowly. "Mine," he says firmly, his low voice wrapping like a fist around my heart. "You can only wear *my* name."

CHAPTER 11

Bailey

IT'S hours later before I get a chance to look over Eli's paperwork.

Did I take it home with me? Yes. Yes, I did.

Because reading over the volunteer application of my crush turned maybe soon-to-be husband—a thought so unreal I'm going to keep qualifying it with maybes and *ishes* until it becomes verifiable with documentation—is something to savor. I choose to savor it with the Bueno from his bouquet, hot tea, and reruns of *Project Runway* streaming on the TV.

There are lots of interesting facts on the actual application. The one I'm still hung up on is Hagrid. I decide, after looking up the publication dates for the first Harry Potter book as well as Eli's birthday, that Hagrid *must* be a family name. Eli is just barely too old for Maggie to have read the books while picking baby names.

He also listed his previous employment as delivering pizzas and babysitting, complete with reference phone numbers—in Canada. Adorable.

Under reasons he wanted to apply, he wrote three. *I love dogs* being the first. Unsurprising, but still cute. The second is about the importance of volunteering, which rings true for him but also sounds a little like what a quick Google search might tell you to put on an application.

It's the third one that has me smiling so hard I got a cheek cramp. *To see my favorite dog handler*, he wrote. Then, in parentheses, he added *(Leelee aka Bailey aka hopefully the person reading this application)*. I read over this multiple times. While massaging my cheek.

The man is almost sweet enough to make my teeth ache. But there's a little squeeze of naughty that just keeps him from being *too* nice.

It takes all my restraint to read the first page thoroughly, slowly before I flip to the second. And then, I almost choke on my Earl Grey.

The page is covered with pink sticky notes, a message scrawled out one word per note in Eli's blocky handwriting: *I know you said yes, but I thought you might appreciate some character references.*

He doesn't say yes to *what*, specifically, but I don't think he means going to the hockey game. Probably smart not to mention the marriage stuff to prevent any kind of paper trail. Even a pink sticky-note paper trail.

I'm grinning as I flip to the next page, careful not to dislodge any of the sticky notes. I'd like to put this whole thing under glass like ancient documents in a museum, install special lighting and buy the kind of gloves museum curators use to aid in preservation. Maybe if I had money for anything extra, I would.

It looks as though Eli asked half the team to write something. Because *of course he did*. I'm starting to see just how much attention he pays to detail, how Eli likes to turn even little things into events.

Most of the notes are fairly generic, and unlike Eli's neat print, most are written in an almost illegible scrawl I can only decipher through squinting and some guesswork. Also, several of them aren't all that convincing, like one from someone named Wyatt, which makes me snicker: *I don't know Eli well, but he seems like a good guy. (And if he's not, I will not be held liable or in any way legally culpable for his actions.)*

Culpable, huh? I could submit this as proof to contradict anyone who still equates athletes with stupidity.

Stay away from hockey players. We stink. Literally, someone named Nathan writes.

Probably true. Though every time I've been around Eli, he's smelled delectable. Men's cologne covers over a host of smell sins, but I doubt it would fully blanket hockey stink. Nathan's note doesn't deter me in the slightest.

Bring it on, hockey stink. Working here has uniquely prepared me for any olfactory assault.

Alec writes, *Eli's a good guy, but if you're looking for someone great …* Then he added a phone number. Presumably his.

Did Eli even read these? I'm not sure he would have included them all if so.

Then again, it's Eli. He might have assumed his charm would outweigh anything negative his teammates said. (He would be right.) Or he knew I'd read these for what they are: his teammates lovingly giving him a hard time.

My throat gets a little tight when I read Van's message: *This guy would do anything for people he loves. Anything. Count yourself lucky if you fall into that category. And whatever you do, don't hurt my boy.*

Surprisingly tender, coming from the guy who hit on both Shannon and Jenny the other night, plus flirted with the snack bar attendant at the bowling alley, a random woman in the parking lot, and the group of older women in the lane next to us. Maybe some of that's just for show? Or maybe Van is a ladies' man who has some hidden depth.

Whatever the case, he's a little misguided if he thinks I would ever be in a position to hurt Eli. *Try the other way around, pal.* Wasn't my crush on Eli completely obvious to everyone around us the other night? I felt as transparent as rice paper.

If anyone's going to get hurt in all this, it will be me. Hands down.

And yet, even knowing this, I am undeterred. If I expected to regret saying yes to this ridiculous marriage thing, I don't. I've felt surprisingly calm and sure about the whole thing. Partly because of the way the ever-present tightness in my chest eases when I think about having financial help. But partly because being around Eli more won't be a hardship.

Not until it ends.

I light that thought on fire, then read through the rest of the notes. Though they don't share any actual details about Eli I didn't already know from spending time with him, I do get a sense of the impact he has on people in his life.

Every hand-scrawled note shows how much the guys *like* him. It's so clear that he's the kind of man who is a beacon to those around him. Drawing people in. Making them feel warm and accepted.

Not that I need to be told this. But it hits different seeing it in these notes, all written in various shades from playful affection to genuine admiration.

The issue at hand isn't whether I need a reason to trust Eli. It's whether I can trust myself not to fall canyon-deep in love with him.

Because somehow, I don't see Eli having the same struggle when it comes to me.

———

"Bailey!"

I'm not sure how I hear my name over the noise of the stadium. Maybe because it's Eli's voice. At this point, I'm like a sad little compass who can't stop being magnetically attuned to him. I might as well start calling him North.

I scan the ice, where the guys are warming up. At a glance, they all look the same in their gray uniforms and helmets and gloves. I don't get to look for long, because I'm trying to keep Maggie from being jostled in the teeming crowd of people.

"Watch the elbows, buddy," she says, throwing her shoulder into a big man who seemed totally unaware of her presence.

He steps back, pulling his cup of beer closer to his chest and tipping his chin. "Sorry, ma'am."

Guess Maggie doesn't need me looking out for her after all.

Shannon grabs my elbow and shakes me with a little too much violence. "There he is!"

As though I could miss the man now skating toward us with a huge grin on his face. My heart transforms into that of a teen girl at a boy band concert. It's a wonder I don't pass out as he reaches the plexiglass in front of us.

"Aw, this is adorable," Beth says with a sigh. "Young love."

I almost choke. "It's not—"

Shannon pokes me in the ribs, eyes wide. Right. As far as everyone needs to know, it absolutely *is* love.

Shannon and Jenny are the only ones I've told about this whole arrangement thing. I needed someone—okay, *two* someones—to know the real story. Jenny couldn't come tonight, which makes Shannon my anchor. Eli said a few guys from the team know. He also muttered something about what sounded like a vow of ... violence?

I wonder if they're as on board with it as Shannon. She started calling us Bonnie and Clyde—I guess because of the illegal aspect of it—though we're certainly not robbing any banks. Just the government?—and seems convinced we're going to fall madly in love and stay married forever and have adorable babies.

Which ... isn't going to happen. Lovely idea, though. One I'm keeping locked up tight for about twenty-three hours and fifty-three minutes a day, allowing myself just seven minutes —an approximation since I'm not actually pulling out my stopwatch to time it—where I'm allowed to daydream about this possibility.

Then, with a show of monster self-control, I put the thought away, and pummel myself with a litany of words like arrangement, agreement, contract, fake, and—the one I hate most of all—*temporary*.

I mean, I'm assuming we aren't doing this as some kind of lifelong not-real marriage thing. Another clutch of worry grips me tight at the reminder of all the things Eli and I still haven't discussed. Between his busy schedule and my own, we just haven't managed. It's only been a few days, but considering the timeline, that's maybe ten percent of the time we have left before getting married.

My knees do a quick wobble, and I grip the metal railing

until cold seeps through my fingers and I'm steady again. *Somewhat* steady. I have a sneaking suspicion I won't be all-the-way steady for a long time. Like the kitchen table in my apartment, only level when a piece of paper is folded just so under one leg.

My eyes don't leave Eli as we near the ice, though it feels like parts of me have left my body. Like, for example, my heart. I think it's hovering around him like some kind of winged bird, ready to light on Eli's broad shoulders. When he leans forward, chin resting on the gloved hand holding his stick upright, a little sigh leaves me too.

At our row, which is right by the ice, Maggie, Shannon, and Beth sit down, leaving me standing by the plexiglass. Standing in front of Eli. There must be thousands of people in The Summit, but right now, with my pulse pounding in my ears, it's just us.

"Hey, Leelee." Eli's muffled by the layer of clear plexiglass between us. That doesn't lessen the impact. The low rumble. The nickname. The smile that feels somehow private.

I feel suddenly desperate, like I could rip away the sheet of plexiglass with my bare hands, Hulk style. Instead, my words get stuck behind an invisible blockade, my tongue thick and mouth dry. I give him a little wave instead.

His grin widens as his gaze does a quick tour of my body. Then, another slower one. Specifically focused on the top half of me. "Parker found you, I take it?"

I nod, smoothing a hand down my jersey. "She did."

Parker, the Appies' social media manager, was waiting inside The Summit for me, her brown hair swinging in a cheerful ponytail, her smile wide. After giving me an enthusiastic and unexpected hug while whispering, "I hope we can be friends," she pressed a jersey into my hands. A mirror of the one Eli's wearing, it's light gray with turquoise accents and the Appies logo in black and turquoise on the front.

And, as he insisted, Eli's last name and number on the back.

Eli leans closer, practically plastering himself against the plexiglass. "Do me a favor," he says, his voice sounding low and husky, though I'm sure he's practically shouting to be heard. Maybe it's the wild look in his eyes that seems to color how his words hit me. "Turn around."

"What?"

His smile melts away, his eyes blue flames as he stares. "I want to see you wearing my name."

Oh.

I know I'm blushing as I hazard a glance at Eli over my shoulder. His mouth stretches into a grin that is one hundred percent pure, unadulterated, smug male pride. I turn back around to face him, swaying closer toward him.

"My name looks good on you," he says, and then he lifts his left glove to the glass.

I'm not sure how I know he's waiting for me to line my hand up with his, but somehow, I do. And when I press my palm against the plexiglass, I'm rewarded with an even bigger smile. This one softer.

Moments like this, I can almost forget it isn't real.

"Enjoy the game, Leelee," he says. "I'm playing for *you.*"

He skates away, leaving me shaky and a little breathless as I make my way to the seat between Maggie and Shannon. The moment I practically collapse into my seat, Maggie gives me a sly look.

"He's showing off for you," she says, pointing.

I watch Eli fly over the ice with a dexterity that seems incongruous for someone his size. He zips right by a few guys, effortlessly countering their efforts to steal the puck, and lines up a shot. I don't even see it hit the back of the net, but the goalie bends to scoop it out, shaking his head.

Eli turns right toward us, beaming. He blows a kiss my way, and I remind myself AGAIN that it's *not* what it looks like to everyone else. Not what it *feels* like.

There's a squeal and a scream from behind us, ripping me out of my Eli haze.

"Did you see that?" a shrill voice says. "He blew me a kiss!"

My head whips around to see a gorgeous woman behind us also wearing Eli's jersey. She has tiny shorts on underneath, and her legs go on forever. Her tan indicates she either just got back from the Bahamas or she spends a fair amount of time at a tanning booth.

An ugly part of me hopes it gives her premature wrinkles.

I'm feverish with jealousy, I realize, and glaring at this woman like I have any right to. I mean, I guess I technically do, but the emotion feels out of place somehow. Unearned. Alien.

I'm about to put my focus back to the ice where it belongs, when Maggie turns all the way around.

"That kiss wasn't for you," she says.

Tiny Shorts sneers. "He was looking right at me. And who are you, anyway?"

"Maggie," I whisper, but she ignores me. "You don't need to—"

"His mother," she says, then hooks her arm through mine. "And this woman is the only one my son's giving any kind of kisses to."

Tiny Shorts turns her gaze to me, the cocky look fading into confusion. "I thought he was single."

"*Was*," Maggie says, then curls an arm around my shoulders. "Past tense. And you're looking at his present and his future."

I almost fall out of my chair when Tiny Shorts says, "Sorry. I don't go for taken men."

A sliver of my faith in humanity is restored as I give the woman a small smile and turn back around. Maggie winks at me.

Beth snorts and leans across Shannon and me to high-five Maggie. "Go, Mama Eli!"

Guilt needles its way through me. Eli's mom *does* like me. And I adore her. But I'm also lying to her. My present and future are going to be filled with lies to her.

Every day, lying.

Clearly, something of the sick feeling in my belly shows on my face because Shannon leans close. "Hey. Stop that. Remember—this is for her too."

"Don't worry, dear," Maggie says, patting my arm. "I'll fight off any puck bunnies."

I cough to cover my laugh.

"Do people really call them that?" Shannon asks. "Like, it's a real thing?"

My stomach turns, thinking of the women draped over him at the bar the night of my birthday. As though sensing my discomfort, Maggie gives my hand a squeeze.

"They exist for every sport or for any public figure. Different names, of course." She chuckles. "Personally, I think *puck bunnies* is a particularly apt name. But"—she angles herself to make sure she catches my eye—"my Eli has always known better than to mess around with that type. He's a romantic."

Shannon pokes me again. "They are adorable together, right? Now, Mrs. H—explain hockey to us poor sports-illiterate people."

A hand grabs the back of my jersey and yanks me back into my seat. "Calm down, Cujo," Shannon says with a laugh.

I glare and shrug her off. "But did you see that? The guy hit him with his stick! That's not okay!"

Maggie laughs. "You'll get used to it. Though I applaud your enthusiasm, and I agree. It was a bad call."

The buzzer sounds to end the second period, and I relax only slightly as the guys skate off the ice. The Appies are up three to nothing, but it doesn't make me feel any less anxious. It was one thing when Eli was warming up with the team, and something totally different when the actual game started.

It's brutal. I always thought people exaggerated when they talked about hockey fights and guys losing their teeth. So far, there have been no actual fights, but I am surprised *anyone* has their teeth with how rough it is.

Yet it's also graceful, with intricate, precise movements. So fast I have trouble keeping my eye on the puck. It's a surprising dichotomy to see such big men in heavy gear be so quick, so graceful.

Beautifully brutal.

"Come on, you." Shannon tugs on my arm, and I see our whole row is standing. "Bathroom time."

"I don't need to go," I say. "I'll stay and keep our seats warm."

I *did* need to go earlier. But I swear, the stress of watching Eli play made whatever was in my bladder evaporate or something. Is that a thing? Probably not.

Shannon is undeterred. "Come on before it gets too crowded."

Maggie gives me a nudge from the other side, and I finally

cave as our little troop of people vacate our row. Shannon groans as we see the line for the bathroom spilling out of the room and almost to the concession stand.

"I could go for a beer and a hot dog," I say, suddenly ravenous.

But this train of thought is derailed by Parker, appearing as though out of nowhere.

"Come on," she says, taking my hand and waving our little group forward. "Secret bathroom. Perk of working here."

I give the hot dogs a longing glance but follow Parker as she shuttles us all through a metal door, giving the beefy security guard a pat on the shoulder as we walk through and into a mostly empty hallway.

In here, the sound of the bass and the crowd reverberates through the cinder block walls, giving the weird sensation of hearing through layers of water.

"This way," she calls, practically sprinting down the hallway.

"What's the rush?" I ask, wondering how far away this stupid private bathroom is. I could be eating a hot dog by now.

Parker tightens her grip on my hand. If we're going to be friends, we'll have to talk later about how I'm more into strolling than speed walking.

"Almost there," she says. "Just through this hallway."

The music is suddenly much louder as we make a turn. I balk as I realize Parker isn't leading me toward another random hallway in the bowels of the Summit.

No—this looks a whole lot like an entrance onto the ice.

"This isn't the bathroom."

Parker manhandles me into a metal folding chair. "Sorry-not-sorry about this," she says. "Don't hate me, okay?"

Glancing back, I see Maggie, Beth, and Shannon all stopped, watching this unfold with knowing grins on their faces. Traitors. Clearly, this is some kind of conspiracy. I'm beginning to suspect I know exactly what kind.

"I don't—"

And now I'm being lifted up by two guys. Not just any guys. Two hockey players who are somehow carrying me, chair and all.

"Hold on and don't wiggle." I realize one of the guys carrying me is Van. "Eli would murder us if we dropped you."

"Um, yes, please don't drop me. Thanks."

I'm white knuckling the seat of the metal chair, which suddenly feels very flimsy. What if it decides to fold itself back up right now?

"We've got you."

The other guy's voice is gruff. I can't make out much besides dark stubble and dark hair, but his expression is intense. I swallow back an apology. I mean, this wasn't my idea, after all. I'd one hundred percent rather be just about anywhere other than being carried out of this tunnel and onto the ice.

"Um, Van? Could you maybe put me down or take me back or, you know, just not do whatever this is?" I beg.

"No can do," Van says with a grin. "I've got orders."

The other guy only grunts. I shrink down in the chair as much as I can while it's being held in the air. The very last place I ever want to be is the center of attention. And at the Summit, the ice is pretty much the center of attention.

Is this … a proposal? I'm smart enough to recognize the signs, even if I stupidly thought we weren't to this point yet. I'm still adding to my mental list of things to discuss. Surely, Eli wouldn't spring a proposal on me.

Then I think of him showing up with a homemade candy bouquet. The way he made my birthday an event. The pages of references from his teammate.

Oh, yeah. Eli absolutely would surprise me with a huge proposal.

It makes sense, being public and all. I'm sure this will go viral, which will only help solidify our quickie marriage story. But I'd rather be stuck in a room full of rabid feral cats than be proposed to like this. And that's saying something.

The crowd amps up, and the screams and shouts all meld into a deafening roar as the guys deposit my chair right in front of one of the goals. Another player skates up and hands me a helmet.

"You're going to want this." I'm momentarily distracted by his perfect white teeth, again wondering if hockey players losing teeth thing was a rumor.

"I am?"

That sounds foreboding. Maybe this isn't a proposal after all? Because where I'm from, the ring isn't usually accompanied by a helmet.

Maybe this is just another part of the entertainment, like the way they had fans don T-rex suits and fight over an exercise ball after the first period.

"Here—let me help. I'm Alec. Team Captain."

"You gave me your number," I say, and he laughs.

"All in good fun." He removes his gloves to help fasten the strap underneath my chin, then taps me twice on the top of my helmet. "You look worried. Don't be worried."

"You just told me I need a helmet," I argue. "I'm pretty sure I have reason to be worried."

He gives no answer other than a last smile as he skates off, abandoning me in my metal chair. It was cold in the stands, but it's freezing down here, and I wrap my arms around myself now that I don't need to cling to the chair for dear life.

I wonder if I could make it back to the exit before whatever's about to happen happens. But I don't wholly trust my ability to make it on the ice without falling. When it comes down to being embarrassed while sitting in a chair or being embarrassed falling down in front of the crowd, I'm gonna stick with the chair.

Suddenly, the lights drop, leaving me in a blinding spotlight. A second spotlight appears at the tunnel. Eli makes his way out as the music shifts to "Marry You" by Bruno Mars.

Definitely a proposal.

The crowd cheers as Eli skates toward me, dribbling a puck and wearing a big grin. He's not wearing a helmet, and blond hair whips around his face.

I hope I don't look like I'm on the verge of a panic attack, even if that's exactly how I feel. Not that I've had a panic attack. According to the articles I've read and the quizzes I've taken online, I don't have social anxiety. I'm just shy.

But the tightness in my chest and the black dots I'm seeing in front of my eyes scream otherwise.

I try to focus on Eli and not on the blur of faces. The cheering. The question of what the heck did I agree to?

Eli picks up speed, circling behind me, behind the goal. The ten-ton pressure on my chest eases when he appears again and I see the smile that's becoming so familiar, his bright eyes that almost always look like he's plotting some kind of mischief.

Anchoring myself on these things helps a little, but I still find myself clutching the bottom of the metal chair, fingertips nearly numb. I clench my jaw to stop my teeth chattering. I don't feel cold anymore.

Honestly, I don't feel much at all. Just a growing tension climbing my spine like a ladder, leaving tightness as it goes.

Dread rather than anticipation fills me as Eli does another lap. It's probably only been a minute since he's been on the ice, but I've lived a decade right here. The helmet is a pleasant barrier against the sound—at first.

Then, I start to feel it too tight around my temples. Too heavy, making my neck ache.

Breathe, I remind myself. In and out. *Slowly. Just ... breathe.*

I've had moments of acute stress in certain situations, especially when I felt like the center of attention. There's a real reason I managed to weasel my way out of every possible school assignment which required speaking in front of the class. I could never explain to my parents, who spent their working days behind a lectern in front of packed seminar rooms or on a stage. Never did I feel like such a confusing disappointment as when I failed the test that lost me valedictorian. I think they suspected the truth—I did it on purpose to get out of making a speech.

Breathe.

I force my eyes to follow Eli, only Eli, while talking myself through what's happening.

It's simple biology. My amygdala sent a panicked S.O.S. to my hypothalamus, telling it we're in grave danger. Because clearly my amygdala is a little dramatic.

My hypothalamus responded instantly with "sir, yes sir" and passed orders down to my adrenal glands.

And they deployed hormone soldiers like cortisol, adrenaline, and a handful of others, who didn't march but RAN into battle. A battle I'm now losing because of those very soldiers.

Thinking my way through the process might sound ridiculous, but it helps me more than any breathing technique. It's the equivalent of a parent assuring you that it was just a dream after a very realistic nightmare, scratching your back and speaking in soothing tones to ground you in reality.

In reality, I'm not in danger.

No need for fight or flight.

It's simply a VERY public proposal. A moment I'd prefer to be private, not acted out in front of thousands of strangers.

Okay—maybe I should have stuck to thinking about the brain science stuff.

Eli finally skates through the center of the rink toward me, stopping about fifteen feet away. Bruno Mars is still singing in what must be the longest song in the whole world. Between the noise of the crowd and the blood pounding in my ears, I can barely hear the music.

I definitely don't hear whatever Eli says before he lines up the puck and sends it my way.

I can't help it. I flinch.

Which is totally silly because he barely nudges the puck sliding my way. It comes to stop right at my feet, joined a moment later by Eli, who slides onto both knees before me.

Only then do I notice the ring box taped to the puck.

Breathe, Bailey. Breathe.

Eli rips of his gloves, prying my fingers off the side of the chair and curling his hands around mine.

"Bailey? What's wrong?"

I open my mouth, but it takes several tries before I can croak out an intelligible response. "I think I'm having an anxiety attack. Or maybe not officially? Maybe I'm just freaking out."

His arms are suddenly around me, tugging me against his solid chest. He feels different with the pads on—smells a little different too, which I'm going to ignore—but his warmth is familiar. His strong arms, banded firmly around me, ease the tightness in my chest. Even if only a little.

The crowd must assume I said yes to the fastest proposal ever because the cheering reaches deafening levels. My heartbeat kicks up again.

"I'm sorry," I whisper. "I'm ruining your whole thing."

"No, *I'm* sorry," Eli says fiercely, lips grazing my ears.

His arms tighten protectively around me. The more pressure, the safer I feel and the more my heart rate slows.

"Is the helmet helping?" he asks. "Or is it making things worse?"

"Worse," I say. And though things get louder and feel closer the moment he removes it, there's also another notching down of tension.

"I'm so sorry," he says again, and one of his hands slides up my back, gently rubbing.

"There's no way you could have known. I've never actually had an anxiety attack. If that's even what this is."

I'd place a hefty bet that it is. But the last thing I want is Eli feeling worse about it.

"I absolutely should have known. You've mentioned being shy. I just didn't think about it because you seem so different with me."

"You make me feel safe," I confess.

And it's true. So true that my breathing is now even. I can't hear the rushing of blood in my ears anymore either.

"I *did* make you feel safe." His voice has a hard edge. "Then I went and did something stupid."

"No, Eli—"

"Let's get you out of here."

As he gets to his feet, Eli keeps me cradled to his chest like I weigh no more than a piece of paper. And that's when the music changes.

"Oh no," I whisper.

Because Bruno Mars's never-ending song has given way to "Kiss Me."

And the crowd goes wild.

I mean, of COURSE after a romantic engagement, they'd expect people to kiss. People who are getting engaged for *real*. Not two people doing this for reasons not having to do with romance. And have never, in fact, kissed.

Oh, and also, Eli never got that chance to ask and I never got the chance to say yes.

Eli pulls back slightly, and his startled eyes meet mine just as people in the stands start stomping and shouting, "KISS! KISS! KISS!"

My heart starts thumping again, and a wave of dizziness returns. I wait for the inevitable panic to set in. But it doesn't.

Instead, I think my adrenal glands are releasing a whole different set of hormones. Ones not related to fight or flight but anticipation. And desire.

I should NOT be thinking about kissing Eli right now.

Not with the anxiety I just moved through, which still lingers around my edges. Or the fact that this isn't real and a kiss isn't required.

Also, I am not and have never been a fan of PDA.

So, why is my heart careening wildly with anticipation like some spun top and why are my eyes focused on his lips like they hold the key to unlock the universe's secrets?

Eli shifts his hold so he's pretty much curled around me, hiding my face from view. Though there are people on all sides of us, the way he's positioning me and the way his head is tilted probably makes it *look* like we're kissing.

I can't help the surge of disappointment.

"I'm not going to force you to kiss me because of a song,"

he murmurs, his lips so very close to where I actually want them. "Not because fans are yelling for it. Not when you look like you're feeling panicked and unsafe, Bailey."

His mouth brushes my jaw as he speaks, likely lending even more weight to the appearance of us doing as the people demand. It also makes tendrils of desire unfurl inside me like wisps of smoke from a fire.

I shiver. Eli tightens his hold on me, likely thinking I'm cold or scared—not overloaded with a bright bolt of electric desire. Which is even more potent mixed with what I suspect is a bit of post-stress euphoria.

He again starts to skate toward the tunnel.

"Wait," I say.

The speakers are still playing "Kiss Me," and though I think Eli did his best to give an appearance or suggestion of kissing, the crowd is still chanting, unappeased. If they didn't fully SEE it, it didn't happen.

And in this moment, held like precious cargo in Eli's arms, I make a decision. Not because the people are demanding it, though I am well-aware of my people-pleasing tendencies.

No—I want to kiss Eli. Here. Now. Like this, with fear crouching at the door of my mind, nervousness a steady whisper in my blood.

Reaching up to curl my hand around the back of Eli's neck, I pull him toward me and press my mouth to his.

CHAPTER 12

Eli

SHE'S ... kissing me.

Bailey is kissing me.

Kissing. Me.

And I'm not kissing her back because this shocked me so badly, I am now a statue. A monument whose plaque reads To the Man Who Was Once Kissed Straight into Paralysis.

Thankfully, my frozen state doesn't last. Because the very last thing I want, after all I just put Bailey through, is for her to think I'm rejecting her by not kissing her back.

She just handed me a free pass to the theme park of kissing, and I'm running through the gates.

"Bailey," I murmur against her mouth as I angle her body higher, closer, tighter against me. "You never stop surprising me."

"Good. I ... surprised me too."

She lets out a tiny laugh, and I capture the sound as I kiss her again in earnest. Bailey's lips are soft, her kisses light and playful, her movements sure. One of her hands tangles in the too-long hair at my neck and her other grasps a fistful of my jersey, holding me captive. Though I am one hundred percent here by choice.

I tilt my head, kissing her softly but deeply, not breaking away for even a second.

Who needs to breathe? Oxygen is definitely secondary to this kiss.

And this—*this* feels like exactly what my mouth is made for.

Bailey. Only Bailey. Forever Bailey.

The realization is sudden and forces a sharp intake of breath. It's a laser-guided missile finding its target in the center of my chest. The settling after the last aftershocks of an earthquake, seeing a whole new landscape. If I weren't already breathless, this knowledge would have stolen all my oxygen.

I *more than* like Bailey as a person. *More than* think she's pretty. *More than* like kissing her.

She snuck up on me like the slow creep of a vine. But now, as her fingers tangle deeper in my hair and she makes a small, happy sound I want to hear again and again, there's nothing hidden or slow. Emotion swells in my chest, tightening my throat and zipping up my spine.

But ...

The thing between us isn't *supposed* to be real. Or feel this good.

I file these thoughts away for Later Eli, though that's partly how I got in this mess to begin with. He'll figure it out. Now Eli wants to get lost in the moment, to take what Bailey gives me for as long as she'll offer it up.

She releases my jersey and drags her hand up my chest until her fingertips touch my jaw. Tentatively at first, then dragging over my stubble. I feel her smile, taste it, and want to drink in even more.

A whistle blows somewhere, and I blink my eyes open to see the entire team just a few feet away, crowded in the tunnel and looking like they just cannot wait to give me hell about this later. And congratulations too. But hell first.

With a sigh, I pull back, only enough to rest my forehead against hers. This close, it's hard to read the emotion in her eyes, but she blinks slowly, smiling sleepily. If nothing else, kissing me eased her anxiety about the very public surprise proposal I really didn't think through.

She lifts her fingers to her lips, tracing them like she's reading the memory of our kiss. The guys take to the ice, and I skate Bailey to the edge of the tunnel, depositing her on the floor. But I keep her close, my hands on her lower back, tugging her tight.

"I've got to go back to work, Leelee."

"You're good at your job," she whispers.

"Yeah?"

"Don't act like you don't know it, hockey player."

"Is this how it's gonna be—you giving me trouble?" I ask, sliding one hand up her back, watching her shiver as my fingertips graze her neck.

"Maybe," she says, then her expression shifts, a tiny furrow appearing between her brows. "We should probably talk about that. You know, expectations?"

"We will," I promise. "We will."

Bailey's lips curve up into the smallest smile. But it's a genuine one.

A smile I can't help but kiss lightly. Just once more.

Fine—*twice* more. I reluctantly let her go. I *really* need to get back to the game. Hockey waits for no man. Not even a newly engaged one.

———

The third period ends with me scoring twice more. I'm flying. No one can touch me. Or stop me. Despite the other team singling me out—probably just because of the proposal—I barely register them. And my guys don't like that and give it back just as hard. Maybe harder. I'm somewhere above it all, and though I don't allow myself to look up at Bailey, knowing she's there is enough.

My blood is still singing from her kiss, an electric current humming beneath my skin.

Just after the buzzer, I finally glance over to see Bailey practically pressed up against the glass, my mom beside her. Both of them screaming, jumping up and down, losing their minds.

One more thing about all this that feels right—Bailey with my mom.

The biggest wrong thing, maybe the *only* one, though it's a biggie, is the fact that really liking Bailey means I've severely messed up the timeline of things.

It calls to mind a memory of Mom, sitting patiently with me at the table in the one apartment we had where the heat barely worked in any room but the breakfast nook, where it blasted like a commercial oven. For hours she tried to help me remember the order of operations, something that just would not stick in my mind. It simply didn't make sense why brackets, which in sentences seem to include something extraneous, would get priority in math.

With Bailey, it's like I've skipped the starting point and gone straight to addition, which was last. No, wait—was it subtraction? Either way, I've jacked up the order of operations. And I'm not sure how to undo it.

"Forget something, lover boy?"

As we enter the locker room, Van presses an object to my chest with the force of a punch, his grin wide.

It's the ring box.

The one I never removed from the puck. Never gave to Bailey.

Because I actually never got around to asking her to marry me.

Worst. Proposal. *Ever*.

Van must take in the shift in my face, which probably looks something like a seven-year-old sugar-crashing hard twenty-minutes after chasing a candy bar with a soda. He gives my shoulder a squeeze meant to be comforting but is actually painful and says, "No worries, man."

"If she says yes without looking at the ring, it's for real," Dumbo adds.

Van and I exchange a look. That's what it might *normally* mean. But in our case … it does not.

Only the guys at Felix's the other night have any idea what's really going on. I didn't fill them in on how we got from point A to point proposal less than a week later, but I'm assuming they connected the dots. I think the rest of the team shares Malik's belief that I was already seeing someone and just kept it quiet. Until it got very, very loud.

"A ring is sort of important in the typical engagement process," Alec says, grinning.

Like anything about this is *typical*. Still. I'm glad for his comment, which is so *very* Alec. It allows me to unclench the fists I didn't know I was making, one hand gripping the ring box.

"Must have been some kiss if it made you forget the ring."

Van smirks. I shove him. And we're all back to normal.

I tuck the ring into my bag and strip off my shirt, dropping onto a bench so I can fully gear down. I'm eager to get showered and get back to Bailey. I'm hoping she stayed with Mom and will be waiting in the family room. We didn't talk through all those details, and now I'm wishing we had so I'm not left disappointed if she goes home.

After the way I overwhelmed her with everything ... she just might go.

"So, dude—did she say yes?" Tucker asks.

I fumble with the laces on my skates before recovering, untying them so fast I practically give myself rope burns. "What?"

"Didn't you see the kiss?" Dumbo says. "Looked like a yes to me."

"He *played* like she said yes. You could have saved a few goals for the rest of us, man." Van tosses a sock my way.

"You should've tried harder."

Without thinking, I use two fingers to pick up the sock, which is damp and came directly from his foot—*disgusting!*—and toss it toward the locker room's laundry bin. It misses. But Van can take care of his stupid sweaty sock. I probably shouldn't have even touched it. Now I need to soak my hand in antibacterial gel.

Passing by on his way to the showers, Logan gives me a nod and says, "I thought it was great. Took some mental notes."

Parker will be thrilled about that.

I'm grateful for Wyatt's vow of violence suggestion because every guy who was at Felix's seems to be acting as my own personal defensemen. One of them runs interference, changing the subject when the other guys ask questions about Bailey or make cracks about how fast I'm moving. It's like I've got my own personal force field, made up of a bunch of sweaty guys in various states of undress.

A guy could get used to this.

I've never showered so thoroughly, so quickly in my life. I ignore the slaps on the back and congratulations—as well as the snide remarks about the old ball and chain that have me wanting to kick the patriarchy right out of a few people—and practically sprint down the hallway. Droplets of water trail down the ends of my hair to the neck, making me shiver as I push open the door.

Faces in the room turn expectantly toward me, but there's only one person I see.

Bailey. She's still here. For *me*.

And still wearing my jersey.

I briefly wondered while getting dressed if maybe the sense of rightness I had when she kissed me was exaggerated. A product of the moment, snowballed into feeling like something more than it was. Nope. Seeing her now, even across the room, there's a tug in my gut, and my feet respond, carrying me toward her with purpose.

Her smile is slow, a little tentative at first before it blooms into something that takes over her whole face, making her eyes crinkle and a not-quite dimple appear in one flushed cheek.

Huh. Never noticed that before. Wonder what else I haven't noticed about her? Probably plenty. But I'm not going to miss anything else now.

I cut through the crowd, seeing no one, hearing nothing, until I reach Bailey. With no hesitation, she walks right into my open arms. I pull her into a hug so tight, her feet lift off the ground, dangling against my shins.

She's warm and smells so good and fits right here: arms linked around my neck, face tucked against mine. A wave of emotion swells and crests before tumbling through me. Bailey is the kind of perfect I could get used to. A permanent fixture. The kind I'd fight to keep.

I want to kiss her again, but I don't know if that's allowed. I don't know if she would want me to, or if kissing me once was a green light for kissing any time. We never sat down and talked this through, and now I've catapulted us ten steps ahead. I have no idea where we stand with anything at all.

Her lips brush my ear as she says, "What took you so long, hockey player?"

"You miss me or something, Leelee?"

I expect her to say something smart back to me, keep up this teasing dance of words. Instead, she surprises me again when she's flat-out earnest.

"Yeah. I think I did."

CHAPTER 13

Eli

I FIND Parker in the hallway the next morning, humming, with her face locked on her tablet screen. Per the usual. Before she looks up, I curl my hands around her shoulders. She lets out a squeak, but I am undeterred.

I steer her inside her office, closing the door. Down the hall, I hear a couple of the guys laughing—laughing at me, I'm sure—the sound now muffled. I ignore it.

"I need your help, Boss."

Parker must miss the desperation clawing at the edges of my voice because she laughs and plops into the pink chair Logan gave her. "Again? Already? The proposal was perfect. And it's viral, so if you needed social proof for the whole"— her voice drops to a whisper—"visa thing, you got it. Everyone loves that she said yes without looking at the ring."

It's true. Both the video on the Appies's main account and

the one on mine blew up overnight. People couldn't get enough. My mom told me there was a mention on Sports-Center. I'm not sure when she started watching *that*, but okay.

I get it. I was there, and yet I watched no less than twelve times, finding some fan videos so I could see different angles. Reliving the moment.

The surprise of it. The taste of Bailey on my lips, like the desserts I sometimes sneak even after the trainers tell us to make every calorie a good one. *Food is fuel*, they like to say. But food is also *fun*. Kissing Bailey somehow felt like the very best of both.

Watching the video also made me want to kick myself for the whole stupid idea because it made Bailey so uncomfortable. I won't make that mistake again.

Parker sighs, a happy little exhale, heart-eye emojis practically hovering around her in a pink cloud.

I shake my head. "The problem," I say, "is that I like her. I like Bailey. Like, really *like* her like her."

"That's too many *likes* in one sentence, Hop." Parker tilts her head. "And I fail to see the problem."

I rap my knuckles on her desk. "I'm not *supposed* to like her. The plan was to get married and then ..." I trail off because I have no idea how to finish this sentence. I shrug instead, feeling helpless.

"So, you have feelings for the woman you just proposed to—and this is a problem because?"

"It's a problem because feelings weren't involved when we agreed to do this. Now they are. And we're getting married. It's like ..." I fumble for an explanation, an analogy to straighten out my tangled thoughts. "It's like a Trojan horse. Bailey let me in the city because I said it was about me getting a visa and her getting money. But inside the horse—"

"But inside the horse you've got a whole feelings army you're about to let loose," Parker finishes.

"Um, yes?"

Parker taps a pen on her desk, which is covered in an array of multi-colored sticky notes. The tiniest of smiles lifts one corner of her mouth. I bet she's probably already thinking about whether or not she could trademark *feelings army*.

"I can see how that's complicated," she says. "Things shifted, and now you're doing things out of order. Do you think Bailey might have feelings too?"

When I do a mental inventory of our interactions, Bailey has seemed, at the least, *happy* in all of them. Smiling, blushing. Her teasing could maybe even be labeled as flirting. Her shyness or maybe just her personality makes her a more difficult study. Usually, I'm better at picking up on vibes.

Then I think of the kiss—the one she initiated and seemed just as into as I was. I remember how she blinked slowly afterward, like she was waking up from a happy dream, the way she clutched my jersey in her tight fist.

"Maybe? I think she could, but I don't know. It's all jumbled up." I stand, wiping my palms on my jeans. "I'm just going to ask her. Right now. I'm going to drive over to her work, maybe find out what flowers she likes first, and then—"

"Whoa! Sit down, Hop." When I hesitate, Parker narrows her eyes. "Now."

There's a reason we call her Boss. Despite her cheerful disposition, when Parker means business, *she means business*. I sit.

"Let's think this through," Parker says. "I know you're a big feelings guy. Which I appreciate, being a big feelings person too. Sometimes big feelings can ... overwhelm a person."

"I don't—"

I stop myself from saying I don't overwhelm people because ... *oh, yeah*. My last serious girlfriend—years ago—said something about me being *too much*. She wasn't the first. It's a common refrain I've heard from girlfriends and dates. The word *overwhelmed* might have been used once. Twice. *Whatever*.

I slump down in my chair with a sigh and wave a hand. "Go on."

"From the little time I spent around Bailey, she seems to be someone who might get overwhelmed. Who might need to ease into things. Who might be surprised that last week, you talked about this as an arrangement, and this week, you're making declarations and demanding to know how she feels. Do you see how this might be a little fast?"

In a conversation in which the underlying assumption is that I've gone from single to marrying someone in a few weeks, I'm not sure how to gauge speed. "Yes?"

"Have you talked to Bailey about expectations?"

"What does that mean?"

"You know when Logan and I started dating, it was pretend, right?" When I nod, she continues. "So, we sat down right here in my office and talked about expectations. How long would this go on? What were we comfortable or not comfortable with? Would we be kissing? That kind of thing. That was just for dating. You and Bailey have a whole lot more questions to figure out. Like, for example, how long will this marriage last? You kissed during the proposal—is kissing totally on the table at all times now? What are the sleeping arrangements going to be at your house?"

I slide down in the chair, feeling the weight of these questions pressing in on me. "Yeah. I can see how we need to talk about some stuff. But what does this have to do with feelings? If we both have feelings, it doesn't matter. It won't end. Kissing and the sleeping arrangements and all that will be a moot point."

"And what if Bailey doesn't know how she feels? What if it takes her a minute? Or if—and I can't see how this would possibly be true because you're amazing—she doesn't feel the same way? Would she still want to go through with the marriage knowing you have feelings and there's all this pressure?"

My head is starting to spin at dizzying speeds. Parker must sense she's overwhelmed me because her voice gets soft.

"Hey, listen," she says. "Let's start with one thing at a time. You and Bailey talk about expectations for the marriage and how this will look. I can help you outline some things to discuss. How does that sound?"

"Okay, I guess."

"You could tell her how you feel and ask if she feels the same, or"—Parker's eyes spark with fresh fire as she leans forward—"Or *don't* tell her. Yet."

"You want me to lie?"

I've already got enough lying in my life right now. Starting with the one I'm spinning for not one but two governments. Not to mention my Mom. I rub a hand over my sternum, like I can smooth away the sting of that one. I keep telling myself it would hurt more to see Mom ripped away from her life here. But it's not easy. Especially seeing how excited she was about Bailey.

When I told Mom I was going to propose, I'm pretty sure they heard her scream in Canada. I thought maybe I'd have to do a lot of explaining—why we were moving so fast, why I didn't mention my plans sooner. But Mom was all-in, no questions asked. Well, a lot of questions, but more the excited, clarifying kind, not the doubtful kind.

Either Mom was way more desperate than I realized to see me married off or she really loves Bailey. Maybe both.

Her excitement only made my stomach drop with an anchor of guilt. And she told Annie before I had a chance to call my sister myself, so now I'm dealing with Angry Annie texts. These come in the form of a barrage of GIFs or long audio messages featuring her singing off-key or reciting what sound like limericks. I've been gearing up to call her, but so far, the guilt has stopped me.

That and my fear of the force that is Annie coming down hard against me for keeping this huge secret. We don't talk often, but we're lazily close. The kind of siblings who may accidentally slip into a few weeks without talking, but then dive right into any topic with barely a hello.

I should absolutely have talked to her instead of letting Mom do it. I'm surprised I haven't been feeling the rumbles of Annie's resentment rolling down from the north like a winter storm.

"I don't want to lie any more than I have to," I tell Parker. "Or pretend I don't have feelings when I do."

Her fingers begin to dance along the edge of her desk, her whole face bright and open, the same look I've seen when she's gotten an idea for a new way to spin a TikTok trend on the ice.

She leans forward. Any farther, and she'll do a belly flop on the desk. "Don't think of it as lying. More like … you're giving her *part* of the truth. While easing her into the *other* truth."

"Still sounds like lying," I say.

"Think of it this way—if you spend more time with her

and realize this isn't what you want or what she wants, you haven't committed to more than the arrangement. You've lost nothing. But if you *do* still want more ..." Parker's smile is slow. "You've already jumped the line, so to speak. And you both live happily ever after."

This makes sense. Or a sort of sense. But only if you squint real hard.

"You're going to woo your wife." Parker clasps her hands under her chin, staring dreamily somewhere above my head. Probably daydreaming about Logan, marriage, and having a whole brood of hockey-playing babies.

I tip over a small container of pink paper clips on Parker's desk and start to arrange them, nudging them into a perfectly straight line. "I don't think I know how to do that."

Parker is still for a few more seconds, clearly deep in thought. I'm about to walk out and tell her to forget it and I'll figure something out when she grabs a fresh pad of sticky notes and gets to her feet.

"Pen," she says, and I hand her one with a pink puffball on top.

She pulls a whole section of sticky notes with her neat handwriting on them down from one wall, setting the stack in a messy pile on her desk. Probably some new plan to take over the world, one TikTok video at a time. Pulling off one pink sticky note from a new pad, Parker slaps it on the wall and turns to me with a grin, pen poised over the paper square. "Let's hash this out and come up with a plan."

And *this* is why I came to Parker.

Half an hour, twenty-seven pink sticky notes, and three square feet of wall space later, Parker and I have talked our way through a semblance of a plan. We're leaning into the whole Trojan horse feelings army thing—I totally knew Parker wouldn't let that go—which essentially means me doing my best to win over Bailey like I would any other woman.

Only she'll already be married to me.

"Feel better?" Parker asks, turning to me with a smile.

Yes? I mean, sort of. Maybe. I don't know that I ever fully recovered after the meeting in Mr. Pebbles's office when I found out about the visa issue. I've been off kilter ever since. So, trying to suss out my feelings is more like doing some kind of blind taste test.

Parker chews her lip. "Because we could always—"

The door flies hard enough to bang into the wall, sending a few sticky notes fluttering to the floor. A pen rolls off Parker's desk and lands by her shoe.

Logan stands there, dark eyes intense as he glares around the room. His gaze stops on my face, and his frown deepens. He slams the door and then looms over me. "Someone said Eli bodily dragged you into your office. With his *hands on you.*"

He's speaking to Parker while burning holes through my shirt with laser beam eyes. I sometimes forget about Logan's intensity because Parker has smoothed out so many of his sharp edges. But other than Nathan, Logan is probably the one guy I wouldn't want to get on the wrong side of. Especially not when it comes to Parker.

I hold up both hands. "Reports have been greatly exaggerated."

"Easy, killer," Parker says with a laugh, looping her arm through Logan's and tugging him away from me. He allows it but doesn't stop glaring, even when she stretches up, pressing a kiss to the corner of his mouth.

"Then what are you two doing in here?" Logan asks. "And why does Eli have a sticky note on his face?"

Do I?

I reach up, fingertips brushing against paper. I have a vague memory of Parker giving me a quick smack to the forehead. More of a pat, really. I guess it came with a sticky note, which is pink and reads *Woo*. Guess that's my new word of the month.

"Oh, I'm just helping solve all Eli's problems," Parker says loftily, running her hands through Logan's hair.

Finally, he stops looking like he wants to murder me. But now he's looking at Parker like he wants to do things I should definitely not be present for.

I stand. "Thanks, Boss. I owe you one."

"And I can't wait to collect," Parker says with a laugh that turns into a sigh as Logan leans forward and kisses her neck.

I escape into the hallway not a moment too soon, with a tiny bubble of hope rising in my chest. Right alongside the dread for whatever Parker's going to make me do.

———

"Aw, my baby boy's all grown up."

"Mom!" I gently swat her hand away as she tries to wipe what I'm sure is a smudge of nothing from my cheek. "Stop. I've been on dates before."

She grins. "Yes, but never with a *fiancée*. I still can't believe my baby's engaged."

"Call me *baby* one more time. See what happens."

Mom only laughs. I duck into the tiny half-bath tucked under the stairs, the one where the top of my hair brushes the ceiling. I give myself a last look in the mirror, smoothing a hand down the front of my blue button-down shirt, one Mom said brings out my eyes.

And yes—I asked my mom what to wear on this date with Bailey. She has good taste.

"What is it?" she asks, locking eyes with me in the mirror.

There's a crease between her brows—partly worry but also partly pain. When I got home from The Summit this afternoon, Mom was still in pajamas, a heating pad and a bottle of pain relievers on the coffee table. I should carry her back to the couch, tuck her in, stay home, and let her pick a cheesy romance movie. That's become our thing on days she's feeling low, whether from joint pain or the exhaustion stemming from fibromyalgia.

But I know she wouldn't let me skip a date. And I really don't want to. Even if I'm feeling unsteady after my conversation with Parker.

"*Eliander*," she says, propping her hands on her hips. "What is it?"

"I'm nervous," I admit, not realizing just *how* nervous until I say it out loud. I turn away from my reflection.

Mom cups my cheek in one hand. "She already said yes, sweetheart. I don't think there's any reason to be nervous." She grins. "But it's adorable that you are."

"Doesn't *feel* adorable," I mutter, tilting my head so I don't have to meet her gaze.

But Mom takes my face in both of her hands now, basically corralling me into an intense staring contest. I blink first.

"You are someone who emotes with every fiber of your being. Always have. Most little boys buried their feelings—especially their tears. Not you." Her smile is gentle. "You were a tempest of emotions and didn't start to hide them until you were a teenager. Even then, you still cared deeply and left more out on the surface than most."

It's true. And as I realized while talking to Parker, my big feelings have been an issue in my relationships. "I don't want to be … too much."

Mom gives my cheeks a rough pat. Not quite, but almost a slap like you'd give someone you're trying to wake from a drunken stupor.

"Be in your feels, son. If you're nervous, well, that just shows how much you care about Bailey."

That—and it's also related to the fact that I'm going on a date with a woman I legitimately like who is also my fiancée and who also doesn't know I really like her. Also, I'm still getting to know her. I've done a whole lot of unintended recon while hanging out with her and the dogs over the past few months, but that's barely scratching the surface of who Bailey is.

File this under: it's complicated.

I'm about to walk out the door when Mom calls my name. My *actual* name. I turn, and she gives me a wide, warm smile. "One more thing—you will never be too much for the right woman. You'll be exactly enough."

CHAPTER 14

Bailey

"HOW WAS YOUR DAY?" I ask Gran.

She snorts instead of answering, then pats the side of her wig. Today it's the Dolly *9 to 5* wig, which makes her head look like a curly blond Q-tip.

I straighten the blanket at the end of her bed, needing something to do since Gran's not in a talkative mood. Mom crocheted this blanket—her only attempt before giving up on the hobby altogether. It's ugly and poorly constructed and almost unraveling. But when I packed up their house, I couldn't bear to throw it out, so I brought it here. Gran seems to like it. Or, at least, she hasn't tried to stuff it in the trash or set it on fire, so that's something.

I trace one of the too-big gaps with one finger, missing Mom and Dad with a sudden and severe ache. I wish they were here to discuss all of this with me—Eli, the proposal, our upcoming date tonight. Of course, if they were here, I wouldn't be considering a marriage proposal for the sake of money. They also never were the greatest at dispensing advice. Or being interested in the details of my life.

I've found one of the hardest things about losing people you care about is the guilt of remembering the things they weren't so great at. Thinking about their flaws and disappointments makes me feel like a traitor. I'd love to picture Mom sitting down with me over coffee to talk about Eli, but it's hard. Because we never did that. Not because she didn't care, but more because we didn't have that kind of relationship ever. And had she lived, I'm not sure we ever would.

The thing is—I'll never know.

For this reason, I keep pushing with Gran. When I start to sit down on her bed, she waves me away with the television remote, a look on her face like I'm carrying cooties.

I thought maybe she'd notice or ask about the giant ring on my finger. The one I can't stop looking at or touching, spinning it around and around when I'm thinking. I'm surprised Gran didn't complain about it blinding her. It's *that* big. Way bigger than Eli needed to get for our situation, or what I'd ever ask for, but the classic round diamond in a platinum band is beautiful.

Gran is too distracted to notice my ring because *The Bachelor* season ten thousand is on. A rerun, I'm guessing, since it's not even six o'clock yet. Gran is a hardcore member of Bachelor Nation. She's seen every episode of every season, plus watches *Bachelor in Paradise* or *Bachelor Island* or *Bachelor in Space* or whatever spin-offs the network vomits up.

Unlike many avid viewers of the franchise, Gran hate watches. Back in the day, before we had to take away her internet access due to her excessive trolling and one tiny bomb threat, she aired her grievances in multiple *Bachelor* subreddits. I wish I'd thought to print screenshots and have them bound up in a book so she could reminisce about the good old days before Bailey took the Wi-Fi away.

"You could learn something from this, you know." Now, Gran points the remote at the TV, which is on mute with subtitles scrolling across the screen. A woman with mascara streaking down her face is weeping in a limousine, wondering why she isn't enough.

At least, I *think* that's what she's wondering. The subtitles haven't been entered correctly, so it actually reads, *Why am I not a cough for him?*

"What can I learn, exactly?"

"Always wear waterproof mascara," Gran says. "You never know when someone's going to break your heart."

———

I'm too antsy to wait in my apartment for Eli to pick me up. I changed my clothes twice—which feels reasonable, all things considered—then cleaned the kitchen and the bathroom and started folding my underwear before deciding a short walk to the parking lot might dispel some of this nervous energy.

The only thing it does is make me clearly see all the reasons Eli slept outside my front door not even a week ago. It *is* dark—too dark. I find myself scurrying from one pool of light to the other all the way to the parking lot, where I stand near my car, directly under the sole working streetlight. Every time a door slams or I hear a raised voice from an apartment somewhere, I jump.

Okay, so my limited budget doesn't cover safety. Noted.

When Eli's dark SUV pulls into the lot, my nerves hit a

crescendo, like a tiny orchestra is playing furiously and with wild abandon inside me. It takes effort to wait for Eli to park. Part of me wants to run, take a leap, and slide across his hood like people always do in cop movies. Only ... there is no world in which I possess that level of coordination.

Eli parks and hops out, his smile wide as he brushes his hair away from his eyes. He's growing out his facial hair, it seems, and my fingers twitch with the urge to touch the short whiskers, a smidge darker than the hair on his head. Almost the color of lightly toasted bread, and I happen to love toast.

"Hey," I say, stepping forward and giving him a little wave.

Eli's smile widens, but he fumbles and drops his phone, which goes skittering underneath his car somewhere. He leaves it.

"I was going to come to your door," he says, joining me on the sidewalk.

I'm glad to know I chose my outfit well—what I'd call nice casual, which perfectly matches what Eli's wearing. We're both in jeans, Eli with blue-checked Vans sneakers and me in boots. The blue shirt he's wearing makes his eyes pop, even in the dim light.

"I couldn't wait," I say. "I probably shouldn't admit that but ..." I shrug and look him over again. It's a really nice view. "Hey—you're still not wearing a coat."

"I'm fine," he says, then fidgets, lifting his hand like he's trying to decide whether to hug me or shake my hand or nothing at all, which is what he finally decides to do, stuffing his hands deep in the pockets of his jeans.

I wilt a little. Because I really could have used a hug.

As though I've broadcast these thoughts across my face like a lit marquis, Eli pulls his hands out of his pockets and wraps me in a hug so quickly that my forehead hits his collarbone and my arms are trapped between us. I wiggle them out, sliding them around Eli's waist. Now I understand him not wearing a coat. The man is a furnace.

"Sorry," he whispers.

"Don't apologize. I like hugs from you."

"Then I'm sorry I didn't do it sooner. But next time I'll try not to slam your face into my collarbone."

"I like your collarbone too."

Go ahead, Bailey. Just confess all the things. Might as well tell him you can't stop thinking about kissing him and also that you have more than friendly, more than contractual marriage *feelings for him.*

After a moment, Eli sighs and lets me go. But not completely. He takes my hand, opening the car door and helping me inside. I suck in a breath when he leans across me to buckle my seatbelt, the scent and heat of him overwhelming me. If I were a bolder person, maybe someone with Shannon's level of confidence, I'd lean forward and brush my lips across his cheeks.

But I'm me, so I just imagine how his whiskers would feel against my lips while my heart stutters out a panicked rhythm.

The belt clicks into place, and he pulls away. "Safety first."

I laugh. "I could have done that myself, thank you." *But I'm glad you did,* I don't add. Just before he closes my door, I remember his phone. "Oh! Don't forget your phone under the car."

As Eli climbs into the car, his stomach makes an unholy sound. I bite back a laugh as he presses a hand over his abdomen like he's trying to shush it. Then he puts the car in gear—and bumps right into the curb. Apparently, he put it in drive, not reverse.

"Are you okay over there?" I ask. I'm not sure I've ever seen him so … unsteady.

He puts the car in park and runs a hand through his hair, pretty much glaring at the dashboard. "I'm sorry."

"Why are you apologizing?"

Without fully turning, Eli tilts his head my way. "I'm nervous, and it's making me totally awkward."

Well, that makes two of us. I just happen to not be the one attempting to operate a motor vehicle.

"Can I confess something?" I ask.

"Please do."

I lean across the center console and whisper, "I'm nervous too. And awkward is my natural resting state. So … maybe we can just be happily awkward together?"

"Awkward together." Eli's grin is fast, and it makes me unreasonably happy to know I put that smile on his face. Warmth rolls over me in a wave, spreading through my chest until even my fingers tingle with it.

But when his gaze drops to my mouth, the warmth gives way to heat. Is it possible I'm not the only one who keeps thinking about the kiss we shared on the ice?

Eli quickly turns back to the wheel, putting the car in reverse this time.

Our conversation slides into something easy and comfortable, Eli asking me about work and about Doris, who's adjusting but still hasn't found a home.

"Any cat incidents?" Eli asks, his grin mischievous.

"Not a week goes by." I pull back my sleeve, revealing the edge of my latest battle wound. A bite this time, the result of trying to administer deworming medicine to a new arrival.

"Ouch."

Eli winces, then reaches across to brush two fingers across my wrist, just shy of the pink skin. His touch is gentle, yet it sparks something not-so-gentle in me. The kind of urgent yearning for more that makes my skin tingle with restlessness.

When he puts his hand back on the wheel, I ask, "What's your hockey schedule like this week? Any more games?"

He shoots me a boyish grin. "You want to come to more of my games, Leelee?"

"I didn't really understand any of the rules, but I liked watching."

And by watching, I mean watching *him*. Though by the end, I found myself screaming for the Appies right alongside Maggie and the other fans in our section. It was thrilling. Definitely a lot more fun than sitting at home watching Netflix.

I might have even screamed, "You suck!" at a player on the other team who knocked into Eli. Which was much nicer than a lot of things people were yelling. But meaner and louder than how I've ever behaved at a public event.

"Any time you want, I'll get you tickets. Mom goes to most of my home games, usually alone."

"Really?" I don't like the idea of Maggie sitting by herself. "Well, then count me in for any upcoming home games."

Eli doesn't seem to take in the fact that this means I have absolutely zero social life and just seems happy enough that I want to watch him play. Apparently, he's got a lot of travel coming up. Two straight weeks on the road with the team playing regular games, some exhibition games, and a lot of fan events, organized by the team owner in an attempt to capitalize on—and monetize, from the sound of it—their social media fame.

"Will we get married before or after you go?" I ask, toying

with the ring. Trying to wrap my brain around the question I just asked.

Because this ring means we're getting *married*. I let go of the ring in favor of a button on my coat.

Maybe Eli's struggling to wrap his head around the idea too because his hand knocks into the wiper lever. The blades screech across the dry glass, and he winces as he fumbles to turn them off. In the process, he flicks on the brights, and someone honks.

"Sorry. I, uh, hadn't planned that far ahead," he says, white-knuckling the steering wheel. "But I guess we should get married before?"

"Which means in the next week."

I swallow, twisting the button until it feels ready to pop off, then letting it spin back. A thousand things flood my mind. Things we need to do. Things we haven't done. Things I don't know how to do. Google is about to get a hefty workout as I search everything I need to know in order to plan a wedding. In a week.

"Wow. Can we do it that fast? I guess if we're just doing a courthouse wedding, it'll be fine. With the judge or whatever?" My brain starts to spin out, totally unchecked and careening right toward the edge of a cliff. "Unless there's a waitlist for that or something. I've never been to the courthouse, but the building's pretty. I love that whole area of town. It's so—"

"Bailey."

"Hmm?"

I blink rapidly until I'm back in the car. Aware of my fingers, still spinning the button on my coat. Of Eli, looking and smelling so good just a foot or so away. Of the fact that I was just babbling.

"Do you *want* a courthouse wedding?" Eli asks.

No. The answer is immediate in my mind, even if it takes a moment to wrangle my tongue into submission.

"I mean, we don't really have time for anything else. People spend a year or more planning weddings. And this isn't—this is just, um ..."

I'm not going to say it's not real. I can't. Because for me ... it is real. Or *some* things are real. Right now, slightly drunk on Eli, I'm not sure.

Eli pulls into a parking spot at the restaurant, then turns to face me, one hand on the wheel and the other on the back of my seat. I want to lean into his hand. I can practically feel the heat coming off him.

"What would you like to do?" Eli asks, his gaze piercing. "If this were the wedding of your dreams, what would you like?"

I glance down, still toying with the button on my coat. Eli drops his hand, lacing our fingers together.

"I never really gave it much thought," I say, studying our hands. I look up, meeting his gaze. "Have you?"

"Would it surprise you if I said yes?"

Not in the least. I smile. "Actually, no. You seem like—" I stop, unable to finish the sentence I started.

"How do I seem?" he asks.

I draw in a breath. "You seem like a romantic, hockey player."

"You're very observant, Bailey ... Wait—I don't know your last name. How can I not know your last name?"

I drop my head back, laughing. This seems like the most perfect kind of irony. Is irony even the word? Probably not. Still—being ready to take the last name of a man who doesn't know mine is ridiculous.

"We sort of skipped over that part, huh? My last name is McKinney."

"Well, Bailey McKinney, soon to be Bailey Hopkins—it sounds like we've got a wedding to plan," he says. "Let's discuss the details inside. With breadsticks."

I smile. "Always with breadsticks."

Eli apparently made a reservation, which shouldn't make me as happy as it does. Our table is by the fireplace, which would be cozy—maybe even romantic?—except that the table closest to ours has three children all watching different shows on iPads. Full volume. No earphones. I wish I didn't know who Blippi is, but I do. And now he'll be joining us on our date because the little girl in the highchair apparently loves him.

The waiter drops off our waters, and Eli suddenly gets jumpy. Fidgeting in his seat, wiping his hands repeatedly on his thighs, looking around the restaurant everywhere but at me. It's honestly kind of adorable to see him struck with the same kind of affliction I deal with on a somewhat frequent basis.

"So," Eli says loudly. "Food!"

Reaching for the menus, he somehow knocks over both of our glasses, sending a sea of water into his lap.

He jumps to his feet, patting at his jeans with a napkin, but there is very little hope. His jeans are more wet than dry, specifically in the upper parts of the legs and crotch.

"Wa-wa!" the little girl at the next table says, Blippi forgotten in favor of Eli's entertainment. She slaps her tiny palms on the table with a manic grin of pure delight, and I cover my mouth to hide my laughter.

"That's why we have lids," one of the little boys says, pointing to his plastic cup. His very serious expression is tempered only by the fact that he's missing both front teeth. "I'm sure they'll give you one if you ask."

"It looks like you peed your pants," the other boy adds.

He's younger and looks like he recently took scissors to his bangs. "Jason peed his pants after recess, and he looked just like you."

Poor Eli. Now, even the parents are trying not to laugh.

"We keep extra clothes in our cubby," the boy continues. "Do you have extra clothes?"

Eli gives up trying to dry his pants, tossing his napkin into the booth with a sigh. "My dude, I don't even have a cubby."

"That sucks," the toothless brother says, nodding.

"Fenton," his father says. "We don't say *sucks*."

"But it does," Fenton argues. "It *totally* sucks."

"Wa-wa," the little girl squeals again, clapping her hands.

I can't help it. I giggle. Eli's head snaps up, and he narrows his eyes at me, but he returns my smile, then points at me.

"You're the one who said awkward was fine," he says.

"It is. Awkward is amazing. It can also be very *amusing*."

"Well, good. Because I seem to be stuck on the extreme awkward setting."

And then he's sliding into my side of the booth, crowding into me, his big body taking up most of the seat. I can't say I mind being this close to him, his thigh pressed up against mine, his body heat making me want to snuggle closer like he's my personal electric heater.

"My side is wet," he says.

I shrug. "You don't need an excuse to sit by me, hockey player."

Our waiter appears then with replacement waters and a busboy who mops up the mess. Fenton, the toothless brother, tugs on the busboy's sleeve and asks if they can bring Eli a cup with a lid.

"Wa-wa!" his sister shrieks again, and I can't hold back my giggles.

Eli mock-glares, then tells the waiter we're going to need a few minutes. The moment we're alone again—aside from the children who are way too invested in our date—Eli groans, dropping his head to the back of the booth.

"What is it?" I nudge his shoulder with mine.

"I'm screwing this all up," he grumbles.

I let my cheek fall to his shoulder just for a moment. "I can assure you, you are *not* screwing this up."

He tilts his head, peering at me. "I'm not?"

"You're not. I can't remember the last time I laughed this much."

"*At* me. You're laughing *at* me."

I grin. "Do you really mind?"

"Nope."

I don't mind either. But I also feel badly that Eli seems to be so nervous. Is it the wedding plans? Or the fact that we might be engaged but are also on our first date? Whatever the reason, I have a sudden idea that might just help us both feel more comfortable.

"But if you're game, I have an idea that involves getting our food to go."

And maybe will make us both feel slightly more comfortable.

Twenty-five minutes later, Eli and I are in the back room of the animal shelter, perched on the countertop, eating breadsticks and hot slices of pizza straight from the box. Every so often, I stop by at night to check on the animals, something I've been doing more since Doris arrived. She just seems so sad and lonely. Now, she's happily wandering the room, sniffing every little thing and looking up at our pizza hopefully.

This thankfully seems to have banished the awkwardness. Though Eli's never been in the back room like this, we've spent more time together in the shelter than anywhere else. It's kind of our origin story.

Eli finishes his current slice, which I think is his sixth or seventh, and wipes his hands on a scratchy brown paper towel—the best I can do as far as napkins, which we forgot to get from the restaurant. Gripping the counter, he leans forward, catching my eye. We're sitting catty-corner, close enough that I can playfully kick him with my socked feet. He still has on his shoes, but my boots got uncomfortable, so I slipped them off when I sat down.

The look Eli's wearing is intense and makes me suddenly self-conscious about how I chew. I cover my mouth with my hand. "What?"

"I can't believe you like spinach on your pizza. What's the other stuff?"

"Arugula," I answer, keeping my mouth covered in case either of the green leafy toppings is in my teeth. "It's like a peppery kind of leafy green."

"Gross. You're basically eating salad pizza."

"And you've got meatza," I shoot back. "Is there a kind of meat you *didn't* ask for?"

"Canadian bacon. Not a fan." When I start to laugh, he says, "What?"

"Oh, the irony. The Canadian doesn't like Canadian bacon."

"I don't claim Canadian bacon. It's a poor representative of both bacon and Canada. It has no taste!"

"Funnily enough, if I'm getting meat, that's the one I *would* get," I tell him.

Eli shakes his head. "Bailey, Bailey, Bailey—how is this

marriage going to work when we can't even agree on pizza toppings?"

I finally finish the bite I've been chewing and wipe my mouth, considering the question. Which I know he meant as a joke, but it's got me thinking about marriage. You know, the thing we're about to do together, for better or for worse, fraudulent or not.

"Maybe that's what marriage is," I suggest. "Arguing over pizza toppings." Eli's brow furrows, so I continue. "I mean, no two people automatically start agreeing on everything once they say 'I do.' So, they learn their differences and how to navigate them. What things are fine to disagree on—like pizza toppings—and where they need to come to a consensus. That's marriage."

My parents seemed to me like the very definition of two peas in a pod, which left me feeling a little bit like the third wheel. But when I said as much one time, Mom told me she and Dad had tons of things they disagreed on. And okay, all of them were kind of nerdy, like whether *Battlestar Galactica* or *Firefly* was the better show. She said that over time, they learned which arguments needed resolution and which ones were healthy to keep in the name of individual autonomy within a marriage. Her words.

"Speaking of marriage, I had a thought. You seemed a little overwhelmed when I brought it up in the car."

I smile weakly, placing my palms on the countertop to steady myself. "Overwhelmed is an understatement."

"How about this: you let me know if there are specific things you want, and I'll handle all the details," Eli suggests.

The relief at this suggestion is palpable. And yet, I don't want to put this all on him. It feels wrong. "You don't need to plan the whole wedding, Eli."

"I don't mind. Actually ..." His smile is a little sheepish, and his cheeks flush the lightest pink as he says, "I kind of want to do it. If that's okay. I know I screwed up the proposal—"

"Eli. Stop. You didn't."

"Bailey, I did," he insists, leaning closer. "Don't try to make me feel better about it. I didn't think it through. But I promise to do better with this. If you trust me, that is."

"I trust you."

I gently tap his shin with my foot, and he traps it between both of his, giving it a gentle squeeze before releasing me. I smile, feeling a sudden satisfaction that has less to do with the pizza I just ate and more to do with the man whose sweetness keeps surprising me.

"We should also talk about expectations," he says, shattering the sense of calm I'd just been relishing, replacing it with jittery nerves.

"Expectations," I repeat.

"Not for the wedding, but after. Like, what this will look like between us in practical terms. I made a list," he says, clearing his throat and shifting his weight to pull something out of his back pocket. A pink sticky note, just like the ones he used on his volunteer application.

What is it with the pink sticky notes?

I want to ask but quickly forget my question altogether when Eli reads the first item on his list. "As far as sleeping together ..." I'm not sure what expression my face makes, but he quickly adds, "We don't need to sleep together. Uh, as in, there are two bedrooms upstairs. Two beds. Mom doesn't usually come up there because stairs are hard on her knees. So she won't know that we're not sleeping together. In the literal *sleeping* sense."

I may be an adult, capable of talking about adult things,

but right now, I'm blushing like a schoolgirl. "Sounds good," I manage.

"Wow." Eli chuckles, dropping his gaze to the sticky note in his hand, which is quickly becoming rumpled as his fingers flex. "I thought having a list would help me."

"Awkward together, remember?" I say gently, knowing my cheeks are burning. "What's next?"

It's not a long list, and after the whole sleeping conversation, we move a little quicker. With fewer double meanings. But no less blushing on my part as we decide when I'll move in—as soon as possible to get me out of what Eli calls my "unsafe living situation"—and how finances will work—despite my protests, Eli insists he's going to cover costs of just about everything, from the wedding to vet school to groceries.

"I do make money," I tell him, more than a little defensively.

Eli gently nudges my foot with his.

"I've been on my own for a while."

Which leads to him asking about my parents. I do my best not to get choked up about it. Their loss is like a scabbed-over wound that so easily gets picked off and goes back to painful.

Eli puts his hand on mine. "You're not alone, Leelee. Not anymore."

If he thinks that kind of statement is going to make me less emotional, he is very, very wrong. I dip my chin, swallowing back a sob at the sudden wave of emotions. Happiness, sadness, grief, hope, and the nagging sense of how much it will hurt when this ends.

"How long will this last?" I ask, my voice sounding a lot steadier than I feel.

Eli is quiet, and I finally take a breath and tilt my head up to look at him. I can't quite read his expression, which looks as jumbled up as I've felt through this entire conversation.

"I don't know," he says finally. "Maybe … we can table that discussion for now and revisit later?"

I'm all too happy to do that. I think I'd happily table any further talking and end the date before I collapse from the emotional weight of it all. Doris has the right idea—snoring a few feet away, her head resting on one of my boots.

"Last item," Eli says, and I almost groan. "What about kissing?"

Cue my face turning red. Again. Maybe I should start wearing blush in copious amounts so that when I get embarrassed or uncomfortable or any of the other emotions that spark the rush of blood to my capillaries, no one will be able to tell the difference.

"Good question," I say. "Actually, wait—what's the question?"

Eli's hand closes around the sticky note, and I wonder if he even realizes he's crumpled it into a ball. I watch, fascinated, as his Adam's apple visibly moves.

"I know there are times that might call for kissing," he says. "Like, uh, the proposal. And the wedding ceremony. I just want to make sure you didn't think I expected you to have to kiss me all the time."

"You say that like it's a hardship," I mutter.

If I had my choice, we'd have spent a better portion of the night kissing rather than having this awkward but necessary discussion.

Wise? Probably not.

Helpful in terms of guarding myself from falling harder for Eli? Definitely not.

Enjoyable? Absolutely.

"I just don't want you to feel pressured," he says.

"You've never made me feel that way."

"Good." Eli opens his hand, blinking down at the crushed pink paper. He tosses it toward the trash can. A perfect shot. He scoots off the counter and gets to his feet, stretching. I watch the way his biceps strain against his shirt, glad my cheeks are already hot so they don't give anything more away. "I guess we're settled."

Settled is the last thing I feel. "On what?"

Eli's gaze meets mine. "On kissing only when the situation requires us to."

Is it just me, or does he sound as disappointed as I feel?

One thing that has come up over and over in my past relationships is my struggle to vocalize how I feel. What I want and what I don't. I'm not sure if it's my inherent shyness or that I never felt fully comfortable, even around my longest-term relationships. Which weren't all that long.

But I find myself needing things to be different here. Not because this is an arrangement, not something real. I want to speak the truth to Eli. Even if it's uncomfortable. Even if it's a bad idea.

Even if it might reveal my true feelings for him.

"Do we need to take non-required kissing off the table?" I ask.

He goes completely still. Not a relaxed sort of stillness either. I can see the flex in his jaw. The tightness in the way his hands are fisted at his sides. Tendons in his neck are tight.

"Tell me what you want, Leelee."

Eli's voice is a low rasp, and it tugs at something in my chest. A ribbon of want unfurls inside me, slow and lazy.

"I don't think we need to stop kissing," I say. "Or that it needs to be done strictly when necessary."

"No?" He takes a step closer.

"No," I breathe. My hands tremble, but I hold his gaze steadily, feeling brave and reckless, ignoring the tiny voice telling me the ice is too thin here. It won't hold me. I don't care. "I mean, it might seem a little unbelievable if it's not something we're comfortable with."

"Comfortable, hmm?" Eli takes one more step toward my spot on the counter until he's standing so close, my knees bracket his torso and my dangling feet brush his thighs.

"I like the way you look with a blush on your cheeks," he says, his gaze moving across my face. "Especially when I'm the one who puts it there."

"You do?"

"Yeah. I do."

Eli brushes a fingertip over the swell of my cheek, then over the slope of my nose to the other cheek. My eyes are on his, but his are following the path of his finger. The blue of his eyes is dark, a heavy storm cloud over a tumultuous sea.

"You blush like a sunrise," he murmurs, the rumble of his voice making my breath hitch. "First a light pink, then a deeper flush, and finally, rose red. Not just in your cheeks. Here," he says, tapping the end of my nose, then sweeping two fingers to my jaw and trailing them slowly down my neck. "And here."

I swallow, and Eli seems fascinated by the movement, tracing my throat with his fingertips.

"You know," he says, his eyes still on the place he's touching me. "You're right—if we don't spend time kissing in private, it might not look believable to other people when we're in public."

"We can't have that," I whisper. "I won't let them deport you, hockey player."

His eyes snap to mine. "No?"

I shake my head. "I think I'd like to keep you."

I mean to add *for a little while* or *for as long as I can*, but the words don't come. Probably because they're not true. I don't want this to be temporary. I don't want this to be an agreement, a list of talking points on a sticky note, balled up and tossed away.

But I'm not brave enough to say all that. Telling Eli this little bit I want feels like a start. A tiny step in the right direction.

"Will you kiss me?" I ask.

Eli slides his hand around the back of my neck, then up into my hair. He makes a humming sound, leaning in until our noses brush.

"That is," I say, my eyes fluttering closed as his lips brush my cheek, his short beard prickling against my skin. "If you don't think it will make things confusing."

It's too late for me. I am nothing if not a tangled knot of confusion, of warring wants and fears, but right now, my longing for Eli's mouth on mine eclipses them all.

"I'm not confused," Eli says.

And then his lips find mine. A light, teasing pass at first, a whisper of a kiss. Then another. But when a low noise escapes my throat, something in him seems to snap, and his mouth moves over mine, hot and sweet and so overwhelming, I'm immediately lost to him.

It's better than I remember. Better without the whole stadium of people watching.

Better with no pressure and no hurry, even though we're kissing with desperation. As though these are our final moments, a goodbye kiss. It feels like we're at the bottom of an hourglass, sand spilling over us faster every moment.

I grip his shoulders, pulling him closer as he gently tilts my head to the side, his mouth finding my cheek, my jaw, my neck.

Until he pulls away suddenly. I blink at him, trying to orient myself to the harsh lighting above and the jar of cotton swabs to my right, the sound of dogs barking incessantly in the kennel nearby.

It only takes a second for me to see why Eli stopped kissing me. Doris is staring up at us both while lifting her leg and urinating on Eli's shoe in a steady stream. Totally unrepentant. Brazen, even.

And we're both frozen. At least, until Doris finishes and darts away, chasing the paper towel Eli dropped earlier.

"Really, D? It's like that?" Eli asks, and the steadiness in his voice is alarming.

Because I am wrecked.

Eli is teasing Doris while I am trying to remember how to breathe. I lean forward, resting my head on his shoulder. He can't see my face this way and notice my disappointment.

But then, he said he wasn't confused about kissing me. I'm the one who asked him to kiss me, and I'm the one confused.

"Are we okay?" he asks, his hands gently kneading my shoulders.

He's so kind, I think. Too kind. I need to stop mistaking that for something else. Even if ... even if I really thought maybe it was more.

"We're fine," I tell him. "The question is—are your shoes okay?"

This makes him smile, which is what I want. Even if I also want to die a little. And for him to kiss me again. And to tell him he can't kiss me again because I was wrong—we're not fine and I'm completely confused. Even if he isn't.

But what is he not confused about?

Is he not confused because he can casually kiss people without catching feelings? I really, *really* hope that's not what he meant. Maybe he's not confused because we just set up expectations for our arrangement and kissing is just one more part of that?

Or ... is he not confused because he has feelings for me, which are not confusing?

His lack of confusion only sends me spinning into more.

As we head for the door, I quickly bend and rescue the balled-up pink sticky note from the trash, stuffing it inside my pocket before I follow Eli out into the darkness.

CHAPTER 15

Bailey

THE THING about planning a wedding in a week is that you end up having very few choices. Which can be good or bad, depending on if you're a glass half-full or half-empty kind of person. On the glass-half-full side, fewer choices can mean less decision fatigue. (It also helps if the groom takes on the wedding planning, which I'm so grateful for.)

On the glass-half-empty side, it means I'm stuck in a big-box bridal store trying on dresses off the rack so covered in sequins or ruffles or lace that it feels more like I'm dressing for some kind of drama performance than a wedding. Then again, this wedding kind of is a performance, so trying on dresses doesn't quite have the emotional *oomph* it would if I were planning a real wedding to a man I really wanted to marry.

And I'm going to keep telling myself that Eli *isn't* a man I really want to marry. An obvious lie. One that gets harder the more time I spend with him, the more I kiss him.

The more I wonder why he kisses me back and what he's not confused about.

Does it mean for him anything close to what it means for me?

Shannon tells me to be bold, to ask what he wants, to tell him what I want and how I feel. But the whole kissing conversation blew my boldness budget for the month. I'm not a person who can discuss what I hope for in a relationship the way I can place an order at the drive-through.

Um, let's see … I'd like to order plenty of kisses, double up on the flirty grins, hold the heartbreak please!

"This one is … special," Jenny says, ripping my thoughts from where they drifted to Eli's mouth on mine, his thumb's gentle press on my throat. "Unique."

Shannon makes a sound somewhere between a snort and a scoff. "It's covered in feathers, J. She looks like some kind of bird of paradise bride of Frankenstein."

I pluck at the feathers circling my waist. If a dress is going to have feathers, you know where it shouldn't have them? Around areas of the body you want to look *smaller*. I look like Big Bird's pregnant albino girlfriend. I think I prefer Shannon's description. You know it's bad when a bird of paradise bride of Frankenstein is the better of two alternatives.

"A bird of Frankenstein," I say, which makes both Jenny and Shannon laugh.

I smile too, but it's not helping me feel any better about this. The wedding dress shopping. The realization I'm still trying to wrap my brain around how I am the one trying on legit *wedding dresses*. The on-ice proposal—or *almost* proposal since I'm wearing the ring but he didn't ask and I didn't say yes—didn't make this whole thing feel real. Neither does this.

Not even after our date, in which Eli was adorably awkward —almost like it was a *real* date—and then kissed me into a haze at the shelter. I really should stop kissing him. Just to, you know, have *some* reminder of this as an arrangement. But now that the box has been opened, I'm not sure I can put kissing back inside.

I was both grateful Doris cut our moment short peeing on Eli's shoe and also ready to withhold all future dog treats for reminding me this will have an expiration date. One more thing we haven't discussed. It feels like for each thing we nail down, there are twenty more we need to talk about. I'm exhausted, a wrung-out piece of laundry drying on the line.

"Can I take a picture?" Shannon asks. "I need to remember this moment."

"Gee, I'm so glad I brought my best friends to help me pick out a dress," I say.

Shannon shrugs and takes a sip from her travel mug. It's full of champagne. And ice. Since David's Bridal doesn't offer complimentary champagne while shopping, Shannon claimed it's a BYOC kind of situation.

Jenny and I stuck to coffee. Which I quickly realized was a terrible idea because I'm so terrified I'll spill on an ugly dress and have to buy it. Now Jenny is balancing both of our travel mugs. She keeps forgetting and drinking out of mine, then making a face because she's a monster who doesn't like sugar in her coffee.

"Do you want me to lie?" Shannon asks. "Or would you prefer I tell the truth when you look like the newest Marvel character—the bird bride of vengeance?"

"Ooh," Jenny says, pushing up her glasses with a forearm,

nearly spilling both coffees. "And she only goes after men who cheat on their girlfriends with their former high school rivals."

Shannon pats Jenny's arm sympathetically at the not-so-vague reference to Jenny's ex. Then narrows her eyes and punches her in the shoulder.

"Ow!" Jenny says, jerking away from Shannon.

"Watch the coffee!" I warn.

"It's high time to get over Chet." Shannon bends herself over the arm of her chair to meet Jenny's eyes. "His name is *Chet*. That alone should make it easier. Your high school rival is the big loser here. You know that, right? You are a gorgeous, amazing human, and Chet and what's her face are the tiny cubes that get spit out of a trash compactor. Nod if you agree."

Jenny nods, her smile a little wobbly. "Thanks."

The very young and very bored David's Bridal employee appears, like a bad spirit we've summoned. The expression on her face tells me this sentiment goes both ways.

"And how are things going?" she asks, giving us a sweeping look that's somehow both bored and judgmental. "Finding everything you need?"

"Tell me"—Shannon leans closer to read the woman's name tag—"Becky. Does this dress come in yellow?"

Becky glances at me, and I'll give the woman credit because she keeps a totally blank face.

"No. White and ivory. Anything else?"

"We're good. Great, actually," I say quickly before Shannon can say whatever she opened her mouth to say next. Probably to ask if there's a rolling discount in proportion to the ugliness of the dress.

When Becky's gone, the three of us dissolve into giggles.

The feathers sway as I laugh, which only makes me laugh harder.

"I think we need to buy this one for funsies," Shannon says.

"You could hang it in a field and scare birds away from the crops," Shannon says.

"Or put it outside at Halloween to scare children," Jenny adds.

Twisting uncomfortably, I manage to read the price tag. "Uh, sorry. It's almost a thousand dollars. Too expensive for Halloween decor."

"Okay, well, how many dresses are left?" Shannon asks. "I need to head out to the car for a refill if it's more than five."

"I think only three." Which does not bode well for me finding a dress I actually like.

"I meant to ask you—did Eli's mom not want to come?" Jenny asks, and I freeze, having taken two steps toward the dressing room.

"What?"

Both my friends blink at me, wearing matching expressions that let me know exactly how much I screwed up.

I spin Eli's ring. "Was I supposed to invite her? Is that ... a thing?"

Bridal etiquette is not in my wheelhouse. The last wedding I went to was probably ten years ago. Or more. And I wasn't joking when I told Eli I don't have a dream wedding in mind. It wasn't the kind of thing I pretended or planned as a little girl. I was busy pretending to perform surgery on my stuffed animals.

"It's not, like, required or anything," Jenny says quickly.

Shannon is silent. Which says more than words could. Dread burrows deep, cozying up to the growing sense of guilt I've been carrying around for lying to so many people about this thing. The very last thing I want is to hurt Maggie. Sweet, funny Maggie, who unscrewed half the lightbulbs in her house just to meet me.

Maggie, who leaned close after Eli's hockey proposal, whispering, "I'm so happy to have you as a daughter."

I almost burst into tears and confessed right there on the spot.

Jenny takes a sip of the wrong coffee again and makes a face. "If brides get along with their future mom-in-law, they might invite them to come. Especially if ..." Jenny trails off. She doesn't need to mention the fact that my own mom isn't here.

Honestly, I know the exact uncomfortable look she'd have on her face if Mom *were* here. The way she'd fidget in the chair, trying to get comfortable and finally giving up to pace. Shopping never was her scene. And wedding dresses are the elite level of shopping.

The truth is: as wonderful as my mom was, planning a wedding, normal or otherwise, would have been uncomfortable with her. Awkward. Not fun. Even if she would have been happy for me—it just wouldn't have been her thing.

But Eli's mom, on the other hand ...

I swallow. "Should I call her?"

"Do you want her to be here? We didn't mean to make you feel pressured," Shannon says.

I don't even need to think about it. I'm already going for my phone.

We decide to have brunch in a cafe next door while we wait for Eli and his mom, who were close by in Asheville for an appointment. Best-salesgirl-ever Becky refused to set aside the dresses I planned to try on, yet looks put out when Shannon tells her she's just going to have to get them out again.

"Can't have it both ways, sister," Shannon told her, and I fully expect every mediocre dress I semi-liked to be hidden in the back when we return. The only ones left will be full of feathers.

"Did she sound excited?" Jenny asks.

"You could say that."

I don't tell them how people two states away probably heard her scream.

"And you said Eli's coming with her?" Shannon has switched from champagne to black coffee and is on her third cup. We've been here twenty minutes.

"Yeah." I don't add that Maggie has some health issues, and Eli got on the phone to tell me she's having a hard day.

His exact words were that she's having a flare-up, and they're already nearby in Asheville to see her chiropractor. I'm not comfortable sharing someone else's medical history with my best friends, even if Maggie will probably tell them herself. I was surprised she didn't mention it at the game. But then, between watching Eli totally kill it on the ice and the proposal, we didn't have much time for chitchat of any kind.

"Are you going to let Eli see you in the dresses?" Shannon asks.

Jenny speaks around a mouth full of muffin. "If you do, it's bad luck for seven years."

"I thought that was breaking a mirror," Shannon says. "Or walking under a ladder. I think the wedding dress thing it's just generally bad luck."

"I didn't know y'all were so superstitious."

I take a sip of coffee, then decide the caffeine isn't helping my frayed nerves and switch to water. I've already eaten everything on my plate. I'm a nervous eater, which now means I'm overly full from the bacon grilled cheese and sweet potato fries I basically unhinged my jaw to eat. My full stomach is going to make putting on dresses oh-so fun.

I lower my voice and grip the edge of the table, trying to anchor myself in place. Or test the tensile strength of the furniture. "It doesn't matter anyway."

"Why not?" Jenny asks.

"You know why." I release the table and drop my hands, suddenly overcome with melancholy like a cloud has moved across the sun, leaving me in shadow.

"Stop that." Shannon reaches across the table and pokes me with her fork. The tines press into my arm, and it's not a wholly unpleasant feeling, but I say "ouch" anyway.

"You're so violent," I tell her, rubbing my arm.

"No, I'm just tactile." Without even wiping the fork off, Shannon spears a bite of maple bacon potato. "But seriously. You know you're allowed to enjoy this process. The dress shopping, the planning, all of it. Even the wedding and"—she gives me a mischievous look—"the wedding *night*."

Jenny's eyes go wide, probably in direct proportion to how red my cheeks are. "Are you going to—like ..." She stops, coughs, and then takes off her glasses, buffing them with her napkin before setting them back in place. "How real is this marriage going to be?"

"I don't know. But not ... that real." I swallow, thinking of how my heart practically vibrated in my chest when Eli's lips dragged over my jaw. "I don't think. It's not like a fake marriage with benefits thing."

"Of course not," Jenny says.

But Shannon raises an eyebrow. "But how do you know it's not just a casual kissing thing?"

It might very well be. I know she's right, and I should clarify this with Eli. *But I will*, I promise myself. I will.

Eventually.

"I mean, not that there's anything wrong with kissing," Shannon adds. "Or *more* than kissing. Even the abstinence people would sign off on this. Is it even technically a real marriage if you don't, you know, consummate it?"

I cover my face with my hands. "Please, do not use the word *consummate* again. For the love."

"I don't think the immigration police or whoever are exactly checking for that kind of proof," Jenny says. "The consummatory kind."

"Still. It could be a perk to enjoy," Shannon says. "I know *I* would."

"But you're not Bailey," Jenny says.

I slide down in my chair, wishing my bones would melt so I could puddle under the table and away from this conversation. It's not that I can't discuss sex like an adult. It's more that this is all too real. And, by the same token, unreal. I agreed to marry Eli for his visa. Not for … any other reason.

But if he asked …

"Can we just … not?"

I can't allow myself to think any more about this. There is a very heavy door closed on the topic of physical intimacy with my soon-to-be only-on-paper husband. I mentally add another few bolts to reinforce it.

"But back to the matter at hand today and the wedding dress dilemma," Jenny says, and I could kiss her for steering this ship away from consummating-the-marriage waters. Shannon sighs heavily—at the change in topic, no doubt— but turns interested eyes my way. "For real, though—are you going to let him?"

"Let him *what*?"

The spike of adrenaline at the sound of Eli's voice has me grasping my knife in some kind of misguided fight-flight-or-stab-someone response. I turn and see a sight that's the equivalent of a whole quiver of cupid's arrows finding my heart in unison. Eli, wearing a backwards cap and a Henley, is carrying his mother. Maggie looks tiny in his arms, her smile broad despite the shadows beneath her eyes.

"We made it!" Maggie says a little breathlessly, as though she were the one carrying Eli, not the other way around.

She throws one arm dramatically wide. The other stays looped around Eli's neck. She's wearing loose jeans, a pink cable-knit sweater, and a black and white striped scarf that somehow makes me think about prisoner's uniforms in old cartoons and movies.

I scramble to my feet and attempt to hug her, which ends up being a strange sort of mother-son group hug. Eli's chuckle shifts my hair and sends a shiver skittering up my spine. Maggie smells like flowers and incense, muting Eli's masculine scent somewhat. I find myself taking a deeper inhale with my nose pressed to his collarbone, trying to locate him.

"Planning on stabbing someone, Leelee?" Eli asks as I pull back.

He raises a brow at my fist, still curled around the butter knife I used to cut my grilled cheese in half earlier. I'm lucky I didn't stab one of them during the hug.

"Oh. This." I set it on the table, but the heavier part is over the edge, and it clatters to the floor. I bend to pick it up and hit my forehead on the edge of the table. "Ow." Slumping back into my chair, I rub my forehead and my wounded pride.

"Set me down, son," Maggie says, patting Eli on one of his impressive pecs. "You're causing a spectacle."

He absolutely is—and not just at our table.

The spectacle isn't because Eli is carrying his mom, though I'm sure that adds to it. *He* is the spectacle. His size, which is the evolutionary pinnacle of our kind. And his handsomeness, which has a sort of full-body halo effect. He's just … brighter than anyone else in the room. Clearly, multiple people recognize him, and phones are already out.

And he's mine, some tiny, very misguided part of my brain says. I pop that thought like a balloon.

"As you wish, madame."

With a swoop that makes Maggie squeal, Eli sets his giggling mother on the empty chair next to mine. Despite the dramatic movement, he's careful to tuck her legs under the table and doesn't step back until she's secure. Then he turns all of THAT my way, beaming as he leans forward to press a quick kiss to my forehead.

"Better?" he asks.

I nod, having lost my ability to speak several minutes ago. Apparently, there's something in the air, because my friends are both under the same bubble of silence. But it looks like they *want* to speak, considering the way both of their mouths are hanging open. Eli pulls a chair up beside his mom, keeping her between us, and I'm glad right now for the buffer. I feel far too soft and squishy and vulnerable right now. Under the table, though, his foot finds mine, giving me a soft but solid press.

"Ignore my dramatic entrance. I can walk. But some days my fibromyalgia flares up, and it hurts. That's when I'm happy to take advantage of having a giant of a son who can act as my personal porter." Maggie's voice is warm and her smile wide, despite the slight wince as she settles in the wooden chair.

While my friends are digesting that pipe bomb of information, Maggie turns to me, and I'm surprised when she hugs me again. This one is a lot less awkward than when Eli was holding her. But then I meet his eyes over her shoulder, and something in my chest cinches tight, tight, tight.

"Thank you for inviting me," she says. "You didn't need to, but I'm so very glad you did."

"Would you like to order food?" Shannon asks. "We ate but could totally wait. Or eat more."

"Speak for yourself," I say. "I'm pretty sure I'll be trying on a whole size larger now."

"What were you saying when we walked up?" Eli asks, and I wish he'd forgotten. "Are you going to let me *what*?"

Shannon, Jenny, and I exchange glances. I know we were talking about trying on dresses, but at his question, my mind zipped right back to the conversation before that one. The one about the physical boundaries in our relationship.

"We were talking about whether Bailey was going to let you see her try on the dresses," Shannon says.

"It's bad luck," Jenny says. "But it might be a dumb tradition y'all don't care about."

Eli looks my way, and the heat in his gaze sweeps over me like a solar flare. "Well, Leelee? Are you afraid of a little superstition? Or do you want to let me peek?"

Right now, I think I'd let him do just about anything he asked. Especially when he's wearing that smile. I know everyone in the room can see it—and I think a woman a few tables over just took a picture—but this smile feels like it's just for *me*.

"I, um … what do *you* want to do?"

I love the way Maggie waits for his answer, her eyes bright and expression proud, like no matter what the answer is, she is just so, so proud to call him her son. I swallow hard.

"While I love surprises, Mom will confirm I'm terrible at waiting for them."

"True," Maggie says cheerfully. "Peeked at every Christmas present every single year. I had to start keeping them at a friend's house just so he couldn't find them, and then wrapping random empty boxes from around the house to go under the tree."

I can totally picture that—a miniature version of the smiling man in front of me, missing a front tooth, eyes narrowed in concentration, hair falling over his eyes as he tiptoes toward the Christmas tree in the dark. His fingers, probably at least one with a scrape, carefully peeling back tape and folding away the paper to reveal a forbidden glance at his present. Like Bluebeard's wife, unable to resist the allure.

Only, with Christmas presents not dead wives. *Obviously.*

I find Eli staring, his blue eyes sparkling. I've heard the phrase smiling eyes, but never until Eli have I known what it means. My heart flutters a bit, nervous and a little excited too as I wait for his answer.

Am I a present he can't wait to open early?

"I'll defer to the bride," Eli says, watching me carefully, his smile now a little less sure.

I can't ignore the little squeeze of disappointment. While I appreciate the way Eli is concerned with making sure I'm okay, this response only makes me understand less what *he* really wants.

I'm not confused.

Are his words the other night ever going to stop playing on a loop in my head?

Probably not until you talk to him and clarify things.

Great. Now Shannon's voice is in my head too. Just what I need adding to the overthinking.

Eli is still patiently waiting for me, unaware that I'm in a tailspin. A total downward thought spiral. His soft smile and the kindness in his eyes takes a little bit of the edge off.

And it's his smile which gives me the courage to shrug and say, "Guess it depends on whether you've been naughty or nice."

Which makes Maggie cackle, Shannon stare at me in shock, and Eli—well, the expression on his face and the mischief in his eyes is definitely on the naughty side of the spectrum.

CHAPTER 16

Eli

I KNOW I can't be the only guy who dreamed about his wedding as a kid.

It's not like I went so far as to try on tuxes the way girls might try on dresses. I'm not even sure where my concept of weddings came from—cartoons, maybe?—but for me, this involved setting up the guests, who were primarily stuffed animals and action figures. Sometimes a few tanks or race cars. The officiant was an oversized nutcracker Mom kept out year-round on the kitchen counter. For a long time, I thought it watched over the kitchen, particularly the sweets I tried to sneak out of the pantry.

The main part of this pretend wedding for me was the wife. Who I decided was too important to be played by any of my stuffed animals or things we had around the house. My wife was always invisible—an imaginary, backlit blur of white. I didn't picture hair color or eye color or any clearly defined features. My pretend wife was the kind of vision you'd see if you were squinting with water in your eyes.

Now, that blurry vision moves into startlingly clear reality as Bailey steps out of a curtained dressing room.

I don't mean to gasp. Hopefully only Mom heard me.

Forget it. I don't care who heard me. Or who sees me stumbling to my feet as Bailey hesitantly takes a few steps toward me, her smile soft and slow like a whispered secret.

"Wow," I breathe. "You look …"

Words fly behind my eyes like the numbers on a stock ticker, too fast for them to make their way from brain to mouth. I'll be honest—I don't even see the dress.

A giggle bubbles out of Bailey, and her eyes shift to the floor. "I look ridiculous."

"No." The word fires from my mouth, a single machine gun round.

Bailey stops just in front of me. Close enough to touch, but I have my hands closed into tight fists and can't seem to loosen them.

Would Bailey want me touching her anyway? What's the protocol here? Is she even big on physical touch like I am? The list of things I don't know about my fiancée is growing like some endless scroll. I wish I had more of a sense of what she wants from me.

I wish I knew more clearly what I want from her. From us.

But seeing Bailey in a wedding dress …

It's like all those childhood moments of playing pretend are finding their culmination here. Even though this isn't the actual wedding but a bridal store. And even if the actual wedding won't be the normal, *actual* wedding. Even if we're saying vows and Bailey is wearing a dress.

For the first time, I actually look at the dress. Then frown.

Then realize I'm frowning and attempt to smooth out my expression.

"Oh. It's …" I trail off, trying to decide how to describe what Bailey's wearing. Which is very … "Fluffy. Like a down comforter."

I hear a snort from behind me and am not sure if it came from Mom or one of Bailey's friends. Bailey bites her lip, but she's holding back a smile.

"Not that it's a bad thing! Comforters are great! Soft and puffy and you just kind of want to snuggle up in bed with them—"

The snorts become full-on guffaws. Sweat prickles along my hairline and the back of my neck. "I didn't mean—"

When Bailey touches my arm, my mouth clamps shut. Even through the fabric of my shirt, the brush of her fingertips has an immediate impact. I stand up straighter and my shoulders pull back. I feel like even the little hairs on my arms are standing at attention.

"It's okay, hockey player." Bailey's smile is easy and genuine. "I knew what you meant. And it does look like a comforter."

She looks down, then presses both hands into the skirt of the dress. They disappear inside the fabric. She giggles. "I wonder how many things I could hide in here? Probably a lot. So, that's a plus. Like a Mary Poppins dress."

"But do you *like* it?" Mom asks, and Bailey glances up, still smiling.

"No," Bailey all but whispers, like we're holding this conversation in a library or inside of a church. "I really don't like any of them."

"This is an improvement over the bird of Frankenstein dress," Shannon says, circling Bailey and giving the puff of white on her shoulder a little pet, like it's a dog.

I raise my brows. "A bird of Frankenstein dress?"

"You don't want to know," Bailey says. "Just picture a dress this terrible but ... feathery."

"Um."

I rock back on my heels, suddenly feeling unsure what to say or do next. The thing is—I don't care about the dress. I mean, this one is definitely a little odd. But when Bailey walked out, I wasn't paying any attention to the dress. The mere idea of Bailey wearing a wedding dress to marry *me*, thinking of Bailey walking toward me down an aisle just like all my stuffed animal scenarios—that's all I care about.

"It doesn't matter," Bailey says quietly, her eyes flicking past me to my mom, then back to me, color rising in her cheeks. "It's just a dress."

Maybe. And I know what Bailey's not saying since my mom is here: it's just a fake wedding. Or, since the paperwork will be real, a marriage on paper.

I suddenly find myself wanting to pull Bailey aside, to ask her if she wants it to be just that. Or if maybe it could mean something more. If this could be something *real*. I know she was the one who said she wanted to keep kissing ... but that doesn't tell me everything I want to know. It's not an answer to a question. More like a clue on a scavenger hunt. And I'm not sure exactly where it's leading or how to decipher it.

But I won't put her on the spot like that. At least not with my mom in earshot or even her friends, who I know *know*. More because I don't want to put Bailey on the spot. To risk her face looking stricken as she finds a kind way to let me down easy and tell me it's just about the money or just about helping me.

About anything but ME.

Even so, even if it's just on paper, it's a wedding. And she should have exactly what she wants.

"It does matter," I say fiercely. Maybe more fiercely than I intended because Bailey flinches, then smiles again. The placating kind.

"We don't have a lot of options," she says. "Just with, you know, the time frame."

"Elvis."

I turn when Mom says my name—or rather my *not* name—and she's scooting forward in her chair. Immediately, I walk over and pick her up. I know she *could* stand. She *can* walk. But I also am adept at reading her pain levels and can recognize when the pain is bad. When she'd rather I carry her, even if she won't ask. Today is one of those days. Even after the chiropractor and massage therapy.

I walk her over to Bailey, trying not to notice how Mom feels lighter in my arms, like she's lost more weight. Is she okay? Have I been so busy and preoccupied with my own issues that I've missed what's going on with her?

"I know we don't know each other well," Mom says to Bailey. "Permission to speak freely?"

Smiling, Bailey nods.

"You'd make a gorgeous bride if we wrapped you up in white kitchen trash bags and used cheesecloth as a veil. But a wedding dress is about how you *feel* in it. And I don't get the sense that you *feel* good in this one. Is that a fair assessment?"

"Pretty much. But I don't want to be picky or ungrateful, and I'm on a budget. If we had more time—"

Bailey stops herself, and I know she realizes she's stepping onto the thin ice of our lie. Because the reasons we've given everyone for rushing this wedding—the upcoming Appies tour, the fact that we just *know*, and also, no, Bailey's not pregnant—wouldn't hold if anyone put their full weight on them. They'd crack right through.

Thankfully, my mom doesn't focus on the time aspect of it.

"Please don't try to tell me it doesn't matter or that it's picky to want the right wedding dress." Mom pauses and purses her lips. "I have an idea," she says, and a tiny stab of worry goes through me at those words.

When Mom says those words—and also when my sister says them—there is usually a very risky thought on the other side. Knowing Bailey, she won't be able to say no.

"How would you feel," Mom asks slowly as Bailey's hands disappear again into the poufy fabric of the dress, "if money weren't an issue and if you could have the dress of your dreams?"

I'm not sure where Mom is going with this, but I'd gladly pay anything for Bailey to have a wedding dress she loves. One which doesn't look like a bird or a duvet.

I mean, unless that's what she *wants*.

"I would love that," Bailey says. "But—"

Mom waves a hand, and for a moment I worry she's actually going to cover Bailey's mouth. Instead, she plucks Bailey's hand from the depths of the dress and gives her hand a squeeze.

"Do you trust me?"

I see the struggle on Bailey's face. She seems to be a people pleaser, much like I can be. People pleasers get a bad rap, but unless pleasing others comes at your own expense or you're unable to ever say no, it's a great characteristic. One of the things that draws me to Bailey, actually.

Her burnished honey eyes meet mine, as though looking for permission. I nod. Whatever idea this is might be a little out there, but I have no doubt that whatever my mom has cooked up will be amazing.

I can see the moment Bailey decides to say yes. It's in the

way her eyes soften, the tentative smile, the way she clutches tighter at Mom's hand.

There's something about my mom and Bailey, hand-in-hand, that just about does me in. I clear my throat, glancing away, only to find myself looking at a set of angled mirrors showing a reflection of us a thousand times.

"I do."

Laughing, Mom gives Bailey's hand a little shake. "Save that talk for your wedding day. Now, I can't make promises, but why don't you get out of that Bed Bath and Beyond monstrosity while I make a phone call."

———

Half an hour later, we're pulling up in front of an A-frame house tucked away in the hills west of Asheville. Shannon and Jenny apologetically bowed out because Mom couldn't give a solid time estimate for this mystery outing. I have no clue, other than the address she plugged into my GPS.

Bailey insisted on taking the back seat to give Mom the more comfortable front. I'm starting to see a pattern here. Though I admire it, I want, with as much force, to protect Bailey, to be the one to make sure she's getting what *she* needs.

But saying yes to whatever dress thing my mom concocted isn't a terrible thing, so for now, I won't step in and try to make sure Bailey is prioritizing herself enough.

More than once on the winding drive, other drivers honked at me because I got distracted looking at Bailey in the rearview mirror. I'm grateful when the GPS—which Mom reprogrammed to sound like a *sexy bloke*, her words—directs me to pull into a circular gravel drive. I park behind an ancient Toyota truck with half the letters scraped off so the tailgate simply reads *Toy*.

Dashing around to the passenger side, I open Bailey's door before scooping Mom up in my arms.

"Whose house is this?" I ask, looking up at the house.

"A friend," Mom says sagely, sounding like a fortune teller looking into her crystal ball, a black cat twining around her ankles.

"Is it someone from book club?" Bailey asks.

I wonder if her shyness extends to meeting new people in smaller groups. I'll have to tack this onto the ever-growing question list. Maybe I need to take a page out of Alec's book and make a spreadsheet, maybe two: *Things I know about Bailey. Things I want to know.*

"Nope."

I don't like the smug note in Mom's voice. Forget a fortune teller. She's like the fortune teller's cat who just ate the cream *and* the canary.

"Cute house," Bailey says as we climb the front steps. "Almost looks like a Swiss chalet."

"Just needs snow on the roof, some flower boxes, and a herd of mountain goats," Mom agrees. Bailey still looks unsure, hanging back a little until I move so we're standing shoulder to shoulder. I wish both of my arms weren't needed to hold Mom so I could take Bailey's hand. She looks like she needs a little dose of solidarity about now.

Though she didn't seem happy at the bridal store, we showed up, derailed her whole plan to try on dresses with her best friends, and now are at some stranger's house for reasons Mom won't say but hopefully have something to do with finding Bailey a dress she doesn't hate.

Mom presses the bell, and what sounds like a miniature dog chorus starts up inside the house. Shrill barks. A lot of them. It gets louder before the door swings open, revealing a woman who, even in bare feet, is taller than me. She's wearing black joggers topped with a silk kimono-style robe, her multicolored braids twirled in what almost looks like a crown on her head. Her height is surprising and maybe a little intimidating, but her smile is wide and welcoming. She also looks familiar, but I'd remember if we'd met.

The dogs, all ankle-biters—some actually nipping at my ankles—spill across the porch, a blur of brown and white and gray and black.

"Maggie," the woman says, reaching out to give Mom's hand a soft squeeze. "I'm so glad you thought to call."

"I'm so glad you had time for us. Zella, this is my son, Eli, and his fiancée, the beautiful—though she'll blush and deny it—Bailey."

Bailey absolutely blushes, the color deepening when her gaze snags on mine. Someone should really name a crayon or a paint color after the exact shade of pink in her cheeks. I'm not a huge pink fan, but I could see painting whole rooms in this color.

"Lovely to meet you, beautiful Bailey." Zella clasps Bailey's hand, the sleeves of her kimono falling down her arms, revealing tattoos of vines curling up her forearms.

For a moment, Bailey seems unable to speak, and the color in her cheeks deepens. Maybe I need a whole swatch of paint colors or a whole box of crayons inspired by Bailey's blushes. From the first pale kiss of pink to the deep sunset red now.

Pink might be my new favorite color.

"Don't be strangers." Zella steps back and opens the door wide. "You! Dogs! Inside!"

The dogs immediately obey, and I almost trip over two of them as I make my way inside. I count at least ten, but with them moving, it's hard to know if that's on the low side, or if I accidentally counted some of them twice.

Inside, the house's high ceiling, walls, and floors are all the same dark wood. Despite that, it's filled with light, the whole back wall composed of windows. The large open room is part living room with two mismatching couches facing each other, a coffee table made of a turquoise door between them.

The other part looks to be a seamstress's studio. Not that I've been in one before. But with a large table covered in swatches of fabric, a few headless dress forms draped in rich purples and greens, and two different sewing machines, it's a safe bet. Off to either side of the main room are doorways, a closed one likely leading to bedrooms and an open one giving a view of an ultra-modern kitchen that's all white and doesn't match this main room at all.

Reminds me of Zella herself, with the flowy robe on top and athletic pants on the bottom.

"Make yourselves at home," Zella says, urging us toward the couches. "I have tea."

There's an intricately carved wooden tray at the center of the table with mugs and a large ceramic teapot, steaming. I settle Mom on a couch next to Zella. The dogs snake around our ankles like cats, and Bailey looks like she's trying to pet them all.

I take a seat next to Bailey on the couch, leaving almost a cushion between us without thinking. But a fiancé wouldn't leave a cushion of space. Heck, I wouldn't leave a small throw pillow between me and a real fiancée. And I absolutely don't want space between Bailey and me. I scoot over until I'm practically in her lap, then take her hand, lacing our fingers together. *That's* what a fiancé would do.

Actually, I'd do more. But maybe not with Mom and Zella in the room. This is a *start*.

"I can't believe I'm meeting you," Bailey says. "I mean, I'm a huge fan. I watched your whole season, and you totally should have won."

"Won what?" I ask, and Zella laughs when Mom tosses a pillow at me. I catch it in my free hand—no way am I letting go of Bailey—and set it next to me.

"Oh, my sweet son," Mom says. "I guess I shouldn't be surprised you don't watch *Sew Strange*."

"Is this related to Dr. Strange?" I ask, knowing full well it probably isn't.

Zella laughs, Mom groans, and Bailey leans close, saying, "*Sew Strange* is a design competition. Zella was the runner-up two seasons ago."

"Sorry, Zella," I say. "I don't follow fashion."

"I don't follow hockey. We'll call it even." She winks.

"You and Bailey both," I grumble. "Though I'm working on Bailey." I give her fingers a squeeze. Because I CAN.

"Hey!" Bailey protests, nudging me with her elbow. "Now that I know you play hockey, I'm happy to support you."

And she has. The last two nights, she was there in the stands beside Mom. Wearing my jersey. Red-faced from shouting every time I glanced up, which was often.

Me? I've never played better.

"You didn't know he played hockey when you met?" Zella leans forward, sliding steaming mugs our way. I'm not a tea kind of guy, but it doesn't smell half-bad. Like cinnamon and some other spices I can't name.

Bailey shakes her head. "No idea. I'm probably the only one in town who didn't know and didn't follow him on TikTok."

"Didn't?" I ask, grinning. "As in, you do now?"

Bailey bites her lip, but it doesn't hide her smile. "Maybe."

The idea of Bailey watching my TikToks makes me ridiculously happy. It also makes me want to do a whole new series. Shirtless, maybe.

"You two are adorable," Zella says, lifting the mug of tea to her lips with a smile. "Now, Bailey—how can I help? What I hear is that you need a wedding dress—and fast." Before Bailey can protest, and it's clear she's about to, Zella holds up a hand. "And before we get started, please know that we're friends here. Friends don't talk about money, and they don't apologize. Understand?"

It's more of a challenge than a question, but Bailey shifts next to me, and I can feel the tension radiating from her, through her hand. I squeeze her fingers and offer her a reassuring smile.

"I—yes. But—" she starts.

"Also no buts," Zella says. "That's rule three. Here's how this will work. You're going to tell me what you want, and I'm going to make you a dress. As for payment, Maggie and I have an arrangement, so it will not even be discussed. Is this clear?"

"Yes, ma'am," Bailey says.

Zella levels her with a teasing glare. "But if you call me ma'am again, I'll rescind this offer and the payment will be walking all my monsters once a day for a month."

"Yes … Zella."

"How's Annie, by the way?" Zella asks, taking a sip of tea.

Mom beams. "You know Annie. Bouncing around, living a loud, philosophically nomadic life."

"Philosophically nomadic?" Bailey asks.

"It means my sister changes jobs, apartments, and

boyfriends every few months. She never lands anywhere long," I explain.

"But she does always land on her feet," Mom adds. "She's coming for the wedding. But, of course, I don't know when."

This is news to me. But then, maybe it wouldn't be if I'd called my sister back. Her flurry of texts and voice messages slowed to a slow drip and then stopped altogether. Which means she's probably gearing up for something.

A surprise trip down for the wedding, sounds like. Just when we least expect her—a very Annie move. I'll be looking for her behind every door. I should probably check under my bed tonight.

"I'll get to meet her?" Bailey asks, sounding excited and also a little like she might throw up.

I squeeze her fingers. "She'll love you. Probably overwhelm you a little too."

She looks unsure, and I'd bet it's because Annie will be one more important person Bailey has to lie to. I get it. This is the same reason I've avoided my sister for almost a week.

"Hey," I say softly, hoping Mom and Zella don't hear over their own conversation, which has carried on without us. "We'll be fine. Okay?"

Bailey nods, still a little hesitantly. I'd love to have a few minutes alone with her, to maybe kiss some confidence back into her.

Or is that just because I want to kiss her again? Either way. Both.

Leaning closer, Bailey lowers her voice. "This all feels like so much. Like, the lie is snowballing. Meeting your sister. And getting a free designer wedding gown?" She shakes her head, and her hair brushes against my arm.

I glide my fingers along the lock of her hair, giving it a little tug as I smile. "Hey. I get it. I do. But it's okay to enjoy it," I tell her, even as I'm telling myself the same thing. "You're making Mom happy. Zella too. Annie will be so thrilled she'll probably steamroll you into getting matching tattoos or something."

"And you?" Bailey asks, looking down at our clasped hands. "Are you happy?"

More than I feel ready to admit. "Yes, Leelee. I'm happy."

An understatement, really.

Zella claps her hands, making us both jump a little. "Now, why don't you tell me what you're looking for in a wedding gown? Actually, let's get hands-on. Come over here and let's talk fabrics."

Still looking like she has half a mind to run away or apologize or call Zella ma'am again, Bailey stands. I don't let go of her right away, playfully tugging on her fingers before releasing them slowly, letting my fingertips drag lightly over her palm. She looks back at me once, and I wink, flashing her a smile. Ducking her head, she follows Zella to the large table by the back windows.

I can't stop watching Bailey. The way her brown hair glints gold in the sun streaming through the windows. The way she leans down to pet the white fluffy dog actively trying to climb her leg, while still not missing what Zella is saying. Every movement feels somehow beautiful or significant, carrying more weight than it deserves.

"I love seeing you like this." Mom stares smugly at me over the rim of her mug.

I stretch out, sliding my legs down until my feet are right next to Mom's. Tapping her foot with mine, I raise my brows. "Seeing me like what?"

"In love," she says.

In love.

Two little words. One big lie.

Isn't it? Love for sure is a stretch, though my feelings for Bailey just keep growing. But knowing this started as just a way to keep me and Mom in the country makes guilt rise like bile in my throat. I hate not being fully honest with Mom. But there is no way she can know about the agreement Bailey and I struck. Or why.

And if things progress like I hope they are—and will—Mom never needs to know. Or maybe years down the road if things work out and the marriage becomes real, we'll tell her and all have a good laugh about how it started.

In an attempt to detract from the guilt, I take a big sip of the tea and immediately burn my tongue. How is Mom drinking this? It's way too hot.

"You're so in love you can't even admit it," Mom says with a laugh. "See—I told you the right woman wouldn't ever think you're *too much*."

She scoffs those last two words, and my throat goes dry. I really want that to be true of Bailey.

My eyes find her across the room. She's laughing, and so is Zella, who has a tape measure out and a pencil between her teeth. As though she feels my gaze, Bailey turns my way. I expect a shy look, but instead, she raises her brows and gives me a goofy smile that has me chuckling.

"You really should call Annie, you know," Mom says.

"I know."

But there are big reasons I haven't called or texted Annie back. Lying to my sister is harder even than lying to my mom. Less because of the guilt and more because I don't know if I can pull it off. My mother is a smart woman. But Annie is devious. Where Mom might not ever suspect I'd do something like this, Annie wouldn't put anything past me. Probably because she's right.

"In lo-o-o-ve," Mom singsongs, just as a small white dog

with a blue bow tie attached to his collar jumps up in her lap. Mom strokes the dog's back as it licks her chin enthusiastically.

Could Mom be right? If I'm not in love, am I heading in that direction?

Is Bailey?

I watch as she says something animatedly to Zella, a flush in her cheeks. "Can you blame me?"

Mom pats my knee. "Not even a little bit."

CHAPTER 17

Bailey

THE DAYS LEADING up to my wedding day—I still can't even think the words *my wedding day* without giggling nervously—are a blur of busy. I'm working full-time. Eli's schedule is intense as they prepare for their two-week trip.

And now it's move-in day.

Which means I'm distracted at the shelter, walking with my head down, my focus halfway on the chart in my hands, halfway on the boxes stacked by the door of my apartment—soon to be stacked in Eli's guest room, which I still haven't seen.

"Oh," I say, jumping back as I collide with a person where I didn't see a person moments ago. My fingers flex and I drop the file, papers fluttering to the floor. "Sorry."

Dr. Evie runs her hands down the front of her white lab coat as though checking for damage, then picks at an invisible piece of nothing, her expression just short of disgusted, like I've infected her with some kind of virus.

I haven't exactly been avoiding her since she agreed to write me a recommendation. Not unless you count ducking into the kennels when I hear her voice outside the door or suddenly deciding to walk the dogs early.

I crouch and gather the papers, stuffing them back in the folder. "I'm sorry."

When I stand, Dr. Evie is smiling. A crocodile smile. "Guess I can understand why you're distracted. What with the wedding and all."

I haven't spoken to her one time about this, which means she must have seen it on social media. Personally, I've been avoiding all things internet ever since Parker warned me it could get overwhelming—or ugly. "Don't get me wrong," Parker said, "social media is my job and it's a beautiful thing. But with the way fans tend to obsess over the players, ignorance might be bliss."

Now, I'm suddenly wondering what things Dr. Evie might have seen or might know that I don't. Does she follow Eli on social media? Read the comments? Drop into his DMs? The idea makes my stomach churn.

"I can't believe you met him right here," she says with a shake of her head.

Clearly, that's not all she can't believe. More likely than not, she can't believe someone like *me*—shy, unassuming, pretty but not hot—snagged someone like Eli. Maybe she thinks if she met him first, things would be different.

"What are the odds?"

"It's been ... a whirlwind," I say, pulling the folder tight to my chest, an ineffective paper shield.

"I'll bet." Her tone is crisp, and I swear, I can almost feel her taking stock of me, tallying up my strengths and weaknesses to arrive at a final score. One she finds wanting.

I wish Beth was working today. She makes an excellent buffer. Or Cyn. Everyone stays out of her way. But today, it's just me and some volunteers.

"I'd better get back to it." I give her a tight smile and start to walk away. I hardly remember where I was going, but now I'm going to head out front to reception. Just to be in another room.

Before I can push through the door, though, Dr. Evie says, "Oh, I meant to tell you …"

And I already know this won't be something I want to hear, even while she's assembling her features into what I think is supposed to be compassion? Hard to tell. Other than to know it's completely insincere.

"I've gone over your performance reviews"—*we have performance reviews?*—"and unfortunately, I'm not going to be able to write that vet school recommendation for you after all."

———

I'm only able to shelve my frustration and fury over Dr. Absolutely Evil because the moment I get home from work, my apartment fills with hockey players. They're too big for the space, too loud, too much for my thoughts to fixate on the reality that while I might now have money to pay for vet school applications, I won't have a recommendation to help me get in.

I shelve those thoughts and worries for another time. Maybe around four o'clock on the last Wednesday of never.

My tongue tangle activated when three guys I barely know showed up in my space to help carry boxes. I'm fairly comfortable around Van now, but barely know the quiet Nathan and the flirtatious Alec. What does it say about me that it only takes four people—Eli, Van, Nathan, and Alec—twenty minutes and the back of one pick-up truck to load all my possessions? Hopefully, it says that I'm not superficial and tied to material things. Rather than being a flashing neon sign indicating the smallness of my life.

The worry over what Eli's teammates think of me stacks up neatly next to all my other anxious thoughts, piling hoarder-high. It's too bad there aren't specialists who can deal with thought stockpiling. People who could parse through the worries and negative thoughts and sweep them out and into a dumpster.

Nervousness bubbles up inside me as we arrive at Eli's house in a little caravan. Maggie welcomes me on the front porch with a hug and a wink. When she leans close, whispering, "Don't worry—the walls aren't thin," I giggle maniacally and almost throw up in the bushes.

My nervous giggles give way to nervous hiccups I can't shake, despite all the internet's suggested remedies. Drinking water upside down—harder than it looks and didn't help. Swallowing three times without taking a new breath—also harder than it should be and also nope. I even popped into the kitchen and tried a spoonful of sugar and immediately sucked on a lemon, leaving my mouth tasting funky ... and still with hiccups.

"What's in this box, B?" Van groans, pauses at the bottom of Eli's stairs, and shuffles the box in his arms, clearly labeled *BOOKS*. "Bowling balls?"

"Yep," I deadpan, then hiccup. "But just my favorite ones."

He frowns. "I was kidding. Considering how many gutter

balls you had the other night, I'm surprised. You really have your own bowling balls?"

Eli steps inside the house, adjusting the boxes in one arm so he can smack Van on the back of the head. "You're blocking the doorway. And don't insult my fiancée's bowling prowess. I'd worry more about your ability to read. The box says *books*."

"What kind of books?" Van asks, looking with interest at the line of tape across the top like it will somehow become a window into the contents.

"I read a little of everything. You're welcome to look if you want," I tell him.

"But first—upstairs," Eli says, nudging Van with a box. "Move."

"*Okay*," Van whines, clomping up the stairs.

"Thank you!" I call. Then knock my hip into the wall when Eli darts in for a sneak-attack cheek-kiss on his way by. I press my hand to the picture frames, rattling from the contact. Right along with my rattling heart.

Hic.

"Have you tried snorting cayenne pepper?" That's Alec, walking in with a box in each arm, plus a hanging bag of the few nice things I own draped over his shoulder.

"I'm … not going to try that," I tell Alec through another hiccup.

Alec shrugs and heads upstairs, followed by Nathan, whose face is a perpetual storm cloud. But he does pause long enough to say, "Snorting cayenne isn't a remedy for hiccups. The best thing is to focus on breathing and relaxing your diaphragm."

"Thanks," I say, watching as he goes, passing Eli on his way back down.

Just the sight of Eli's smile seems to make my hiccups do

double-time. I step back slightly, expecting Eli to pass by me in the small entry hall, but instead, he curls his palms around my shoulders and directs me backwards, his smile edging wider and brighter.

"Where are we going?" I ask, my eyes darting left where Maggie is pulling a tray of cookies out of the oven. She grins at the sight of us, waving an oven mitt as she sets the cookies down.

"I have another idea to cure your hiccups," Eli says, and then he's steering me into the cramped bathroom under the stairs, doing an awkward shuffle as he kicks the door closed behind us.

We're plunged into darkness.

Immediately, my other senses engage. I can hear his breath and my pulse in my ears as my heart does its best jackhammer impression. I'm hyper aware of Eli's hands inching across my shoulders, thumbs dragging over my collarbone and making me suck in a hiccuping breath.

"If you're trying to scare them out of me, it's not working."

His scent invades my space as he leans in, the rough stubble he's been growing out brushing against my cheek. His mouth finds my ear, his words and breath sending a cascade of shivers along my spine. "Who said I'm trying to *scare* them out of you, Leelee?"

Well, okay then. I may not be willing to snort cayenne, but I'm happily willing to try whatever *this* is.

Especially when Eli kisses a path along my jaw and up my cheek, like he's mapping his way in the dark. Unhurried yet somehow urgent, like he's torn between prolonging this moment and rushing to get there.

When a tiny sound escapes me that is definitely not a hiccup, Eli's urgency wins. His mouth finds mine in a kiss that's messy and raw and absolutely perfect. My hands take on a life of their own, just as eager as my mouth is as they grasp Eli's shirt, then move to his biceps, then link around his neck, tugging him closer.

We bump into the wall, then the corner of the sink. I'm going to have a bruise on my hip. I actually hope I do. Maybe I can get a tattoo artist to trace around it, shade in something permanent.

Even as I realize how ridiculous that idea is, I lose all rational thought as Eli's hands grip my waist, palms spread wide like he wants to cover as much surface area as possible, even on top of my shirt. I slide my hands through his hair, loving the silky brush of it against my fingertips. He shifts, going for a different angle.

In the process, he must hit the light switch because suddenly we're blinking in the too-bright bulb over the sink. I take the tiniest peek in the mirror and see mussed hair, cheeks reddened from the scrape of his stubble, and lips that appear swollen. Eli is a mirror of me, only instead of looking simply dazed, he looks delighted. Totally unabashed. Totally unrepentant.

I wonder what it would be like to have Eli's confidence in place of my shyness. Even for five minutes. I'm sure it would be revolutionary.

As it is, I'm just glad I had the wherewithal to say I wanted to keep kissing. Because Eli's lips on mine have a sort of drugging power to erase any of my worries and issues. Even while ratcheting up other things, like need. Want. Hope.

"See?" he says, and I can only blink at him.

I don't see. At least, not whatever he's asking about.

Because all I see is the trouble lying ahead when I'm living in close proximity to the man who will soon legally be my *husband*. The man I'm starting to feel like I wouldn't mind marrying for real. The man who seems to have no qualms or confusion about pulling me into bathrooms for passionate make out sessions.

The one who doesn't share my confusion for the whole situation.

"Cured your hiccups," he says, sounding all too pleased with himself.

Right. Those.

CHAPTER 18

Bailey

With every box stacked in the guest room upstairs and the other guys gone, I puddle limply on the living room floor, nose pressed to the carpet, which smells inexplicably like peppermint.

Not *the* living room floor. *My* living room floor? Technically, this is my new residence too. My house. My room.

But maybe because of the lack of bills I'll pay (no rent money was part of the arrangement) or my name not being on the deed (getting my name on the deed was not part of the arrangement), I'm left feeling very much like a visitor. Not quite an intruder, but very much a guest.

I don't know that this will ever feel like *my* place. When was the last time anywhere felt like a home to me? Definitely not my apartment, which I'm honestly relieved to be out of.

Once Eli pointed out all the safety concerns, I couldn't *not* see them. I think I'd been stuffing down my worry with a bright, forced optimism since my budget left no other choices. Before that, I lived in college dorms, college apartments. And no place that smells consistently of ramen noodles and slightly stale weed can feel like home.

Honestly, I haven't had a *place* since my parents died, I discovered they had a reverse mortgage, and I ended up having to give it back to the bank. Ever since their death, I've been floating, I realize. Not only in terms of not having a home, but in having no real anchors. Maybe that's why I try so hard with Gran. She's all I have.

It's these morbid thoughts my brain is circling when I hear heavy steps and then feel something nudging my thigh. I tilt my head slightly to confirm it's Eli, toeing me with one of his socked feet. They're boring white athletic socks, but it's oddly cute seeing him in them. Probably there's no look that wouldn't be attractive on him. *And now I'll be living down a short hallway from him, seeing them all.*

Maybe the sketchy apartment is less dangerous—for totally different reasons. I return my nose to the carpet, squeezing my eyes firmly closed.

"You awake and alive?" he asks, amusement lacing his voice.

I grunt in response, too exhausted and, frankly, depressed, to use words.

"Aw, Leelee."

My heart constricts at the tenderness in his voice, and it becomes hard to swallow. There's suddenly a warm pressure on my back, a firm hand gently pressing as it glides up the length of my spine. Even without opening my eyes, I know he's crouched beside me. I can feel the heat of him there.

It's nice. More than nice.

"Today was a lot for you, huh?"

"Feel like my bones melted," I mumble, aware that his warm hand on my back is both lulling me to sleep and waking up some feelings I'd rather stay in an extended hibernation. I'm also aware I sound like an idiot.

"You look like your bones melted. Are you hungry?"

"No," I say, as my stomach disagrees with a loud groan.

"Hm. Well, Mrs. No Bones—"

"Melted bones."

"Sorry, Mrs. *Melted* Bones—we've got dinner ready. And don't worry about getting up," Eli adds. "I've got you."

If I weren't already in a state of limp sloth, those three words would have immobilized me. I don't think it's ever solidified as a conscious thought before now, but I'm suddenly very sure that *I've got you* might trump *I love you* in my book. Maybe it's the overuse of the latter, the casual and interchangeable way people use love for their favorite ice cream flavor, their sibling, or their spouse.

Or maybe it's just that, given my last few years' of being alone and adrift, the idea of someone *having* me has been elevated.

Eli carefully rolls me over and scoops me up, cradling me against his chest with care. For someone so big, he's gentle, measured in his movements. I think of him on the ice, how amazing it is to watch him—all the guys, really, but especially the one I'm most fascinated with—move all that bulk so gracefully, with such speed and delicate precision.

He holds me the same way. I want to wrap my arms around his neck, but instead keep them folded against my chest in tight fists. Like maybe if I stay still, I won't be able to fall any harder for this man who keeps surprising me with his kindness.

Impossible.

Maggie's laugh when we reach the kitchen is the thing that finally makes me crack one eye open, then the other. I blink, then blink some more.

Because my gaze is caught on the table, all set for dinner with plates and folded paper towels for napkins and silverware in perfectly straight lines. It's not this or the platters of food at the center of the table making my throat ache and my nose burn. It's the place setting right in front of me. With a small place card that has my name written in Eli's neat print.

"We made a place for you," Maggie says.

They made a place. For me.

It's got to be the exhaustion of the day, the emotional overwhelm of the last two weeks, or the way holding in my real feelings is starting to crack me in half, but Maggie's words and these small, simple gestures are too much.

Especially when I think about what Maggie thinks this is versus what it *actually* is. The guilt eases some when I remember that oh, yeah—there is nothing fake about my feelings.

"Oh," I whisper. "Thank you."

I don't miss the look Maggie and Eli exchange just before he sets me down in my chair, pushes it in, and even hands me the paper towel to put in my lap.

"Thank you," I say, gripping his hand tight, the paper towel between our fingers. His deep blue eyes are so kind it brings back the aching tightness in my throat.

"Of course." Eli squeezes my hand and presses a kiss to the top of my head before dropping into the chair next to mine. He looks comically colossal, his legs stretching almost the length of the small table and his shoulders almost as broad.

Maggie smooths her hand over my hair and leans down to whisper, "You don't need to thank us. It's what family does."

I thought it would be Eli, but Maggie is the one who will be the death of me.

And between the longing for family with a place setting for me at the table and the lies resting between us, I spend the whole first ten minutes of dinner in complete silence, hoping the tears backing up inside me won't flood out of me over the plate of grilled chicken.

———

Considering our situation, staying in the second bedroom upstairs is a perfect solution.

Almost.

As I stare up at the slats of light filtering through the gauzy curtains, it's the *almost* my brain keeps snagging on.

There's a whole bathroom in between Eli and me, so it's not like he's right on the other side of the wall or anything. But knowing he's six steps—yes, I counted—down the hall is … something.

Tantalizing? Tempting? Nerve-racking? Insomnia-inducing?

Then there's the fact that Maggie misses very little. I can't imagine she didn't hear the heavy steps of hockey guys carrying things to the opposite end of the hallway. This little charade is one trip up the steps from being revealed. I know Eli says she doesn't come upstairs much because of her joints, but most days I've seen Maggie, she's been spry and energetic.

Like today—she made three dozen cookies for the guys and then dinner too. If she decides to snoop—and she absolutely has *snoop* written all over her—it will take one peek up here to find us out.

Clearly, with her not-thin walls comment, she wouldn't have a problem with us sharing a room. Before the wedding, we could always say that we're waiting. But there's not any kind of reason why I wouldn't be sharing his bed after. And if Maggie happens to come upstairs once Eli and I are married …

I freeze, hearing a creak in the hallway. The soft pad of a bare foot on hardwood.

My whole body practically vibrates with tension at the thought of Eli standing outside my door, barefoot and shirtless, athletic shorts slung low on his hips like earlier when I ran into him outside the bathroom and almost fell into a trance. The sight of so much bare skin, so many stacked muscles, the light dusting of golden hair on his chest—it was all too much for my already threadbare heart, worn thin by all his kindness.

Still wrecked by something as simple as a place card at the table, being told it's what family does.

I strain, listening for more while trying not to move, not to breathe, not to imagine the blocky muscles of his abs. I've never dated a guy who looked like that, never really thought it was my thing. Shannon once said I was weird when I only shrugged at some shirtless picture of Chris Hemsworth she showed me.

"Doesn't do it for me," I told Shannon at the time, thinking I was oh-so-enlightened, a woman interested more in personality than looks.

Ha! Apparently, it just takes the right guy. Then I can go all-in on abs.

When I hear the bathroom door close with a quiet click,

disappointment surges in a hot wave, followed by an equally hot flood of embarrassment. This isn't what we agreed to: feelings, desire, disappointment. It should be easy enough to keep the lines drawn. He gets to stay here and so does Maggie. I get some relief from the financial burdens I'm half-buried under. Simple. Cut-and-dried.

But the moment I kissed Eli, it moved the goal post. I'm not sure it's even planted firmly in the ground. Feels more like it's moving and shifting with each little gesture, each kiss. I think the goal post was obliterated altogether when Eli pulled me into the bathroom earlier.

Until he reminded me he was only kissing me to help get rid of my hiccups.

If that wasn't just an excuse. And I don't think I'm reading too much into Eli's gazes and glances, his touches and kisses. Maybe I'm not the only one considering how things could be between us.

Or it has more to do with the fact that Eli is the most physically affectionate person I've ever seen.

He passes out hugs like parade candy, and always seems to be touching someone. With his teammates, it's everything from high fives and fist bumps to shoves and hair ruffling. His mom gets a gentler, yet still playful, side of him, whether he's carrying her when her joints are bothering her or simply reaching for her hand. It's ... almost sickeningly sweet.

So, how much meaning can I attach to the way he touches me, kisses me? Even with his tactile propensities, I don't see Eli as a casual hookup kind of guy. He isn't careless. Just ... generous with his affection.

If I am the only one with feelings, and all of Eli's gestures and actions are simply part of his effusive and enthusiastic golden retriever personality, I can't fathom confessing feelings and then living here still with an unrequited husband.

Fake, I remind myself. The only thing real will be the marriage certificate, making this legal. Otherwise, it's *fake, fake, fake.*

I'll probably fall asleep tonight counting fakes instead of counting sheep. If I fall asleep at all.

When there's a light knock on the door, I almost leap out of bed. My heart takes off, torn between the knowledge that it's Eli and the split-second when it was simply reacting with fight or flight.

"Eli?" I whisper.

The door creaks open, and his big form appears, backlit by the hall light. "Expecting someone else?"

I may not be able to see his expression, but I hear the smile in his voice.

"Van mentioned stopping by to borrow a book sometime—"

I don't get to finish my sentence because Eli is suddenly striding into the room, kicking the door closed behind him. The room goes dark, and there's a thump and a grunt. The room is still a maze of boxes, and there is one more grunt and then a kind of growl before the bed dips and Eli is climbing in.

"Scoot over, Leelee."

I'm not going to argue. Not with that husky command. I slide over in the double bed to make room. I almost immediately roll back his way when Eli's weight fully settles on the bed. When I try to sit up and leave space between us, he curls an arm around me and drags me to him, my head landing on his bare chest. His hand rests on my lower back, two fingers touching the bare sliver of skin between my shirt and shorts.

The heat of him, the scent of him—it's intoxicating. My fingers flex, wanting to explore the bare skin I feel under my cheek, to know what those muscles feel like beneath my palms. Under the soft glow of the nightlight I plugged in earlier, Eli's eyes are hooded, his beard looking darker.

"Having trouble sleeping?" he asks.

"I wasn't until someone interrupted me."

"Liar. I could practically hear you worrying." I don't bother protesting this time, and Eli adds, "Want to talk about it? You don't have to. But you can. I'm also fine with just being here for as long as you need, just being quiet."

"Really? Because you haven't stopped talking since you walked in the room."

Eli's hand on my back presses in, giving me a playful shake. "Wow. Nighttime Bailey is feisty. Or is all this big talk how you are once you're really comfortable around someone?"

"Guess you'll find out," I say.

He chuckles then shifts slightly, lifting his other hand until he's stroking my hair. The light scrape of his nails against my scalp, the soft press of his fingertips—it's almost enough to lull me to sleep. But it stirs awake longing too, making my skin hum and my belly flutter.

"Having second thoughts?" he asks.

"No." I'm honestly shocked by the question. But then, maybe that's how he's interpreting my behavior today. How quiet I was at first with his friends and then again at dinner with Maggie. I'm nervous. I have worries. But I'm not rethinking. Just … overthinking. "You?"

He's quiet for too long. Shame burns hot in my throat and my eyes, and I start to wiggle away. His hand on my back presses forward, holding me in place as his fingers stroke my hair with a little more pressure.

"It's harder than I thought," he says. "The lying."

It is. Even harder as my feelings grow. Because I'm not just lying to Maggie and others about what Eli and I really are to each other, but in a way, I'm lying to him about what I want us to be. I'd prefer to steer us away from this conversation before I do something stupid, like make a declaration in the darkness.

"I had an issue at work today," I say, and when he hums encouragingly, I proceed to tell him about Dr. Evil refusing to write my recommendation.

I can feel his anger growing in the way he tenses beneath me. Without allowing myself time to overthink it, I reach up, running my finger over the whiskers on his jaw, remembering the way they left my cheeks pink and raw after kissing in the bathroom. He sighs under my touch but doesn't completely relax.

"Why would she do that?" he asks.

"She isn't a very nice person." Which is being generous. "And I think she might be ... jealous."

"Of what?"

"Of you, dummy. Or, I guess, of *me* for having you."

"Well, that sucks."

I can't help the laugh that bursts out of me. I'm not even sure why—maybe because Eli's answer was so simple. Some people might have blamed themselves unnecessarily, when this is clearly a Dr. Evie problem, not anyone else's. It's also a relief to talk about something—even if it's a stressor—unrelated to the marriage situation.

"It does suck," I say. "Especially considering I need to turn in applications soon."

Two professors from my undergrad program at UNC-Asheville wrote recommendations, but it would be better to have someone from a work environment.

"You know," Eli says, "I think one of the women in

Mom's book club works for a vet hospital. Give me a few days, and I'll see what I can do."

"No one's going to write a recommendation for someone they don't know," I protest.

"Give me a few days," he insists. His hand glides up my back, then down again in soothing strokes.

I want to protest more, to tell Eli he doesn't need to fix all my problems. He's definitely trying—earlier he insisted that when he's out of town, I'll be driving his car while mine gets a tune-up and some new tires. I couldn't argue my way out of that either.

And honestly? After being completely on my own for a few years now, it feels so incredibly nice to have someone taking care of me.

"Now that we've solved all your problems for the night" —Eli ignores my snort at this—"go to sleep."

"If nighttime Bailey is feisty, nighttime Eli is bossy."

I swear, I can feel him holding back whatever it is he wants to say, but after a moment he only huffs out a small laugh. I'm almost asleep when that deep voice rumbles again, his lips brushing my forehead.

"And Leelee? I don't want Van borrowing any of your books. Or coming anywhere near your bedroom."

"Bossy," I murmur.

"You have no idea."

———

I wake when the bed moves again. It takes a moment to shake off sleep and remember Eli climbing in here with me. I smile, rolling to face him, missing his warmth and his hand on my back.

But as I turn and find myself staring at a pair of navy eyes, it takes me a few seconds to make sense of what I'm seeing.

Because it's not Eli next to me in bed.

I bolt upright in bed, clutching the comforter to my chest. The woman —who shares Eli's eyes and his winsome smile —bolts up right next to me.

"Sorry to scare you," she says, grinning and not looking the least bit sorry. "I'm Annie. Nice to meet you."

CHAPTER 19

Eli

"YOU CAN'T JUST climb into a stranger's bed, Annie!"

I press my palms over my eyes, wishing when I opened them again, my sister won't still be sitting cross-legged at the kitchen table, hands circled loosely around a mug of tea.

Like she didn't just drop-kick the idea of boundaries and personal space to the curb by climbing into bed with Bailey.

I don't *really* wish Annie would disappear. It's good to see my sister. I can't remember how long it's been. Long enough for her to bleach her hair lighter, chop it shorter than mine in a pixie cut, and get a few new tattoos, one of which is peeking out of her shirtsleeve as she lifts the mug to her lips. She and Van could have quite the showdown.

"It wasn't a stranger's bed." Annie's placating tone only ratchets up my frustration. "It was *your* bed. In *your* guest room."

262

She lifts a shoulder in an innocent shrug as though to say, *See? Totally normal and not in the least inappropriate or leaping over any personal boundaries.* Bailey, who was locked in the upstairs bathroom when I dragged Annie downstairs by the collar of her t-shirt, might disagree.

Are we too old for the kind of knock-down-drag-out fights we had when I hit middle school and got tired of Annie picking on me? Probably. Still, it's tempting as my sister takes a casual sip of tea.

The only reason I'm not yelling is because Mom hasn't woken up yet. And I'd rather not have Bailey overhear me losing it on my sister. I'm still trying to make a good impression, and pummeling Annie probably wouldn't do me any favors.

"Aren't you glad I'm here, large little brother?"

I drag my hands through my hair, stopping just short of pulling it all out. "Annie—*yes*. So glad. But that doesn't mean—"

"Because," she says, raising her voice to steamroll right over me, "I really wasn't sure, what with all the avoided calls about your engagement you didn't bother to tell me about."

Dropping into a chair, I cross my arms over my chest and heave a sigh. "I should have called to tell you."

"You should have called *beforehand*," Annie says, finally setting down her tea and looking serious. "We could have discussed rings and stuff. And I would have talked you out of doing a cliche hockey proposal and given you some truly sweet *original* ideas. I want to be part of your life, Eli. Even if you defected to the states. You're getting married, dude."

Though her words made my chest tighten, the grin she gives as she delivers that last sentence has me grinning back. "I know, dude." She leans forward and smacks me on the shoulder. Hard. "You're getting married!"

Guilt chooses this moment to remind me it's still here, hanging out like that friend who crashes every party. I choose to ignore it.

"I'm getting married," I repeat, grinning.

"I like her," Annie says, and I shake my head. "What? You can get a good sense about someone watching them sleep."

I cover my face with my hands and groan. "*Annie.*"

She only laughs, pressing on my bare foot under the table with hers. Despite the chasm of differences between my free-spirit sister and me, we share some common traits: specifically a sunny personality soaked in optimism and a serious leaning toward all things tactile. Mom's the same way. We are happy, hands-on sort of folks.

"Why are you sleeping in separate bedrooms, anyway? You know Mom wouldn't care."

I go completely still, my hands still covering my face. Thankfully—I wouldn't want Annie to see whatever expression I'm wearing now. Because I just had a realization I maybe should have had the moment I learned Annie was here.

Staying in separate rooms upstairs worked. When we weren't worried about another person noticing. The only guys I asked to help move were ones who agreed to the vow of violence. I told Mom we were putting some of Bailey's stuff in the guest room so she wouldn't wonder why she heard people moving around up there rather than my room.

Now, my guest room solution has totally blown open with Annie here, all up in our space.

"Oh," she says slyly. "You're waiting for the wedding night? That's so sweet. My little romantic of a brother."

One thing Annie and I don't have in common is her need to overshare. More than once, I've had to run from the room, hands over my ears, when she starts getting into too much detail about things I don't want to know about my sister and the guys she dates.

I drop my hands to my lap. "How long are you staying, by the way?"

"Trying to get rid of me so soon? And changing the subject at the same time?"

"I'm not trying to get rid of you. I just wondered how long I'm going to be sharing a bathroom with *two* women."

Annie cackles at this. "Good thing I helped normalize periods for you years ago. If you're lucky, we'll all sync up in a period trifecta."

"Annie, *please*." I may not freak out at the sight of a tampon, but I also don't want to chitchat about periods. Especially not with the unanswered question of how long Annie will be here. "I need to know how long you're staying so we can talk about logistics. Namely, which couch you're going to sleep on since I'm not moving Bailey out of the guest room for you."

"You're going to relegate me to the couch after not talking to me in forever and not telling me about your engagement yourself? Really?"

"Laying it on just a little thick with the guilt there, Annie."

"Or maybe I'm letting you off easy. Have you ever tried to sleep on a couch?"

"I haven't fit on a couch since I had a growth spurt at sixteen," I say, and Annie presses her foot a little harder into mine under the table, opening her mouth to clap back when Bailey speaks from the doorway.

"I don't mind sharing."

I tilt my head back, looking at Bailey upside down. She's just as adorable this way—hair sleep-messy and a little makeup smudged under her eyes. I like her short sleep shorts just a little too much.

"See?" Annie says. "Your almost-wife and my soon-to-be BFF doesn't mind also being my bedfellow."

"Bailey, you don't have to—"

"It's fine," she says with a little wave of her hand. As she takes the chair next to mine, Bailey drags soft fingers across my shoulders. A little shiver rolls over me, and I capture her hand, holding it on the table with my fingers loosely curved around her wrist where I can feel her pulse. She gives me a soft smile.

Annie holds up three fingers. "I hereby solemnly swear not to snore too loudly and only to steal the covers a little bit. Just enough to prepare you to share a bed with this brute." She nods to me. "Think of it like spring training. You've got to be forewarned and fully ready to deal with an unrepentant sheet-stealer who has a deviated septum. Unless you've gotten that fixed since we last talked and it's one more thing you didn't feel like telling me?"

"I don't snore."

"He snores," Annie says to Bailey, who's biting back a smile, her teeth digging into her lip. "But he wouldn't if he got his nose fixed. Maybe you can convince him."

"You have a deviated septum?" Bailey asks, looking concerned. I like that look on her face. Makes my heart pick up into a hearty jog.

"I've had my nose broken a few times," I tell her. "It's fine."

"Doesn't sound fine when you're sleeping, bro."

"I think he'd actually do it if you asked, Bailey." That's Mom, who is now awake and turning this into a very clear three-against-one battle as she sits down in the last empty chair. "He's a lovesick puppy and would do anything for you."

"Awwww," Annie says, a wicked grin stretching across her mouth. "Wittle Ewi in wuv."

Bailey laughs, and my cheeks flame hot. "Is this how it's gonna be?" I ask, looking at the three women.

And I'm somewhere between terrified and all kinds of sentimental when my mom, my sister, and my fiancée all respond as one: "Yes."

———

I'm dragging the next morning at practice after so little sleep, and so of course, the guys bring the Speed Bump moniker back. Along with a lot of extra hits and comments, which I think have more to do with the fact that I'm refusing to have a stag night, aka a bachelor party.

For one—I'm not in the least interested in the typical things guys do for those events. I've never understood how getting wasted at strip clubs is considered a celebration of marriage. And while Felix offered to plan something more like just a guy hangout night, which I would be okay with, there simply isn't time. As it is, I barely managed to throw together a non-courthouse wedding and am still not entirely sure something won't fall through in the next two days. Mom delegated some tasks to her book club friends, but my teammates are handling the lion's share.

In the locker room after practice, I pull up my checklist and start barking out questions. "Logan—you're picking up the flowers?"

"For the seventh time, yes."

"I'm a go on food," Nathan offers before I can ask. He

doesn't sound happy about it but I also know he'll do it if he says so.

"Camden—drinks?" When he nods, I point my pen at Wyatt, who's only wearing a towel. "You're still good picking up the cake?"

"On it. And I watched both videos on how to correctly transport a wedding cake in a vehicle, so thanks for sending those," he says drily.

I ignore his tone. I'm not taking any chances after I read about how many cakes get damaged in transit.

"Gracie's string quartet is all set for the ceremony," Felix says, cutting me off before I can ask. "And I'll be on duty with Bailey's grandmother."

"Perfect." Bailey warned me that her gran is cantankerous (her word), but I decide not to warn Felix. He can handle one grumpy grandma.

"Why don't we have jobs?" Tucker whines, rubbing a towel over his reddish-brown hair.

"Yeah," Dumbo echoes.

"You do. You'll be valets the day of."

"Sweet," Tucker says, leaning over to high-five Dumbo. "*The Fast and the Furious*, baby."

Trusting them with vehicles might be a mistake, but it was easier to give what I consider the main jobs to the guys who know the reality of the situation. We've got our own group chat and everything.

"More like: protect the Douglas's landscaping so I don't get blamed," Logan says, narrowing his eyes at them.

Parker strong-armed her dad into letting us have the wedding at his fancy house, and since Logan is still not his favorite person, it would probably come back on him if we mess things up. Parker's mom, on the other hand, was on board in an instant. With all the charity functions she hosts, she already has a tent, chairs and tables, and outdoor heaters since it will be cold all week. She even offered to pay for one of the companies she often uses to help set things up, decorate the tent, and serve the food.

"I think she's considering this a trial run for me," Parker whispered, clearly not wanting Logan to hear and feel pressured. She doesn't need to worry. He told me he's already picked out a ring.

Fast? Yes.

But not as fast as me, so maybe this helped move Logan along.

"Then I think we're all good," I say, scanning the sheet one last time.

"Forgetting something?" Van asks, rolling up a towel and whipping it toward my bare chest. "Don't worry; I've got a perfect playlist for the reception."

I *am* worried. But honestly, I didn't trust Van with anything else but music. Do I think there will be a lot of inappropriate songs geared toward getting people freaky on the dance floor? Yes. Is that my biggest concern right now? No.

My biggest concern isn't the wedding at all. It's the reality that I don't know how Bailey really feels about me, and I'm still on the Parker plan of wife-ing, then wooing her. Even as backwards as it seems.

"Also, why didn't you tell me your hot sister's in town?" Van asks. "Don't tell me you're going to be one of those overprotective brothers."

I laugh. "No. Have at it. Annie will chew you up and spit you out. We'll find your remains scattered over three states."

The guys laugh at this, but I'm only half kidding. Annie has needed a protective brother exactly zero times in her life. I won't tell them how, a time or two, she played the overprotective role for *me*. My nickname would probably change from Speed Bump to something worse.

"Cool," Van says with a smile, and I make a mental note to tell Annie how much I'd like to keep my best friend in one piece.

"And I," Alec says with a flourish, "am ready to be your officiant."

I still can't believe Alec is legally ordained in the state of North Carolina, but it did save me a couple hundred bucks and the headache of finding an officiant. I'll worry about why and how he got ordained later.

"Nothing weird, right? You're going to keep it short and simple?"

"What do I look like?" he asks.

"The kind of guy who'd enjoy having a little fun messing with Eli on his wedding day," Felix says. "And I highly suggest you don't."

"So, Eli," Alec says, and if he hoped I wouldn't notice the subject change and his lack of an answer, he's going to be disappointed. "After seeing how organized and focused you can be, I thought maybe I, as official team captain, would ask you to be team secretary. I can get you a little plaque, a pretty pink pen, and—"

"Shut up." I toss the clipboard in my bag.

"Whatever you say, Madame Secretary." Alec salutes me, and I think I've just earned another nickname.

If we had more time before the Appies head out for our long time on the road, I'd do more. As it stands, I feel pretty good about everything I've done. Shannon probably wishes she'd never given me her number because I've blown up her phone on a daily basis to make sure I know everything Bailey would want, from the number of people (not many) to the kind of flowers (calla lilies) to the flavor of icing (chocolate buttercream). I wasn't about to have this be like the proposal, when I surprised her with the exact opposite of what she would have wanted.

Now, I just need all the things to come together.

And what I really don't need is to get called into a meeting with Larry right as I'm about to leave the Summit. Especially when I see Malik slumped in a chair looking apologetic and Grant leaning against the wall looking ticked.

"If it isn't our groom!" Larry says as I walk into the office, his smile as false as his celebratory tone of voice. "When will I be getting my invitation?"

I hadn't planned on giving him one, honestly. I sit down in one of the hard chairs across the desk after giving Malik a quick nod and avoiding Grant's face altogether. "We're having a very small ceremony."

"I don't mind small," Larry says.

Yeah, but *I* do. The last person I want at my wedding is our team owner, whom I like less the more time I spend with him. The only people invited are the team, Mom's book club, and a handful of people Bailey asked me to invite.

I decide that keeping my mouth shut is the best option. I'm choosing to ask forgiveness rather than permission.

"Interesting timing for your wedding," Grant says, peeling himself off the wall to stand next to Larry's chair. "Very … fortuitous and some might say *coincidental* timing."

"Give it a rest," Malik says. "We talked about this—there's nothing wrong with pushing up a timeline. It's fine."

"We did talk about it." Grant glares down at me, looking like an angry vulture with his beady eyes and sharp nose. "And I was very clear that I couldn't stand by while you committed fraud."

Malik groans. "It's not fraud."

"Sure, it's not," Grant says.

Larry waves a dismissive hand toward the team lawyer, who looks about two seconds shy of steam coming out of his ears. "Eli, let me be frank. I'm thrilled with the whole proposal thing. I love it. Fans love it. Everyone loves it." He pauses, leaning forward to steeple his fingers on the desk. "No one will love it if you're lying and marrying someone just to stay in the country. But that's not what you're doing, is it?"

"No."

The single syllable is sharp and solid as a punch. I hope Grant can feel it—right in the solar plexus.

I hope he also feels the truth behind the word. It *is* true. Maybe this all started as something else. It may only still be an arrangement for Bailey. But it's become something else to me.

"You're making a big gamble, son," Grant says, shaking his head as he storms out of the office.

I am. But the biggest gamble, the one I'm most concerned about, isn't immigration. It's whether my marriage has a chance of becoming something real.

CHAPTER 20

Bailey

"OH, NO YOU DON'T." Shannon's fingers curl around my shoulders and shuttle me away from the window.

The one I was trying to climb out of. Or, at least, I was trying the locks. I'm pretty sure it's painted shut. Though this house is way too fancy to paint windows shut. Maybe there's a special key or something? They're rich-people windows. Something I know nothing about.

"Parker's family is loaded," I grumble.

Shannon sits me down on the sofa I was on before I tried to escape. "They sure are, though I'm not sure what that has to do with you trying to climb out a window. Wanna talk about why you're trying to escape, Houdini?"

"It's hot in here. This dress is ... itchy."

The dress Zella made for me is in no way itchy. It's

perfect. From the fit to the fabric to the design. I'm not sure how she gathered anything from our conversation at her house, where I mostly fan-girled and babbled, but somehow, she managed to create something better than I ever could have dreamed up for myself.

Soft and romantic in the skirt and the sleeves—which I requested because of the cold—and fitted in the bodice without being too modest *or* too low-cut. When I walk, I look like I'm floating, the gauzy top layer of the skirt trailing me like romantic wispy smoke. I want to wear it forever. I also want to lock it in a standing safe so nothing can ever hurt it.

So, no—the dress isn't the problem.

What's itchy, I suspect, is the guilt. And the mild panic that's been clawing at me for days.

"Your dress is gorgeous. And probably worth more than your car so I'm not letting you rip it while trying to shimmy out a window." Shannon gives me a look. "For real—let's discuss, and quickly. Considering there's only half an hour before Parker returns and tells us it's time to start."

Parker has been acting as the unofficial wedding planner for the day, making sure everyone has everything they need, watching the schedule, and keeping Eli out of sight. His one request for the wedding was not to see me before I walk down the aisle.

Though I'd really like to talk through this panic with *him* —the only other person who could possibly know what it feels like to enter into a marriage under these circumstances —I couldn't deny Eli this one thing. It's … sweet. Further proving my suspicions that he's a romantic.

But why does he want to be romantic when this isn't about romance? Wouldn't he want to save this for a real wedding? The one that could happen once we split up. Which is … still not a thing we've talked about.

I rub my arms, the soft fabric on my palms soothing me ever so slightly.

Shannon snaps her fingers. "You. The window. Talk."

I open and close my mouth. If there are thoughts, they're not making their way into words. They're a log-jammed in my brain, stacking up high, the pressure I've felt all morning mounting to an almost unbearable level.

Shannon sighs and sits down at my feet, adjusting her emerald-green dress so it won't wrinkle before pulling a handful of Twizzlers out of exactly nowhere. Maybe from her cleavage? She holds one out, and I start to shake my head, then change my mind and snatch two.

"How about I make guesses, and you tell me hot or cold." Shannon doesn't wait for a response before firing off the first question. "Second thoughts?"

Shockingly, no. I still want to marry Eli. It's just … maybe not for the same reasons I agreed to do so.

"Cold," I croak, my voice squeaking like an old screen door.

"Worry about all the legal stuff?"

"Warmer."

Shannon bites off the end of a Twizzler, chewing thoughtfully. "Scared?"

I shrug and fold a whole rope of candy into my mouth. The answer is, of course, *hot*. Pizza oven-hot. Earth's core-hot. Shannon might say Hemsworth-hot, which is the highest heat level on her personal rating scale.

"Ah. There it is."

"Where what is?" Jenny bursts through the door, breathless in a cloud of pink chiffon, returning from a Gran-check.

I decided maybe against better judgment, to have Gran attend the wedding even if she doesn't remember who I am. Eli promised that Felix, the team's goaltender, will be her date-slash-caretaker. His girlfriend, Gracie, is playing cello in the string quartet, so Felix offered to help with Gran. Which is super sweet. According to Eli, Felix had a special relationship with his grandmother and was looking forward to this job.

Even after being warned about some of Gran's escapades.

"Your gran is totally fine. Felix watching her is about the most adorable thing I've ever seen, and now I need to find a guy who loves grandmas." Jenny pauses, touching the pink flower tucked into her braids. "Uh-oh. What'd I miss? I see you brought out the big guns."

She gestures to the Twizzlers, then pulls two out of the fistful Shannon still has. They seem to be multiplying. Is magical cleavage licorice a thing?

"Bailey tried to climb out the window," Shannon reports, sounding every bit like a toddler tattling.

Pushing her glasses up her nose, Jenny blinks owlishly as she takes a seat next to me on the couch. "But your dress!"

"I know, right?" Shannon shakes her head.

"I'm glad everyone's first concern is the dress," I say.

Jenny nibbles on a Twizzler. "Obviously, we're more concerned about you."

"But you don't want to talk," Shannon adds. "This is how we wear you down."

I drop my head in my hands, wishing this were a fainting couch, not just the regular kind in one of many living rooms inside Parker's parents' house. I could use a good faint. Maybe a nap. Or a coma. I could wake up, already be married, and then carry on from there. If Eli and I had a totally normal relationship first, I could see marrying him. Not in a two-week period of time like this. Probably not. Then again, maybe.

I'm shocked at how my original crush has grown and deepened into something else at rapid speed. And it's only getting worse. Every look from Eli, every touch, every kiss makes a swell of emotion balloon in my chest, tightening and expanding until I feel ready to burst.

Every kindness too.

There was last night before he left, when Eli gave me a single, soft kiss while cupping my face so tenderly, I actually felt breakable. Like his care with me meant I'm made of the thinnest blown glass. Every brush of the whiskers in his neatly trimmed beard felt like a distinct electric current, jolting my system with tiny shocks.

Then he said, "See you tomorrow, Leelee," picked up his bags, and left to stay the night with one of the guys.

Not even a little piece of that felt like it was fake.

Then, when I showed up today, I realized that somehow, Eli managed to put together a whole wedding in the span of a week. All because I didn't like the idea of getting married in a courthouse. Shannon wasted no time telling me how he's been hounding her for information—what flowers I like, what I'd like to eat for the reception, the kind of cake I want, what music I like. It's all about me.

When I then peeked inside the tent and saw big flower arrangements and candles and gauzy fabric stretched across the top of the tent, transforming it into a beautiful kind of dream, black dots filled my vision and I had to grab onto a chair so as not to topple over.

It's all too much. Too real. Too perfect.

And Eli did all this for *me*.

The same knot that's been in my throat tightens until I wonder how it's possible for me to swallow. Or breathe.

"You okay, B?" Jenny slides an arm around my shoulders,

being careful of the dress and my hair, which she painstakingly curled into soft waves earlier.

"She looks like she's about five seconds away from passing out," Shannon says. "Maybe you should put your head between your knees? Never mind—you might get makeup on the dress."

"I could put a pillow there to keep the makeup from—"

"Will you both shut up about the dress?"

These words come out of me in a wheezy whispered hiss. I sound like some kind of harpy, straight from the pages of a fantasy novel and ready to drop some curses.

Jenny gives my shoulder a squeeze. "What can we do? Talk to us, Bailey. Tell us how we can help."

"Or tell us how you're feeling," Shannon says. "Jenny and I will come up with a plan. Even if that's running away. Just … not through a window."

"Why didn't y'all try to talk me out of this?" I ask, looking between them. It's not an answer to either of their questions. But it's where I need to start. "When I first told you I was going to marry Eli essentially for money, neither of you protested. Not really."

The night I asked them to come over, I drank a very full glass of wine out of a coffee mug before blurting out the way Eli's offhanded joke about marriage (and my subsequent choking) turned into something I seriously considered … and then agreed to while sleep- (and a little Eli-) drunk. Rather than freak out—okay, Jenny did do this high-pitched scream thing that made my ears ring—my two besties asked a few questions and then calmly told me I should go for it.

Almost totally in sync too, which was mildly creepy.

They gave none of the arguments I'd expected, none of the ones I've been arguing with myself. They didn't laugh.

They didn't tell me I was selfish or ridiculous for even thinking about an arrangement like this.

Shannon and Jenny give me too much time to worry while they exchange a glance as though trying to silently make sure their stories line up.

I expect Shannon to be their spokesperson, but it's Jenny who says, "We like Eli. And *you* like Eli. Maybe we just thought ..."

I swallow. "You thought what?"

Jenny doesn't answer, just presses her lips together in a forced smile that looks more like she's trying to hold in a really big burp. Shannon presses up on her knees, taking both my hands in hers. The pleading look she gives could rival the cutest begging dogs ever. It would beat a begging baby goat, even.

"We thought maybe ... it would just sort of work itself out. Like, over time it would become less of an arranged marriage and more of a real one. You know, how they do."

"How *they do?*" I'm back to the harpy's hiss. "I don't know that people *really* have this kind of thing in real life. And if they did, it wouldn't just—*poof!*—become a real marriage."

"Not *poof*," Jenny says. "But over time. Like a friendship becoming more."

I groan, pressing my hands over my eyes. But lightly, because I'm not about to mess up the makeup Shannon took forever to do. I barely sat still the first time. If she comes at me again with a mascara wand, I might punch her.

I'm on the cusp of arguing, but I can't. Because I've had the same thought. More like ... a hope. That maybe over time, Eli might start to see me as something more. More like the way I see him. He certainly *acts* like I'm something special, whether that's in the way he looks at me, the tenderness in his voice when he calls me Leelee, or the way he steps in to do things like help me find a new job at a veterinarian's office.

Turns out, one of Maggie's book club friends didn't just work at a vet, her husband *is* a vet. And he offered me a full-time position, saying he had no doubts he could write a recommendation once I had a few weeks under my belt. This is my dream, and it means I don't have to work with Dr. Evil anymore.

So, yeah. Eli has gone above and beyond for me in big and small ways. And he definitely doesn't seem to mind kissing me.

But then, I've done way too much unhealthy late-night googling related to hockey player dating habits and spent far too long over-analyzing any photos of Eli ever with another woman on his social media. There's also the unhelpful memory of my birthday, finding Eli in the bar with a woman attached to either side like a pair of hot leeches. A hard mental image to uproot, that's for sure.

My conclusion: kissing may or may not mean much to Eli. The kind things he does may or may not be just part of his personality

Right now ... I'm not brave enough to ask him directly. Even if I'm allowing a warm hope to unfurl and bloom inside me.

If Eli does have or develops feelings for me, this marriage thing could be a sort of head start. A putting of the cart before the horse. Cutting the line to get into the club. The *marriage* club.

I peek through my fingers, looking between them and ask, "You know I like him. A lot. And you think I should still marry him and then hope it becomes more—like a real marriage with real feelings?"

"That's exactly what we think," Jenny says. She pats the top of my head, and I half-expect her to follow up by offering me a dog treat.

Close—she grabs one of Shannon's Twizzlers and hands it to me.

"Worst case scenario: you're shacking up in a cute little house with the kind of guy who would do all this for you, plus his adorable mom, and you're having vet school paid for. Everybody wins."

Unless I lose my heart. Which I may have already done.

"It's almost time," Shannon says, and suddenly my throat is tightening up again. "Let's get you out there. And when you say your vows, say them for real. Then blow out your candles and make a wish that Eli's doing the same thing."

I don't bother reminding Shannon that wedding cakes don't have candles for wish-making.

———

"Everything is perfect," Parker gushes.

She's wearing a huge smile, hugging a clipboard to her chest, and wearing an earpiece I'm pretty sure she doesn't need for a wedding this small. To Parker, wedding planning is a serious business. Even one I know she knows is more about visas and avoiding student debt and less about love. We're standing just inside the back door of her parents' house—one of the *many* back doors, I should say—and everyone else is in the tent. Ready. Waiting.

While I'm rethinking the whole escape-out-the-window plan and debating about whether I'm going to vomit halfway down the aisle.

"You look gorgeous," Parker says. "Eli is going to lose it. I predict tears."

"Oh, I highly doubt—" I start to argue, but Parker boops me on the nose, a move that surprises me into silence.

"*Trust me*," she says through clenched teeth, in the kind of tone a kidnapper might use to threaten their victim into compliance.

It works. Or, at least, I'm prepared to walk through the door. But before we can, a figure in a suit jogs out of the tent, up the back steps, and inside. It's Van. Gone is his usual smirk. His face is a study in fierce intensity, instantly making me want to panic.

"Is Eli okay? Did he …"

I can't quite make myself form the words, *Did he change his mind?* But they're right there on the tip of my tongue.

Van's brows dip and he shakes his head. "Everything's fine. Except the big dummy failed to mention you didn't have anyone to walk you down the aisle."

"Oh. I was just planning to walk myself."

Shannon and Jenny both offered, but I decided in addition to not having a traditional wedding party, I didn't need to have an escort. After all, I'm giving myself away.

Van runs a big hand through his hair, glancing away with a quick nod. "Right. Sure. Good. You can do whatever. I just didn't want you to not have the choice of someone standing beside you."

He starts to turn away, but I grab his arm and link mine through it, ignoring the burning in my eyes and nose and the tightness in my throat. Parker tries to hide a tiny sniffle.

"I'd love to have you walk me down the aisle, Van."

"Yeah?" he asks, his dark eyes regaining a little of their usual swagger.

I nod, and Parker steps in front of us both, opening the

door and grinning, her eyes bright with unshed tears. "It's time."

As Van and I step through the door, he slows the pace and looks down, catching my eye. "You good, B?"

Something about him using the nickname my friends call me makes my chest cinch tight. "I think so? Ask me tomorrow."

CHAPTER 21

Eli

I GLANCE around the big tent in Parker's backyard and realize I wouldn't change a thing. Except maybe one: groomsmen.

Because as I stand up here alone, waiting for Bailey to appear, I desperately need someone beside me. Felix telling me it's going to be fine or Van whispering insults under his breath—either one. Both.

Or someone to catch me if I happen to pass out, which feels at this moment like a very real possibility.

"For a fake wedding, you sure do seem to have a lot of feelings, bro."

Oh, right. I *do* have someone standing up here with me. Alec.

Perhaps the last person I might want, who just chose this moment to remind me of the thing I want to forget—that

284

this isn't a typical wedding. Without turning away from the back of the tent, where Van just jogged off for what's probably the worst timed bathroom break I can imagine, I give Alec a healthy dose of side eye. Only to see him smirking back.

I speak quietly, moving my lips as little as possible. "You know, as someone officiating a fraudulent wedding, I'm pretty sure you'd be on the hook for some hefty fines too, *bro.*"

I'm making this up. Though it seems legit.

Alec leans in closer, putting a hand on my back as he says, "But that's the thing, Hop. Nothing about this seems fraudulent to me. Especially not the lovesick look in your eyes." He pauses just as there's movement at the back of the tent, unseen people outside pulling apart the flaps. "And not the look in hers either."

His voice fades as the small group of guests gets to their feet, turning. I suck in a breath.

Bailey steps into the tent, clutching Van's arm like she's in as much need of support as I feel. Her eyes are only on mine, but I can't hold her gaze. I need to look *everywhere.*

Beautiful, beautiful Bailey. How did I ever think she was just pretty? Not even that, but the kind of pretty I didn't react to but noticed like I might appreciate a waterfall or a nice sunset.

Now, her beauty hits me like a solid punch. It knocks the breath clean out of me, just as sure as if someone really did hit me right in the diaphragm. Long brown hair in waves cascading over her shoulders, a dress that floats around her like she's the princess in a fantasy movie—almost magical. If a team of birds suddenly appeared, carrying the train of Bailey's dress in their beaks, I wouldn't bat an eye.

Seeing Van escorting Bailey is not what I expected when

he ran from the tent a few minutes ago. The expression he's wearing is also surprising. At most, he's been tolerant of this idea and *only* because it means I get to stay. He's bitten his tongue about the whole marriage aspect, but I happen to know how he feels about monogamy and long-term commitment—not great.

But right now, his smile is a little wobbly at the edges, and though he's trying hard not to show it, the set of his jaw and the way he can't stop blinking tells me he's fighting off some pretty big emotions.

Ones which echo in my chest as my heart kicks up. Today is about Bailey and me. But the teammates in my close circle have never felt as much like brothers as they have this week when they were all busting their butts to help me throw this wedding together. Van walking Bailey down the aisle—something I should have thought about but didn't—means the world.

I give him a quick nod, my jaw clenching, then I focus my attention back on Bailey.

As she moves closer, her smile gets bigger. Her grip on Van's arm loosens, and her pace picks up, like she can't wait to get to me. I have half a mind to jog down the aisle and meet her in the middle.

We're doing a lot of other things differently—why not have the ceremony right in the middle of the room?

I might have done it too, had my feet not cemented themselves to the floor.

Alec's hand never left my back, and now, he slides it around to my shoulder, giving me a little shake. "Breathe, Hop," he says with a little huff of laughter. "Breathe."

I draw in a shaky breath. I don't think I've been breathing since Bailey stepped inside the tent. Not good if I want to avoid passing out. I focus on slow, steady breaths and not locking my knees as Bailey nears. There's the slightest tremor in my fingertips, and I close my hands into fists, needing the bite of my fingernails in my palms to ground me. I want to be completely present in this moment, and the tiny bite of pain helps me focus.

"Hi," Bailey whispers as she and Van stop.

I'm grinning, but I swear, I just felt the slide of a tear on my cheek. "Hi," I murmur back. "You look beautiful, Leelee. Perfect. Radiant. Am—"

"We got the point, Mr. Thesaurus," Alec mutters. Then, louder, in his captain voice, he says, "Welcome! Close friends, family, teammates, and book club."

This earns him laughs and a few wolf whistles I'm sure come straight from the book club ladies, but my eyes don't leave Bailey's face.

Not until Alec goes off-script.

"Who gives this woman to be married to this man?" he asks.

I do turn away from Bailey then, trying not to show the full extent of my frustration. I made it clear to Alec we weren't doing the giving-away part of the ceremony. Bailey and I planned to leave it off, considering her father isn't here. When we talked about it, I saw the sad look in her eyes, the one she tried to hide. I don't want her to have to think about too many sad memories today. More than she already is. I know there's no way she hasn't thought about her parents missing this day. I barely remember my dad, and even I felt the tiniest twinge of something when I thought about him not being here.

In addition to all that, Van doesn't get the right to give Bailey away just because he happened to escort her down the aisle.

But Alec just winks at me as Van clears his throat. And

then there's a chorus of male voices joining Van as they say as one, "We do."

It takes effort to swallow past the lump in my throat. The whole row of my closest teammates spoke up. Every single one.

And as I'm processing this, blinking back embarrassing tears, Van leans close and presses a quick kiss to Bailey's cheek, making the whole emotional thing worse.

"You're just what he needs," Van says quietly to Bailey. Then loud enough for the whole tent to hear, he adds, "If this guy gives you any trouble at all, let us know. We'll make him suffer."

Bailey giggles at this, and a blush rises in her cheeks, painting them a perfect pink as Van, who has recovered from his overly emotional moment earlier, hams up the act of placing Bailey's hand in mine before giving me a half-hug and then murmuring something about *prima nocta* in my ear that has me laughing and shoving him back toward the rows of seats.

The moment Bailey and I turn to each other and I clasp both of her small hands in mine, something shifts and settles inside me. A sense of place I've never had before, a peaceful confidence about what we're doing here.

It's more than what we said it would be. This isn't what we agreed to between us. I know I'm not imagining the emotion in her face, the earnestness in her trembling voice as she recites her vows, the piercing way she holds my gaze. The way she squeezes my fingers as she slides the wedding band in place on my finger.

And when the blur of the quick ceremony ends with Alec telling me to kiss the bride as the whole tent erupts in cheers, Bailey's lips on mine feel like forever, not fraud.

"You don't have to carry me," Bailey murmurs into my neck while snuggling even closer to my chest and tightening her arms around me. I think at this point, if I let her go, she might stay attached. A Bailey barnacle.

"Of course I do," I tell her, tightening my hold with one arm as I fumble with the hotel key. "It's tradition."

"But this isn't a threshold," she says through a yawn. "It's a hotel room."

"A threshold is a threshold. And if I need to carry you into our house tomorrow, I will."

She giggles, her breath ghosting over my skin and creating a cascade of goosebumps. I drop the key card.

"Hang on, Leelee." I crouch, keeping her cradled to my chest as I fumble for the card, finally coming up with it.

"Just like when we were dancing," she says sleepily, and I notice her eyes are closed now.

I dipped her more than once tonight when we were dancing to the surprisingly appropriate playlist Van made. Every time I tilted Bailey back, her cheeks flushed and her grin grew. I wanted to keep that look on her face all night, and I did—up until she got sleepy after hours of dancing and a glass of champagne that hit her hard. It was right after Van's dance-off with— shocker of the night—Wyatt. Bailey and I held hands and ran to the limo through two lines of our guests, all waving sparklers. I'm pretty sure Bailey's gran tried to burn me with one.

"That's right," I say. "You're quite the tiny dancer."

"I'm only tiny because you're a giant," she argues, poking me in the chest.

"Sure," I say agreeably, finally getting the card positioned just right to see the green light flash on the door of the suite.

Bailey gives a soft sigh as I walk us through the door, her weight settling more fully against me.

Is she asleep?

I tilt my head, peeking down at the dark lashes resting against her cheeks, still wearing the flush they've held all night. Totally asleep. And it's no wonder.

The emotional exhaustion of the day is starting to catch up to me. I feel it seeping outward from my bones. We did a big thing today. Maybe not traditional in the typical sense of the word, today carried the same weight as any other wedding. Maybe more, considering the underlying duplicity.

Or … lack of duplicity?

Today didn't feel like an act. It didn't feel like an arrangement. I know on my part, it was all sincere. But it seemed to be the same for Bailey. From the way she looked at me during our vows to the firm press of her mouth and the smile she wore when Alec announced us as Mr. and Mrs. Eli Hopkins.

And then there were all the other emotions, ones tied to my mom and sister, who definitely believed it all. Annie, who never cries, even got teary when she hugged Bailey after the ceremony. I think she also squeezed all the oxygen out of Bailey's lungs and possibly made some kind of threat—probably to come after me if I hurt Bailey, not the other way around.

I've never seen Mom so happy or smile so big. Which made the guilt twine itself around the happiness into a heavy rope looped tight around my chest.

Because what happens if Mom or Annie find out the truth? Or what if instead of this becoming more, it ends?

I hope they never know, just like I hope Parker's idea to woo my wife will result in something real growing from the seeds of what started as practical necessity mixed with a little insanity. Today made me hopeful. If I wasn't actively thinking about the way this began, I got completely lost in the genuine emotion of it all.

Despite Parker's recommendation to wait, I wanted to talk to Bailey about it tonight. But hearing the conviction in Bailey's voice when she said her vows, the way her eyes never left mine, I don't feel like I need to wait. The whole night felt like a big green light.

Only now as I'm seeing Bailey's physical and emotional exhaustion, I know this wouldn't be the right time. I want her fully awake and fully cognizant when we talk about our real future.

I also don't want to mess with the perfection of today.

As I cross the suite's living area, I toe off my shoes, leaving them by the couch, which will likely be my uncomfortable bed for the night. One of the guys booked this room for us, and while I would have picked a suite with two rooms, Wyatt chose the honeymoon suite.

To be funny? Or maybe because he's also rooting for us?

Either way, I'm not going to share a bed with Bailey all night without her express, coherent consent. I won't trust any decisions she makes in this sleep-addled, exhausted state. And I won't have her waking tomorrow with regrets.

It's not easy to peel back the comforter and sheets while balancing Bailey against my chest, but I manage. Only ... I hesitate once I've got the bed ready. Would she want to sleep in this dress? *Can* she sleep in this dress?

I know nothing about fashion, but I am aware that a custom wedding gown from a designer like Zella wouldn't be cheap. And it's a gorgeous dress. Likely not one Bailey wants to get wrinkled and possibly ruined in sleep. But if I'm not willing to share a bed without consent, I'm not exactly going to take off her dress. The thought of it makes heat flood my neck and cheeks. I suddenly can't wait to get out of this suit.

I stand there, cradling Bailey as I debate. Put her to bed in this dress, or wake her? I finally lean down, brushing my lips across her temples.

"Bailey, sweetheart?"

"Mmm?"

"Do you want to sleep in your dress, or do you want to change first?" Annie dropped our bags off in the suite earlier today, her one contribution to the wedding plans. And honestly, I'm shocked she managed even that. But my duffle is in the corner, next to a purple rolling suitcase that must be Bailey's.

Way to come through, Annie.

"Change," Bailey says with another yawn, her eyes still closed. "Is my bag here?"

"Yeah. Hang on." Careful not to bunch the dress up under her, I rest Bailey on top of the sheets. She sighs and tucks her head against the pillow, her hair fanning out across it.

I stand there, staring for a moment, memorizing the way she looks in the soft white dress against white sheets, eyelids fluttering as though she's already fallen into a dream. Maybe she has. But then her lids crack open slightly and she gives me the smallest smile.

"What?" she asks.

I grin and look away, rubbing the back of my neck. "Nothing. Just … nothing."

It would be too much right now to tell her how beautiful she looks, wouldn't it? I told her on no less than a dozen occasions tonight. I meant it every time. And every time, she blushed.

"You look good in a suit," Bailey says, her eyelids fluttering closed again. "And in a jersey. And in those shorts you sleep in. Even a muumuu! I'm pretty sure you'd look good in anything. It's not fair."

Chuckling, I cross the room and unzip her bag. "Not *anything*. I couldn't pull off scrubs like you do."

Bailey snorts. "Scrubs are the least sexy things ever."

"You make them look good, Bailey."

My voice is gruffer than I intend, but maybe that's because I'm imagining her lying in that bed in her normal work attire, hair tied up in a ponytail. I like this idea a *lot*.

Maybe scrubs *aren't* inherently sexy, but I wasn't lying when I said she makes them look good. I like Bailey in everything I've seen. I'm sure she'll look great in whatever pajamas she's packed.

Only … as I unzip her bag, I realize I never should have trusted Annie. Not with a single, simple task.

Bailey's whole suitcase is full of nothing but lingerie.

Not the kind that could double as a nightgown either. The kind I think can only be purchased at some kind of adult gag store. It's all lace and strings and mesh. I'm not even sure there's enough fabric in here to make a single outfit if someone quilted them together.

I drop my head to my chest and groan.

"What's wrong?"

When I glance over, Bailey is leaning up on an elbow. Still looking sleepy, but more awake than she's been since she first conked out in the car on the way here.

"We might have a problem," I tell her, zipping the suitcase back up. I can't keep looking at all this lace. I might get … ideas.

"What kind of problem?"

I stand, fisting my hands on my hips and swallowing hard. "Annie took it upon herself to repack your bags. Probably mine too." I don't even want to open mine, now that I've thought about it.

Bailey sits up fully. "Repacked them *how?*"

"With, um, lingerie."

"Oh. *Oh.*" Bailey giggles. "This doesn't surprise me, somehow."

"I'm sorry."

"Don't be. I love Annie. And I appreciate her … enthusiasm? I'm not sure if that's the right word."

"The right word is probably intrusive. Nosy. Obnoxious. Difficult."

"Funny," Bailey corrects, then lifts a hand to her mouth as she yawns again. "But what do we do? I can't sleep in this. Is there anything I can wear?"

I'm not sure what expression is on my face, but Bailey laughs. "Okay, guess that's a no."

"I've got an idea," I say, already shrugging off my suit jacket. I drape it over the back of a chair then start unbuttoning my shirt. I freeze on the second button when I realize Bailey is staring at me, unblinking. "What?"

She simply shakes her head.

I make quick work of the buttons, then pull the shirt off, holding it out to Bailey. "Here. It may not be the most comfortable thing to sleep in, what with the buttons and all. But it's better than wrinkling your dress."

Bailey takes the shirt, and almost as though it's an involuntary action, lifts it to her nose. I watch as her lids lower with her deep inhale. "Smells like you," she murmurs. "This will be perfect. What about you?"

"I didn't check my bag. I can only imagine. But at least I've got this t-shirt and boxers."

Bailey clears her throat and gets to her feet unsteadily, grabbing the nightstand for support. "I'll go change. You look in your bag. I can't wait to hear what she packed for you." With a smile, she walks to the bathroom, still holding my shirt up to her nose.

I expect something like a whole bag full of condoms and am surprised when I open it to see fabric. Not what I packed, though.

Instead, Annie removed everything I put in the bag earlier, replacing my clothes with what looks like a bunch of towels and one single wearable item: the muumuu I wore on Bailey's birthday. I'm sure she had no idea the significance of this, but it's oddly fitting. Especially since Bailey just mentioned it.

Smiling, I remove my t-shirt and slip the muumuu over my head while Bailey's in the bathroom, then shuck my pants and drape them over my coat on the back of the chair. I've just finished when I hear Bailey call me from the bathroom.

I place a palm flat on the closed door. "Are you okay?"

"I … I think I need help." Bailey opens the door a crack, peeking at me with one brown eye, then laughing when she sees what I'm wearing. "That's what Annie packed for you?"

"She's got some sense of humor," I say drily. "Now, what kind of help do you need?"

Bailey opens the door a little wider. "This gown has a million tiny buttons," she whispers, her cheeks flaming. "Jenny helped me get dressed this morning, and I didn't think about getting them undone."

"No problem," I tell her, twirling my finger. "Turn around."

But when she does, pulling her hair out of the way, I see the problem. Not her problem, though I do see how impossible it would be for Bailey to undo the delicate buttons herself. No—the problem I'm aware of is *mine*.

Because I'm the one who has to undo them.

"Eli?" Bailey tilts her head, looking up at me over one shoulder. "You okay?"

There's a tickle in my throat, but swallowing doesn't make it better. I cough. "Yep."

I'm torn between wanting to curse and wanting to thank Zella for putting so many buttons on the dress. They start just between Bailey's shoulder blades and drop down just below her waist. So small my big fingers struggle to work them. Especially with the way my mind is warring with itself, making it hard to focus. Under the loose fabric of the muumuu, my lower back starts to sweat.

Bailey angles her head, peeking at me over her shoulder. "You okay there, hockey player? I can't imagine a few buttons are hard for a guy who can balance on tiny blades while sending a little puck into a net with a stick."

"You wouldn't think," I mutter.

By the fifth button, the top of the dress falls open slightly, revealing what looks to be the top of some kind of undergarment. Not a bra. A corset, maybe? Or some fancy thing women wear under fancy dresses?

I squeeze my eyes closed and try to move my fingers faster, which only makes me clumsier. And slower. I honestly might do a better job wearing my game-day gloves.

Soon, it's not just my lower back that's sweating but my forehead and neck. Every inch of me is hot and electric. I hope Bailey can't feel the heat when my fingers brush over her skin, dragging over her lower back as I move down, down, down below the bottom hem of her undergarment. Bailey's skin is warm and smooth, and seeing this little bit of it makes me want more.

I bite back a groan.

Two more buttons, and I find something that stops me. I trace around the raised, red mark.

"What?" she asks.

"Leelee, have you been playing with cats again?"

She groans, angling her body as she tries to look. She'd have to be a contortionist to see it. I gently turn her back around.

"I don't think he was playing," Bailey says. "More like trying to use my back as a springboard. Think it will leave a scar?"

"I don't think so. But you should let me put something on it when we go back home. Mom has some antibiotic cream."

"I didn't even know it was there. I guess this is what we do now, huh? Watch each other's backs?"

I grin. "That and argue about pizza toppings. A wise woman told me that's what marriage is about."

As I go back to the buttons, I see Bailey spinning the wedding band I slid on her finger earlier. She requested something simple, so it's a plain platinum band. Except for one thing.

"Did you happen to check the inscription?" I ask.

"You added an inscription?" Bailey slips the ring off and turns the ring until she can read it, laughing when she does. "*Awkward together*," she reads. "From our first date. Eli—I love it."

"Feel like maybe it will be something of a theme. Says the guy wearing a muumuu while unbuttoning your dress."

I expect another laugh, but maybe it's the mention of undoing Bailey's dress that has us both falling silent again. A thick tension hangs in the air like a curtain, only growing more obvious in the quiet. The only sounds are our breaths—both of us a little unsteady—and the sound of my fingers fumbling with the buttons.

I slow as I move closer to her waist, closer to the end. Both relieved I'm almost done and wishing Zella had put buttons down the whole back, down to the floor. When I undo a button just above Bailey's hips, my heart thrumming in my chest, the whole dress starts to slip down, sliding right off her shoulders.

"Oh," Bailey says on a breathy exhale, clutching the top. She barely keeps it from falling into a pool of soft white fabric around her feet. "I guess that's all the help I need. Thanks, Eli."

"No problem." I swallow with difficulty and take a step back, wiping my palms on the muumuu.

Bailey turns to face me, her fingers tight on the top of the dress. For a long moment, we stand perfectly still, as though each of us is waiting for the other to make a move or speak. The air shimmers with a pulse of electricity, and I wouldn't be shocked to see light dancing in the air.

I want to kiss her. I want to *more* than kiss her.

And with the way Bailey's toffee eyes have darkened to liquid chocolate and her teeth are worrying her lip, I think she wants that too.

I hear a faint whisper in my mind, Parker's voice saying *patience … you don't want to overwhelm her …*

Most guys wouldn't think about patience. They wouldn't overthink this. Or think at all. They wouldn't care about talking first, about being sure we're on the same page.

They'd be inside the bathroom, shucking off Bailey's dress and this stupid muumuu, words lost in favor of a tangle of lips and tongues and maybe even teeth. Imagining it has blood rushing through my body, like a clanging alarm bell.

But there's more riding on this. And what I want is more. Something long and lasting. Not a quick decision made in the heat of a moment. The risk is higher now, the cost potentially greater. If I want this to be *real*, I need to work for it. To exercise the utmost restraint until it's safe to unleash it. Until I'm sure *she's* sure.

Otherwise ... I'd be sharing a house with my own personal heartbreak right down the hall.

As much as I want to toss thought and consequence and *future Eli's* potential heartbreak to the side, I decide to choose the patient path. The safe one. The one most likely to transform the label of wife, which Bailey now wears, into more than a title. More than words on a paper. I am after something lasting, not fleeting.

Which means I need to step back. For now.

But, just as she did at the rink during my mess of a proposal, Bailey is the one to take charge. Stepping forward and still holding her dress up with one hand, she hooks the other behind my head and pulls my mouth to hers.

I slide my hands around her waist, tugging her closer. *Needing* her closer.

Bailey kisses me like she's been dying to do so for hours —or days. Like our kiss at the ceremony—quick, sweet, chaste—was only a tease, igniting this level of consuming hunger.

Or maybe that's just how it was for me, and I find myself kissing her back with the same level of desperation.

My fingers find the tiny sliver of skin on Bailey's lower back between where the dress gapes open and whatever she has on underneath. When I trace my finger along the borders of the area, trailing along the hems and the fabric lines, Bailey gasps into my mouth. I swallow the sound and move my fingers slower, softer, needing her to make that sound again.

She does, and a low sound comes from the back of my throat.

This is something more than just kissing. More than an agreement or arrangement or an aligning of what I need—a visa—with what Bailey needs—money for vet school. It's more than I've ever felt kissing any woman, and though I still can hear Parker on a loop in my head saying not to overwhelm, to be patient, though I *know* Bailey and I are barely getting to know each other even if we're wearing each other's rings, it's hard to hold back.

I want to give her everything.

Bailey is the one to pull back, dropping a kiss to my chin before letting her hand drop, grinning at me as she steps back. "I'm going to finish changing now," she says.

"Probably a good idea." Though I have plenty of *other* ideas.

I trail my fingers down Bailey's cheek to her jaw. A whisper touch. A future promise. She shivers in response, gently swaying forward just as I step back and drop my hand.

"You good?" I ask in a voice rough and cracked and more than a little tortured.

Bailey's nod is quick, her smile knowing, her pupils dilated. "I—I'm *something*."

Me too.

I turn then, needing relief from the pinch in my chest, the pull toward this woman who has so quickly worked her way right into the center of me with her kindness and sweetness and the quirkiness that makes Bailey *Bailey*.

"Hey, hockey player," she says, and I pause, back still turned. In the mirror above the dresser, I can see just a sliver of the bathroom door, Bailey's hand with my ring on her finger. "Thanks for helping with my dress."

"Just … let me know if you need any more help."

Bailey closes the door on her laughter, and I smile all the way to the couch. Where I fully intend to sleep unless invited to the bed. Which can just be for sleeping, if that's what Bailey wants.

I yawn, letting my head fall back as I close my eyes.

Tomorrow, I leave for two weeks. And while I'd like to talk to Bailey before I go about what this is, what that kiss meant, and if she wants this marriage to be more—to be real, I don't know how we'll find the time.

I have to be at the Summit most of tomorrow for a last round of training and then meetings about the trip. Our bus leaves around seven p.m., and we'll drive overnight. It's going to be grueling, and while I had been looking forward to it, now all I want is to stay home.

I yawn again, snuggling deeper into the couch cushions, letting my mind wander back over the day. It was perfect. Everything I could have wanted—except the full assurance that it's as real for Bailey as it is for me.

Though I meant to stay awake until Bailey came out, I wake up, disoriented, sometime in the middle of the night to find one of the pillows from the bedroom under my head and a comforter tucked over me. There's a note on the coffee table, written on the hotel stationary, and I squint to read it through the light coming off the EXIT sign.

Goodnight, husband, from your wife, is all it says. I fall back asleep with the note still in my fingers, pulled close to my heart.

CHAPTER 22

Bailey

I WAKE UP MARRIED.

MARRIED.

Married but ... alone.

I shove down the disappointment, which has dulled slightly after being acutely painful when I emerged from the bathroom and saw the empty bed. Then found Eli sitting up, sleeping with his head tilted back and mouth wide open, snoring softly.

Okay, in addition to the disappointment, I was also slightly amused. Had to cover my mouth to keep from guffawing. Eli sleeping, it turns out, is almost as heart-breakingly adorable as Eli awake.

In any case, I wasn't about to wake him. For one, we were both pretty dead last night. Weddings are a killer in terms of exhaustion. Even the not-quite-traditional kind, as it

302

happens. As gently as I could without waking him, I repositioned Eli so he was lying down, giving him a pillow and the blanket I found folded up in the closet. After burrowing his head a little deeper into the pillow, he smacked his lips and ordered, "Head rub."

For half a second, I thought he was awake, and I froze. But then his breathing deepened, his eyelids fluttering those long blond lashes against his cheek.

Maybe I should have left then, to avoid creepy watching-new-husband-while-sleeping behavior, but the man did order a head rub. So, I spent a few minutes sitting on the coffee table, dragging my fingers through his soft hair. Why the man isn't set up with a shampoo sponsor, I don't know. I should send a letter to Pantene or Herbal Essences or whatever the kids are using these days. But then, I hate the idea of even a stylist having her hands on his hair, so maybe not.

I didn't expect jealousy to come standard with the wedding band, but here we are.

After my hand started to cramp, I scrawled Eli a little note, smiling at the use of the words *husband* and *wife*, then came to bed feeling satisfied and also … very alone. I thought the whole kissing him with my dress half undone would have maybe been enough to let Eli know he was welcome to stay with me. If not for consummating the marriage—I want to kill Shannon for cementing that word in my brain—then just to sleep. I could imagine waking curled up beside Eli, his warm weight with me like it had been the night Annie came, when he climbed into my bed.

Anyway. I guess we have time for that? Or not. If that's not what he wants. While I feel almost sure we're on the same page, Eli seems just as reticent to talk about it as me. Probably not for the same reasons—where I struggle with words and saying things I want, the man seems unable to hold back.

Except with me. And I don't know how to take that.

There are too many maybes in my head right now. They're breeding like rabbits and did so until around two o'clock in the morning, when I fell into an exhausted, fitful sleep.

I spin the rings on my finger, taking off the band Eli placed there yesterday, reading the engraving again, then running my fingers over the letters. *Awkward together*. The thoughtfulness and the quirkiness of it makes a huge smile stretch across my face.

I should have come up with something like that for him. His ring is a plain gold band. It's what he asked for, but now it doesn't feel like enough. Though the present I'm planning to give him today is something I know he'll love. *More* than love. I actually can't wait.

In the long run, I know there's no way I'll be able to keep up with Eli's level of thoughtful giving. He's Olympic-level. I'll just need to find my own ways of making him feel special.

I slide the ring back on my finger, staring down at how foreign my hands look with such beautiful jewelry.

A door slams, and then I hear noises from the main room of the suite—a rattle, grunt, and a jangle—approaching the bedroom. I sit up, straightening Eli's button-down shirt. I really thought he had to have been exaggerating about Annie's prank, but he might have downplayed it. When I opened my suitcase, I swear a purple, lacy thong practically shot out at my face. The only time I've seen that much lingerie is walking by Victoria's Secret. Definitely nothing wearable in there. At least, not for *this* particular honeymoon.

But I'm grateful to have had the excuse to sleep in Eli's

shirt, smelling him against my skin while I slept. I'm not going to look this gift shirt in the mouth.

I would have preferred *him*.

There's a knock at the door, and I scoot back against the pillows, pulling the comforter up over my bare legs. "Come in," I call.

As Eli backs into the room, still in his lime-covered muumuu and tugging a silver rolling cart, I realize I didn't wash off my makeup last night. Which means it's still on my face, probably in none of the places it's supposed to be.

To complete this elegant post-wedding look, my hair is a wild nest. I tied it into a knot last night because I hate the feel of hair heavy on my neck when I'm trying to sleep. Now it's loosened but not fully unknotted. When I lift a hand to it, I'm surprised a squirrel doesn't dart out, making a break for the door, stopping for one of the pastries on Eli's cart.

"Morning," he says, stopping at the end of my bed and turning to grin at me. "I am pleased to bring you your honeymoon breakfast service."

Unlike my still sleep-rumpled state, Eli's hair is damp, and the smell emanating from him screams *freshly showered*. There must be a second bathroom in this suite—I didn't get a good look last night when he carried me in half asleep. Unless he snuck in here while I was sleeping and showered in this bathroom. My eyes dart away from the stack of pastries to the bathroom door, then back to the food.

I could worry about if Eli tiptoed through, seeing me sleeping. But: pastries!

"Would you like full-service breakfast in bed? Or would you prefer self-service?" I start to swing my legs over the side of the bed, not wanting Eli to go to any trouble, when he holds up a finger and says, "And if you're choosing self-service to be nice even though what you really want is for me to serve you, put those pretty legs back in bed."

He must see my hesitation, or maybe it's the way I froze when he said pretty legs, but he arches a brow, grinning. "I mean it. Back in bed with you. If it makes you feel less guilty, I'll join you."

Eli rolls the cart closer so I can tell him what I'd like. It looks like he ordered one of everything and two of things that are sweet: chocolate chip pancakes, cinnamon buns, and chocolate-filled croissants.

"I wasn't sure what you would like," he says.

"You know *some* of what I like," I tell him, pointing to my plate laden with sweets. And two strips of bacon as my token protein.

"I'm learning," he says.

I want to be learning too, so I watch as he heaps his plate with eggs and bacon, along with what looks like a salad. Then he climbs into bed next to me, nudging my elbow with his before tucking into his food.

"You made fun of me for salad pizza, yet you're having salad for breakfast?" I tease.

He rolls his eyes. "With all the traveling coming up and the extra games, I'm trying to stick to our meal plan. Which includes more spinach than I'd prefer. Want some?" He holds out a forkful, and I wrinkle my nose.

"Nope. I'm happy with my chocolate," I tell him. "So, you really *do* have a meal plan?"

"It's a bigger deal in the NHL. A lot of our guys are looser with things, though we often have as many games and almost as much training. I don't like being strict with my diet, but I do feel better if I'm more regimented about it."

He pauses, his gaze sliding from my eyes down to my

mouth. And then, too swiftly for me to react, his lips are on the corner of my mouth. He lingers there, unmoving, as my eyelids flutter closed and my pulse hammers through me. Then his lips part, and I feel the tiniest drag of his tongue on my skin.

I almost black out, not sure how such a tiny movement caused such an intensity of *want*. The fork shakes in my hand.

"Sometimes I cheat," Eli murmurs, still right next to my mouth, his lips brushing the corner of mine.

"Cheat?" I whisper, barely restraining myself from turning my head so our mouths fully meet. It's only the fear of my morning breath—thanks to Annie for stealing all our toiletries—that holds me in place.

Eli pulls away, a crooked grin on his face. "You had a little chocolate right there." He points.

I wonder what Eli would do if I dip my finger into the center of the croissant and then drag it all the places I'd like to feel his mouth on me.

Eli's phone rings. Saved by the bell? Or ruined by the bell? I'm not sure.

"It's Annie," he says, picking up. "I hope you aren't looking for a thanks, Ananias. I'm currently in the honeymoon suite bed wearing a muumuu."

But then his face goes still, and when his eyes find mine, they're intense and serious.

"We'll be back soon," he says, then hangs up, already moving out of bed.

"Mom's having a rough morning," he says. "I'm sorry to cut this short, but do you mind if we—"

"Let's go," I tell him, all thoughts of chocolate and kissing set aside.

"I'm sorry for ruining your honeymoon," Maggie says, and I reach across to the passenger seat and touch her hand. "I know you only got like twelve hours of wedded bliss."

"No worries," I assure her, meaning it. I pull out of the doctor's office parking lot, heading back toward our side of town.

Eli was able to skip morning practice today, but he had to be at The Summit for training and meetings all afternoon since the team leaves tonight. My stomach clenches at the thought. Our honeymoon—more like a *tiny* moon—always would have been quick. Though our morning might possibly have been a lot more fun if Annie hadn't called.

After arriving home in our wedding clothes again—which made Annie snort-laugh—I assured Eli we could handle things. Annie practically shoved him out of the house, and she and I drove Maggie to her doctor.

On the one hand, yes—it's disappointing the way hockey is stealing Eli from me so quickly. But I'm weirdly grateful for the space. I already know I'm going to miss him when he leaves tonight, but I hope this will help me process everything happening between us.

Yesterday was … intense. I need a minute to get a handle on my emotions.

Annie pokes her head between the seats and gives me a wicked grin. "I'm sure they enjoyed a lot of wedded bliss in those twelve hours."

Maggie only laughs, and I shake my head, groaning.

"And yes," Annie adds. "In case you were wondering, you can always expect this level of intrusion and violation of your privacy."

"How long are you staying again?" I ask lightly.

Annie laughs and pats me on the shoulder. "Did you hear that, Ma? This is a whole new side of sweet Bailey. Salty Bailey. I love it."

"You can always expect this level of giving as good as I get," I say, echoing her words and making Maggie laugh, which then turns into a grimace as she presses a hand to her chest.

"You okay, Ma?" Annie rubs a hand down Maggie's arm.

"Don't mind me," Maggie says, but Annie and I exchange a look.

The doctor was thankfully able to work Maggie in for a steroid shot. A corticosteroid shot, to be exact. I took notes, wanting to make sure I know as much as possible to help me in the next few weeks. And anytime Eli travels. The shot should help with some of the pain and inflammation, most likely exacerbated by all the activity this week. I'll try not to feel guilty that our fake-ish—or not at all fake?—wedding exacerbated her issues.

When the doctor gave Maggie a look and told us to make sure she takes it easy, Annie muttered, "If you can give us a straitjacket, that would help."

But I don't think it will be hard to make Maggie rest. I've never seen her so worn down, limping and wincing with even the smallest movements. Not even the day we looked for dresses and Eli carried her around. It would have been great to have him around for that today, though with Annie and I helping support Maggie, we did okay.

"What are we doing here again?" Annie asks as I pull into a parking space in front of the shelter.

I told them I needed to make a quick stop before heading back to the house. I glance up at the building where I've worked for more than a year. But I didn't tell them why we needed to stop.

"I'm putting in my notice." Honestly, the only thing I'll miss about the place is Beth. And the animals. But I can't wait to start my new job at an actual vet hospital. With a vet who isn't Dr. Evil. "Thanks to you"—I give Maggie's hand a quick squeeze—"and Eli being nosy, I have a cushy new job starting soon."

"You're quitting your job?" Annie asks. "Ooh, I want to come!"

"I'm just handing in a letter. I'm not, like, pulling a Jerry Maguire or anything."

"Jerry who?" Annie asks.

Maggie laughs. "Okay, I know what movie we're watching when we get home."

I can't convince Annie it won't be boring, so she joins me inside, where I've got one other thing to do before I officially hand over my letter. Beth is up front and comes around the desk to give us both hugs.

"Aren't you supposed to be spending the day doing married people things?" Beth asks, her eyes twinkling.

Annie laughs, and before she can make any kind of comment, I say, "Eli has training and meetings today. The team leaves tonight."

"Aw." Beth frowns. "That's too bad."

"I'll be fine." If I keep saying it, maybe I'll manifest it instead of feeling sick thinking about Eli being across the country. "I'm just here to give my official notice," I tell her. "And to pick up Eli's surprise."

I hand Beth the adoption paperwork I filled out a few days ago, and she slides it into a folder, then gives my arm an extra little squeeze. "How will I survive without you?"

"I'm sorry."

"Don't be. You need to move on. And Dr. Evil's arrows don't pierce this armor." She pounds a fist on her chest, and Annie laughs.

"Is she here?" I ask.

"Unfortunately," Beth says. "Last I saw, she was in her office."

"You're not supposed to come back here," I tell Annie as I head toward the door, but she steps up next to me, giving me a look. "But I'm not going to fight you over it."

"Good. You'd lose. I'm scrappy," she says, fake punching the air.

I have no doubt. She's also not as tall or muscular as Eli, but she has a very athletic build and at least six inches on me. Even if she weren't scrappy, it wouldn't be much of a contest. Honestly, I don't hate having her beside me as I hand in my official letter of resignation.

Even if that means getting the death glare from Dr. Evil as I knock on her office door. "Who's this and why is she back here?" she asks, barely glancing at my typed letter of resignation. Maybe she assumes it's me trying again to get her to write a recommendation or something.

"I'm Annie." She reaches out a hand, but Dr. Evil ignores it. Because of course she does. Though if she knew Eli is Annie's brother, I bet the reaction would be a whole lot different.

"I'm just giving you my notice." I point toward the paper, now on her desk next to the monitor, where she's playing Free Cell.

Frowning, she picks it up between two fingers, her expression souring as she scans the page.

"Bet she's a peach to work with," Annie mutters close to my ear. "Can't imagine why you're quitting."

Dr. Evil finally sets down the paper and pushes back her

chair to stand. Clearly, she means to be intimidating as she looms over me, but Annie steps closer and looms over the vet. It's such an Eli move, I almost laugh.

"No need to finish out your two weeks," Dr. Evil says, backing up a little. "You can consider it unpaid vacation for the *honeymoon*."

She says the word with so much derision, Annie makes a little growling sound next to me. I lean my shoulder against her, just in case. The last thing I need today, when I told Eli to trust me with his family, is for Annie to get arrested on my watch.

"That works," I tell her. Though if it weren't for Eli pretty much bankrolling my life, this would be an issue. But I don't need to have this battle. Not today. "Thanks for ... everything." I have nothing specific to thank her for, and *everything* feels generous, but I'm ready to get out of here.

Poor Beth. I wish I could take her with me. Maybe I can recommend her to my new boss if they have any other openings.

But as I guide Annie away from the office and toward the kennels, Dr. Evil trails behind us. "That's the wrong way," she says. "Exit's up front. Also, no one who isn't official staff or a volunteer should be back here."

I only offer her an insincere smile. "I'm just going to pick up all my things. Then you won't have to see me ever again."

And vice versa. One more thing I owe Eli for. That list really is starting to stack high. But I decided something in the middle of the night when I wasn't sleeping, thinking of Eli on the couch and Eli saying his vows and Eli kissing me after helping with my dress. I decided I want to be bold. To tell Eli how I actually feel and what I actually want.

The problem, again, is that I'm not good at this. I need time to figure this out. Which I guess his two weeks on the road will give me. I should be thankful, but I still just don't want him to go.

In any case, while I figure out how to use my words, I'm going to start with actions. To match Eli's kind thoughtfulness with my own. And I cannot wait to see his face.

CHAPTER 23

Bailey

I HOPED this would go better. It was a great plan. I could totally picture Eli's face when he opened the box to see the squirming surprise I managed to stuff in there as he pulled into the driveway.

But that was before Doris got nervous in the box—something I should have seen coming—and managed to both poop and pee. It also looks like she rolled around in it.

Which means when Eli walks into the house, what he gets instead of a new dog in a box with a bow is me lifting a poo-smeared and urine-soaked Doris out of a box that needs to be taken outside and burned immediately.

"Is that Doris?" he asks, dropping his keys right next to the door.

I freeze as Doris starts wiggling in my arms and wagging

her tail, both things sending unwanted substances around the front hallway as well as all over me.

Great. Even when I try, I suck at this surprise kindness gift-giving thing. You win, Eli. You win.

"Surprise?" I say. "And also, sorry. Doris got nervous, and now I need to go give her a bath. And I think I need a bath and maybe to do some laundry—"

"I'll help," he says.

No hesitation. No concern for getting poo on his person. Just drops his bags, plucks Doris from my hands, and starts up the stairs, cooing in her ear like she's not the canine embodiment of a portable toilet.

Is it possible to fall more in love with someone when poop is involved?

You wouldn't think so. But as I join Eli in the upstairs bathroom and help him clean Doris up, I absolutely fall harder. Farther. Whatever. Just ... all the falling.

"Look at how good you clean up, D!" Eli says, toweling her off in front of the mirror. She looks at him with adoring eyes, like she didn't pee on his shoe just last week when we were kissing in the shelter.

Somehow, that feels like years ago.

I lean against the wall, watching Eli in the mirror as he baby-talks to Doris, who isn't *quite* the ugliest dog I've ever seen. Her fur is growing back, which helps, but she's definitely more in the so-ugly-she's-cute category. Whatever kind of mix she is, there's pug in there somewhere. I can tell by the almost comically bulging eyes and short, snuffly snout.

"I can't believe you got me a dog." Eli turns his megawatt smile my way. "Got *us* a dog," he corrects and my heart shimmies happily. "I've always wanted a dog."

"I know," I say softly. "Happy wedding, hockey player.

Sorry she's a day late. I figured the timing would be better after."

Eli's smile falters. "I have to leave soon."

"I know."

"I don't want to go," he says, and I'm already nodding.

"I don't want you to go."

This moment feels huge. It feels like way more than a post-dog-bath kind of moment. More significant than any conversation that should happen in a bathroom.

And why, now that I'm thinking about it, do Eli and I have so many bathroom moments? We really need to fix this.

I don't realize I'm rubbing my sternum until Eli's gaze drops to my hand and he frowns. "Are you okay?"

He's probably so used to picking up on cues from his mom that Eli legitimately thinks I'm in physical pain. How do I explain that my heart is aching at the thought of him leaving?

I already miss his smiles and his touches and just him— the way he's able to lighten any room he walks into with his presence alone.

"I'm just—"

Whatever words were on their way to coming out of my mouth—maybe just nervous babble, maybe a confession, like *I'll miss you* or maybe even *I think I love you*—I'm interrupted by a horn honking outside.

Like, obnoxiously honking.

It has to be Van.

Eli sighs heavily. "I think that's my ride. Are you okay?"

"I'll be fine." I hold out my arms for Doris. Eli gives her a little squeeze, looks like he's about to kiss her head, then rethinks and hands her over.

Good call. Wet dog hair on the lips is not something anyone wants. Ever.

Especially not when you're planning to kiss a human, which I guess he was, as he surprises me by leaning in quickly, kissing me so thoroughly that I stumble when he releases me. His big hands find my shoulders and squeeze lightly.

"Take care, wife. I'll text. And call. And video call."

"Any chance of adding teleportation into the mix?"

His grin is fast and sweet and makes me want to chase after him, stuffing myself in the bigger of his two suitcases.

"I wish," he says. And then with a last look that I swear is full of enough longing to make my hope in this sprout wings, Eli pounds down the stairs, grabs his bag, and is gone.

———

Eli: Any point I score in tonight's game is a gift for you.
Bailey: Should I take it personally if you don't score?
Eli: I'm taking it personally that you're even thinking I WON'T. You've been watching the last few games, right?
Bailey: Yes. I've been watching. Every game, I'll have you know. With your mom, Annie, Doris, and sometimes Jenny, Shannon, and the book club ladies. Gran even came once.
Eli: How did Gran do? I think she hates me, by the way. She kicked me in the shin at our wedding.
Bailey: Sorry. It's not personal. She hates me too. She kind of hates everyone. Except Felix. And Doris. They bonded. But it was fine having her over. Other than when she tried to steal a steak knife. For what purpose … I don't want to know.
Eli: You really have watched every game?
Bailey: All the ones streamed on YouTube. Which is all of them so far. I don't even get up to pee until there's a commercial, which might be TMI, but too bad.
Bailey: You're kind of good at the whole scoring thing.

Eli: Kind of?

Bailey: Didn't take you for the kind of man who needs a good ego stroking.

Eli: We're still getting to know each other. Maybe I've been hiding my giant ego from you all this time.

Bailey: Doubtful. I may not know ALL the little things about you, but I'm a good judge of character. I'm observant. And I've been snooping in your room.

Eli: Our room.

Bailey: Still feels like yours. Other than the half a dresser you cleaned out for me. Thanks for that. But especially for the Buenos. I've been finding them all over the room. How many did you hide?

Eli: I'll never tell.

Bailey: Well, thank you. It's very sweet.

Eli: It's a small thing. And we can work on making the room feel like OURS when I get home.

Bailey: I like that idea. Back to your ego—you don't have a giant one hidden somewhere. Not even a small one. You have healthy confidence.

Eli: Gee, thanks?

Bailey: What?

Eli: Healthy confidence sounds just like what every woman is looking for in a guy. Goes hand-in-hand with being a nice guy.

Bailey: You'd be surprised. Healthy confidence is incredibly sexy.

Eli: Thanks. It's nice to know you find me incredibly sexy, Leelee.

Bailey: I was wrong about you not having an ego, hockey player. Also, thanks for using punctuation in your texts for me.

Eli: Anything for you. But honestly, this is hard. I've used more periods in texts this week than ever in my life.

Bailey: It's like a bouquet of periods!

Bailey: Okay, that sounded really bad. Ew. EW! EW! EW! Sorry. SO sorry. Let's roll that back.

Eli: How about a bouquet of commas?

Bailey: I accept.

———

Eli: New idea: every point I score equals a point with you.

Bailey: Come again?

Bailey: And if this turns into some kind of misogynistic thing that has to do with scoring, I'm going to block your number.

Eli: Not that kind of scoring! Also, please don't block my number. I won't make it through the rest of this trip without seeing your face in our nightly chats. Thanks for staying up for me, by the way.

Bailey: I like seeing you too. Even if having you in Pacific Standard Time sucks. You're totally worth the lack of beauty sleep, husband.

Eli: And you don't need sleep to be beautiful, wife.

Bailey: Aw, flattery will get you everywhere. Now, tell me more about this non-misogynistic point-scoring thing.

Eli: Now it sounds stupid.

Bailey: Tell me anyway.

Eli: I was thinking maybe as I accumulate goals, I could earn Bailey Points.

Bailey: Oooh! I like this. It's kind of like my own kind of currency?

Eli: If that's how you want to think of it.

Bailey: And what do Bailey Bucks—fully leaning into the currency thing—get you?

Eli: I don't know. Maybe this idea got away from me.

Bailey: Liar. You know what you want. You just can't say it.

Eli: I sometimes have trouble with that.

Bailey: Me too.

Bailey: How about I suggest things and you can say yes or no.

Eli: Yes.

Bailey: Good job! You got the hang of that quick. Okay, how about head rubs?

Eli: YES.

Bailey: Wow. That was enthusiastic.

Eli: You gave me a head massage on our wedding night.

Bailey: I thought you were asleep.

Eli: I was. Mostly? I thought it was a dream. But it was a really lovely one.

Bailey: Noted. Another option: I could cook for you?

Eli: No offense, but no.

Bailey: Offense taken! Why not?

Eli: Last night, when we were doing our nightly Q&A thingy from that book you found, you said you couldn't cook. That you once forgot water was boiling until it all evaporated and then ruined a pot.

Bailey: I thought we agreed that our little get-to-know-you exercise wasn't to be used as ammo against the person.

Eli: Not ammo! Just knowledge. And now that I know you can't cook, I think it's best we keep it out of Bailey Bucks.

Bailey: Fine. Back massages?

Eli: YES YES YES YES

Bailey: Don't you have a trainer or something for that?

Eli: The team has a massage therapist come in sometimes, but she's not you.

Bailey: SHE? Your massage person is a woman?

Eli: Jealous?

Bailey: Honestly, yeah. I hate the idea of other people touching you. Does that make me a terrible person?

Eli: No. You're my wife. You can feel that way all you want. I like it a lot.

Eli: And trust me when I say I DO NOT like or want any guy touching you. He won't like it either if he wants to keep his hands. Or face.

Eli: Did you fall asleep texting again? Or did my violent side scare you?

Bailey: I don't hate it.

Bailey: Okay, fine. I kind of love it. But …

Eli: This but is taking a long time…

Bailey: I just don't always know what to expect here. What's real and what's … just the arrangement.

Eli: We should probably talk about that.

Bailey: We probably should.

Bailey: I'm not great at talking about things. I wanted to before you left, and then I chickened out.

Eli: Really? Because I wanted to before I left and I sort of chickened out. But also I've been trying to wait.

Bailey: Why?

Eli: I was advised that patience might be a good virtue in this particular situation.

Bailey: Patience is overrated. Any other reason?

Eli: I've been told I can be too much.

Bailey: You are NEVER too much for me, Eli. And I don't want you to hold back.

Eli: Noted.

Eli: Hate to go now, but Parker needs me for a TikTok video.

Bailey: Likely excuse.

Eli: Trust me—I'd much rather talk to you. Video chat later after the game?

Bailey: Can't wait.

Eli: Awkward together?

Bailey: Awkward together.

———

There's a difference in watching Eli play hockey while in the same building and watching while at home on the couch.

Not just the lack of screaming fans and energy—Annie and Maggie have a lot of energy, and we all do a lot of screaming—but it somehow ratchets up my worry. When things got physical on the ice at the few games I went to at the Summit after the proposal, there was a comfort in knowing I was right there. Just in case anything happened. Not like I could do anything. Or that he'd necessarily want me if he got hurt. I doubt I could have even gotten to him, considering I don't know my way around the building and security wouldn't let me just wander around.

But we had proximity.

Watching him on the TV screen, knowing tonight he's somewhere hours west—Arizona? Texas? Nevada?—in a whole other time zone, makes me twitchy. I can't eat much, and I find myself spinning my rings incessantly, wishing they worked like Dorothy clicking her heels together, sending me to the no-place-like-home that is, apparently, my husband.

"What happened to little bro's game?" Annie asks, tossing a piece of popcorn toward her mouth. Missing. Plucking it from her lap and offering it to Doris, who gobbles it up.

I choose to ignore it because a few pieces of popcorn won't be an issue. Even if, on a whole, Annie's insistence on feeding Doris anything she begs for could result in a long-term health crisis, namely obesity. I also ignore Annie's question, which was probably rhetorical anyway.

"He's just having a bad night," Maggie says, brow furrowed. Then she points a finger at Annie. "Don't even think about giving him a hard time. You know he's too hard on himself already."

"Which only makes it more fun to poke at him about it," Annie says.

Meanwhile, I'm watching for the cameraman or whoever's producing this livestream to pan over the bench, where Eli is currently seated. Hard on himself, huh? I guess it doesn't surprise me that easygoing Eli wouldn't go easy on himself. It makes me wish I were there even more.

Something is definitely off, and I can't help but worry it's because of our text conversation.

We've texted off and on every day while he's been gone. I had to go out and buy a portable charger because my battery won't last, and I'm more addicted than a teenager to my phone. It's either in my hand, tucked into my bra, or in the back pocket of my jeans. Somewhere I'll feel the buzz of an incoming text or see the screen light up.

Sometimes it's just light things. A selfie in a Seattle coffee shop or some other city location that should be significant but I have to google. Pictures of Eli with the guys, him on a bus, him in the locker room. I'm sure he didn't realize in one of those there was at least one guy in the process of taking off his pants. There are also memes and GIFs and jokes. He even started using punctuation for me!

We've also been getting to know each other better. Mostly thanks to a book I found in Book Smart, my favorite bookshop in Harvest Hollow's cute little downtown. It's a book of questions for couples, meant probably to be asked while sharing a meal or something. Over text works just fine too.

We've gone over everything from what objects we'd save from a house fire to favorite and least favorite foods, dream vacation, and biggest fears. Which led to deeper discussions in which I shared more openly than I ever have about what it was like after I lost my parents, and he talked about growing up not knowing his dad.

Honestly, the one big elephant in the text convo is our real feelings. Which ... I think somehow are the framework underpinning our conversations. We danced around them in our last text, and I think that means a real conversation is imminent.

I tell myself not to freak out. It's not wishful thinking to imagine we share the same feelings. I'm not reading into Eli's words, his near-constant communication, the way he lights up when our video chats connect and he sees my face.

This is real. No matter how it started or what we expected.

My heart does a few somersaults and then a few cart-wheels thinking about our call tonight. When we might—finally—be honest about our feelings.

Unless ... that's why he's playing poorly. Why he looks off and distracted. Because it's a bad conversation coming. Or he changed his mind.

I tell myself that's really stupid.

Maggie pats my knee. I'm almost knocked over by a wave of guilt for the basket of lies I've woven for her. "Maybe he just misses his wife."

Or maybe he isn't sure how his wife really feels about him because she's kind of a coward.

"I don't think missing me is the reason."

"Are you kidding?" Annie tosses a handful of popcorn my

way. And even though I'm not in the least bit hungry, I eat it. Mostly to save it from Doris, who is well on her way to developing a popcorn addiction. "You two are disgustingly adorably perfect for each other."

"Are we?"

It's probably the question that gives it away. Something shaky in my voice that has both Annie and Maggie swinging their gazes in my direction. They make eye contact first—something passing between them I can't decipher but very much fear is something like, *Liar! She's a lying little liar!*

When I swallow, my throat catches and I have to try again. "What?" I ask.

Maggie purses her lips, but it's not an annoyed look—or disappointed. It's—wait. Is she holding back a laugh?

"You know we know, right?"

"Know?"

Annie flings popcorn at me, and this time, I don't stop Doris from launching up into my lap to scavenge the pieces. "We know about you and Eli getting married for his visa."

My stomach drops to somewhere in the vicinity of the earth's core as I chew the inside of my cheek, wishing my words wouldn't choose this moment to disappear.

"I wasn't sure why at first," Maggie says. "But then I looked up the timing of his visa, and his sudden rush to get married made sense."

"Oh," I manage, already mentally calculating what it will cost to have my things moved back out when Maggie asks me to go, wondering if my old apartment has been rented or if maybe I should stay in a hotel. At least until I figure out my next steps.

Then I realize she isn't asking me to leave. Not accusing me of lying. And she doesn't look disappointed. She looks *amused.*

"You aren't upset?" I ask.

"Heavens, no," Maggie says. "I don't care how my children find love. I only hope they do."

"And you're clearly in love with him—for reasons I can't fathom, being that he's my brother and all."

Yeah, it is pretty obvious, huh?

Maggie takes my hand and gives me a soft squeeze. She no longer looks amused but tender as she says, "And he's clearly head over heels for you."

"You think?" I whisper.

Maggie nods, smiling with tear-filled eyes that make my chest suddenly constrict.

Annie rolls her eyes. "Can you seriously not tell? He's a smitten kitten." She pauses with a piece of popcorn halfway to her mouth, blinks rapidly, then drops her hand. "Oh, my gosh—you don't know."

"I—" The one syllable chokes out of me, and I can't continue, shrugging instead.

Maggie drapes an arm around my shoulders and pulls me close, the move so familial, so *maternal* that it shakes something loose inside of me. "Oh, sweetie. Has he not told you how he feels?"

"To be fair," I say, my voice finally returning, even if it's wobbly. "I haven't told him either. We've been talking around it. Are you—are you not mad that we lied? That *I* lied?"

"Nope," Maggie says. "I'm just happy at how things have turned out. I've gained another daughter, and my Eli is happy."

It's more grace than I deserve, and I whisper, "Thank you" just as Annie jumps to her feet, knocking the popcorn bowl to the ground. Her eyes are wide, staring at the television, where the game is still streaming.

Only now, the action has stopped and there are medical

personnel making their way onto the ice, one player flat on his back. A helmet is a few feet away, but his head is blocked by someone standing in the way of the camera.

There's a rushing buzz in my ears as I watch the screen, knowing even before the person moves revealing the blond head of hair I ran my hands through just last week. The breath whooshes out of my lungs in a sickening wheeze.

"What happened?" Maggie says, her voice pulled tight.

"I didn't see it," Annie says, sounding dazed. "The announcers said something about his head. He's unconscious."

I don't even realize I'm getting on my feet until I'm halfway across the room. All I can think about is Eli being injured and being alone. Not knowing how I really feel about him.

"Where are you going?" Annie asks.

"To get my purse," I say, not slowing down. "I have to get to him."

CHAPTER 24

Eli

I WAKE up having been run over by a bus and then spat out of a trash compactor. I am a tiny, trash-compacted cube of throbbing pain.

"You're not a cube, you're a drama queen, that's what you are," a familiar voice tells me.

Did I say that out loud? At most, maybe I mumbled it. My mouth feels like it's full of cotton, and I have only hazy memories of being taken off the ice, riding in an ambulance, and having a bunch of bright lights in my face. Voices waking me up, a blood pressure cuff on my arm, beeping monitors. Someone—a doctor?—telling me I have a concussion but will be fine.

I crack open one eye and hope it effectively conveys glaring. Probably not, based on the way Alec chuckles.

"Too loud," I mumble, closing my one eye again. Darkness is a relief. And this hospital room is practically glowing. "And I'm not being dramatic. I'm concussed. Can we turn off the lights?"

"They're off. That's called the sun, dude. Good morning."

Great. So, Van is here too. Doesn't the hospital have a limit on visitors? Or, at least, smart-mouthed hockey players?

"I'll work on the blinds."

Guess the limit is at least three, because that's Felix. And the grunt I hear sounds like Nathan.

"Thanks. Are we having a team meeting in here or what?" I ask. "Did you decide to vote me off the island?"

"Can't we check in on our favorite and most concussed player?" Logan asks.

"How many of you are in here?" I groan. "It's like a clown car. But a hospital room full of hockey players."

"I'm here too," Parker chirps. Then, probably noticing my wince, she lowers her voice to a whisper. "Sorry. We all just wanted to make sure you're okay."

"And that you don't have amnesia," Van adds. "I was kind of hoping you did, just so I could mess with you."

"Thanks? I remember you guys—maybe a little too well. But I don't … I don't remember exactly what happened."

"It was my fault."

This voice I don't recognize as much, and I crack open the same eye again, zeroing in on Wyatt, standing next to a poster about healthy blood pressure. He looks grim. Not that unusual, as he's like Nathan's second-in-command with regards to grumpiness. But Wyatt looks darker now, his eyes shadowed.

"How was it your fault?" I ask.

"It wasn't," Alec says. "He's got a guilt complex. It was as much your fault as his."

"*My* fault?"

Van sits down on the end of my bed and gives my foot a squeeze. "Don't worry, cowboy. You were just defending your wife's honor."

Before I can ask another question, Alec jumps in, explaining how I was in a bad mood today, though no one could figure out why, and Wyatt got on the wrong side of the other team's right winger, who then made a comment to me about Bailey and—

"What did he say about her?" I growl, trying to sit up even though it makes the throbbing ache in my head more of a slamming chisel to the skull.

The reminder of Bailey has me suddenly feeling an urgent tug in my chest. And an ache of longing. It's as nice as it is annoying to have all the guys here, but they're not the ones I want.

No—the one person whose face I'd like to see—*need* to see—is across the country.

"Calm down, big boy," Van says, lightly pushing me in the chest. "No need to get testy."

"We took care of the guy," Logan says, and Parker rolls her eyes.

"You're all a bunch of idiots," she says, and then when Logan bats his lashes at her, she adds, "Lovable idiots. But still."

"How did I wind up with a concussion?" I ask, settling down again with a scowl.

Though I have some memories of *after* filtering in, I can't remember *before*. The last memory I have is … gearing up? Or maybe skating out from the tunnel? Trying to remember makes my head throb.

"Your helmet came off in the fray, and you took a knock to the head, then hit your head again when you went down on the ice," Felix explains.

"Good thing you've got a thick skull," Alec says.

"Where's my phone?"

I need to call Bailey. Especially if she happened to be watching. Does she know I'm okay?

Also: I missed our talk last night. The one when I was planning to actually tell her how I feel and hopefully get confirmation she feels the same way. It feels oddly ironic the way I finally planned to stop holding back—and then got held back by things outside of my control.

If anything, absence has made my heart surer. More sure? Whatever. I know Bailey is the woman I want, and I know I want to tell her.

"You're not allowed to be on screens for a while. Doctor's orders," Logan says.

"*Someone get me a phone,*" I seethe. "I need to check in with Bailey."

"I sent her a message," Parker says. Then her smile tightens. "But I didn't hear back from her."

I clench my jaw, then groan and stretch it. Every little movement hurts right now. But I need to talk to Bailey. I need to—

There's a commotion out in the hallway. Some shouting and a scuffle.

"Sounds like you're not the only troublesome patient," Van says, patting my foot again. I give him a little kick in response.

"You can't go in there!" The voices are getting louder now, and that one definitely belongs to a tired member of the hospital staff. She sounds like she's about half a second from calling security.

A male voice, getting closer now says, "Ma'am. Stop. I don't want to forcibly remove you."

Or ... maybe she already called security.

All the heads in our room swivel toward the door as the first woman yells again, "He already has too many visitors in the room, and you can't just—"

"*I am his wife.*"

The grin stretching across my face *hurts*, but I don't pull it back. Because I know that voice. And as Bailey appears in the doorway looking like some kind of warrior, ready to take on the evils of the hospital staff with her bare hands, warmth spreads through my chest, gliding right to the tips of my fingers and even my toes.

Doesn't dull the headache at all, though, which is going to really make it a challenge to kiss Bailey the way I want to. I can't even get myself out of the bed right now.

"Wife," I say, and refuse to be embarrassed by how much emotion is in my voice. The crying kind.

Van doesn't miss it, though, and must open his mouth to remark on it because I see Wyatt darting away from the wall and hear an *oomph* from Van. But I'm not looking at them. Only Bailey.

"Hockey player," she says.

This time, Wyatt doesn't move quickly enough to stop Van from saying, "Which one?"

I'm the one who kicks him—right off the bed and onto the floor. Which really doesn't do good things for my head, but I regret nothing.

"Everybody out," Alec says, clapping his hands. When I wince at the sharp sound and the way it tunnels through my head, he lowers his voice. "Sorry, Hop. Everybody out."

Parker hugs Bailey, who's still hanging in the doorway, and a few of the guys pat her shoulder or back. Alec manages to sweet-talk the nurse and security guard who were trying to stop Bailey, and in a few seconds, everyone is gone.

But Bailey is still standing in the doorway.

"After all that bravery, telling off the hospital staff, and making marital declarations, you're scared to come in here?"

I pat the bed next to me, unable to really scoot over for her because I just know that kind of movement will kill my head. Kicking Van almost made me puke. Throwing up is the last thing I want to do right now.

"I just ... need a minute," Bailey says, and I frown. Which, like everything else right now, hurts.

Don't I even get a morphine drip in this place?

"What do you need a minute for?" I ask, as she finally, finally walks fully into the room, pushing the door closed softly as she does.

Her eyes don't leave mine. "I needed to see for myself that you were okay. I've been traveling all night, and the last thing I saw was you on the ice, not moving." She stops just short of the bed, and I don't miss the way she's twirling her rings or the way her lips tremble. "Seeing that on a YouTube livestream was ..."

"Come here. Please."

I tug her toward me, trying to move slowly but still wincing because my stupid, stupid head feels like someone is hitting it repeatedly with a rubber mallet.

"Does it hurt to move?" she asks and when I nod, she narrows her eyes. "Then stop moving."

"Then get in this bed with me."

"There's no room."

"Get in the bed, wife."

"So bossy," she says, carefully settling herself next to me. "Are we having our first fight?"

"Only if it means we get to make up later. Ow."

"Does it hurt to smile?" With gentle fingers, Bailey traces my lips.

"Everything hurts," I groan, and she shifts, running her fingers through my hair. "Except that. That feels awesome."

"Then I'll keep doing it. Even if you didn't score any points."

I close my eyes, trying not to laugh. Groaning instead because her fingers feel so good on my scalp. Forget a morphine drip. I need a Bailey mainline. "Did you fly all the way here to tell me how much I sucked in the last game?"

"Yep. That and to tell you I love you."

"Aw, you—wait. Hang on. Did you just say you love me?" I stare at the shy smile on Bailey's face, wishing my brain felt less mushy so I could be one hundred percent sure she said—

"I love you."

This time, I get the full effect. Because I'm watching her as she says it, and I'm slightly more prepared than I was a few seconds before.

"You love me?" I know I sound incredulous, and Bailey's face dims slightly—not what I wanted. At all.

"I know it's soon, and we still barely know each other but—"

"I wasn't aware love had a strict timeline," I say. "Or that you had to exchange social security numbers or something before you could say it. Because I don't know everything about you, and I don't know your social security number, but I love you, Bailey Hopkins."

Her grin stretches wide, and her fingers press harder on my head, making me moan as my eyes flutter and try to shut. But I don't allow them too. I can't stop looking at Bailey. Who *loves* me.

"You don't know my last name, either," she says. "Because I haven't changed it yet. It's still McKinney."

I frown. "Why haven't you changed it?"

"There hasn't been time, hockey player. But I have the

paperwork and plan to do so. Until then, just so people are sure …"

She spins, moving her hair out of the way. I didn't even notice she's wearing a jersey, but she is. And it's mine. I trace the letters of my name across her shoulders.

"I love you, Bailey not-yet Hopkins," I tell her. "And it may be soon, but I've known for longer."

Bailey turns and puts her hands right back in my hair. This time, when my eyelids flutter, I allow them to close. "How long, hockey player?"

"At least a week."

"That's like … a third of our relationship," she says with a giggle.

"Depends when you start counting. I mean, if you consider when I first came into the shelter—"

"You did *not* have feelings for me then."

I open my eyes and, despite the ache it causes, I lift my hand to take Bailey's, then press a kiss to each of her fingertips. "But I loved coming to the shelter for more than the dogs. I made it a personal challenge to see if I could get you to talk. And I loved making you blush. Just like now."

I let go of her hand to trace over her pink cheeks, dipping to her mouth, where I drag a fingertip over her lower lip.

"I'm sorry I didn't tell you earlier," I say. "I wasn't sure how you felt, and I didn't want you to feel pressured or stuck. I wanted to win you over without overwhelming you."

"Can we talk about that?" Bailey asks. "And then, I want to do some not-talking, and then I think you need to rest."

"Okay," I say agreeably, mostly because I like the idea of not talking very much. And I'm also exhausted.

"You do not overwhelm me, Eli. You aren't too much for me. The last thing I want is for you to hold back."

"Good." A tightness I wasn't even aware of loosens in my

chest, and I slide my hand around to cup the back of Bailey's head.

And then I kiss her, not holding back.

Not holding back the depth of emotion I feel for her or the hopes I have for us, not holding back because of fear or worry or uncertainty.

It's only the pain in my head that forces a groan out of me —not a happy kind—and has me flopping back against the pillows.

"Sorry," I say, a little out of breath.

Bailey smooths her finger across my forehead, then goes back to my hair as I let my eyes close again. "Don't be sorry," she says. "Rest. You'll need it. Because"—she leans closer and brushes her lips over mine—"when you're recovered, I don't plan to hold back with you either."

It's with this promise and the knowledge that Bailey is fully, finally, actually mine, that I drift into sleep and happy dreams.

EPILOGUE

Bailey

I SINK DOWN on my bed, holding the envelope in my hands, staring at the return address until the words blur and swim into squiggly lines. It's from the University of Tennessee Knoxville—the only vet school that wouldn't require relocation. And like trying to watch an acceptance-letter pot come to a boil, this has been the last to arrive.

Eli encouraged me to apply to more schools, telling me he would be the Ruth to my Naomi and where I go, he will go, which made me laugh. I never expected to have my husband compare us to a Biblical mom and daughter-in-law duo. But then, Eli does live to surprise me.

So far, I've gotten two acceptance letters. I have options. But I don't want them. I want *this*.

Because I don't want to move. I like our life, the one Eli and I have been building together in the slightly bigger house right next door to Maggie and—most of the time—Annie, who seems to want to stick around too. She's still figuring out work and her visa situation, making too-frequent cracks about having her own marriage of convenience since ours turned out so well. I don't bother trying to dissuade her. I learned quickly that telling Annie no is like shooting a starter's pistol, sending her sprinting in the opposite direction from the one you want.

Even so, I like having more family. And now that I have them, I'm not willing to leave them behind. Or ask them to relocate for me. Not Maggie or even Annie, if she'd follow.

Definitely not Eli. I don't want him to leave the Appies, who are as much his brothers as his friends. And of course, I'd like to stay close to Shannon and Jenny. But the really big non-negotiable is that I can't move Gran. Even though she still might not know me or not fully know in what city or even state she's living—a move is disruptive and it's been a month or more since she threw anything (other than food) at anyone.

All of which makes this letter vastly more important than the others. It's why I've hidden it inside a book on my bedside table for two days. Knowing it's there but refusing to open it.

"Whatcha got there?"

My head snaps up to see Eli leaning in the doorway, Doris tucked under one arm like a little doggy football. All of which I'd normally find sexy—if I weren't so busy panicking.

I go with instinct. Which means shoving the letter right down in my bra. Full circle to the day Eli first joked about marrying me. Complete with a sharp corner in an unwelcome spot. I wince.

"Nothing?" I say. "Just … a thing. You're home early."

"I'm home right on time. And I happen to love *things*."

Eli's grin is wicked as he peels himself off the doorframe, setting Doris down on her dog bed as he stalks toward me. He's freshly showered after practice, and I love the way his damp hair is just a little darker than when it's dry. He smells good too, but the devious look in his eyes has me scuttling back against the pillows. I grab one and hold it in front of my chest like a memory-foam shield. My heart beat picks up and my adrenaline kicks in, a biological instinct in response to a predator.

Which isn't wholly a *bad* feeling.

"Show me," Eli says, his voice a husky rasp as he reaches the end of the bed, pausing with hands on his hips.

I shake my head. "No, thanks."

He *tsks*, then lowers himself and starts to crawl across the bed toward me. Which doesn't take long, considering his height. I press back into the pillows as far as I can as he reaches me, sitting up on his knees and placing one palm on either side of my head.

"Don't make me come and get it," Eli says.

Actually … that doesn't sound so bad.

Sounds kind of great, actually.

Arching an eyebrow, I cross my arms over my chest, hearing the crinkle of the letter as I do. "I'm not handing it over willingly. Do your worst, hockey player."

Grinning, Eli leans in and captures my mouth.

His worst, as it turns out, is the best.

Some time later, when I'm tangled up in the sheets feeling a little boneless and a lot happy, Eli props himself up on an elbow and pulls the letter out from under a pillow. The letter I totally forgot about and also totally lost track of while otherwise … occupied.

Eli holds it up like a prize. "Got it."

Laughing, I say, "Seems like you forgot what you came for."

"Oh, I got what I came for." His smile is slow and satisfied. "This letter is just … something I'm interested to follow up on. Shall we open it?"

As Eli starts to tear open the letter, I grab his wrist. "Wait." He does, and I lick my lips, trying to articulate my thoughts. "What if it's a no?"

He sits up, the sheets pooling down around his waist, leaving his bare torso on full display. At least the view is nice. Even if I'm quietly freaking out. Eli slips his wrist out of my grip and cups my face.

"First of all, they'd be dumb not to take you. Your grades were phenomenal, my sweet little nerdling, and from what I understand, your recommendation was stellar. You're a sure thing. And if they don't take you—well, we can discuss what you want to do. As I said, I'm willing to do whatever. Our life together isn't just about *me*. My career doesn't need to take precedence over yours."

"I want us both to have what we want," I say, leaning into his warm palm.

"What I want most is you," Eli says, brushing his lips across mine so sweetly, it makes something clutch in my chest. "Wherever I can have you, I do love it here. Love our house, love my team, even love this little town. But I'd do life wherever you are, so long as you're my partner in it."

"You say the sweetest things, hockey player." If my voice is a little husky, it's not because I'm about to cry. It's just because … okay, fine! That's why.

With no warning, Eli pulls back and rips into the envelope. It takes only three seconds of me holding my breath for him to scan for the right word. I know from his smile when he sees it.

"'Congratulations,'" he reads. "'On behalf of the faculty, staff, and—'"

Squealing, I throw myself at Eli until we're both laughing and even more tangled up in the sheets. My legs are trapped between his, and we're pretty much cocooned in soft cotton. I couldn't get up if I tried. Good thing I don't want to try.

"I got in," I say, unable to stop my smile.

"You got in," Eli repeats, kissing the top of my head. "Of course you did. Because my girl is amazing."

I lay my cheek on Eli's bare chest, lifting my fingers to stroke his jaw. Right now, he's clean shaven. I love the waxing and waning of his facial hair, which he likes to grow out only to surprise me by shaving. He likes to see how long it takes me to notice the change.

You'd think it would be obvious. It should be.

But sometimes it takes me a whole day to realize the beard from the day before is now smooth skin. The only time I noticed immediately was when he left a thick mustache and I laughed until I cried and then told him I wouldn't kiss him again until he shaved it off.

They may be trendy, but mustaches are *not* for me.

"I like your face," I tell him, stretching up to kiss his jaw.

"I like your *everything*."

I give his neck a little nibble. "Always trying to one-up me with your words."

"I'm not trying to one-up anyone," he says. "It's the truth."

"Well, I like your everything too."

A door slams down below, and Eli drops his head back and groans as Annie calls, "Yoohoo! Lovebirds!"

"We're busy!" Eli calls.

"You're always busy," Annie says, her voice getting louder as she reaches the stairs.

I don't bother asking Eli if she'd really barge into our bedroom. She hasn't yet, but it's *Annie*. I disentangle myself from Eli and find my clothes. My shirt may be inside out, but I'm dressed when Annie throws open the door, one hand over her eyes.

"Annie," Eli says, tossing a pillow at her. "You can't just barge into our bedroom."

"I'm not looking," she says, peeking through her fingers. "See?" Eli snorts, and Annie continues, undeterred. "I need to know if you opened the letter from UT yet."

I exchange a look with Eli. "What letter?" I ask.

"The one that came two days ago. I assumed by now you've opened it, and I've been as patient as I can be."

"Annie," Eli says slowly, "did you go through our mail? You know that's a fraud."

"Is it? I'm not caught up on my US laws. So—did you open it? What's the verdict?"

"Maybe I do want to move," I mutter to Eli, who laughs and shakes his head.

"She's like a barnacle," he says. "We'll never fully escape."

"Hey! This barnacle is still right here, listening to everything. And waiting for you to tell me if you were accepted to your dream vet school."

I consider making her wait, but I just can't. "I got in," I gush.

Annie drops her hand from her eyes—and the guise of giving us any privacy—and throws herself at me in a full-body hug. I'm sure glad I put clothes back on.

"I'm so glad!" she says. "And I was thinking about applying for jobs in Knoxville and maybe we could carpool and—"

"Slow your roll, sis," Eli says. "And maybe get out of our bed?"

"Fine." Annie gives me one more squeeze before hopping back to her feet with the boundless energy she shares with Eli. "But are you going to tell Mom or can I? She and I have both been *dying* since I told her the letter came."

"Is nothing sacred? Can we have *no* secrets?" Eli asks, pressing his palms over his eyes.

"Well," I say slowly, "we do have the *one* big secret."

Eli drops his hands from his face and looks over at me. "Yeah? You're ready to tell people?"

Annie bounces on her toes, eyes shining as she claps her hands. "What secret? Tell me! Tell me!"

Eli reaches across and threads his fingers through mine, nodding to give me the go-ahead. I draw in a breath and hold Annie's gaze for a beat, knowing it's driving her nuts.

Finally, when I think she's about to start throwing furniture, I say, "We're expanding our family."

This is not the news she expected. Clearly not, if her slack jaw and wide eyes are any indication. I take great pleasure in shocking the person who is so nosy she peeks in our mailbox.

"What?" Her voice is barely a whisper. "You—I thought you were going to wait. With the whole vet school and hockey career thing."

Eli lifts my hand to his smiling mouth, still keeping our fingers twined as he kisses my knuckles.

I shrug. "What can I say? We've been thinking about it for a while, and now that we're settled in the house, it feels so big. Too big."

"Plus, Doris is lonely," Eli adds. "She needs a friend."

"Wait." Annie narrows her eyes, glancing between us. "When you say expanding your family, you mean—"

"Adopting a dog," I tell her, keeping the straightest of straight faces.

Until I just can't. Annie's face is too much. Eli howls with laughter, and I wipe tears from my eyes at the way his sister is glaring at us both.

"You ..." she sputters. "I can't believe you two let me think you were pregnant. A plague on both your houses."

"Uh oh," Eli says. "She's bringing out Shakespeare to curse us."

Throwing up her hands, Annie stomps out. "I hate you both. And when and if you do decide to procreate, it's going to take some serious convincing to get me to agree to be your spawn's godmother."

"Bye, sister!" Eli calls.

"And you can tell Maggie about UT!" I add. "And about our new addition."

There's only muttering from downstairs before the door slams, and we're alone again. Doris lets out a loud, drawn-out snore. Alone—with Doris.

"Think she'll ever stop being so ..."

"Intrusive?" Eli suggests.

"I was going to say nosy and overly invested in our lives, but I guess intrusive works."

"No, I don't think she'll ever change. Is that okay? You didn't realize what you were signing onto when you agreed to marry me."

I shift until I can catch and hold Eli's gaze. His gorgeous, Norwegian fjord eyes that I love. Reaching out, I smooth my fingertips over his jaw. "I have not one single regret about marrying you, hockey player."

"No?" He smiles delightedly, like this is the first time I've told him this in the past six months, not the hundredth.

I lean closer, teasing his mouth with mine, pulling away when he tries to capture my lips. "Not a single one."

And then, I let him catch me, one big hand cupping my

head as he pulls me close. "Awkward together," he whispers against my mouth. "Always."

THE END

Want an extra bonus scene PLUS some alternate POVs and deleted scenes? Join my list and read now-
https://emmastclair.com/groombonus

THE APPIES

Just Don't Fall- Emma St. Clair

Absolutely Not in Love- Jenny Proctor

A Groom of One's Own- Emma St. Clair

Romancing the Grump- Jenny Proctor

Runaway Bride and Prejudice- Emma St. Clair

Oakley Island (with Jenny Proctor)

Eloise and the Grump Next Door

Merritt and Her Childhood Crush

Sadie and the Bad Boy Billionaire

Other books by Emma:

Love Stories in Sheet Cake

The Buy-In

The Bluff

The Pocket Pair

The Wild Card

Sweet Royal Romcoms

Royally Rearranged

Royal Gone Rogue

Love Clichés

Falling for Your Best Friend's Twin

Falling for Your Boss

Falling for Your Fake Fiancé

The Twelve Holidates

Falling for Your Best Friend

Falling for Your Enemy

A NOTE FROM EMMA

It's nice to be back on the ice with the Appies and with YOU!

And if you can't handle a long, maybe rambling, possibly unedited and personal author note, just know the TLDR is I appreciate you and I hope you love the book.

When I was writing *Just Don't Fall*, I KNEW that I'd want to give the rest of the Appies stories. I love friendships and family and especially found family—which this team has in spades. And I'm so happy Jenny Proctor and I are in on this together! It feels like the perfect pairing.

After being inspired by the Savannah Bananas and wanting to write a team like that but HOCKEY, I have *so* enjoyed the way readers have supported this fictional team. I also loved learning more about hockey and attending my first games while writing these books.

It seems fitting that I'm taking all three of my daughters to an ice hockey skating clinic. Parker would be proud. Her dad would not, but he can go fly a kite.

When it comes to the end of every book, I reach a point where I love and I hate what I've written, where I'm terrified everyone will hate it, and at the exact same time I think it's the best thing I've ever written. Every. Single. Book.

Then I need to crawl into a cave for a few days, ignore social media (even the lovely posts from readers!), and focus on another project so I don't go POOF in a flaming ball of anxiety. #authorlife

I LOVED writing Eli and Bailey's story. I am preferential to a good grump, but it's so nice and refreshing to write a guy who loves his mom (in a not man-child way) and is a romantic and wants to get married and doesn't mind showing BIG FEELINGS. I also really loved Maggie and Annie—who really wanted a bigger role for herself—and fell even harder for the Appies, who really endeared themselves to me in this book.

I hope you're ready for more of them!

Marriage of convenience (like fake dating) can be hard for me to write. The realist in me doesn't ever fully believe the circumstances of these books EVEN THOUGH I'll happily suspend disbelief when I *read* them.

For Eli's situation, I did a TON of research and consulted a lot with immigration lawyers, all to have a few very vague lines in the book discussing visas for athletes. It's complicated. Truly. And boring.

So far as my research (and my new lawyer buddy) assures me, Eli's situation could happen. Now, as to whether you'd solve this issue by getting married rather than going back to Canada and hoping your team would keep your spot … well, I can only say that's the choice Eli made.

While I don't have a chronic illness of my own, some people very close to me deal with chronic illness or chronic pain, and I wanted to give a little nod to them in Maggie—

who has so much to give and often has to deal with pain or issues that doctors often dismiss. Especially in women. Though that's not a focal point in this story per se, it was important to me to include this.

Please know that if you've struggled with chronic illness or pain, I see you. I can't pretend to know what that's like, but I've learned a lot and gained a lot of understanding watching people I care about struggle with something people often don't understand, refuse to acknowledge, or brush aside. You guys are ROCK STARS.

(Gigi, JacQueline, Kirsty—I'm especially thinking of you as I write this.)

Like Bailey, at one time I dreamed of being a vet and worked at a vet hospital where I did some weird, cool, and disgusting things. I was picturing West End Vet Hospital (somewhat) as I wrote. Shoutout to Dr. Kelley, Dr. Wally, and Lesley—I hope you're all doing amazing. Thanks for putting up with the teenage punk that was me. ;)

Thank you again for reading this book!

If you want to keep up with the various series and the things I'm doing, the best way to be in the know is to join my Facebook group or follow on Instagram.

If you picked up the bonus content for this book, you'll start receiving my weekly emails, which also have updates and book recs.

Happy reading!

Don't miss the rest of the Appies!

-e

PS- Don't forget your bonus scenes for A Groom of One's Own-

https://emmastclair.com/groombonus

ABOUT THE AUTHOR

Emma St. Clair is a *USA Today* bestselling author of over thirty books and has her MFA in Fiction. She lives near Houston with her husband, five kids, and a Great Dane who doesn't make a very good babysitter. Her romcoms have humor, heart, and nothing that's going to make you need to hide your Kindle from the kids. ;)

You can find out more at http://emmastclair.com or join her reader group at https://www.facebook.com/groups/emmastclair/

ACKNOWLEDGMENTS

Jenny, thanks so much for being the bestest critique partner and for telling me when things suck and also for the things that make me laugh in the comments. It's so fun writing alongside you! Sorry for constantly whining at you about, well, everything.

Thanks to Emily of Midnight Owl Editors for editing and not hating me for how many em dashes I use.

And I am always so grateful to my early readers who help weed out the typos that make it through all my edits. Thanks to Devon, Suzan, Bethany, Ali, Abby, Mandy, Bethany, Stephanie, Rita, Arizona, Jordan, Carole, Marinda, Lindsay, Marsha, Megan, Rosalynn, Berly, Marti, Heidi, and Cathy.